# ꙥCELLiES

## JOE FLOOD | DAVID STEWARD II

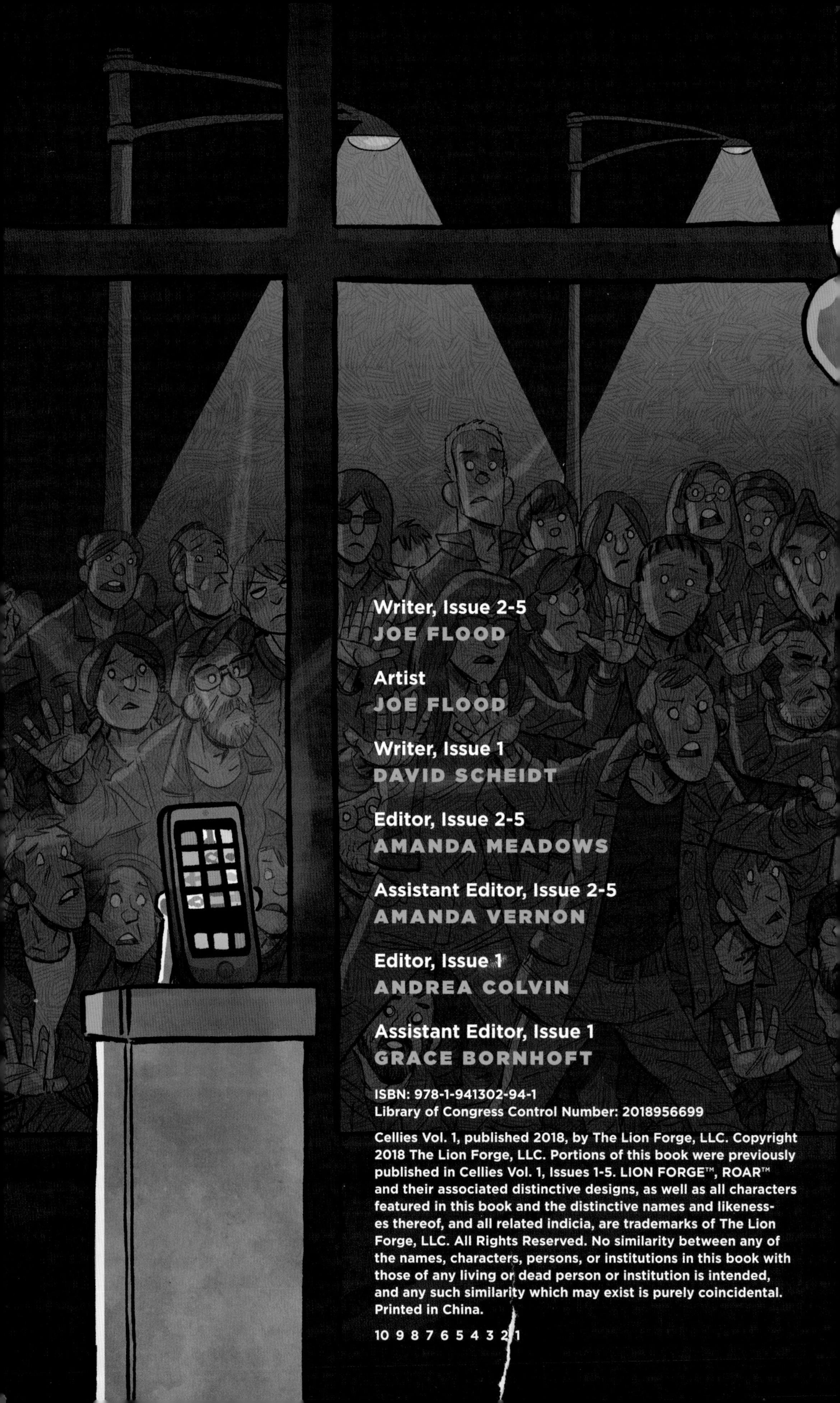


Writer, Issue 2-5
**JOE FLOOD**

Artist
**JOE FLOOD**

Writer, Issue 1
**DAVID SCHEIDT**

Editor, Issue 2-5
**AMANDA MEADOWS**

Assistant Editor, Issue 2-5
**AMANDA VERNON**

Editor, Issue 1
**ANDREA COLVIN**

Assistant Editor, Issue 1
**GRACE BORNHOFT**

ISBN: 978-1-941302-94-1
Library of Congress Control Number: 2018956699





10 9 8 7 6 5 4 3 2 1

# CHAPTER 1

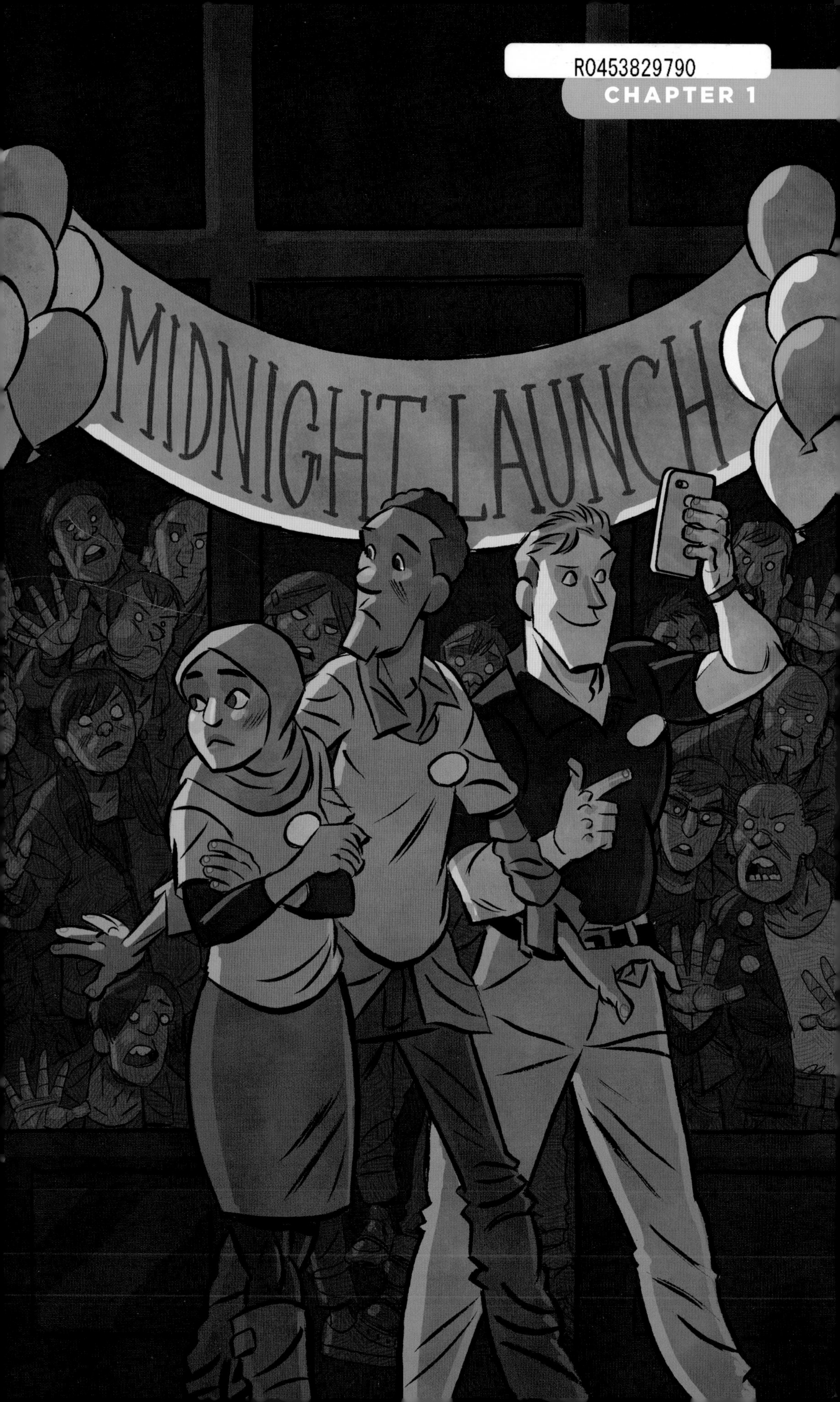
MIDNIGHT LAUNCH

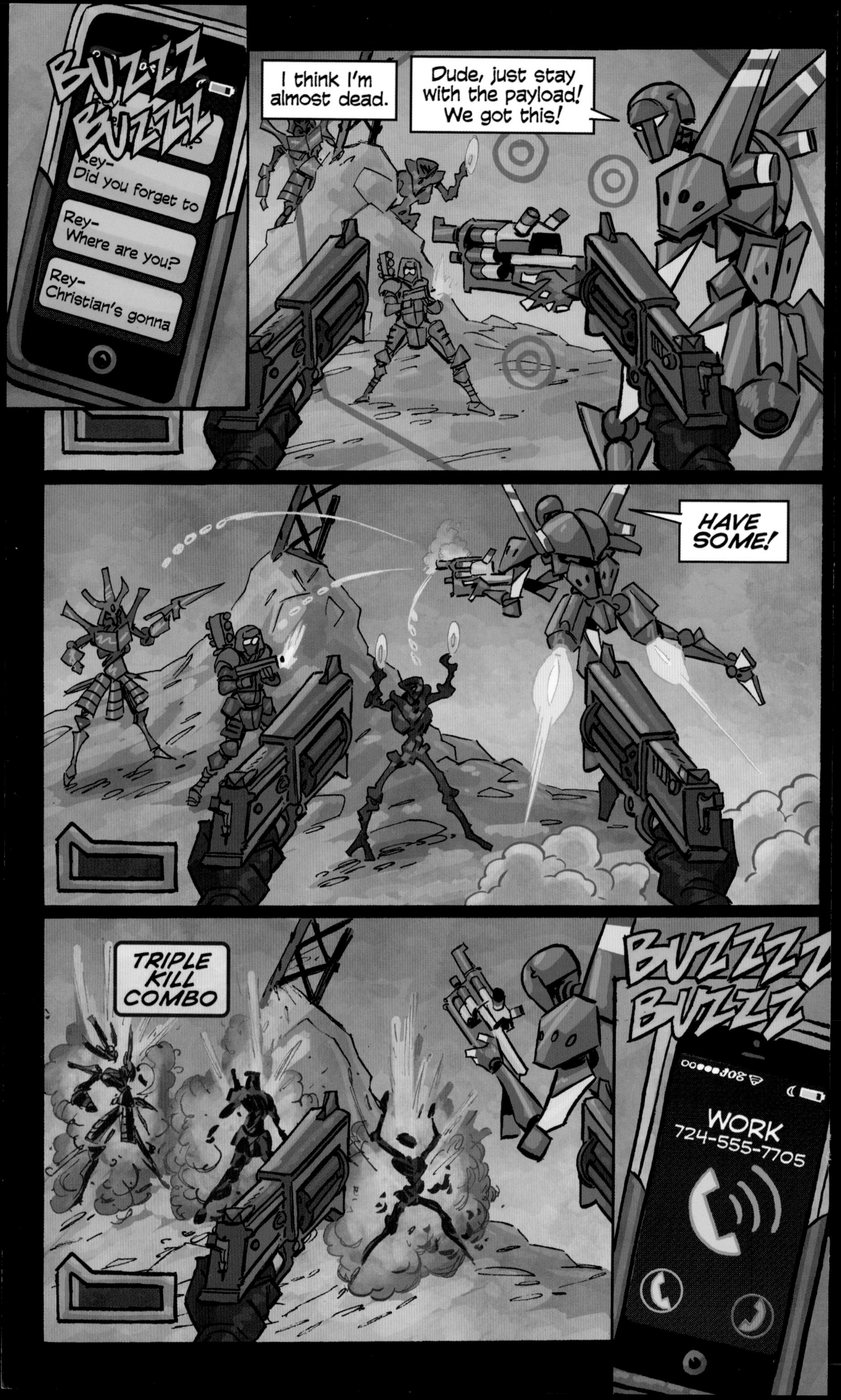
BUZZZ
BUZZZ!
ey-
Did you forget to
Rey-
Where are you?
Rey-
Christian's gonna
I think I'm almost dead.
Dude, just stay with the payload! We got this!
HAVE SOME!
TRIPLE KILL COMBO
BUZZZ
BUZZZ
WORK
724-555-7705

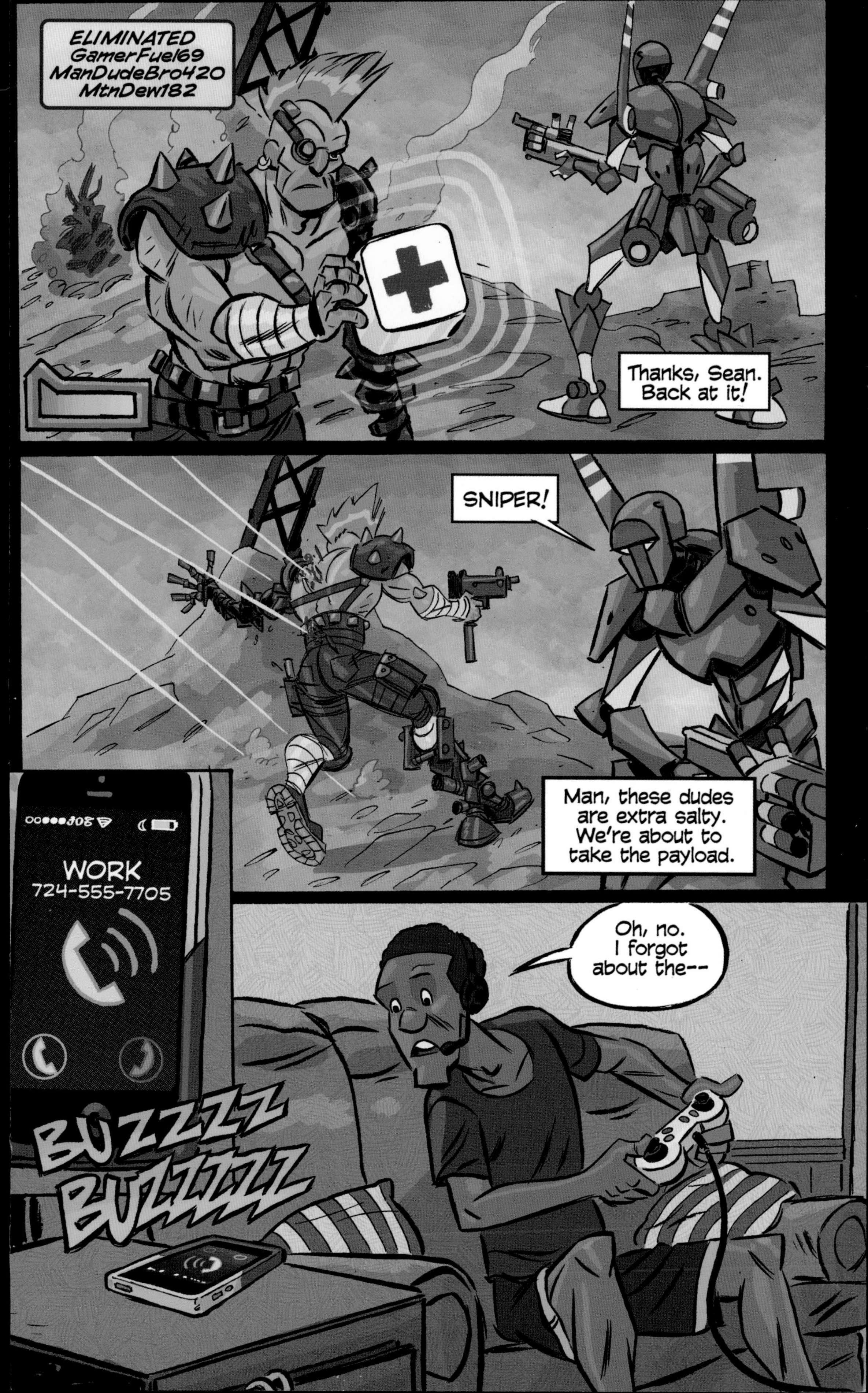
ELIMINATED
GamerFuel69
ManDudeBro420
MtnDew182
Thanks, Sean. Back at it!
SNIPER!
Man, these dudes are extra salty. We're about to take the payload.
WORK
724-555-7705
Oh, no. I forgot about the--
BUZZZZ
BUZZZZZ

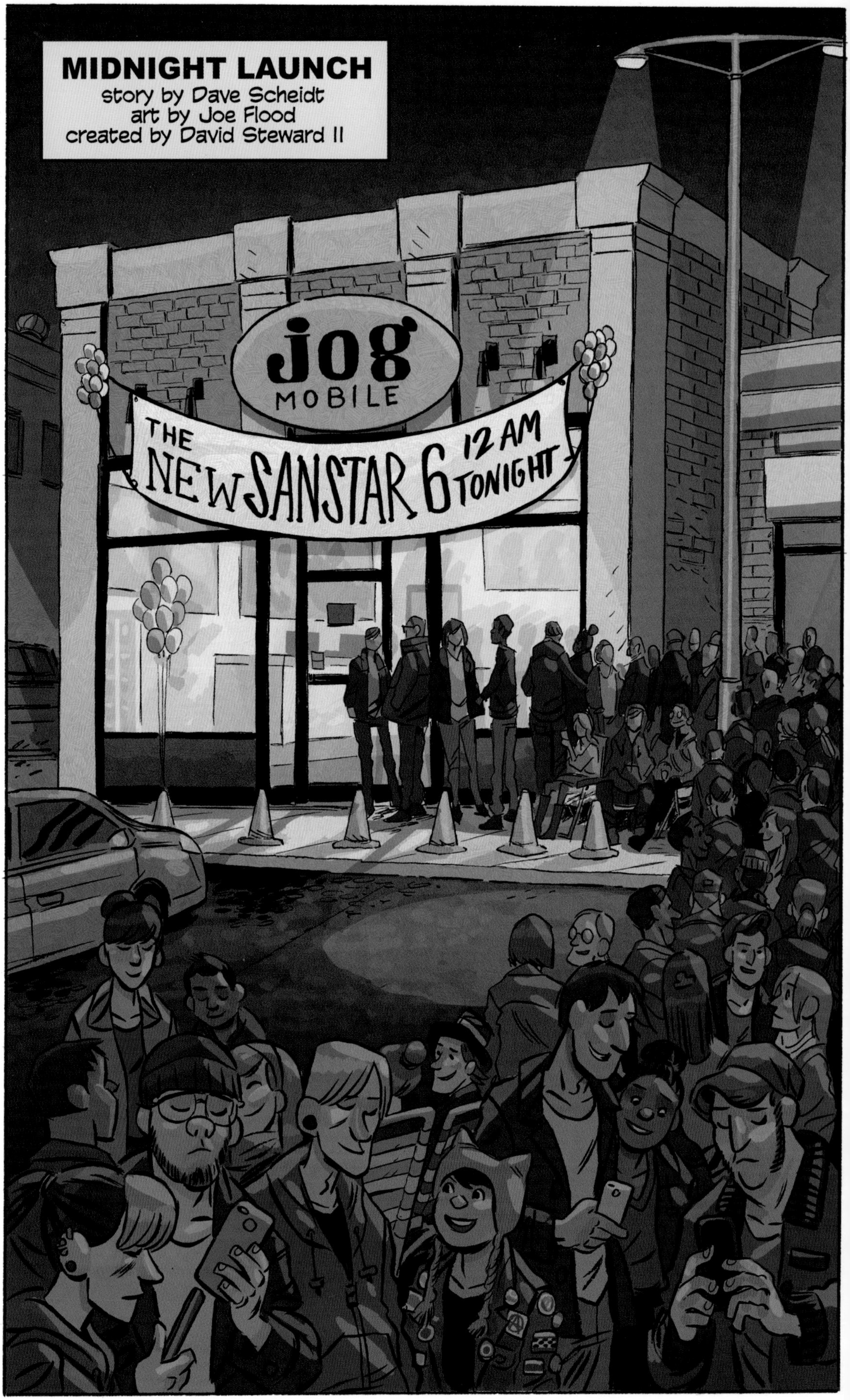
MIDNIGHT LAUNCH
story by Dave Scheidt
art by Joe Flood
created by David Steward II
jog MOBILE
THE NEW SANSTAR 6 12 AM TONIGHT

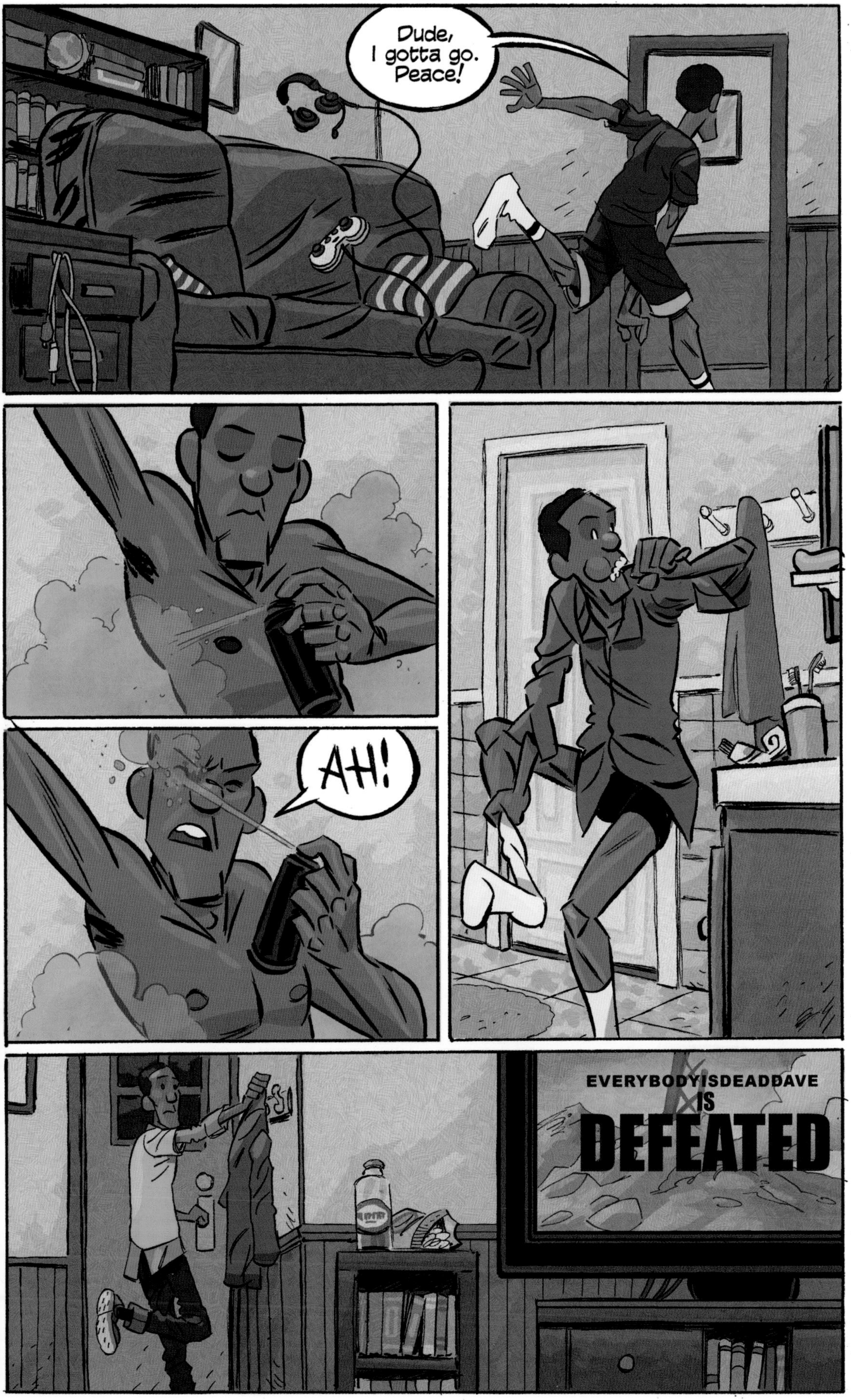
Dude, I gotta go. Peace!
AH!
EVERYBODYISDEADDAVE
IS
DEFEATED

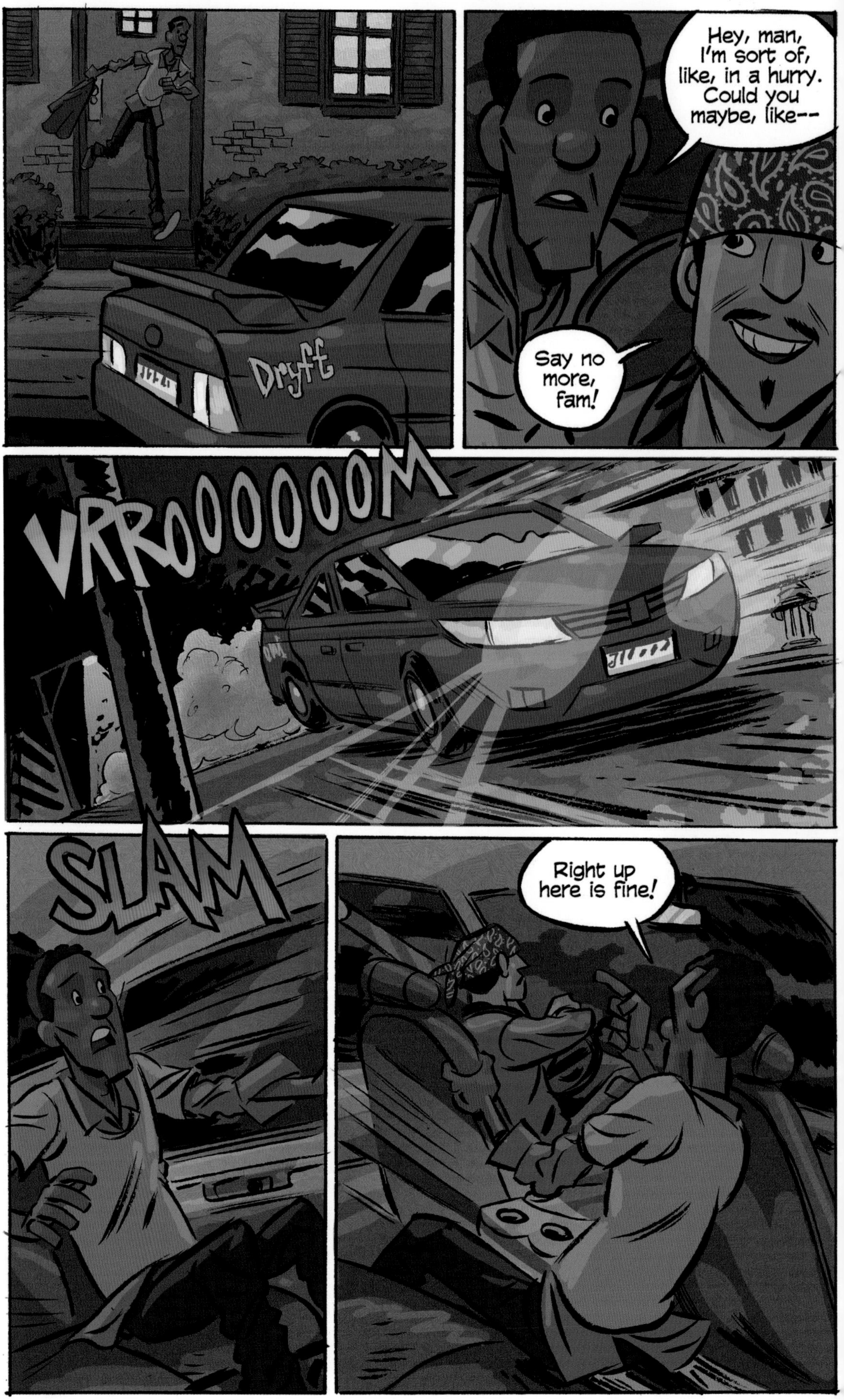
Dryft
Hey, man, I'm sort of, like, in a hurry. Could you maybe, like--
Say no more, fam!
VRROOOOOOM
SLAM
Right up here is fine!

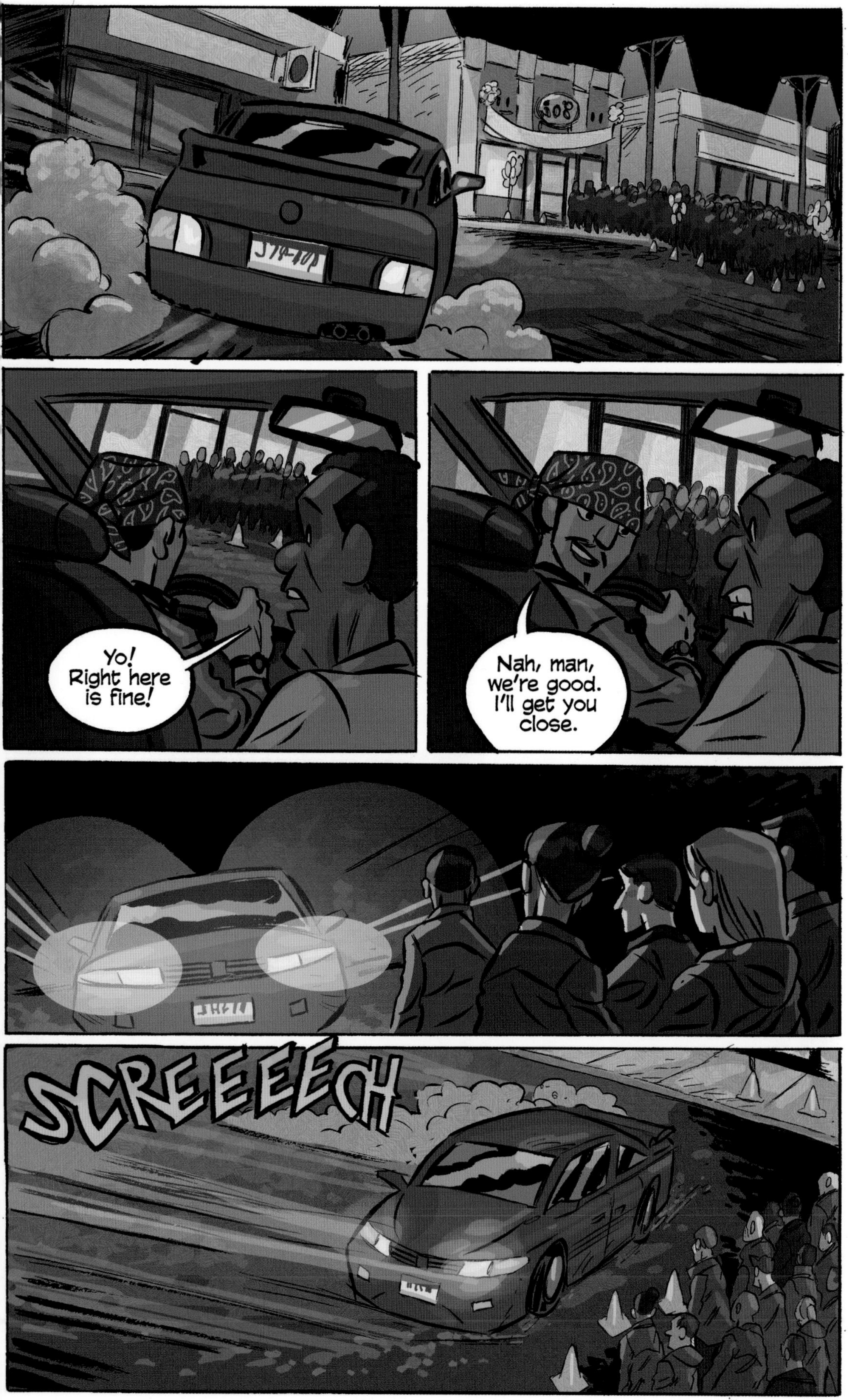
Yo! Right here is fine!
Nah, man, we're good. I'll get you close.
SCREEEECH

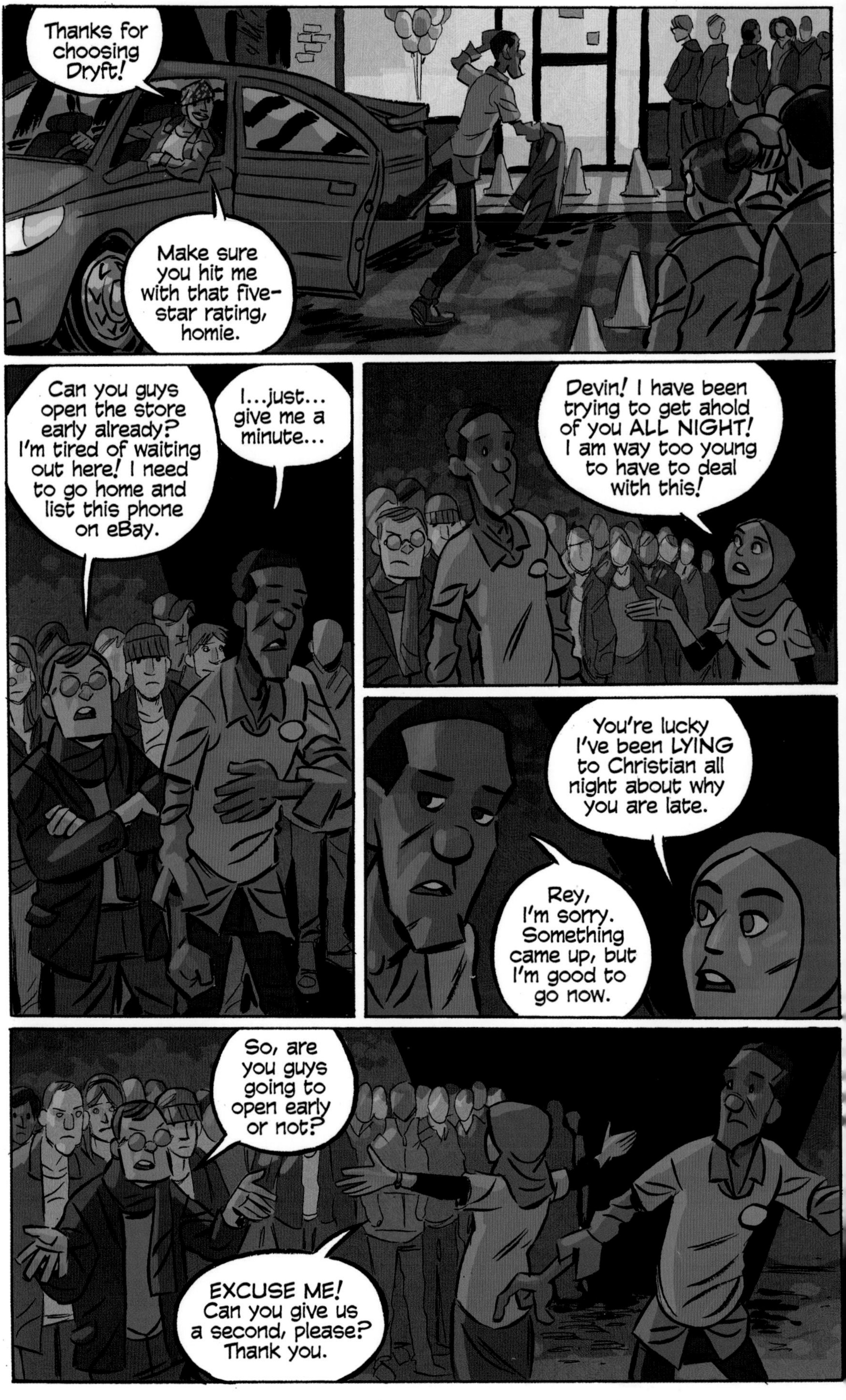
Thanks for choosing Dryft!
Make sure you hit me with that five-star rating, homie.
Can you guys open the store early already? I'm tired of waiting out here! I need to go home and list this phone on eBay.
I...just... give me a minute...
Devin! I have been trying to get ahold of you ALL NIGHT! I am way too young to have to deal with this!
You're lucky I've been LYING to Christian all night about why you are late.
Rey, I'm sorry. Something came up, but I'm good to go now.
So, are you guys going to open early or not?
EXCUSE ME! Can you give us a second, please? Thank you.

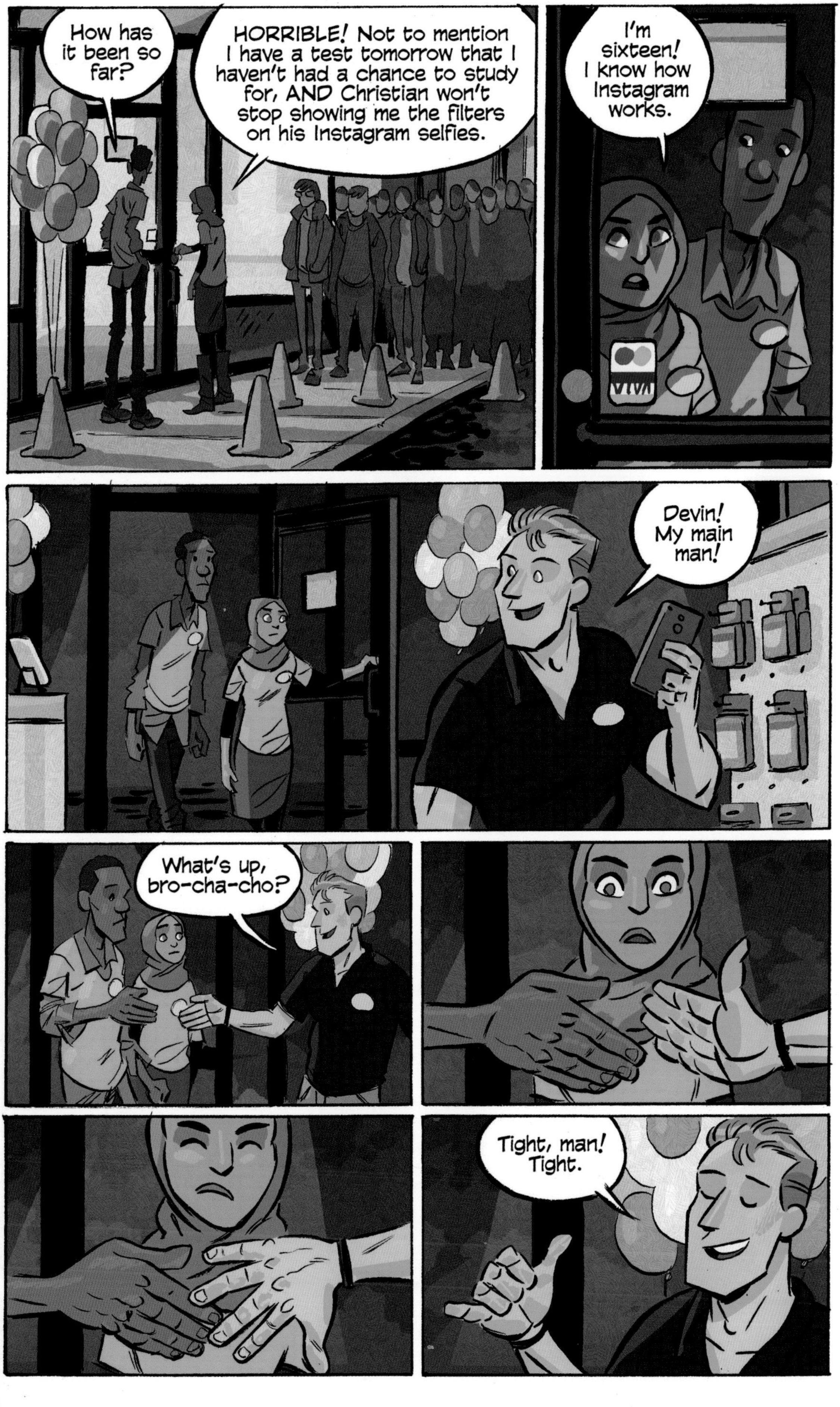
How has it been so far?
HORRIBLE! Not to mention I have a test tomorrow that I haven't had a chance to study for, AND Christian won't stop showing me the filters on his Instagram selfies.
I'm sixteen! I know how Instagram works.
Devin! My main man!
What's up, bro-cha-cho?
Tight, man! Tight.

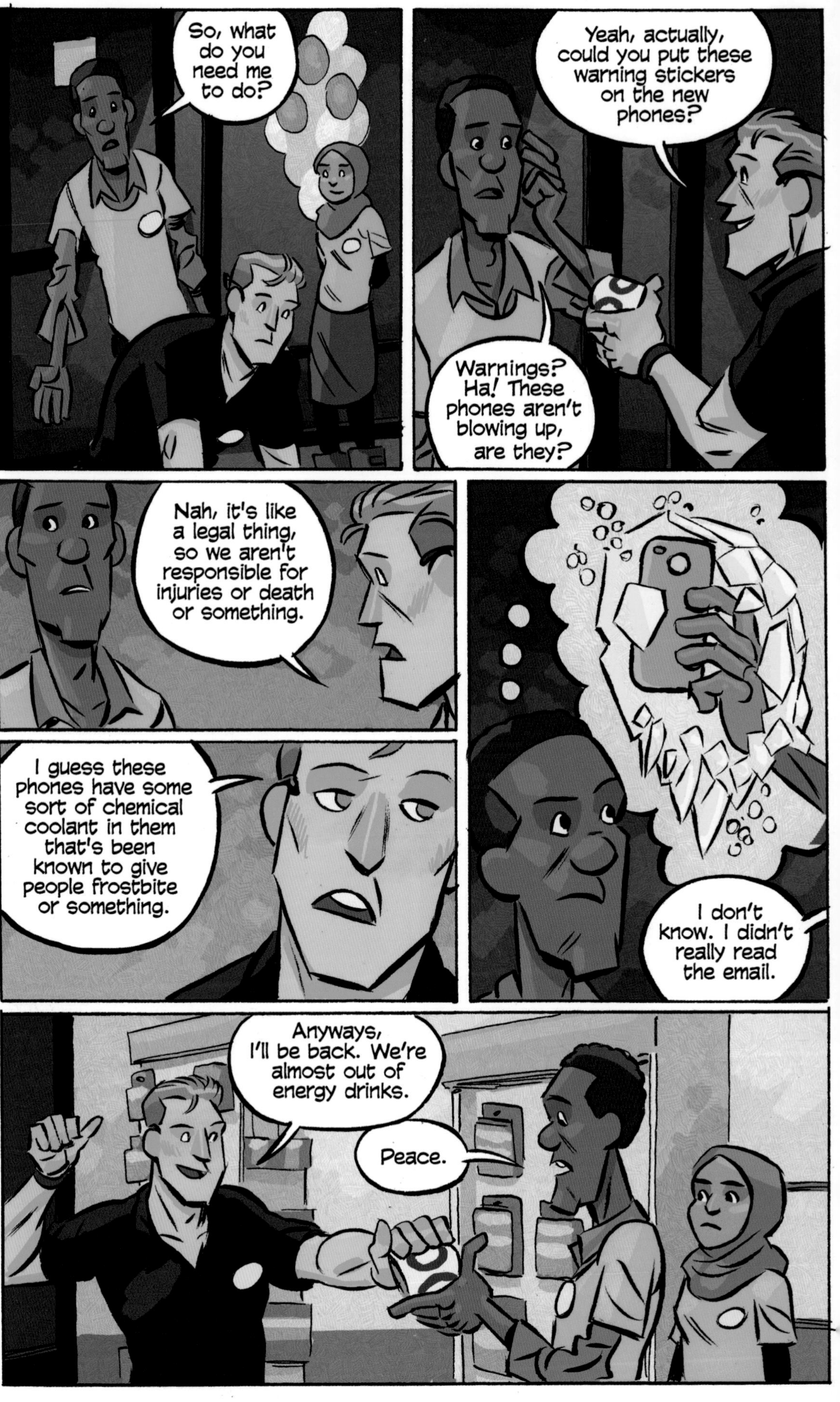

So, what do you need me to do?
Yeah, actually, could you put these warning stickers on the new phones?
Warnings? Ha! These phones aren't blowing up, are they?
Nah, it's like a legal thing, so we aren't responsible for injuries or death or something.
I guess these phones have some sort of chemical coolant in them that's been known to give people frostbite or something.
I don't know. I didn't really read the email.
Anyways, I'll be back. We're almost out of energy drinks.
Peace.

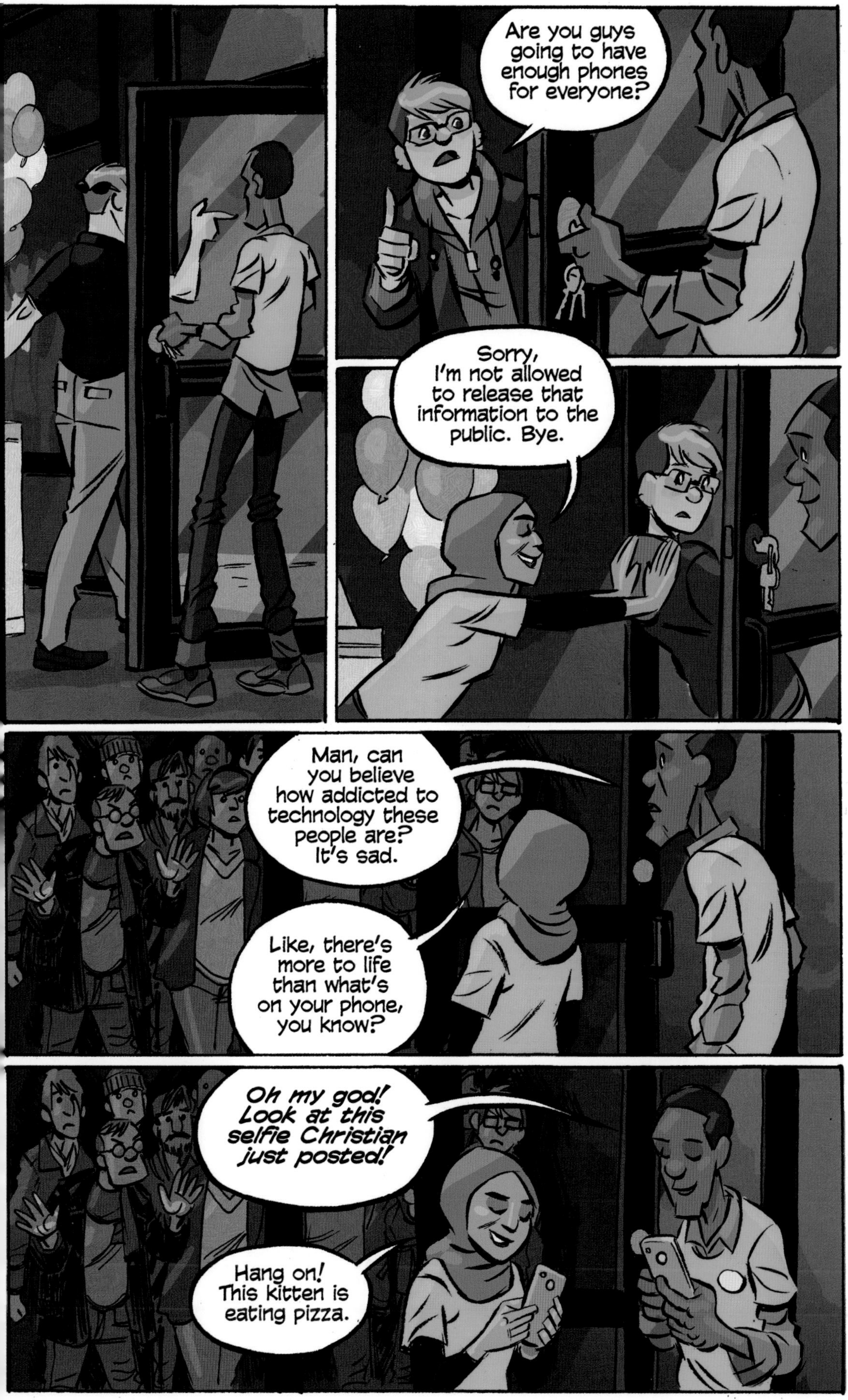
Are you guys going to have enough phones for everyone?
Sorry, I'm not allowed to release that information to the public. Bye.
Man, can you believe how addicted to technology these people are? It's sad.
Like, there's more to life than what's on your phone, you know?
*Oh my god! Look at this selfie Christian just posted!*
Hang on! This kitten is eating pizza.

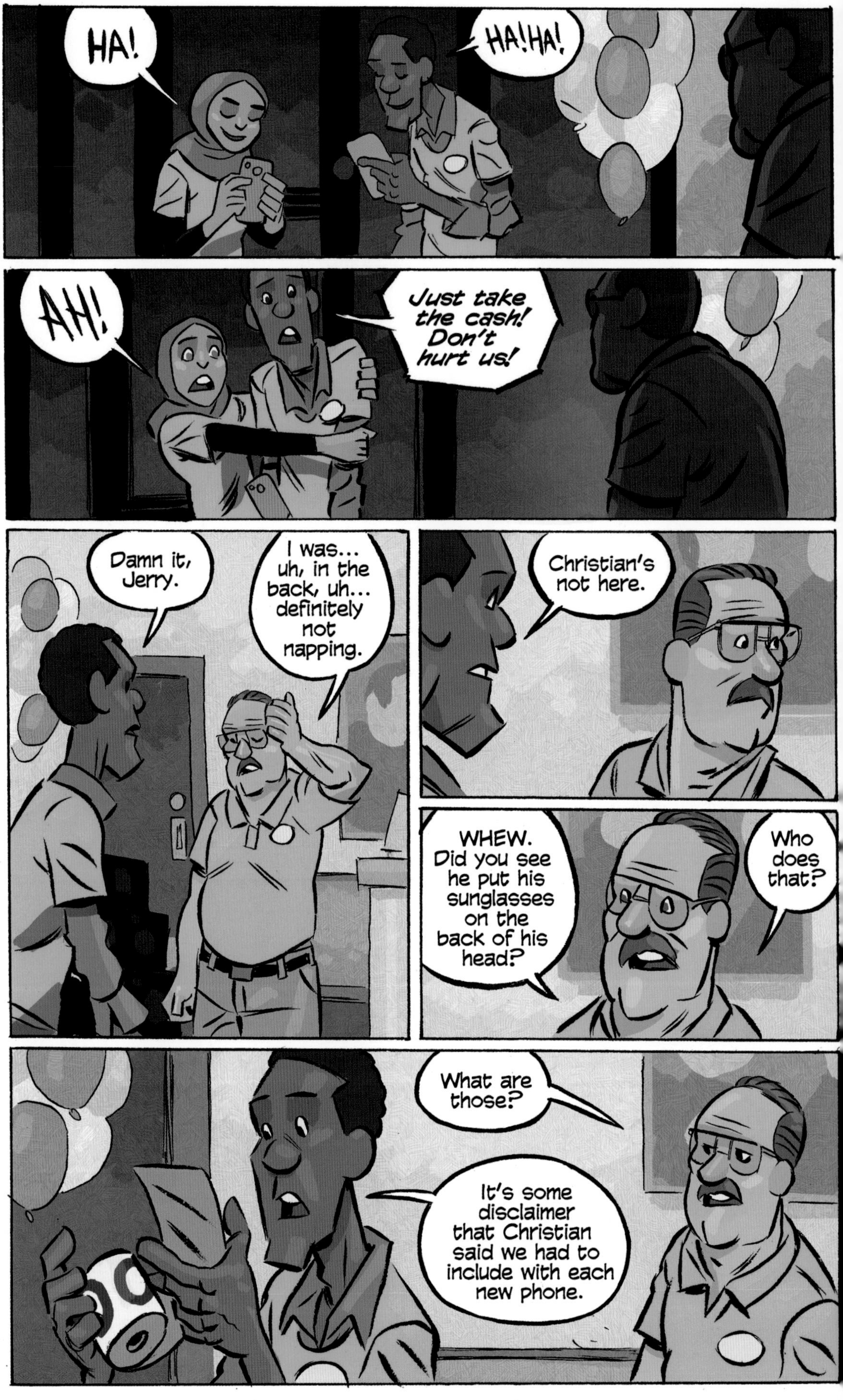
HA!
HA! HA!
AH!
Just take the cash! Don't hurt us!
Damn it, Jerry.
I was... uh, in the back, uh... definitely not napping.
Christian's not here.
WHEW. Did you see he put his sunglasses on the back of his head?
Who does that?
What are those?
It's some disclaimer that Christian said we had to include with each new phone.

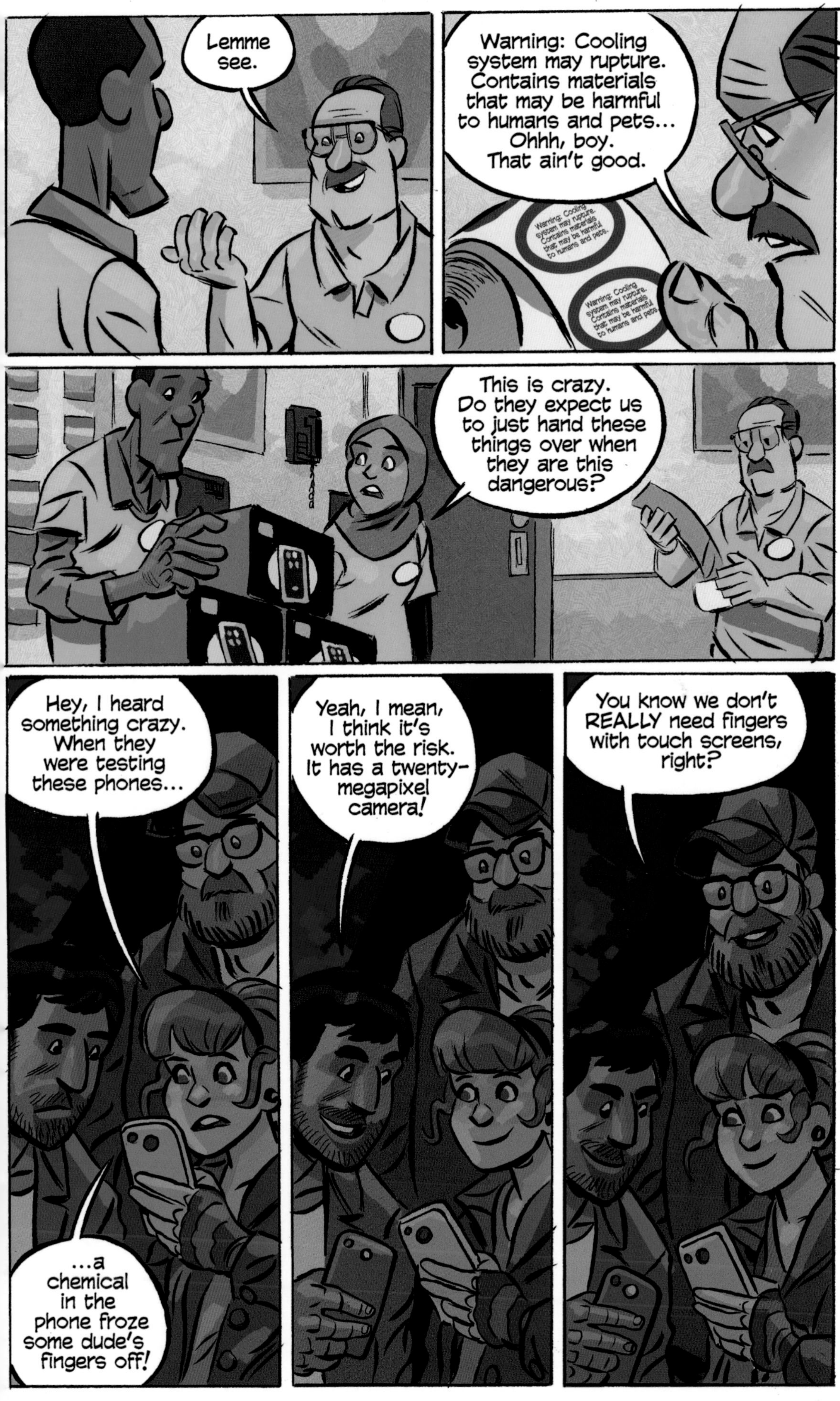
Lemme see.
Warning: Cooling system may rupture. Contains materials that may be harmful to humans and pets... Ohhh, boy. That ain't good.
Warning: Cooling system may rupture. Contains materials that may be harmful to humans and pets.
Warning: Cooling system may rupture. Contains materials that may be harmful to humans and pets.
This is crazy. Do they expect us to just hand these things over when they are this dangerous?
Hey, I heard something crazy. When they were testing these phones...
...a chemical in the phone froze some dude's fingers off!
Yeah, I mean, I think it's worth the risk. It has a twenty-megapixel camera!
You know we don't REALLY need fingers with touch screens, right?

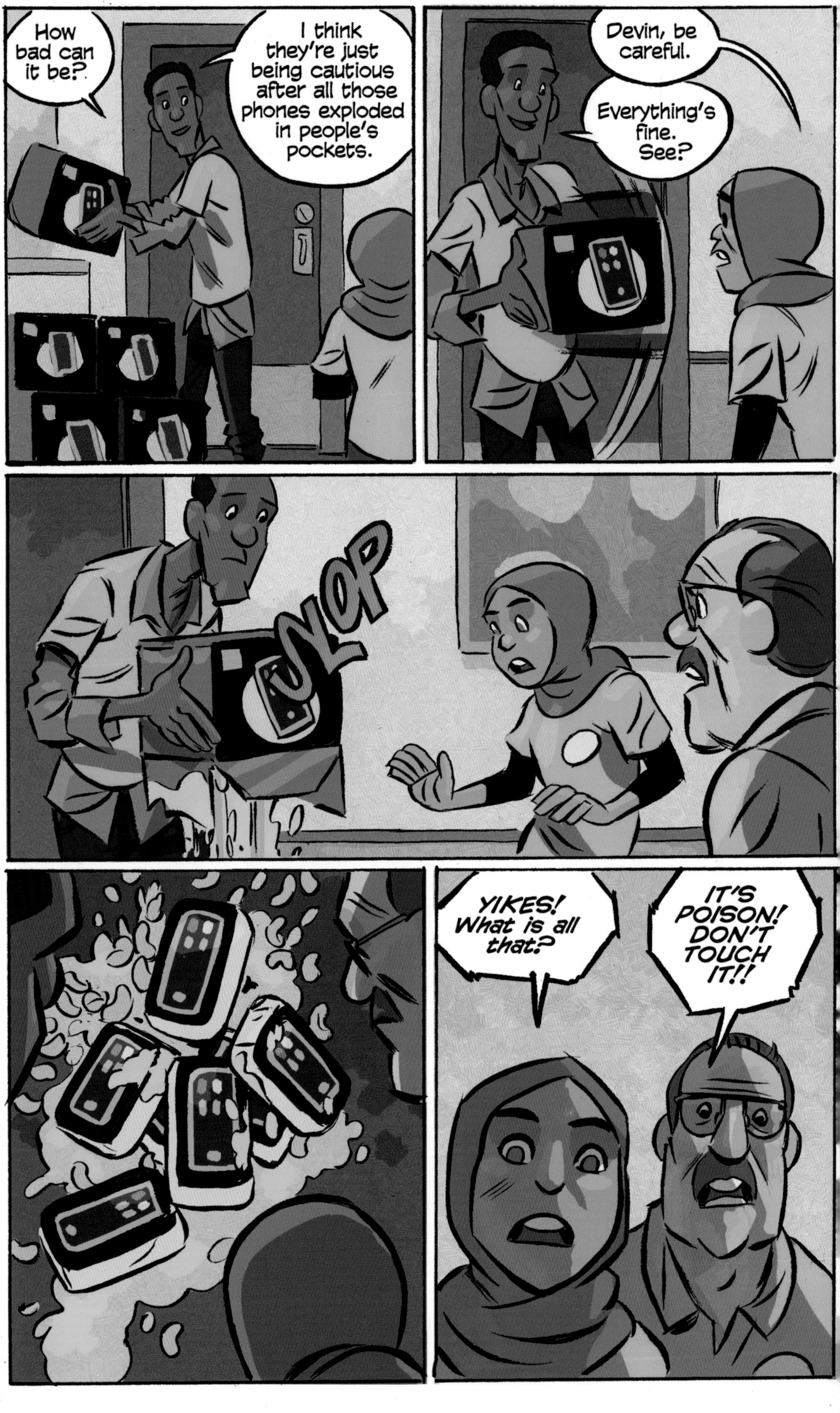
How bad can it be?
I think they're just being cautious after all those phones exploded in people's pockets.
Devin, be careful.
Everything's fine. See?
GLOP
YIKES! What is all that?
IT'S POISON! DON'T TOUCH IT!!

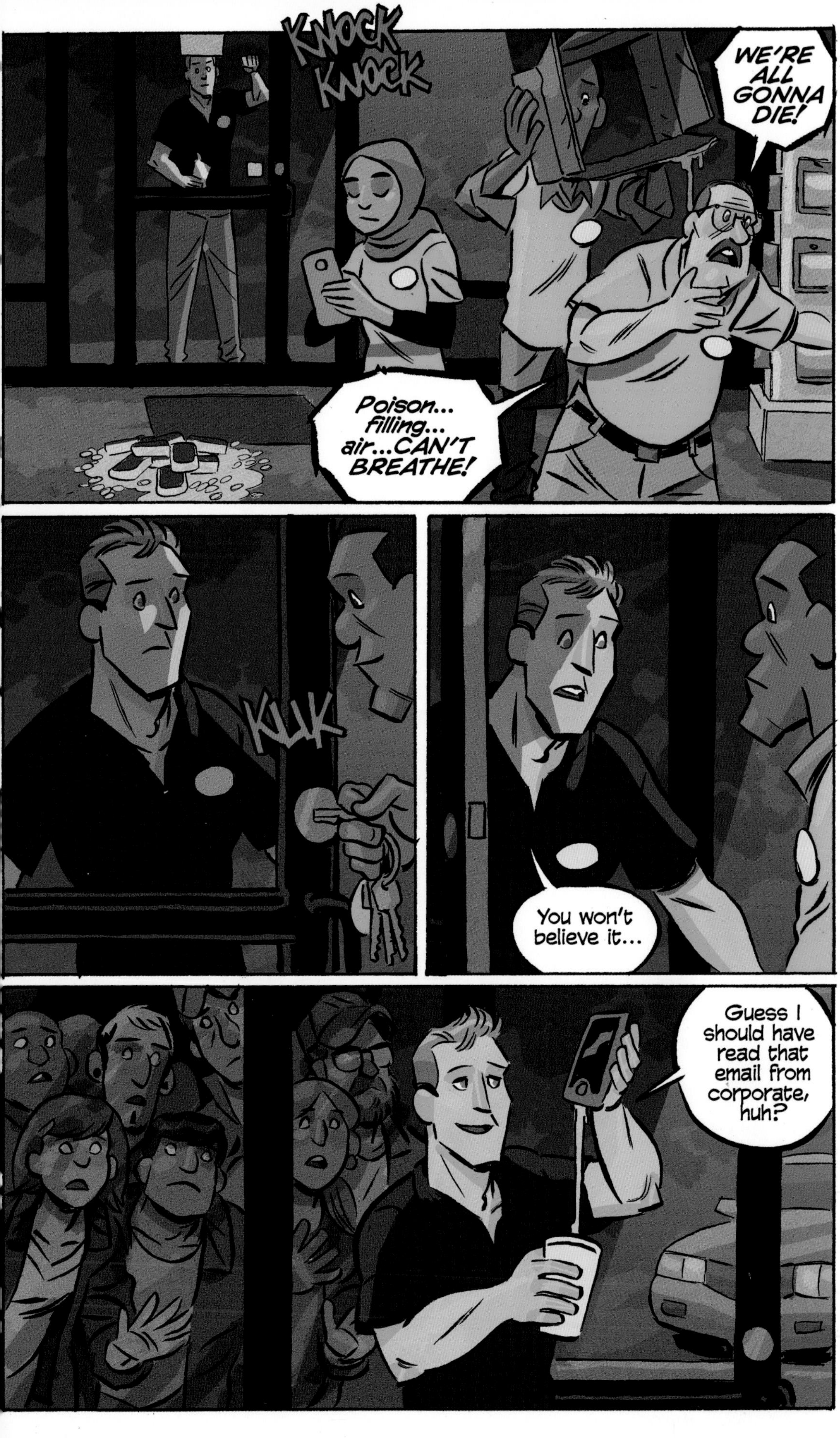
KNOCK KNOCK
WE'RE ALL GONNA DIE!
Poison... filling... air...CAN'T BREATHE!
KLIK
You won't believe it...
Guess I should have read that email from corporate, huh?

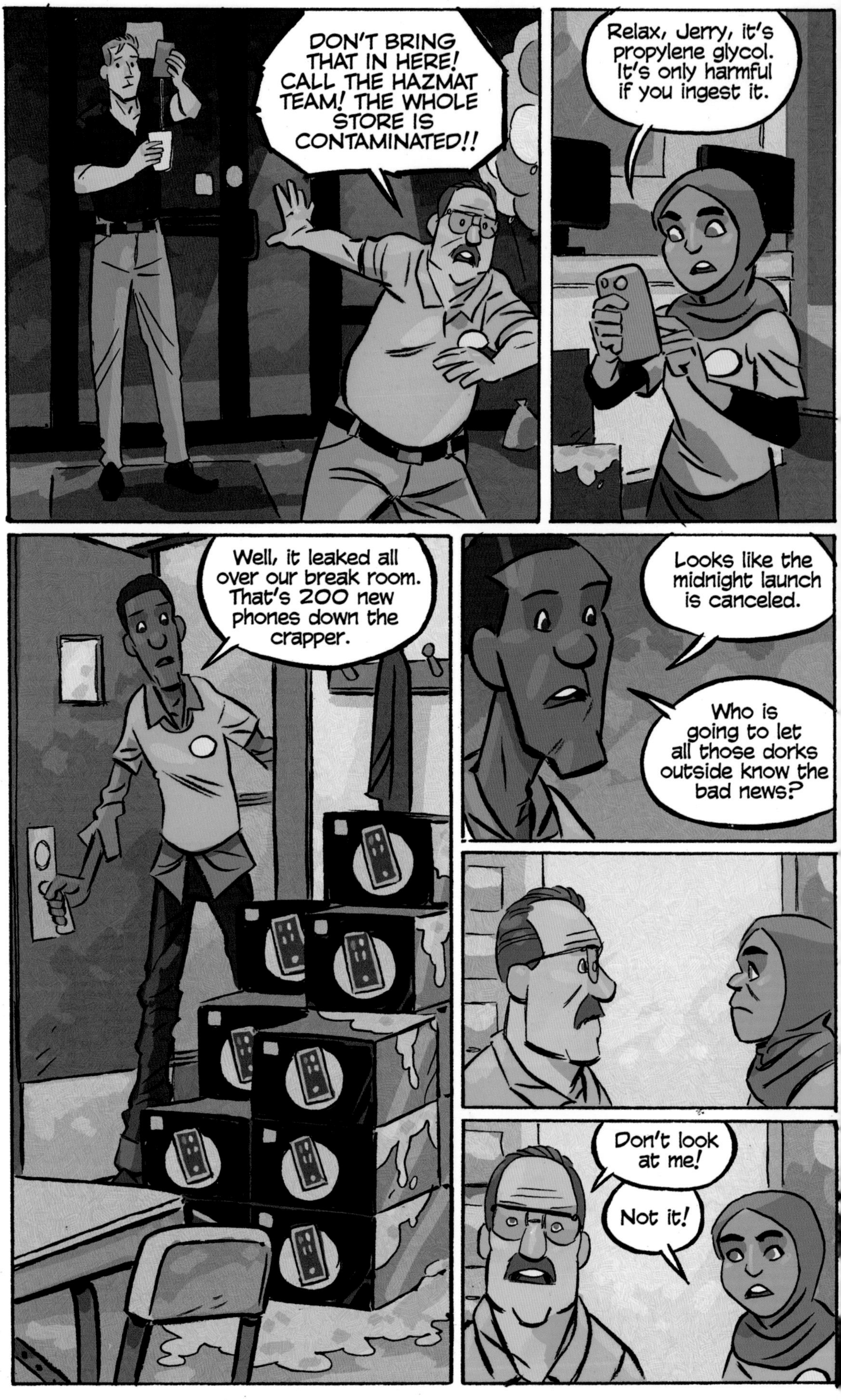

DON'T BRING THAT IN HERE! CALL THE HAZMAT TEAM! THE WHOLE STORE IS CONTAMINATED!!
Relax, Jerry, it's propylene glycol. It's only harmful if you ingest it.
Well, it leaked all over our break room. That's 200 new phones down the crapper.
Looks like the midnight launch is canceled.
Who is going to let all those dorks outside know the bad news?
Don't look at me!
Not it!

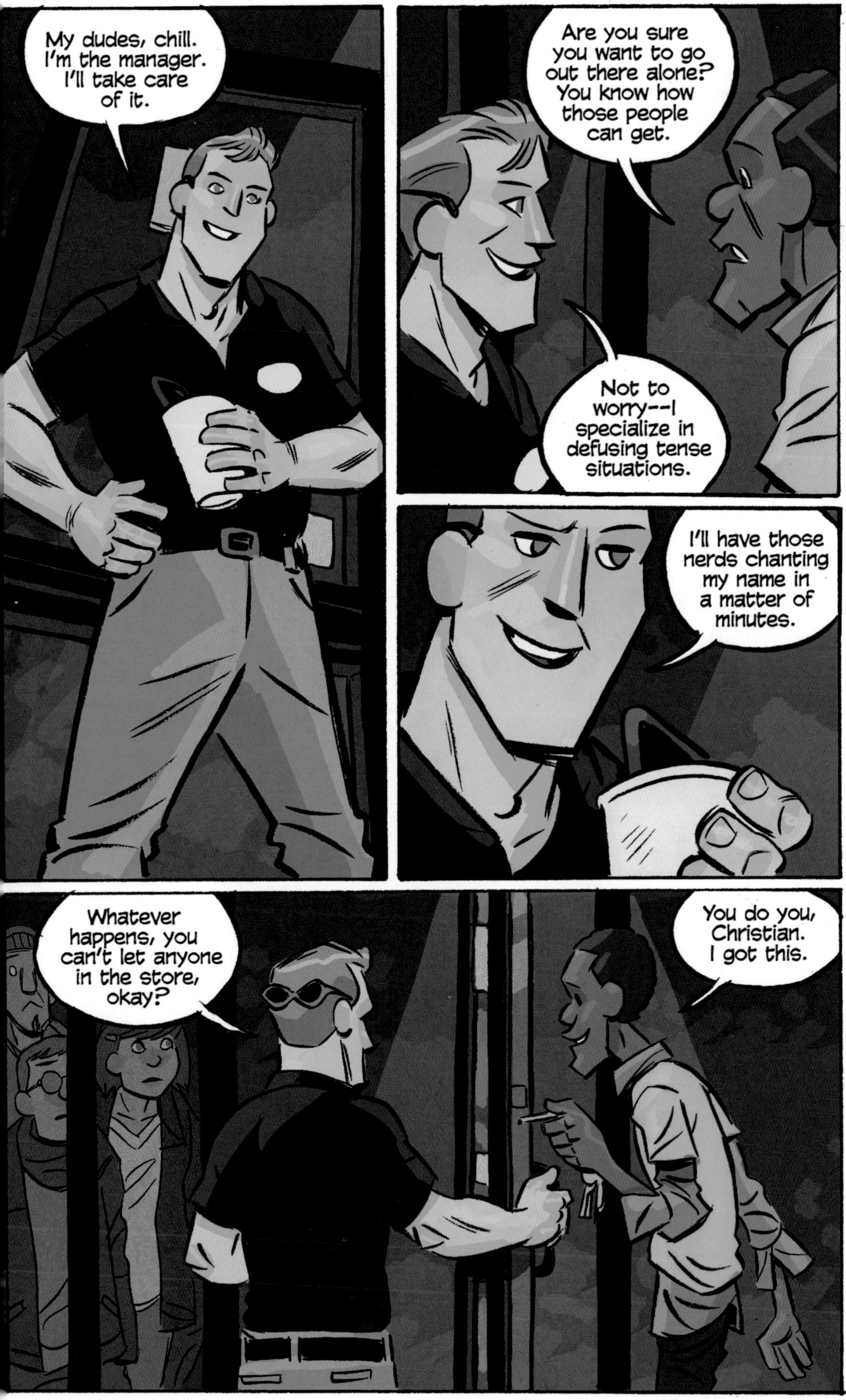
My dudes, chill. I'm the manager. I'll take care of it.
Are you sure you want to go out there alone? You know how those people can get.
Not to worry--I specialize in defusing tense situations.
I'll have those nerds chanting my name in a matter of minutes.
Whatever happens, you can't let anyone in the store, okay?
You do you, Christian. I got this.

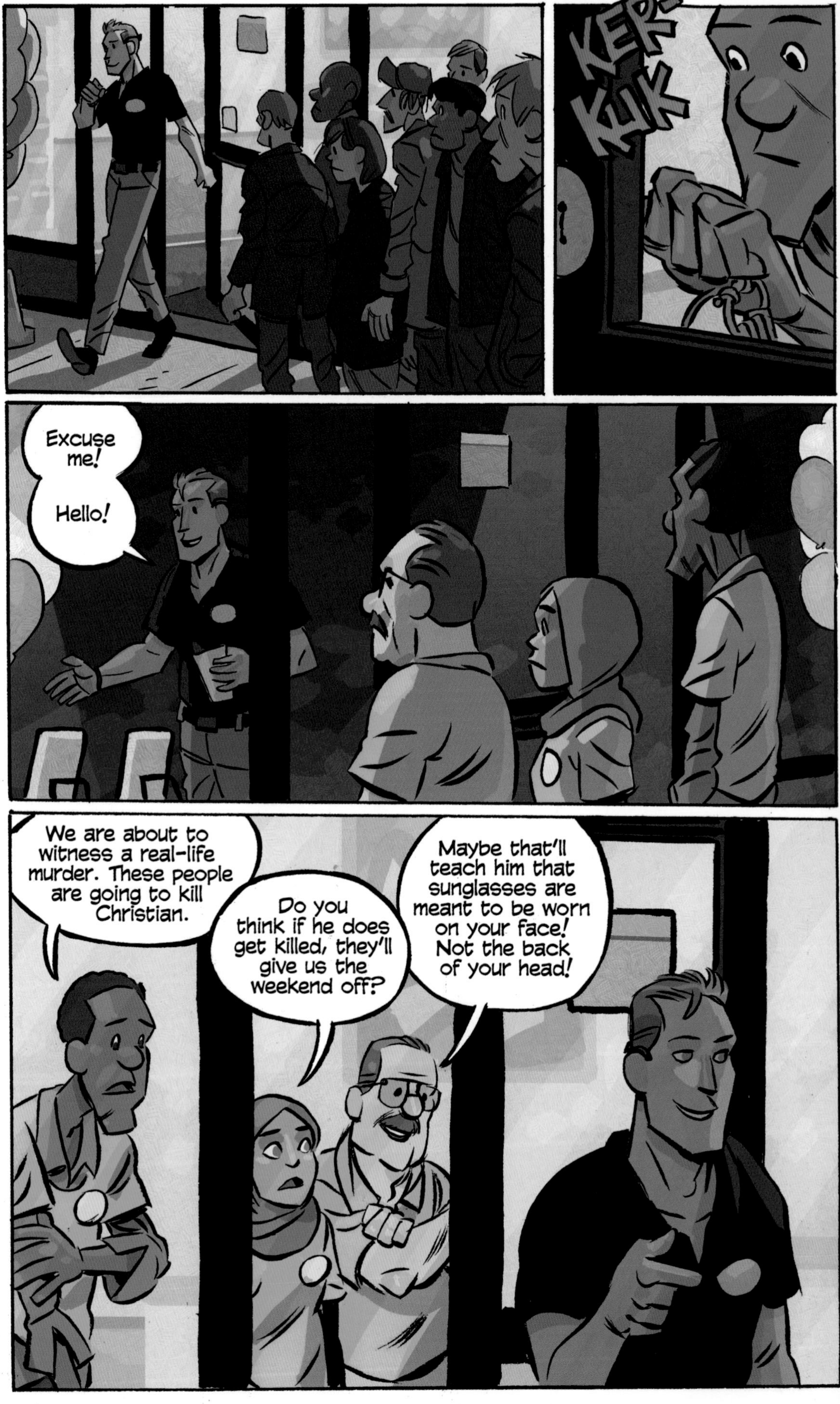

KER-KLIK
Excuse me!
Hello!
We are about to witness a real-life murder. These people are going to kill Christian.
Do you think if he does get killed, they'll give us the weekend off?
Maybe that'll teach him that sunglasses are meant to be worn on your face! Not the back of your head!

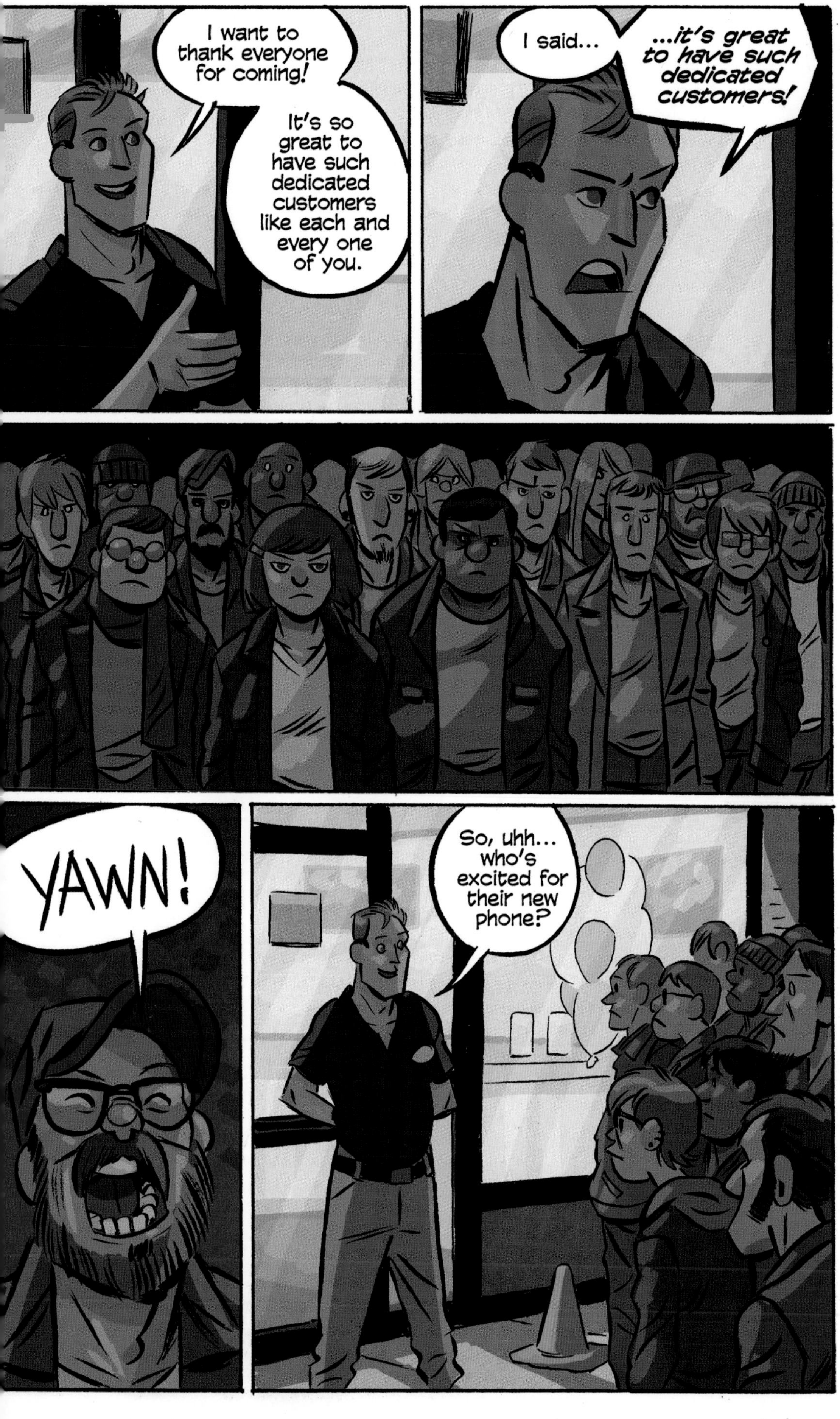
I want to thank everyone for coming!
It's so great to have such dedicated customers like each and every one of you.
I said...
...it's great to have such dedicated customers!
YAWN!
So, uhh... who's excited for their new phone?

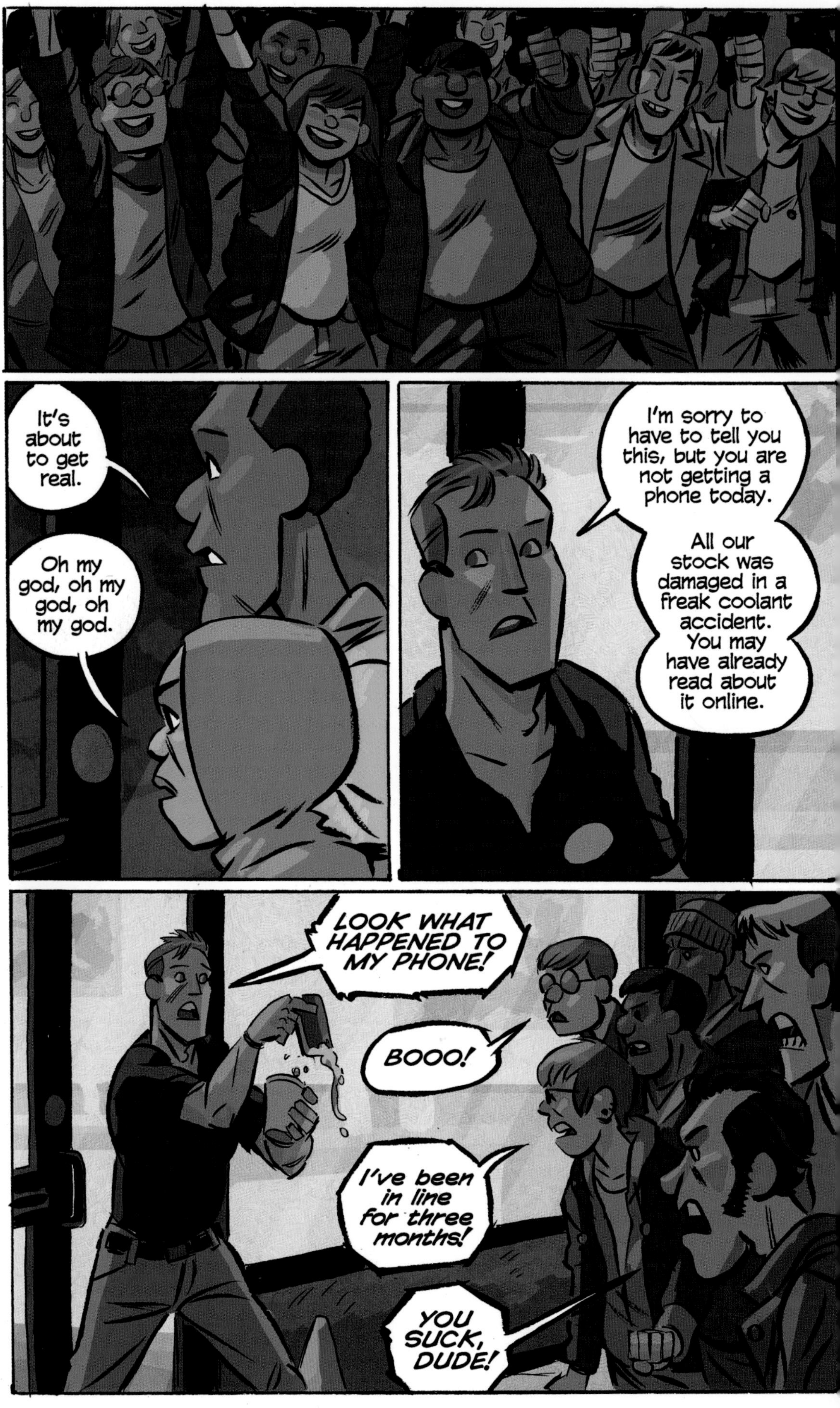
It's about to get real.
Oh my god, oh my god, oh my god.
I'm sorry to have to tell you this, but you are not getting a phone today.
All our stock was damaged in a freak coolant accident. You may have already read about it online.
LOOK WHAT HAPPENED TO MY PHONE!
BOOO!
I've been in line for three months!
YOU SUCK, DUDE!

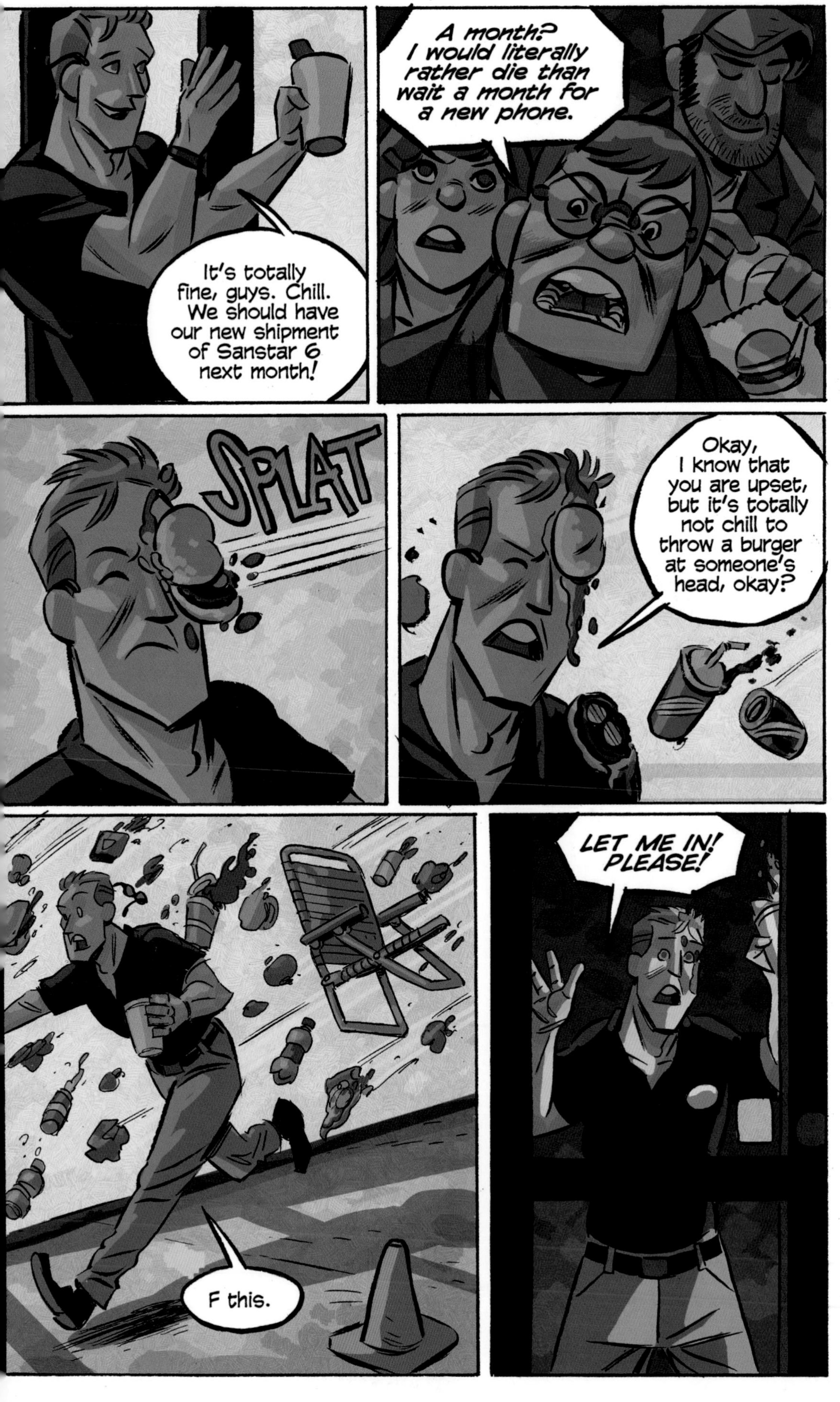

It's totally fine, guys. Chill. We should have our new shipment of Sanstar 6 next month!
A month? I would literally rather die than wait a month for a new phone.
SPLAT
Okay, I know that you are upset, but it's totally not chill to throw a burger at someone's head, okay?
F this.
LET ME IN! PLEASE!

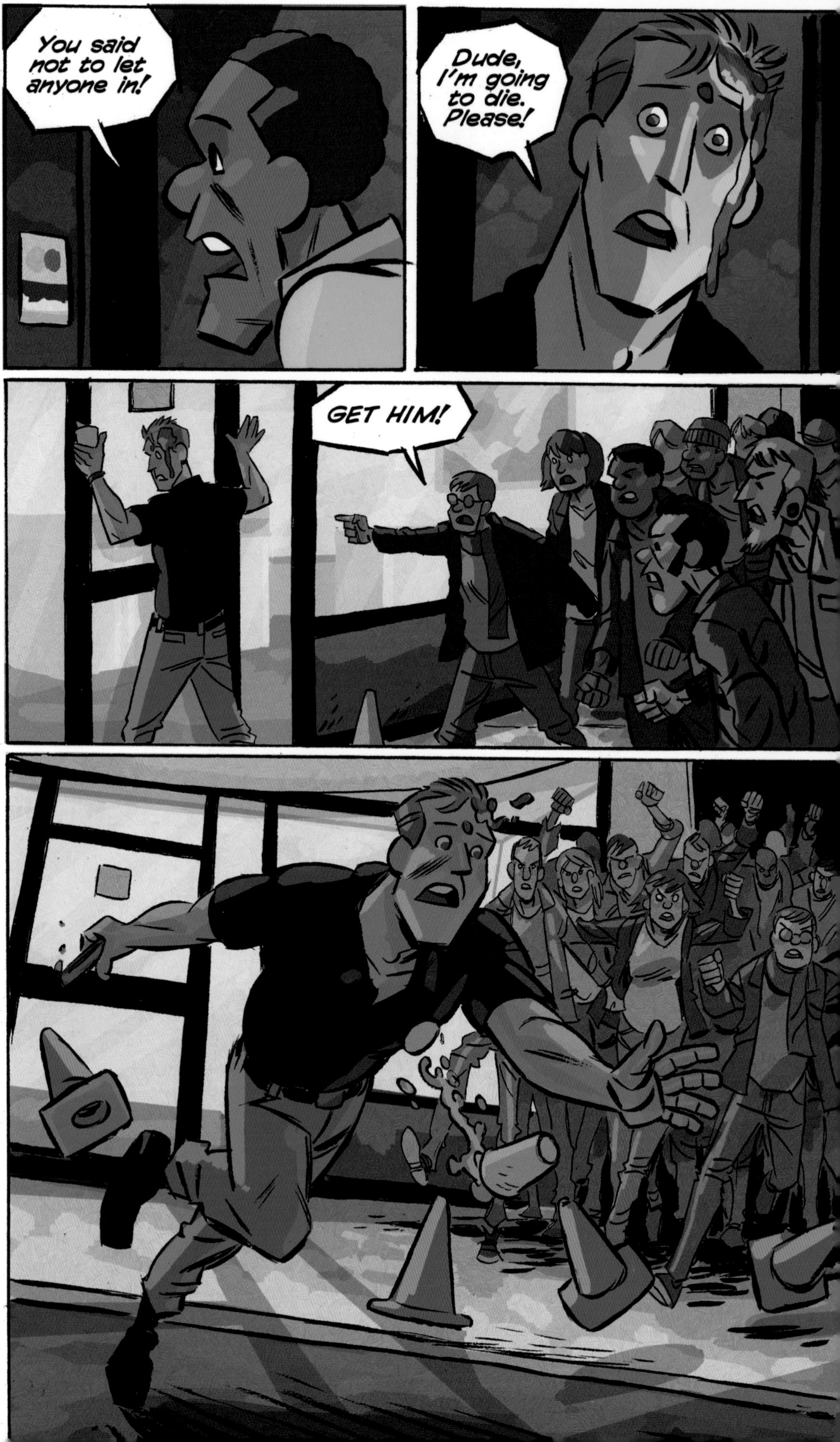
You said not to let anyone in!
Dude, I'm going to die. Please!
GET HIM!

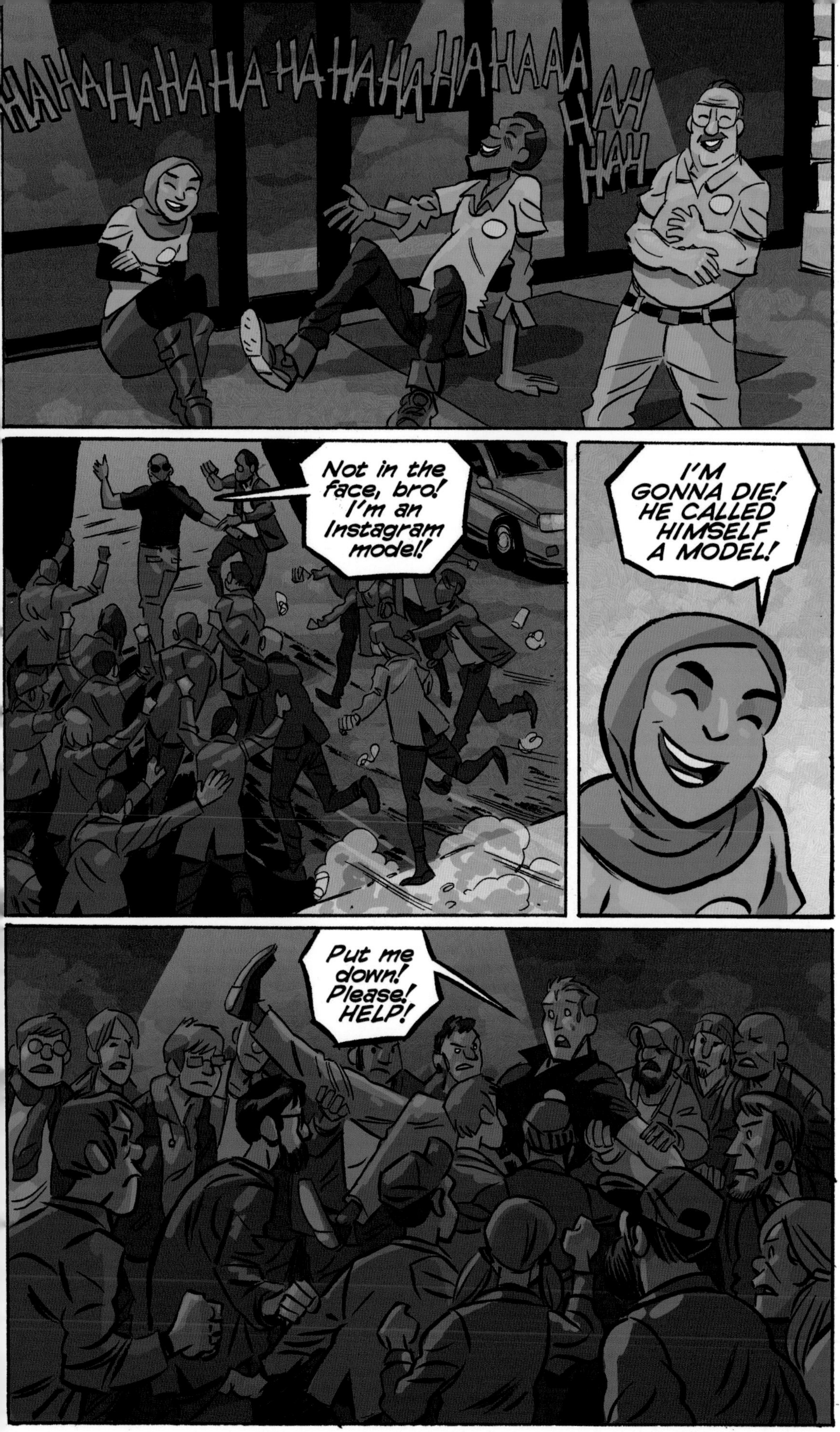
HAHAHAHAHAHA HAHAHAHA HAHAAAAAH HAH HAH
Not in the face, bro! I'm an Instagram model!
I'M GONNA DIE! HE CALLED HIMSELF A MODEL!
Put me down! Please! HELP!

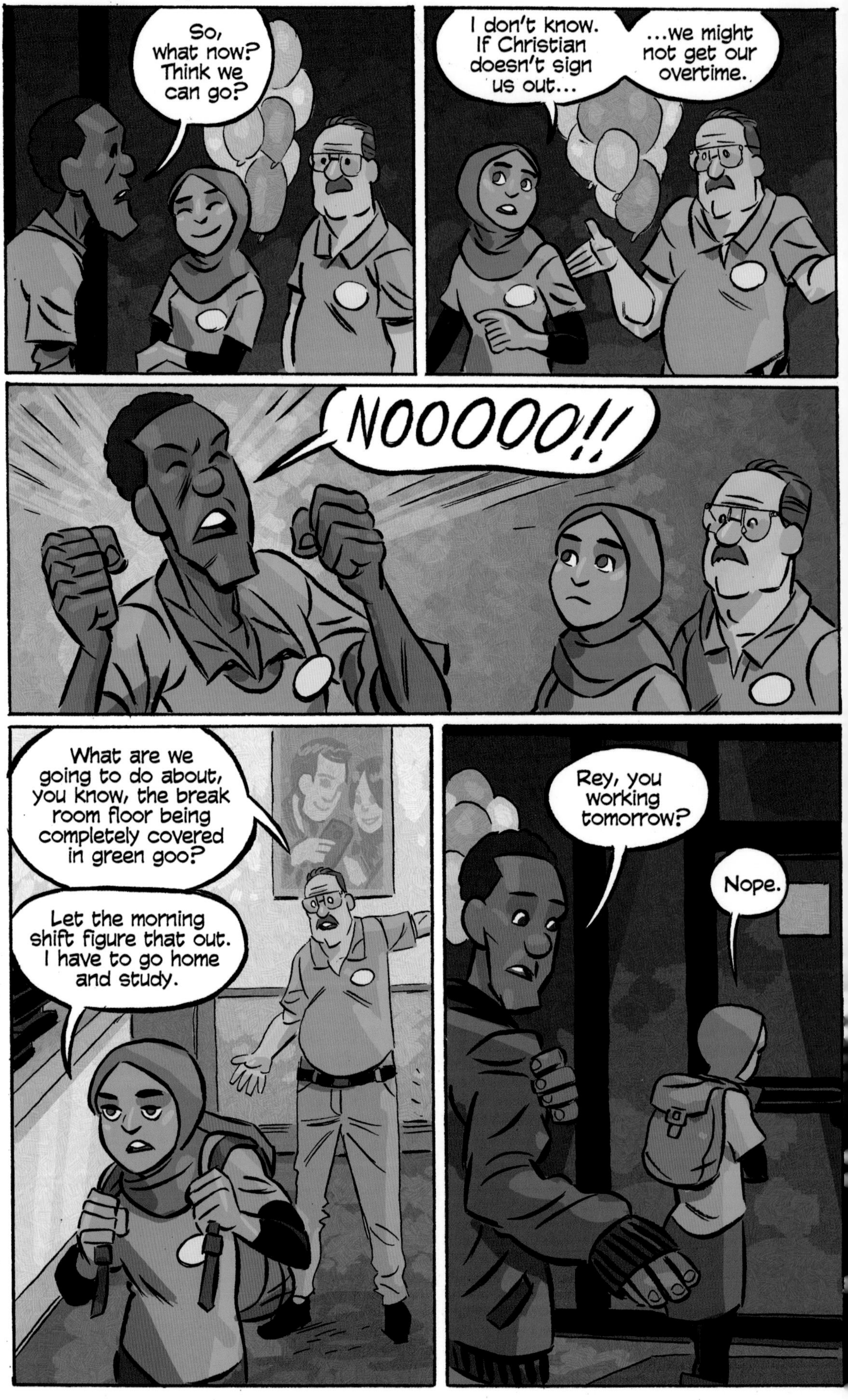
So, what now? Think we can go?
I don't know. If Christian doesn't sign us out...
...we might not get our overtime.
NOOOOO!!
What are we going to do about, you know, the break room floor being completely covered in green goo?
Let the morning shift figure that out. I have to go home and study.
Rey, you working tomorrow?
Nope.

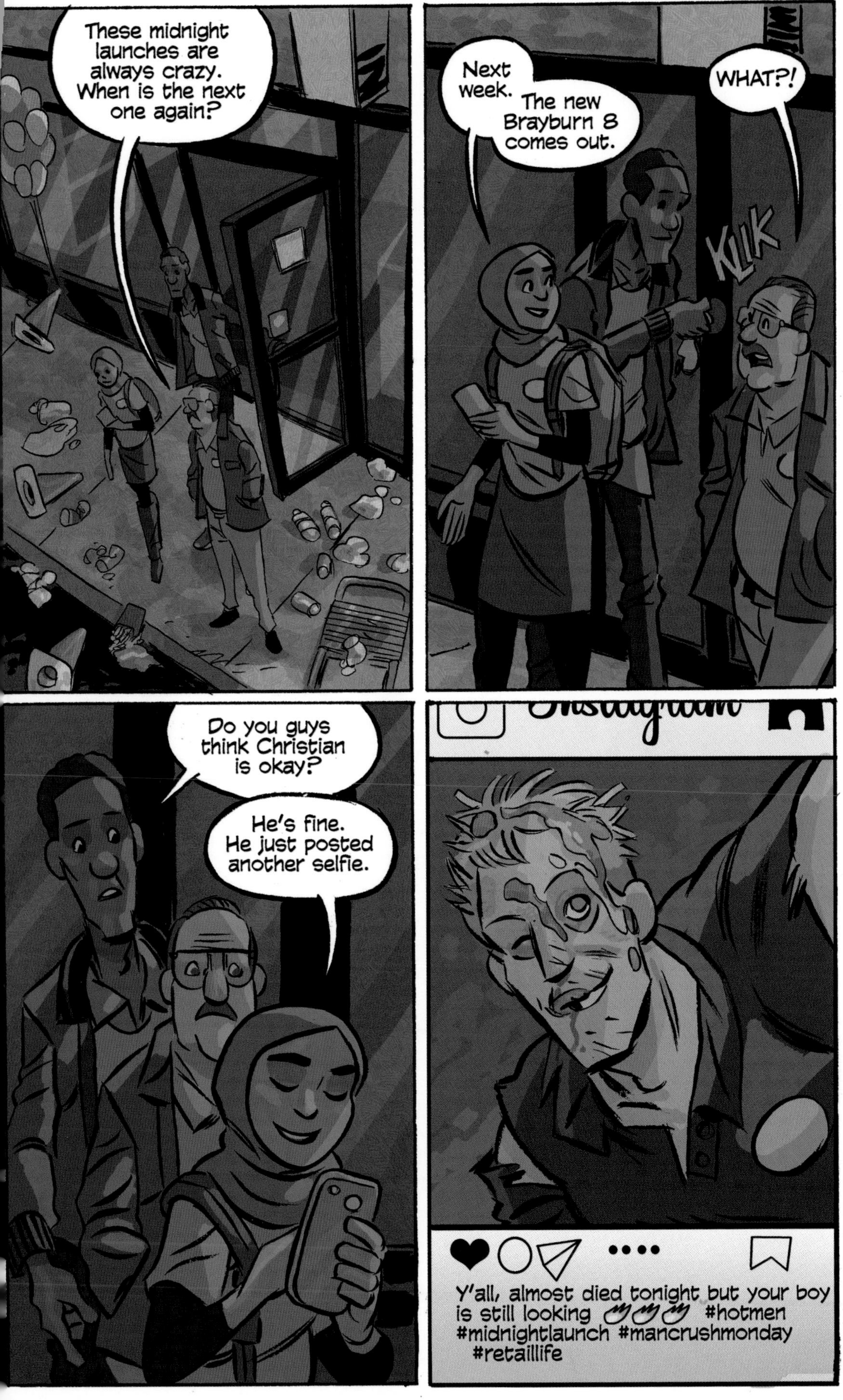
These midnight launches are always crazy. When is the next one again?
Next week.
The new Brayburn 8 comes out.
WHAT?!
KLIK
Do you guys think Christian is okay?
He's fine. He just posted another selfie.
Y'all, almost died tonight but your boy is still looking #hotmen #midnightlaunch #mancrushmonday #retaillife

# CHAPTER 2

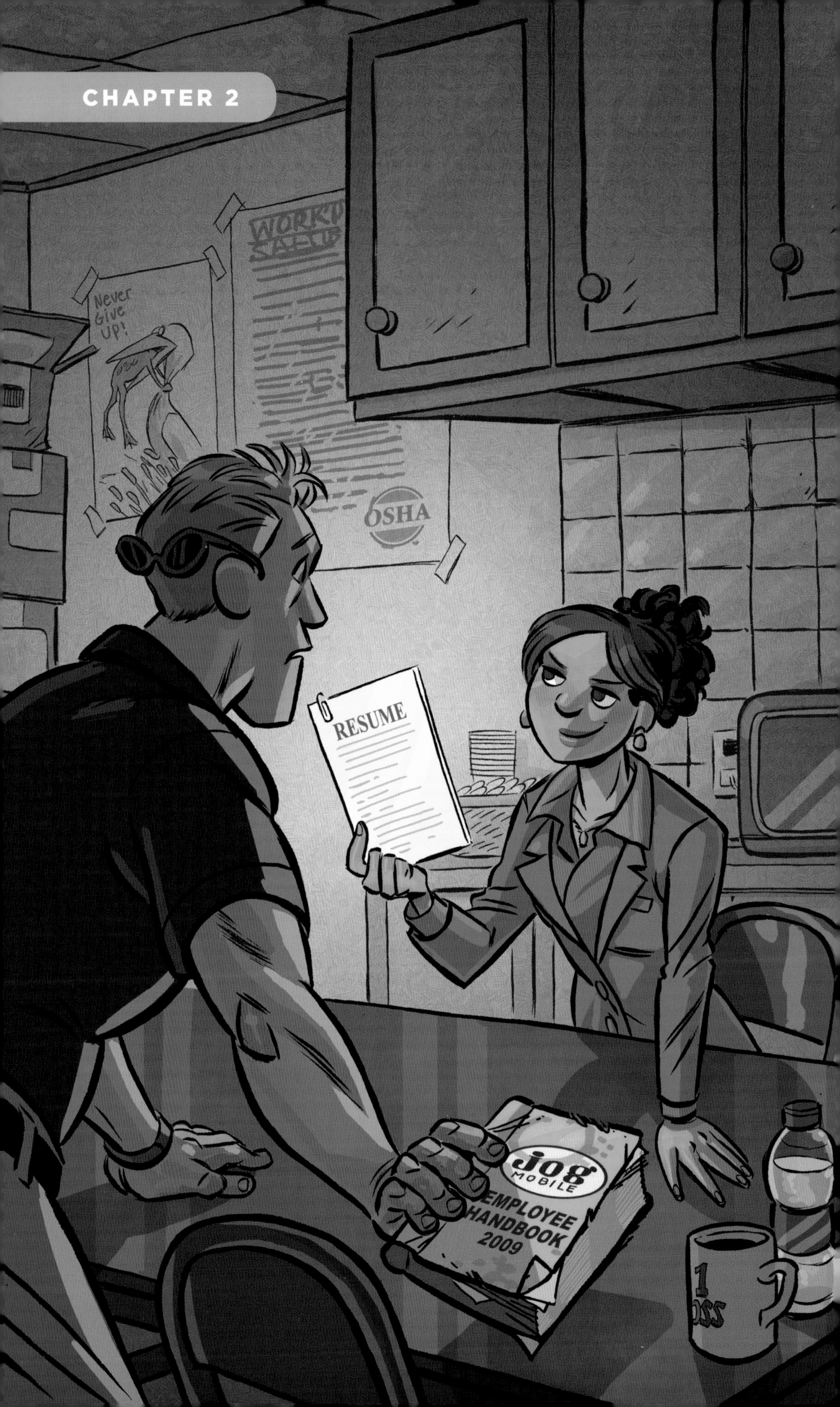
Never Give Up!
OSHA
RESUME
jog MOBILE
EMPLOYEE HANDBOOK 2009

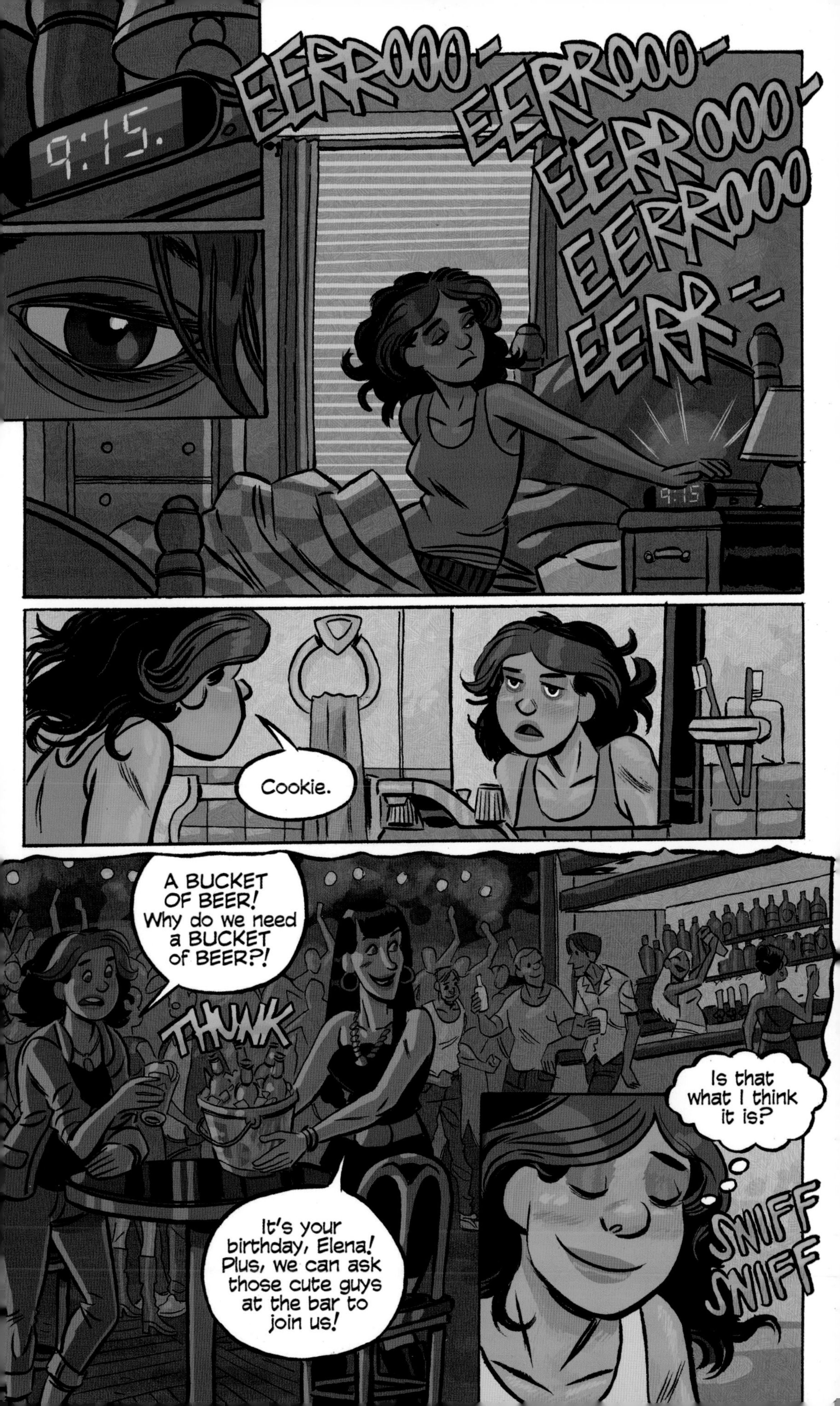
9:15.
EERROOO-EERROOO-EERROOO-EERROOO EERROOO EERR--
Cookie.
A BUCKET OF BEER! Why do we need a BUCKET of BEER?!
THUNK
It's your birthday, Elena! Plus, we can ask those cute guys at the bar to join us!
Is that what I think it is?
SNIFF SNIFF

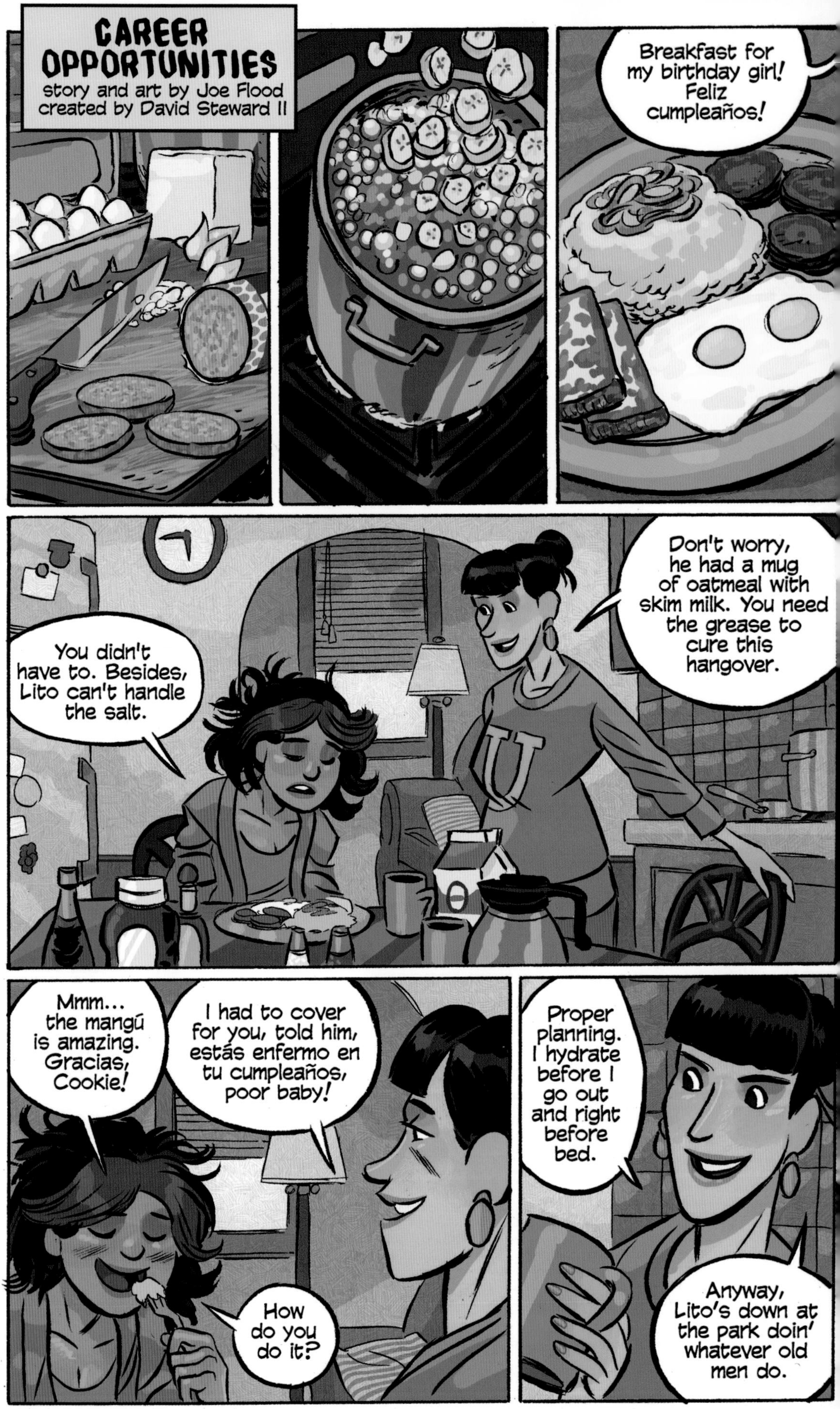
CAREER OPPORTUNITIES
story and art by Joe Flood
created by David Steward II
Breakfast for my birthday girl! Feliz cumpleaños!
You didn't have to. Besides, Lito can't handle the salt.
Don't worry, he had a mug of oatmeal with skim milk. You need the grease to cure this hangover.
Mmm... the mangú is amazing. Gracias, Cookie!
I had to cover for you, told him, estás enfermo en tu cumpleaños, poor baby!
How do you do it?
Proper planning. I hydrate before I go out and right before bed.
Anyway, Lito's down at the park doin' whatever old men do.

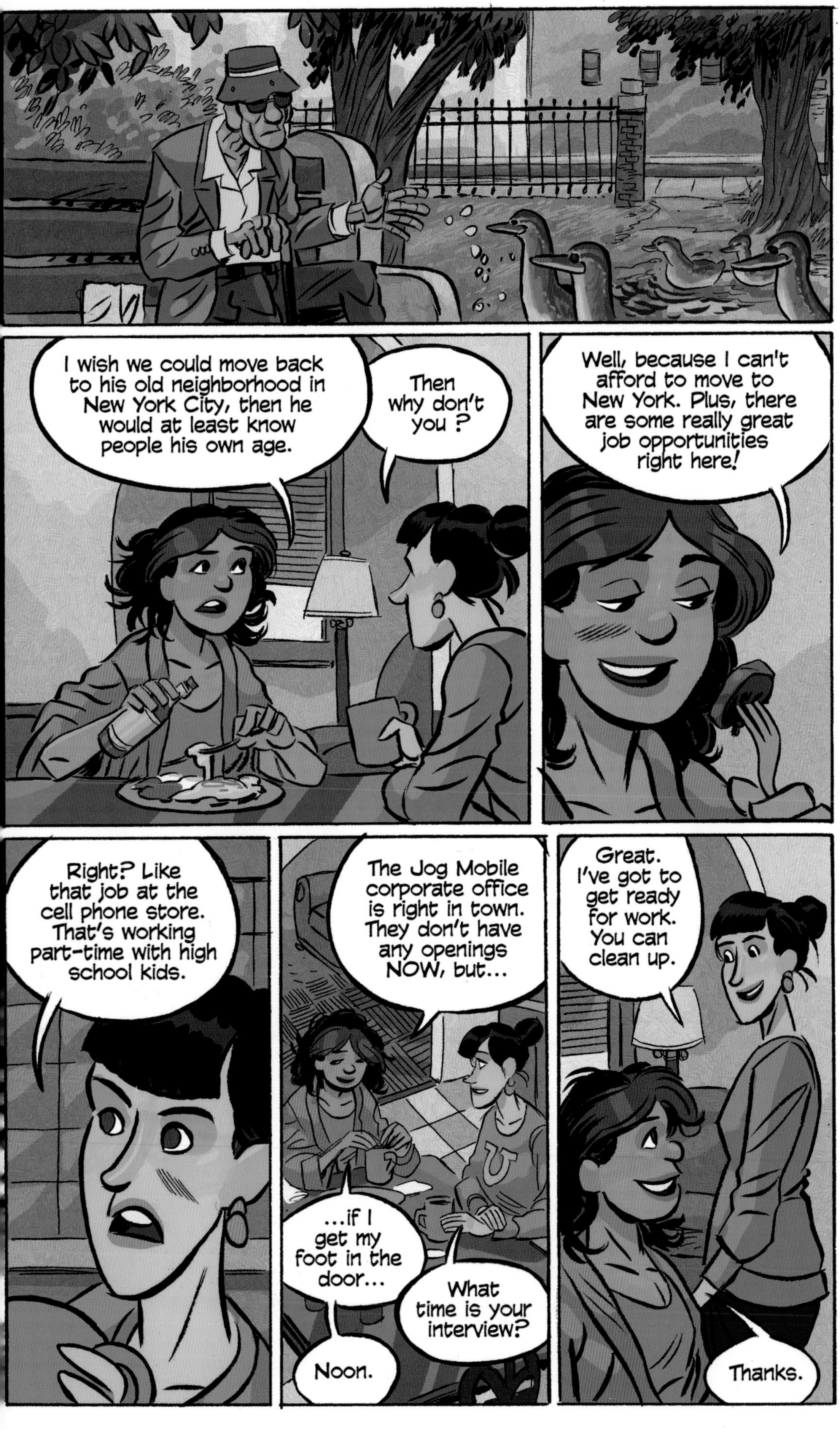
I wish we could move back to his old neighborhood in New York City, then he would at least know people his own age.
Then why don't you ?
Well, because I can't afford to move to New York. Plus, there are some really great job opportunities right here!
Right? Like that job at the cell phone store. That's working part-time with high school kids.
The Jog Mobile corporate office is right in town. They don't have any openings NOW, but...
...if I get my foot in the door...
What time is your interview?
Noon.
Great. I've got to get ready for work. You can clean up.
Thanks.

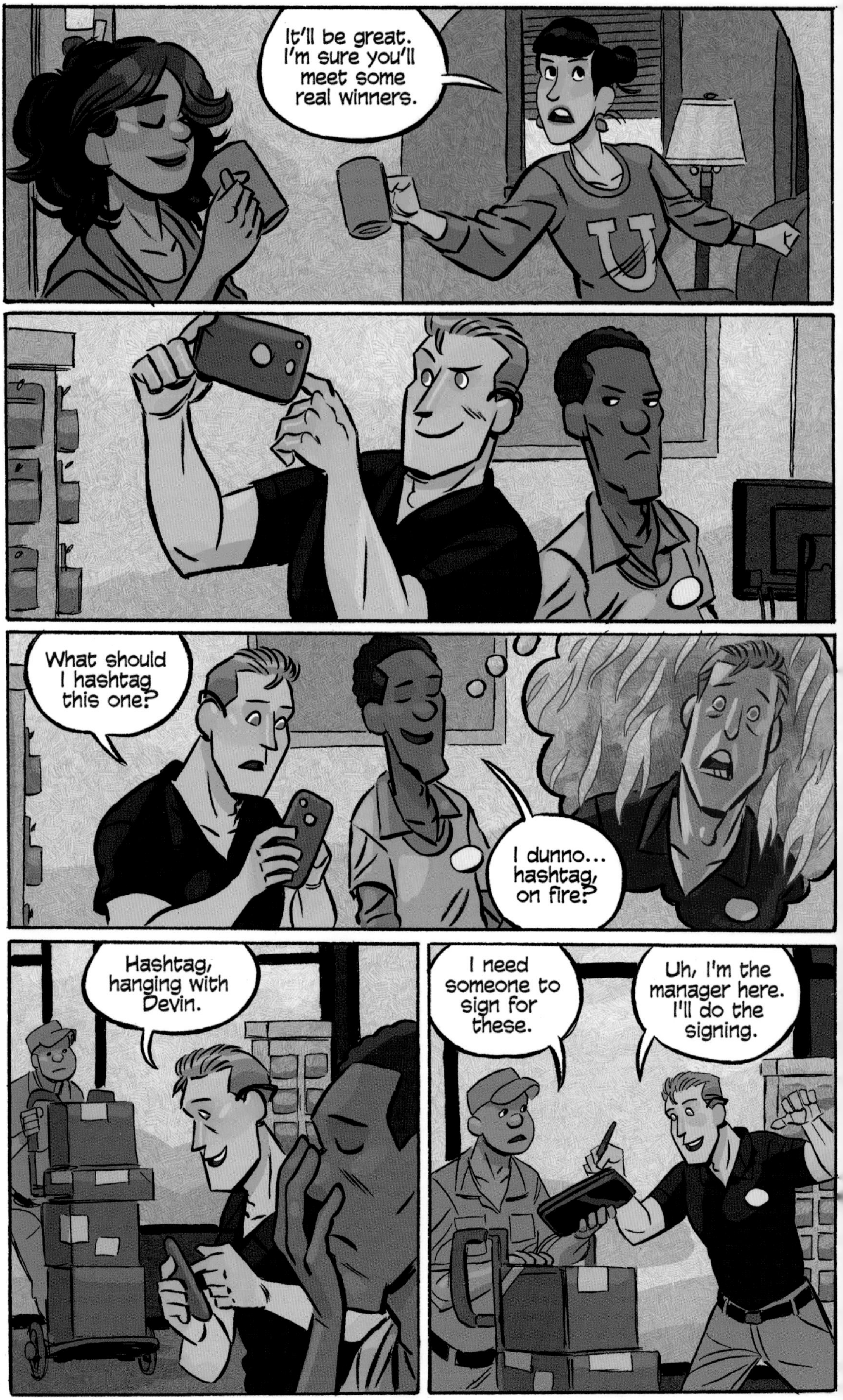
It'll be great. I'm sure you'll meet some real winners.
What should I hashtag this one?
I dunno... hashtag, on fire?
Hashtag, hanging with Devin.
I need someone to sign for these.
Uh, I'm the manager here. I'll do the signing.

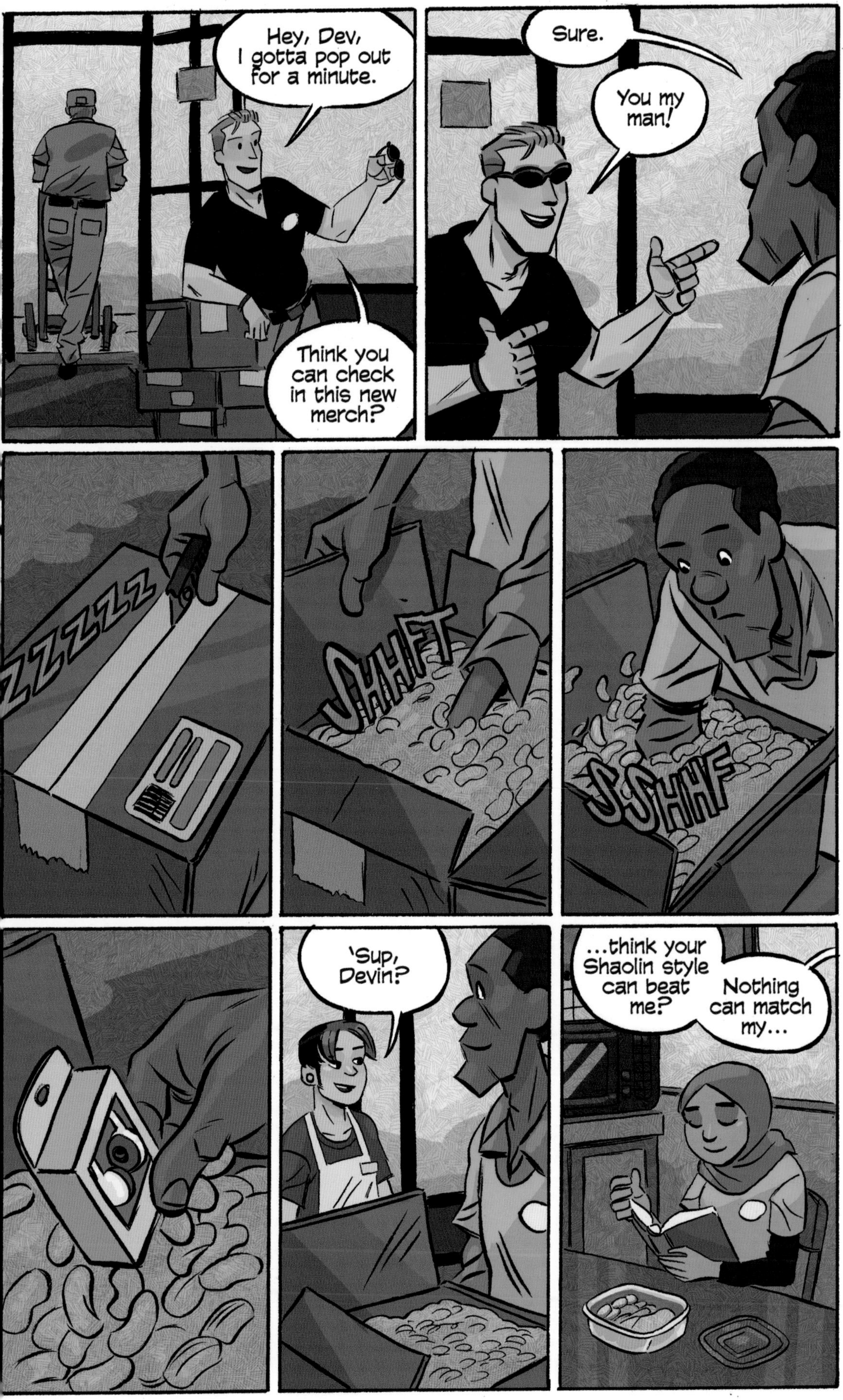
Hey, Dev,
I gotta pop out for a minute.
Think you can check in this new merch?
Sure.
You my man!
ZZZZZZ
SHHFT
SSHHF
'Sup, Devin?
...think your Shaolin style can beat me?
Nothing can match my...

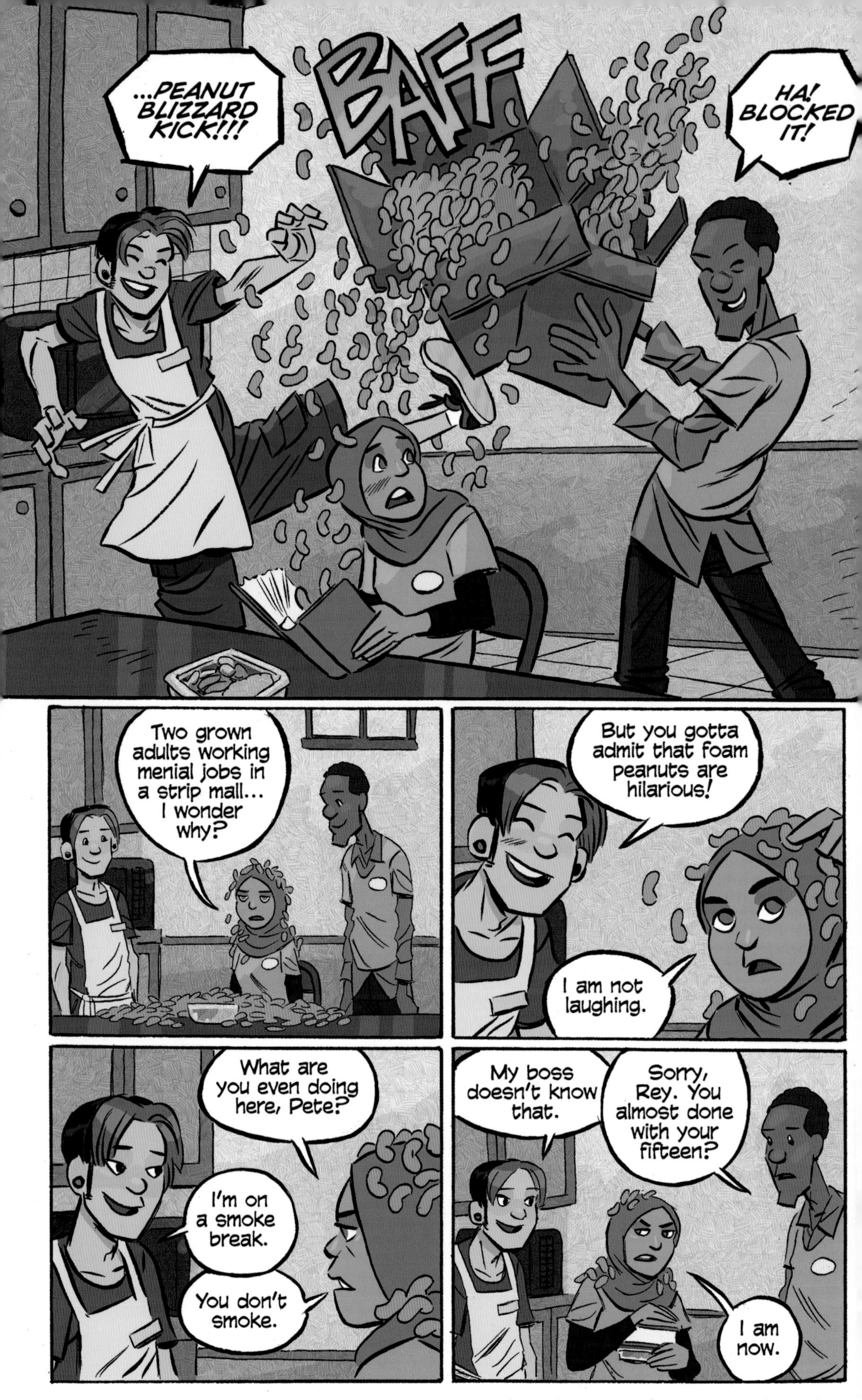
...PEANUT BLIZZARD KICK!!!
BAFF
HA! BLOCKED IT!
Two grown adults working menial jobs in a strip mall... I wonder why?
But you gotta admit that foam peanuts are hilarious!
I am not laughing.
What are you even doing here, Pete?
I'm on a smoke break.
You don't smoke.
My boss doesn't know that.
Sorry, Rey. You almost done with your fifteen?
I am now.

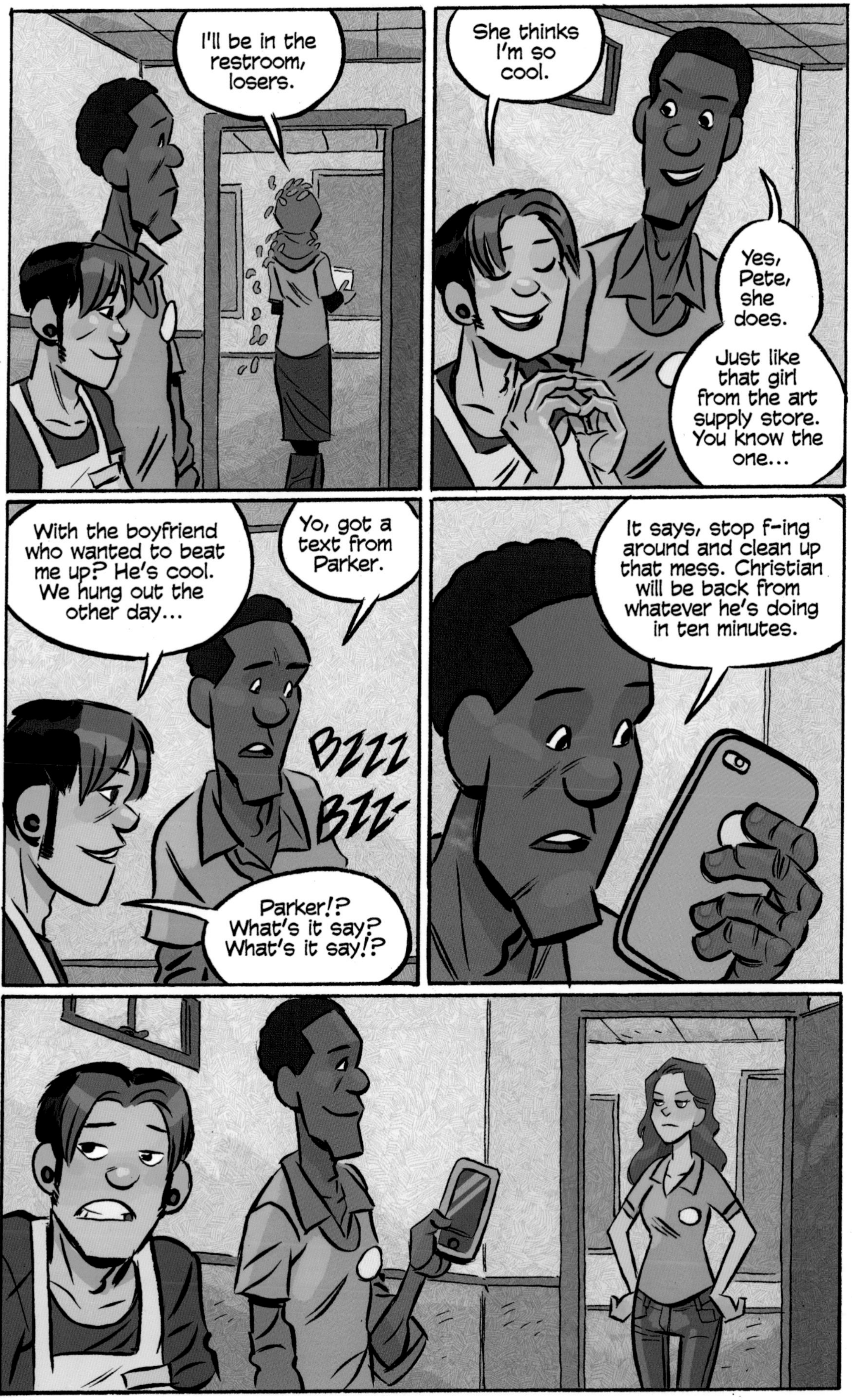
I'll be in the restroom, losers.
She thinks I'm so cool.
Yes, Pete, she does.
Just like that girl from the art supply store. You know the one...
With the boyfriend who wanted to beat me up? He's cool. We hung out the other day...
Yo, got a text from Parker.
BZZZ BZZ-
Parker!? What's it say? What's it say!?
It says, stop f-ing around and clean up that mess. Christian will be back from whatever he's doing in ten minutes.

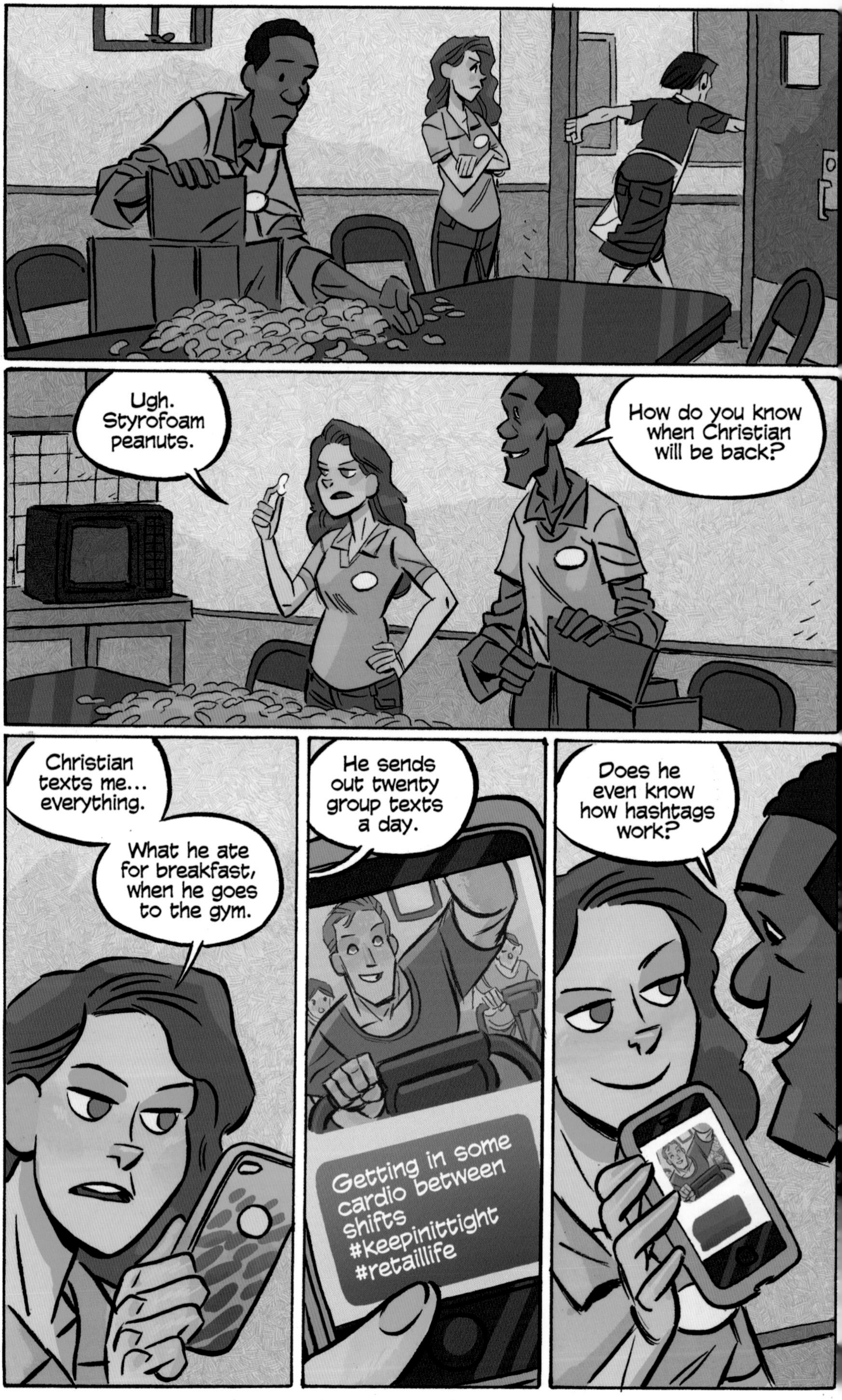
Ugh. Styrofoam peanuts.
How do you know when Christian will be back?
Christian texts me... everything.
What he ate for breakfast, when he goes to the gym.
He sends out twenty group texts a day.
Getting in some cardio between shifts #keepinittight #retaillife
Does he even know how hashtags work?

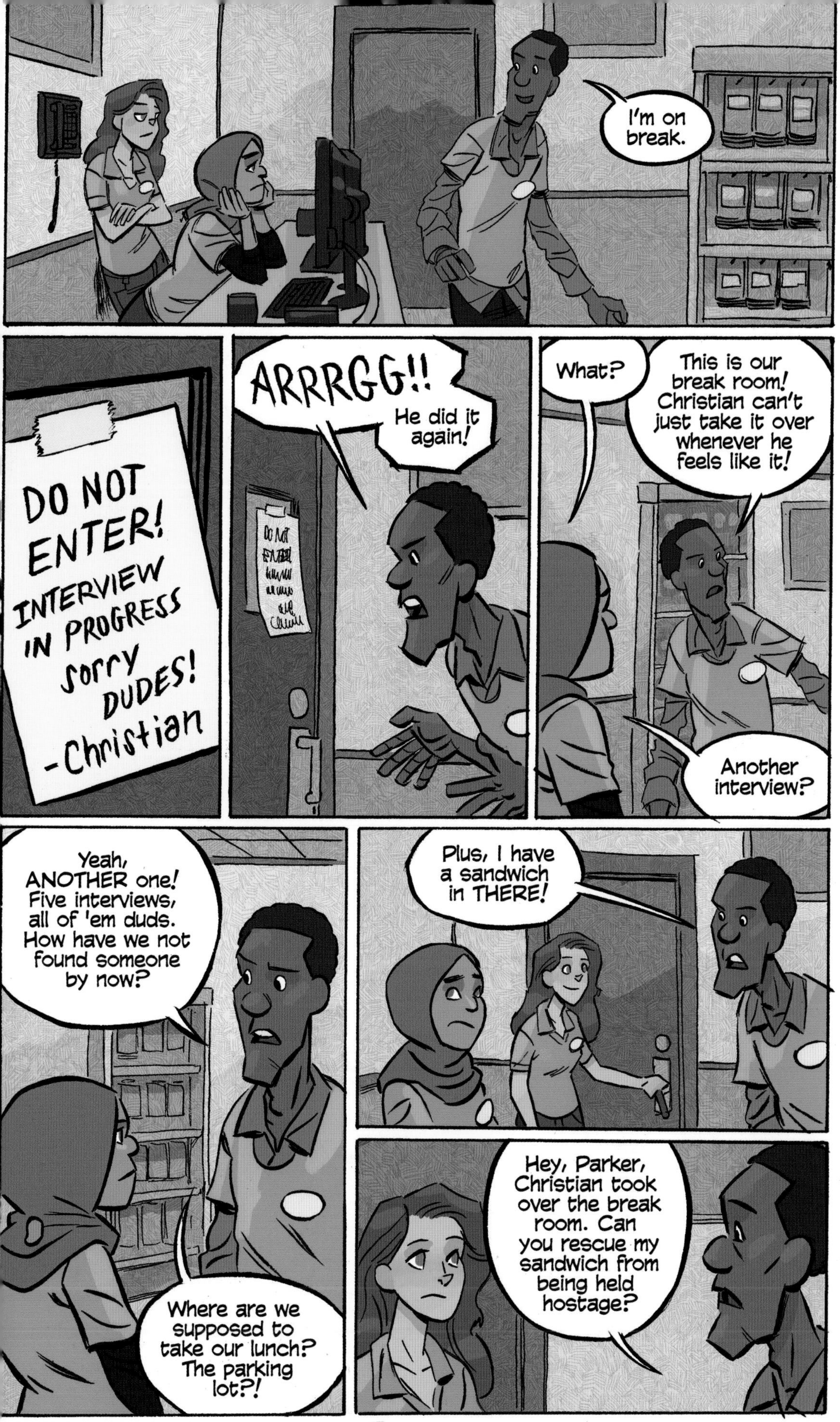

I'm on break.
DO NOT ENTER! INTERVIEW IN PROGRESS Sorry DUDES! -Christian
ARRRGG!!
He did it again!
What?
This is our break room! Christian can't just take it over whenever he feels like it!
Another interview?
Yeah, ANOTHER one! Five interviews, all of 'em duds. How have we not found someone by now?
Where are we supposed to take our lunch? The parking lot?!
Plus, I have a sandwich in THERE!
Hey, Parker, Christian took over the break room. Can you rescue my sandwich from being held hostage?

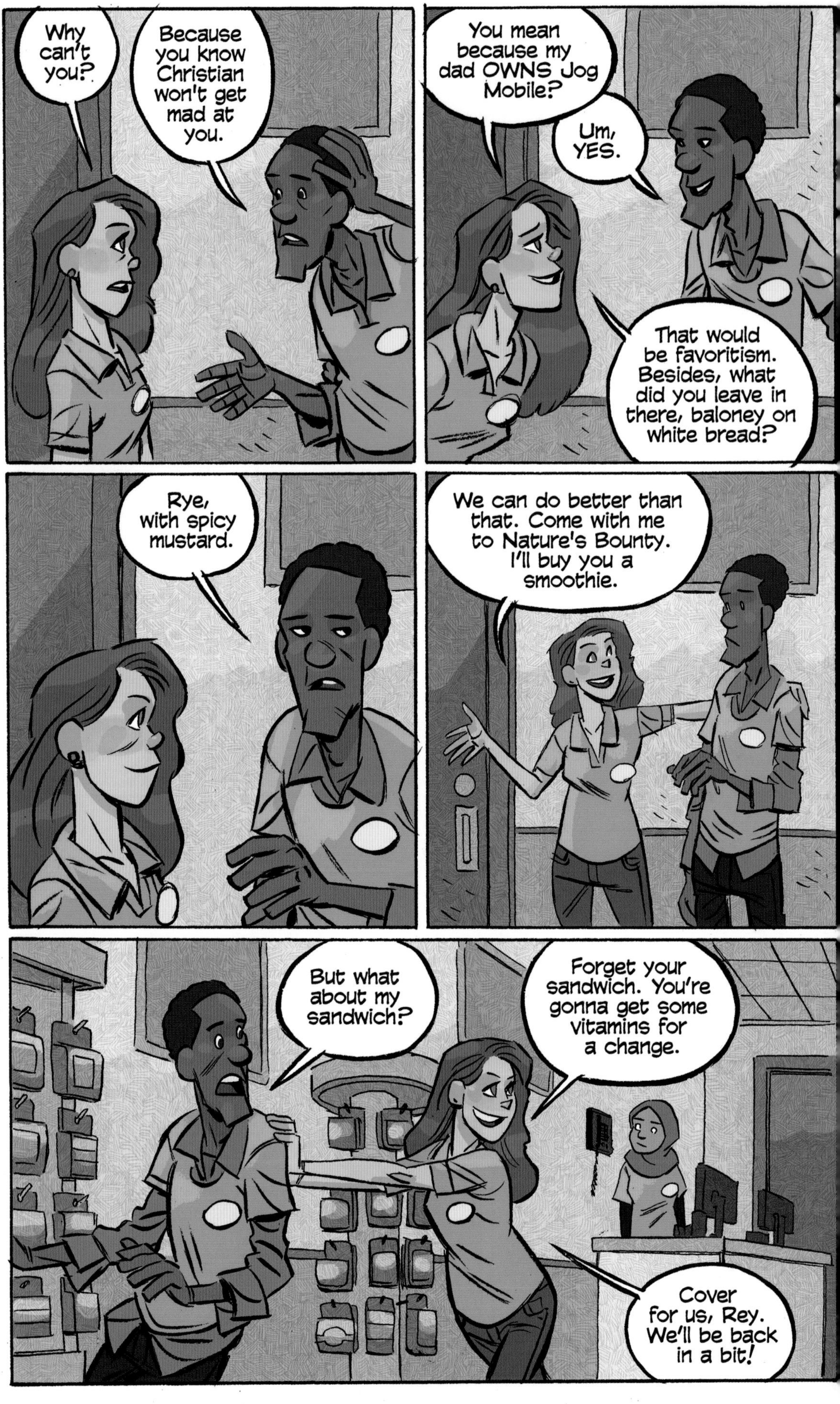
Why can't you?
Because you know Christian won't get mad at you.
You mean because my dad OWNS Jog Mobile?
Um, YES.
That would be favoritism. Besides, what did you leave in there, baloney on white bread?
Rye, with spicy mustard.
We can do better than that. Come with me to Nature's Bounty. I'll buy you a smoothie.
But what about my sandwich?
Forget your sandwich. You're gonna get some vitamins for a change.
Cover for us, Rey. We'll be back in a bit!

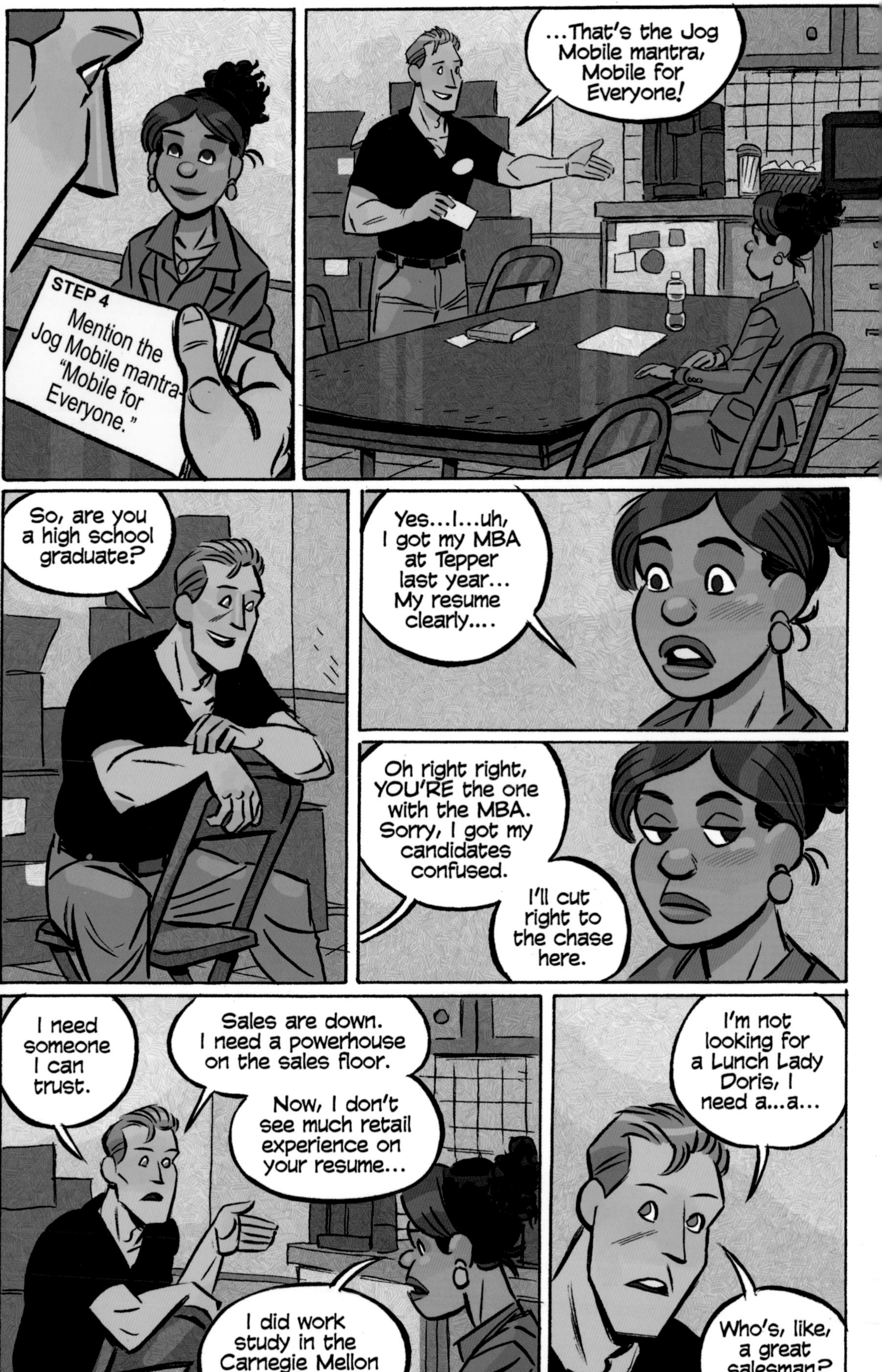
STEP 4
Mention the Jog Mobile mantra- "Mobile for Everyone."
...That's the Jog Mobile mantra, Mobile for Everyone!
So, are you a high school graduate?
Yes...I...uh, I got my MBA at Tepper last year... My resume clearly....
Oh right right, YOU'RE the one with the MBA. Sorry, I got my candidates confused.
I'll cut right to the chase here.
I need someone I can trust.
Sales are down. I need a powerhouse on the sales floor.
Now, I don't see much retail experience on your resume...
I did work study in the Carnegie Mellon ...commissary.
I'm not looking for a Lunch Lady Doris, I need a...a...
Who's, like, a great salesman?

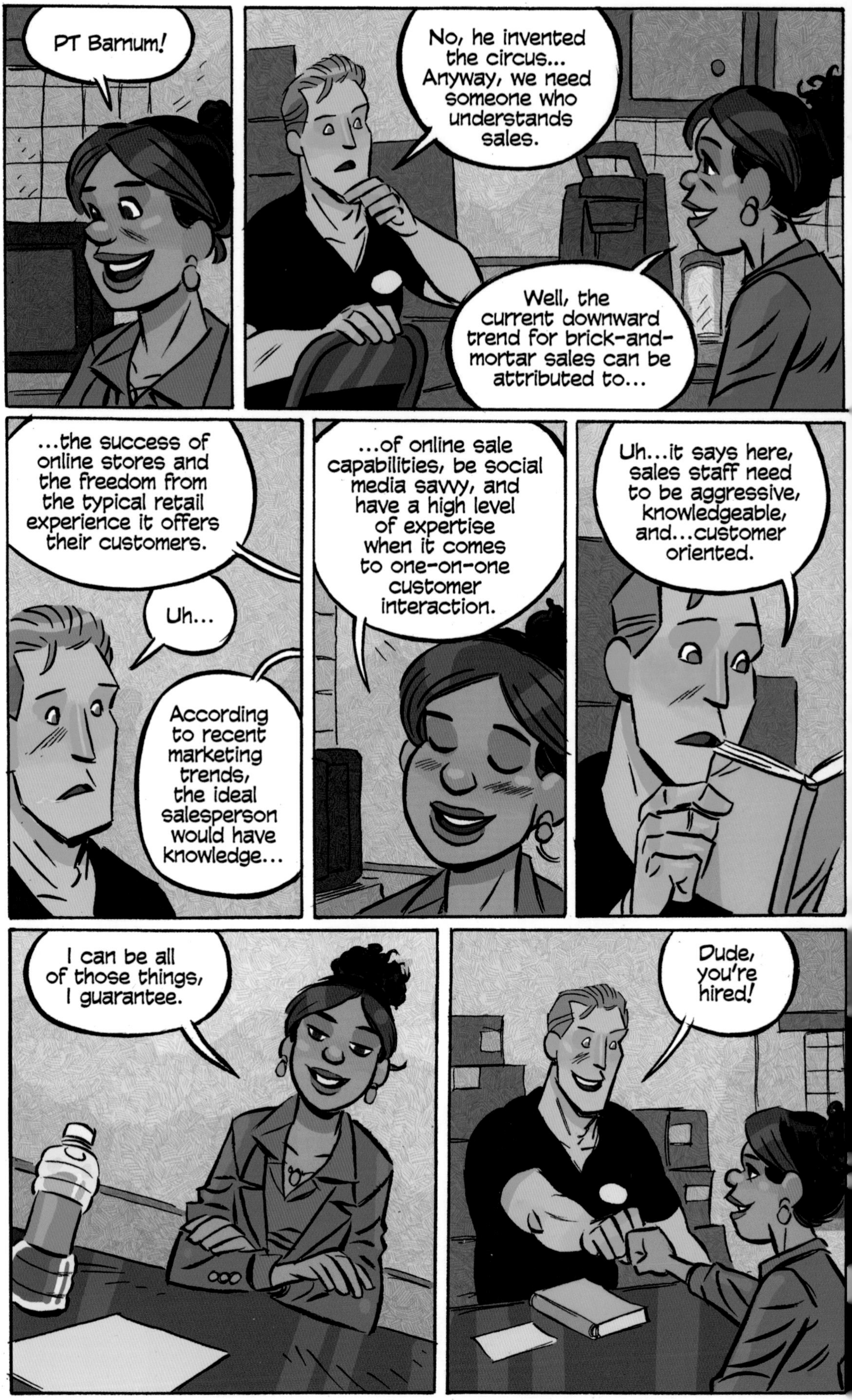
PT Barnum!
No, he invented the circus... Anyway, we need someone who understands sales.
Well, the current downward trend for brick-and-mortar sales can be attributed to...
...the success of online stores and the freedom from the typical retail experience it offers their customers.
Uh...
According to recent marketing trends, the ideal salesperson would have knowledge...
...of online sale capabilities, be social media savvy, and have a high level of expertise when it comes to one-on-one customer interaction.
Uh...it says here, sales staff need to be aggressive, knowledgeable, and...customer oriented.
I can be all of those things, I guarantee.
Dude, you're hired!

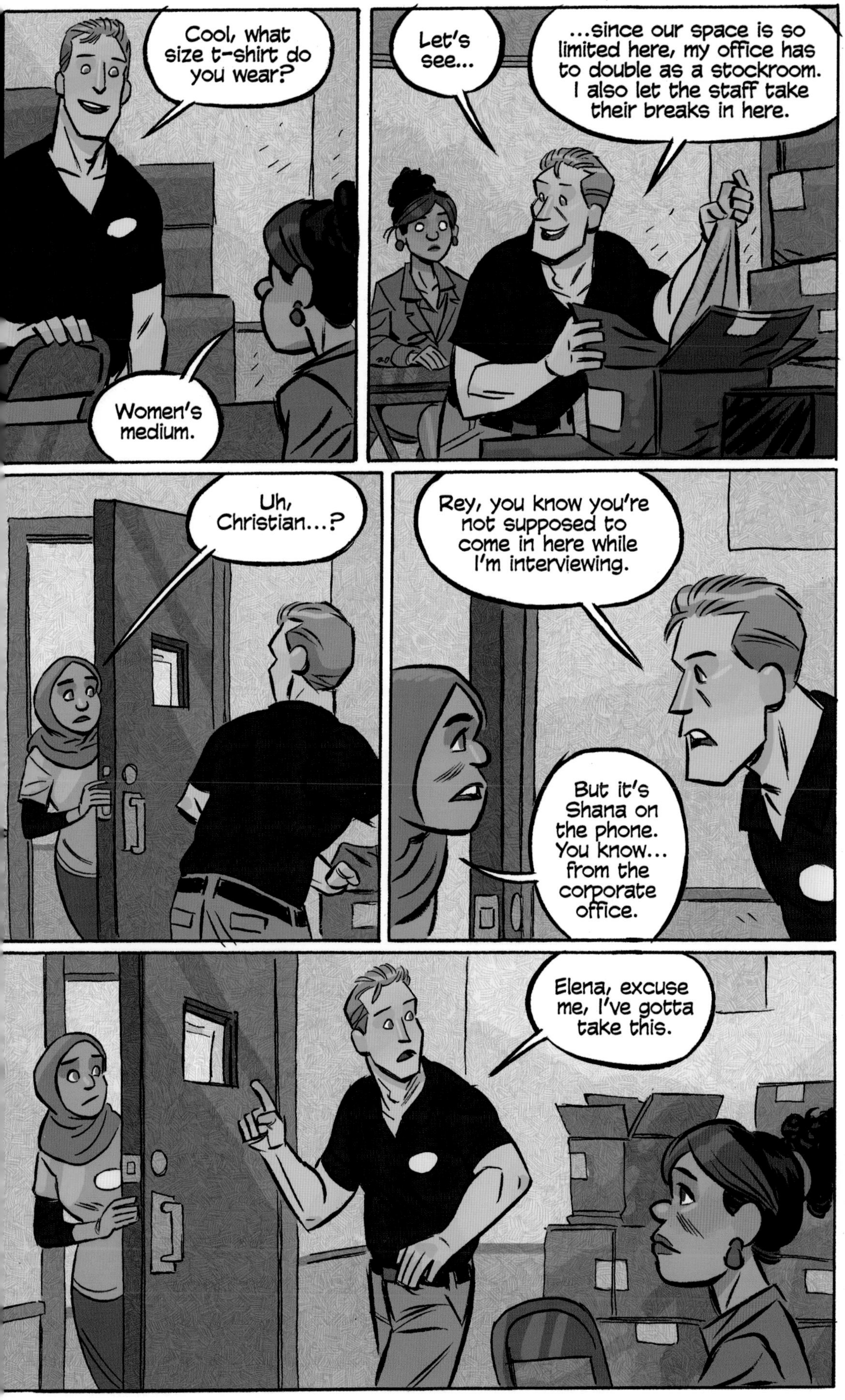
Cool, what size t-shirt do you wear?
Women's medium.
Let's see...
...since our space is so limited here, my office has to double as a stockroom. I also let the staff take their breaks in here.
Uh, Christian...?
Rey, you know you're not supposed to come in here while I'm interviewing.
But it's Shana on the phone. You know... from the corporate office.
Elena, excuse me, I've gotta take this.

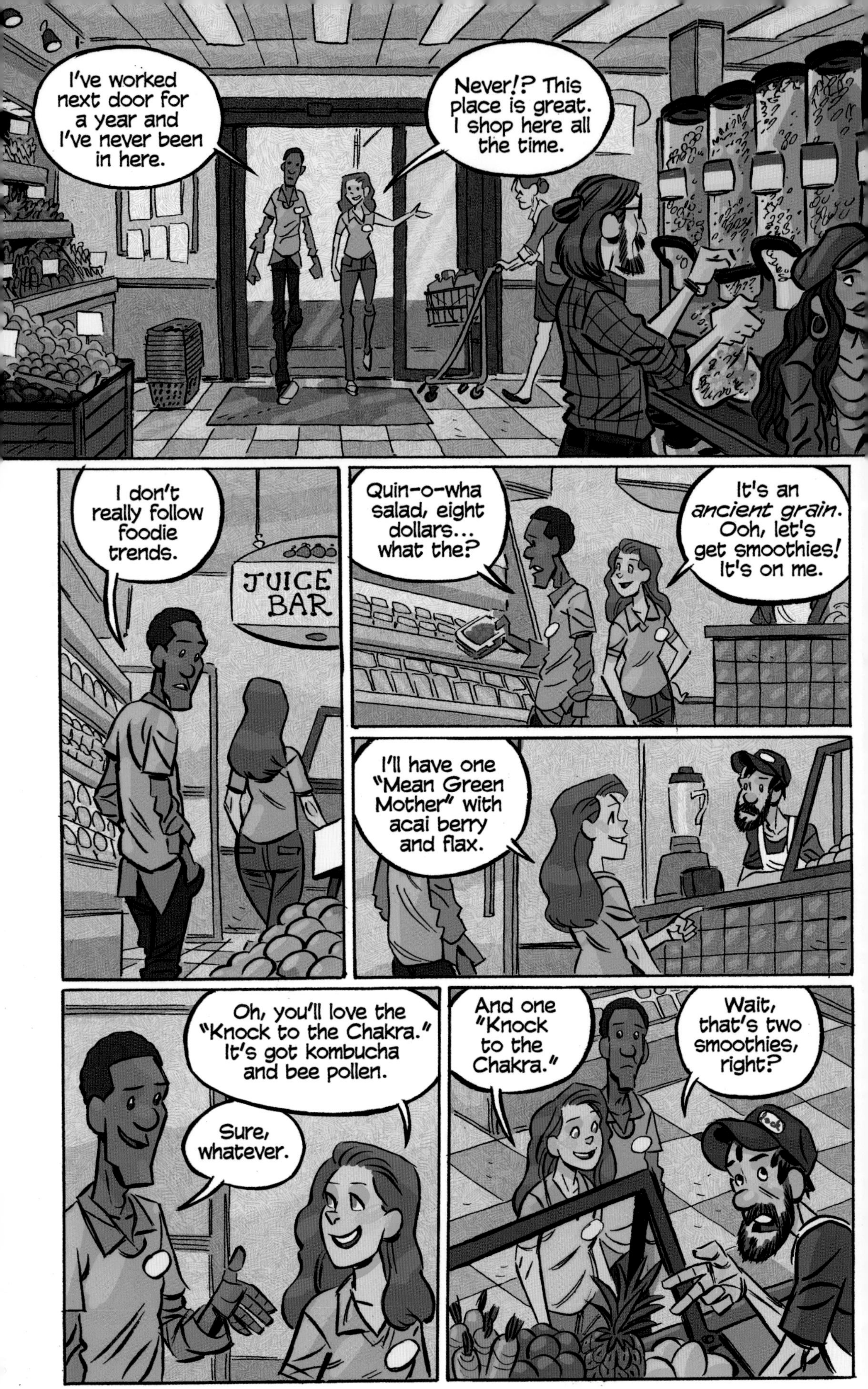
I've worked next door for a year and I've never been in here.
Never!? This place is great. I shop here all the time.
I don't really follow foodie trends.
JUICE BAR
Quin-o-wha salad, eight dollars... what the?
It's an *ancient grain*. Ooh, let's get smoothies! It's on me.
I'll have one "Mean Green Mother" with acai berry and flax.
Oh, you'll love the "Knock to the Chakra." It's got kombucha and bee pollen.
Sure, whatever.
And one "Knock to the Chakra."
Wait, that's two smoothies, right?

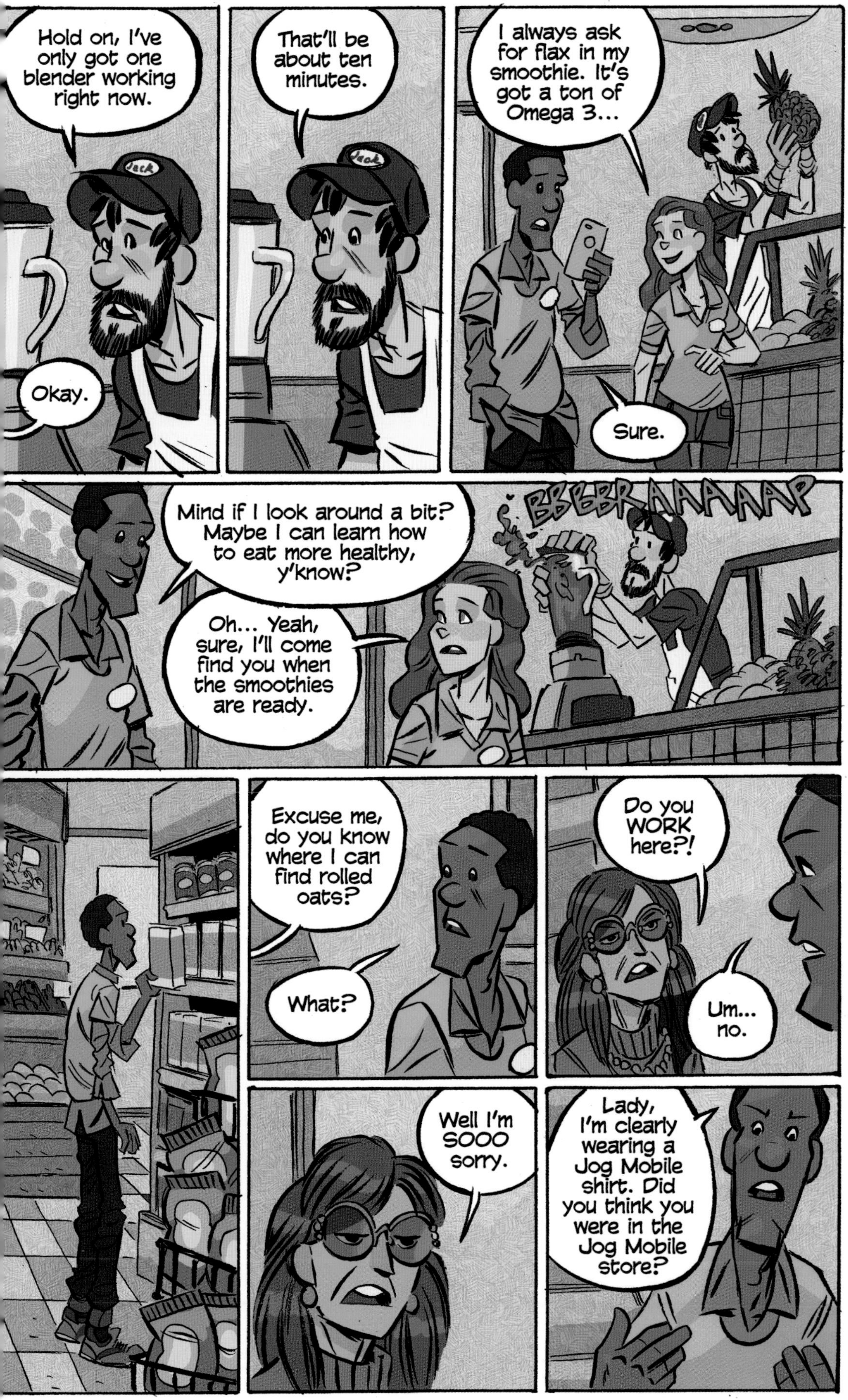
Hold on, I've only got one blender working right now.
Okay.
That'll be about ten minutes.
I always ask for flax in my smoothie. It's got a ton of Omega 3...
Sure.
Mind if I look around a bit? Maybe I can learn how to eat more healthy, y'know?
Oh... Yeah, sure, I'll come find you when the smoothies are ready.
BBBBRAAAAAAP
Excuse me, do you know where I can find rolled oats?
What?
Do you WORK here?!
Um... no.
Well I'm SOOO sorry.
Lady, I'm clearly wearing a Jog Mobile shirt. Did you think you were in the Jog Mobile store?

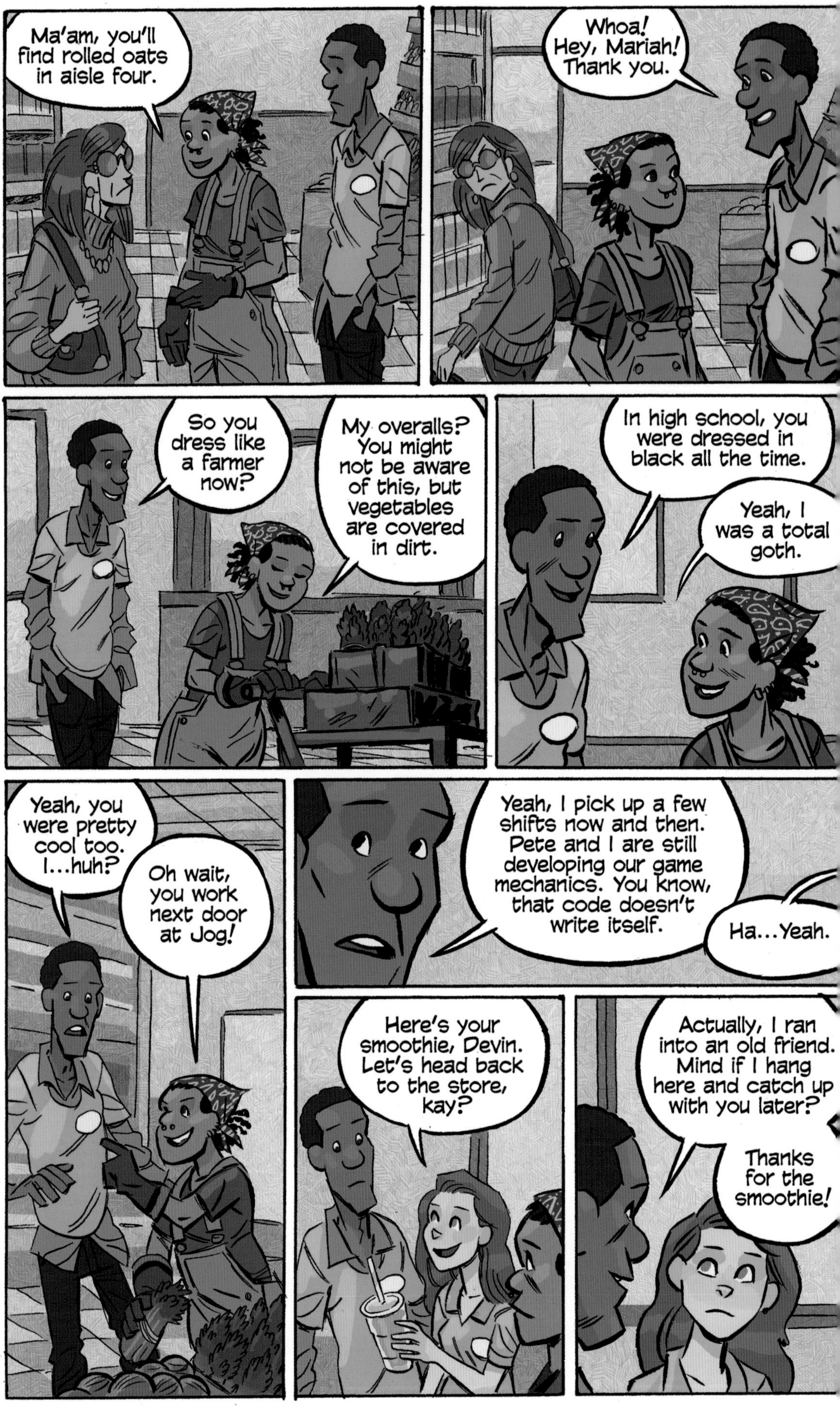
Ma'am, you'll find rolled oats in aisle four.
Whoa! Hey, Mariah! Thank you.
So you dress like a farmer now?
My overalls? You might not be aware of this, but vegetables are covered in dirt.
In high school, you were dressed in black all the time.
Yeah, I was a total goth.
Yeah, you were pretty cool too. I...huh?
Oh wait, you work next door at Jog!
Yeah, I pick up a few shifts now and then. Pete and I are still developing our game mechanics. You know, that code doesn't write itself.
Ha...Yeah.
Here's your smoothie, Devin. Let's head back to the store, kay?
Actually, I ran into an old friend. Mind if I hang here and catch up with you later?
Thanks for the smoothie!

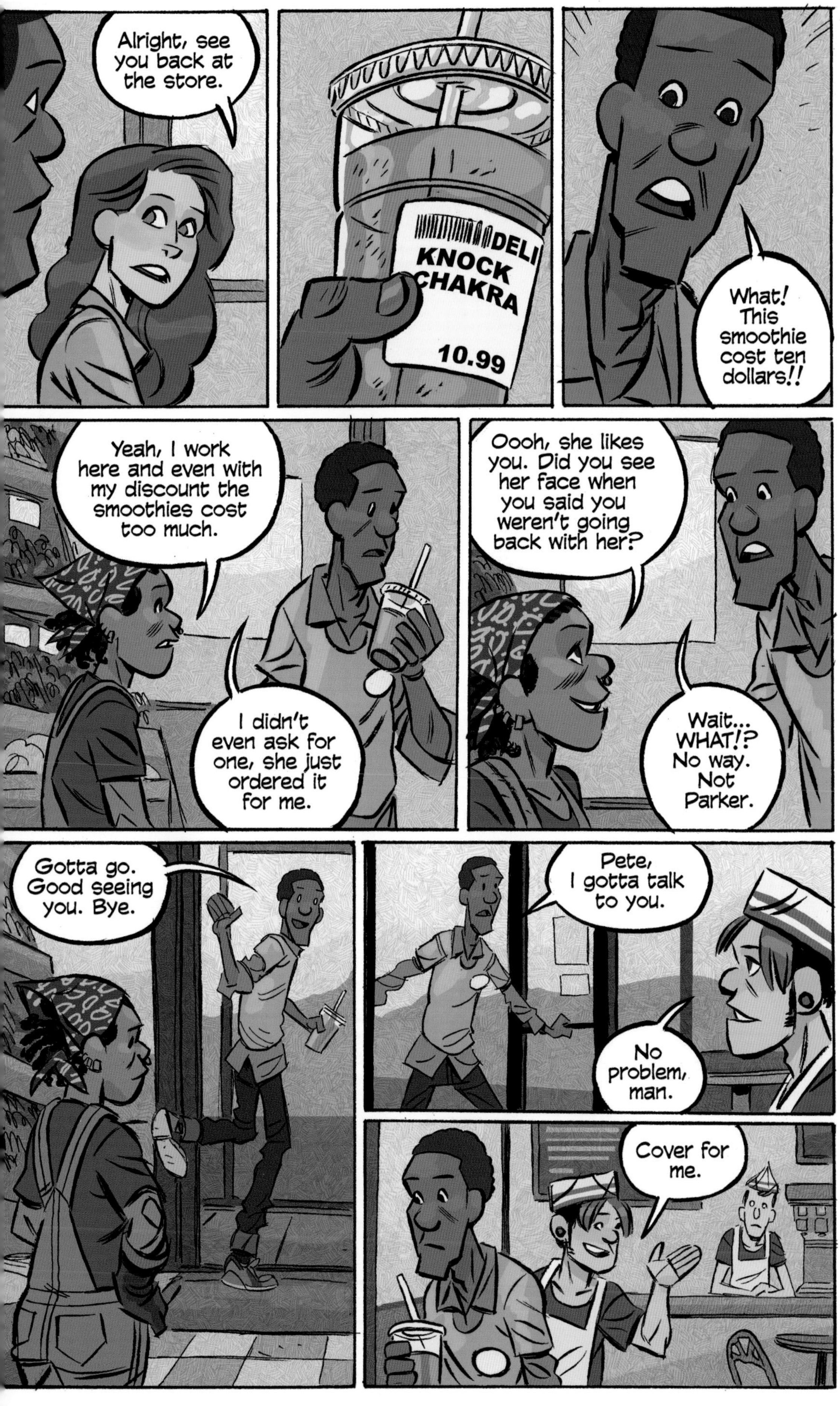

Alright, see you back at the store.
DELI
KNOCK
CHAKRA
10.99
What! This smoothie cost ten dollars!!
Yeah, I work here and even with my discount the smoothies cost too much.
I didn't even ask for one, she just ordered it for me.
Oooh, she likes you. Did you see her face when you said you weren't going back with her?
Wait... WHAT!? No way. Not Parker.
Gotta go. Good seeing you. Bye.
Pete, I gotta talk to you.
No problem, man.
Cover for me.

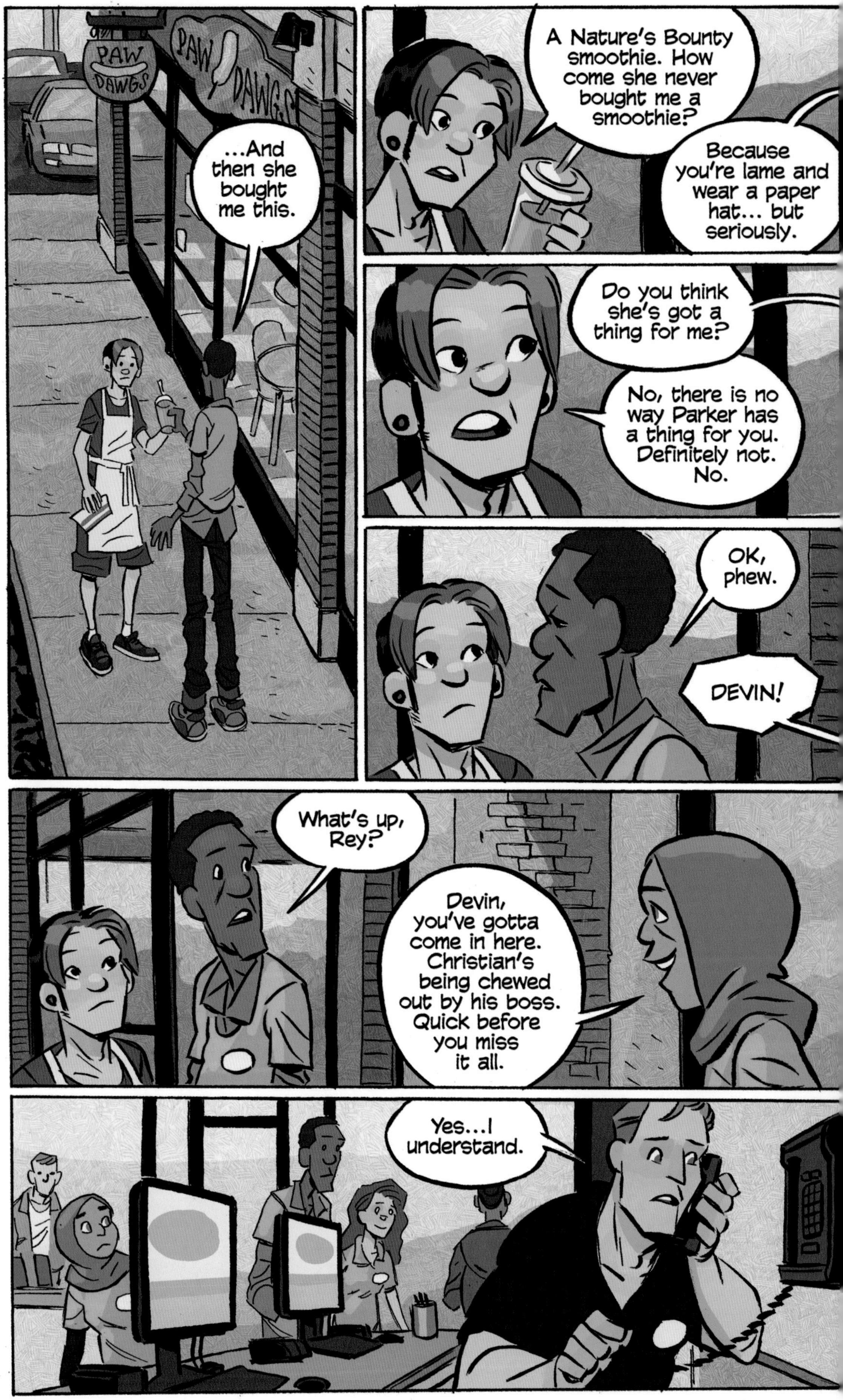
...And then she bought me this.
A Nature's Bounty smoothie. How come she never bought me a smoothie?
Because you're lame and wear a paper hat... but seriously.
Do you think she's got a thing for me?
No, there is no way Parker has a thing for you. Definitely not. No.
OK, phew.
DEVIN!
What's up, Rey?
Devin, you've gotta come in here. Christian's being chewed out by his boss. Quick before you miss it all.
Yes...I understand.

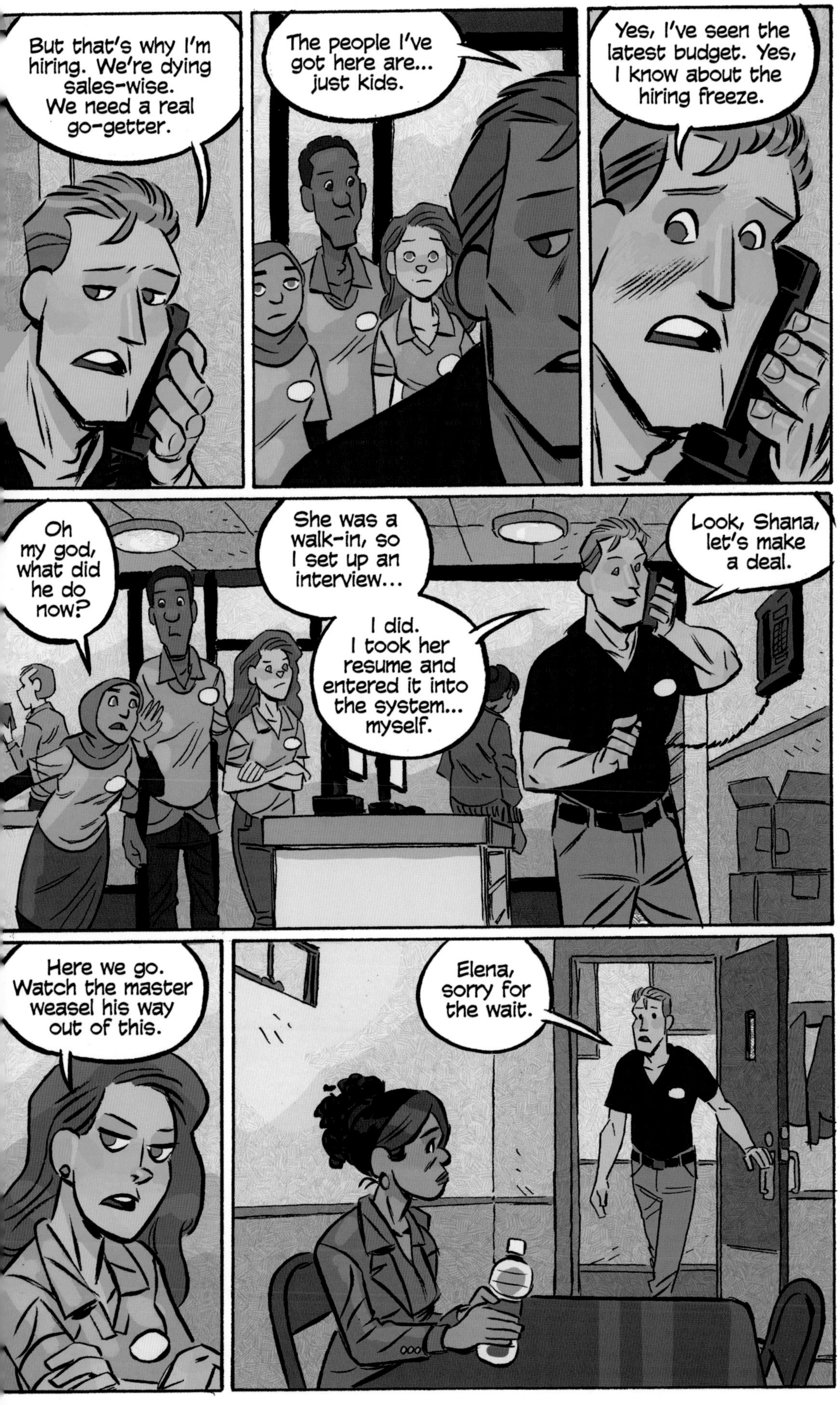
But that's why I'm hiring. We're dying sales-wise. We need a real go-getter.
The people I've got here are... just kids.
Yes, I've seen the latest budget. Yes, I know about the hiring freeze.
Oh my god, what did he do now?
She was a walk-in, so I set up an interview...
I did. I took her resume and entered it into the system... myself.
Look, Shana, let's make a deal.
Here we go. Watch the master weasel his way out of this.
Elena, sorry for the wait.

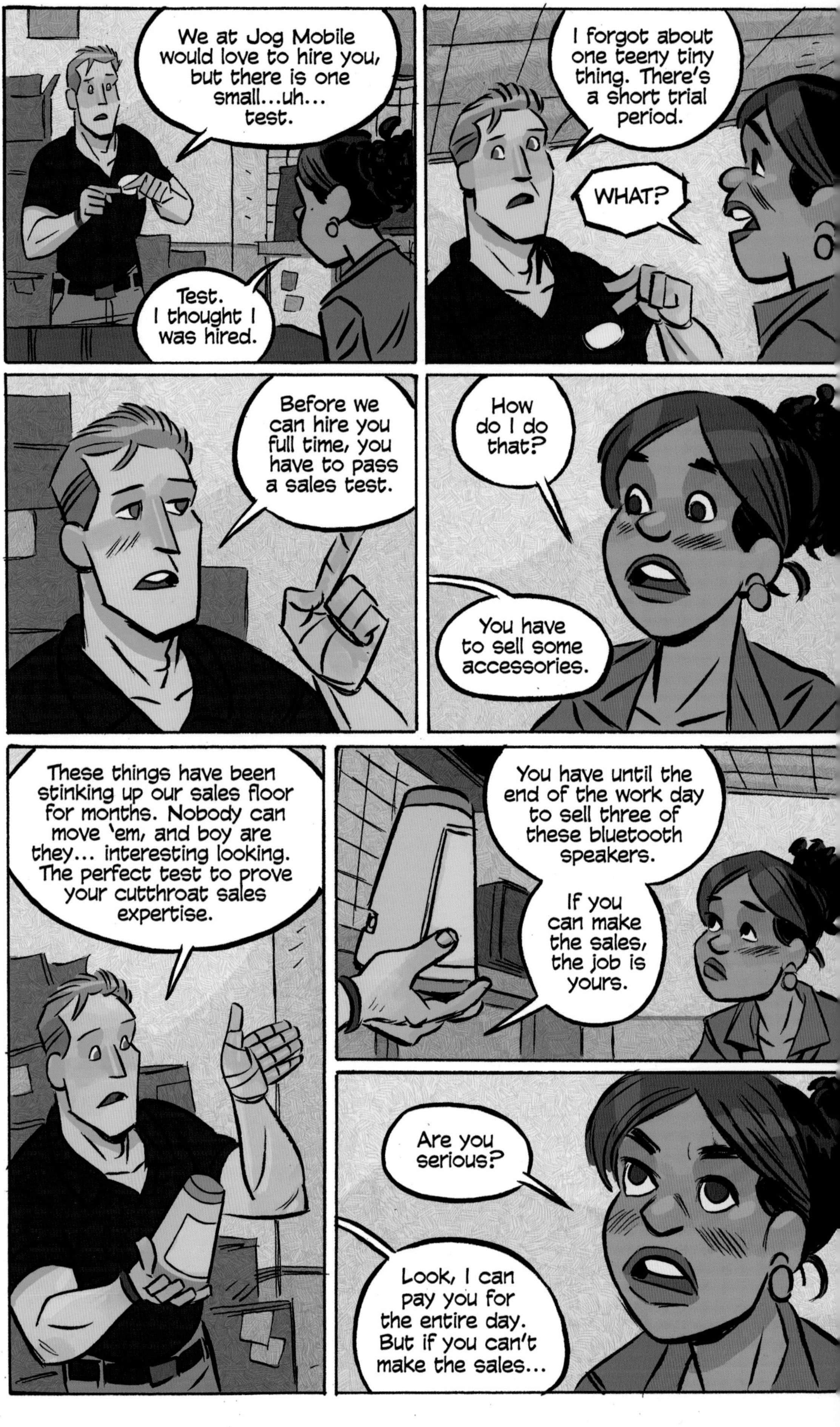
We at Jog Mobile would love to hire you, but there is one small...uh... test.
Test. I thought I was hired.
I forgot about one teeny tiny thing. There's a short trial period.
WHAT?
Before we can hire you full time, you have to pass a sales test.
How do I do that?
You have to sell some accessories.
These things have been stinking up our sales floor for months. Nobody can move 'em, and boy are they... interesting looking. The perfect test to prove your cutthroat sales expertise.
You have until the end of the work day to sell three of these bluetooth speakers.
If you can make the sales, the job is yours.
Are you serious?
Look, I can pay you for the entire day. But if you can't make the sales...

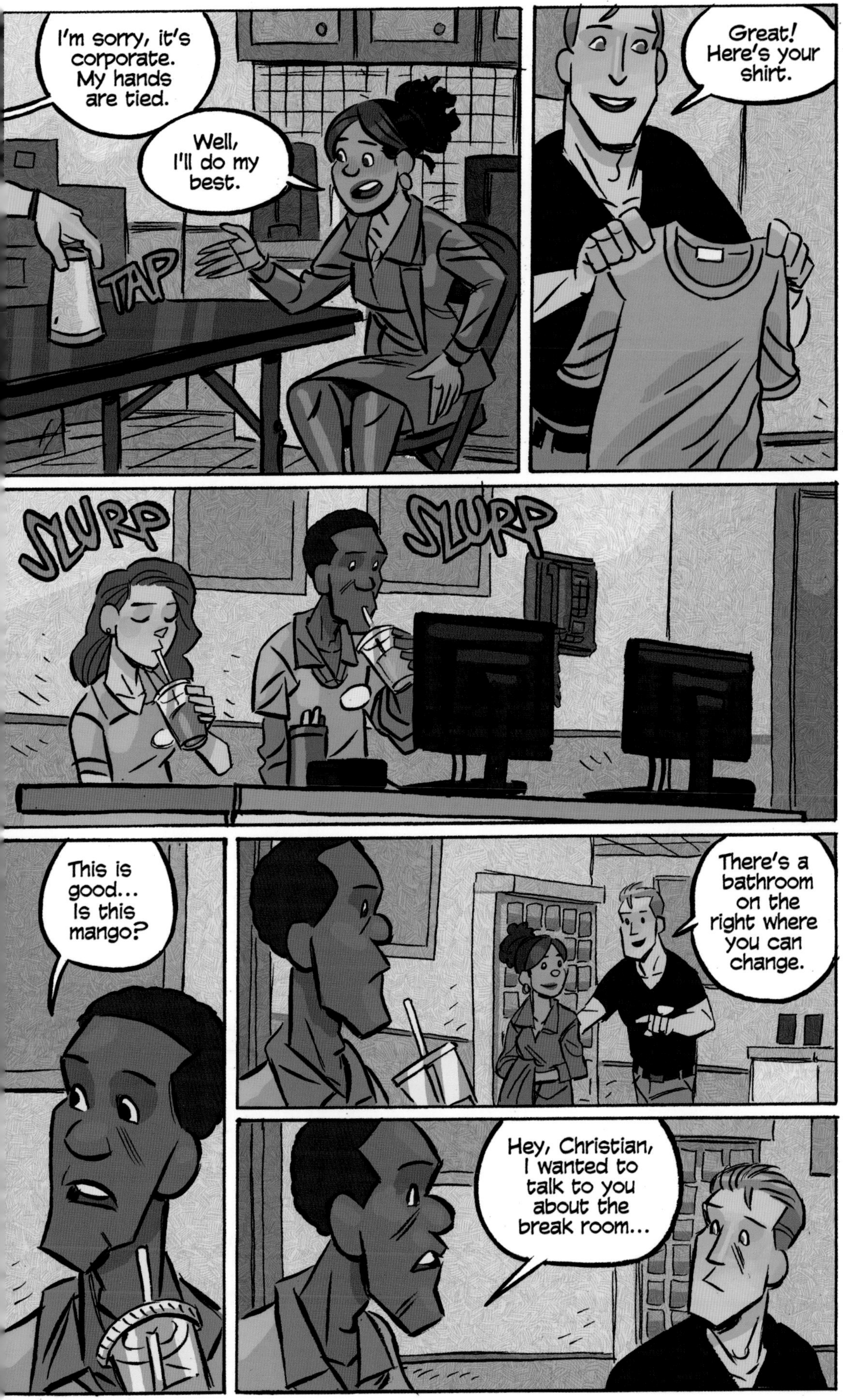
I'm sorry, it's corporate. My hands are tied.
Well, I'll do my best.
TAP
Great! Here's your shirt.
SLURP
SLURP
This is good... Is this mango?
There's a bathroom on the right where you can change.
Hey, Christian, I wanted to talk to you about the break room...

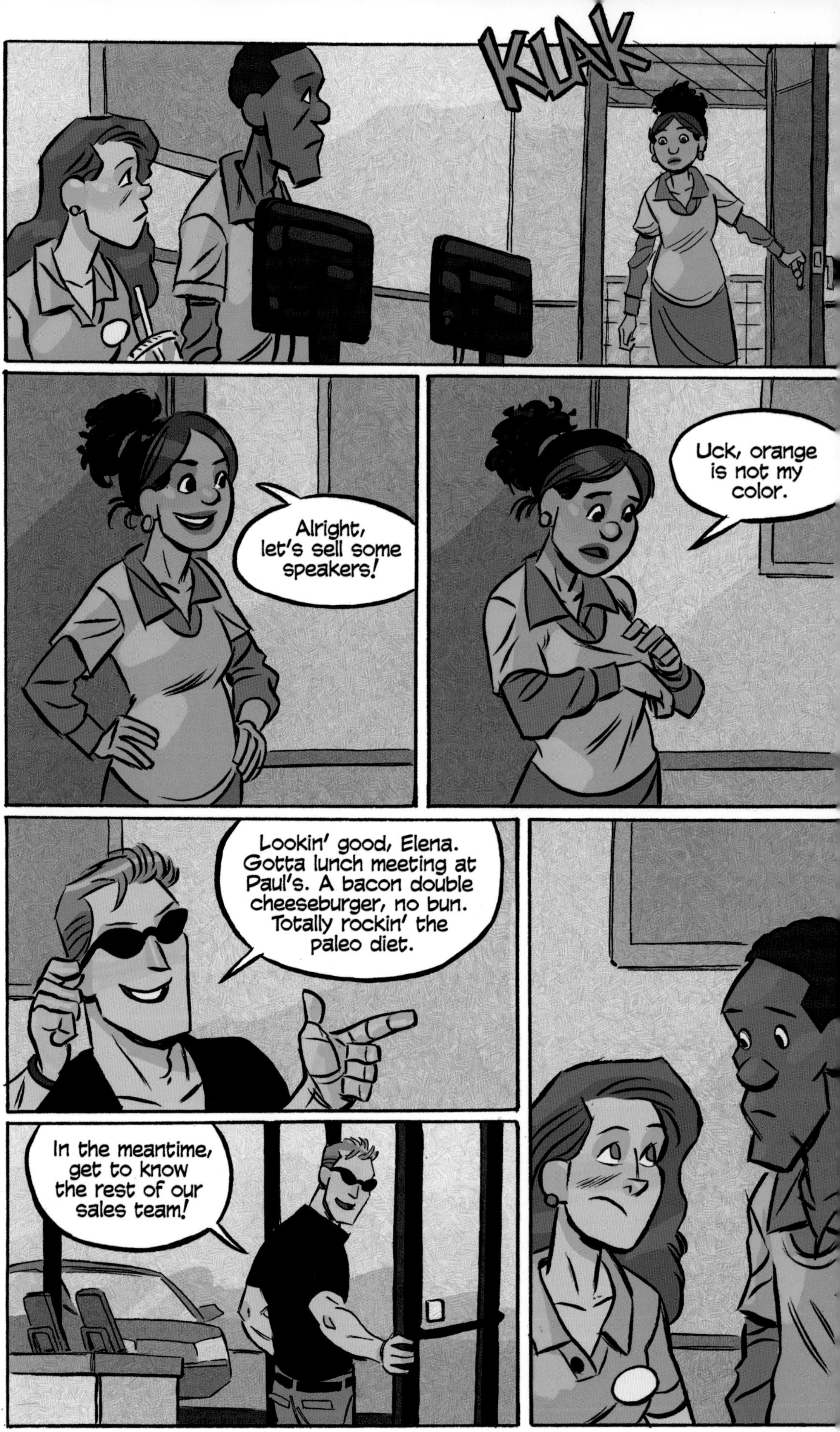
KLAK
Alright, let's sell some speakers!
Uck, orange is not my color.
Lookin' good, Elena. Gotta lunch meeting at Paul's. A bacon double cheeseburger, no bun. Totally rockin' the paleo diet.
In the meantime, get to know the rest of our sales team!

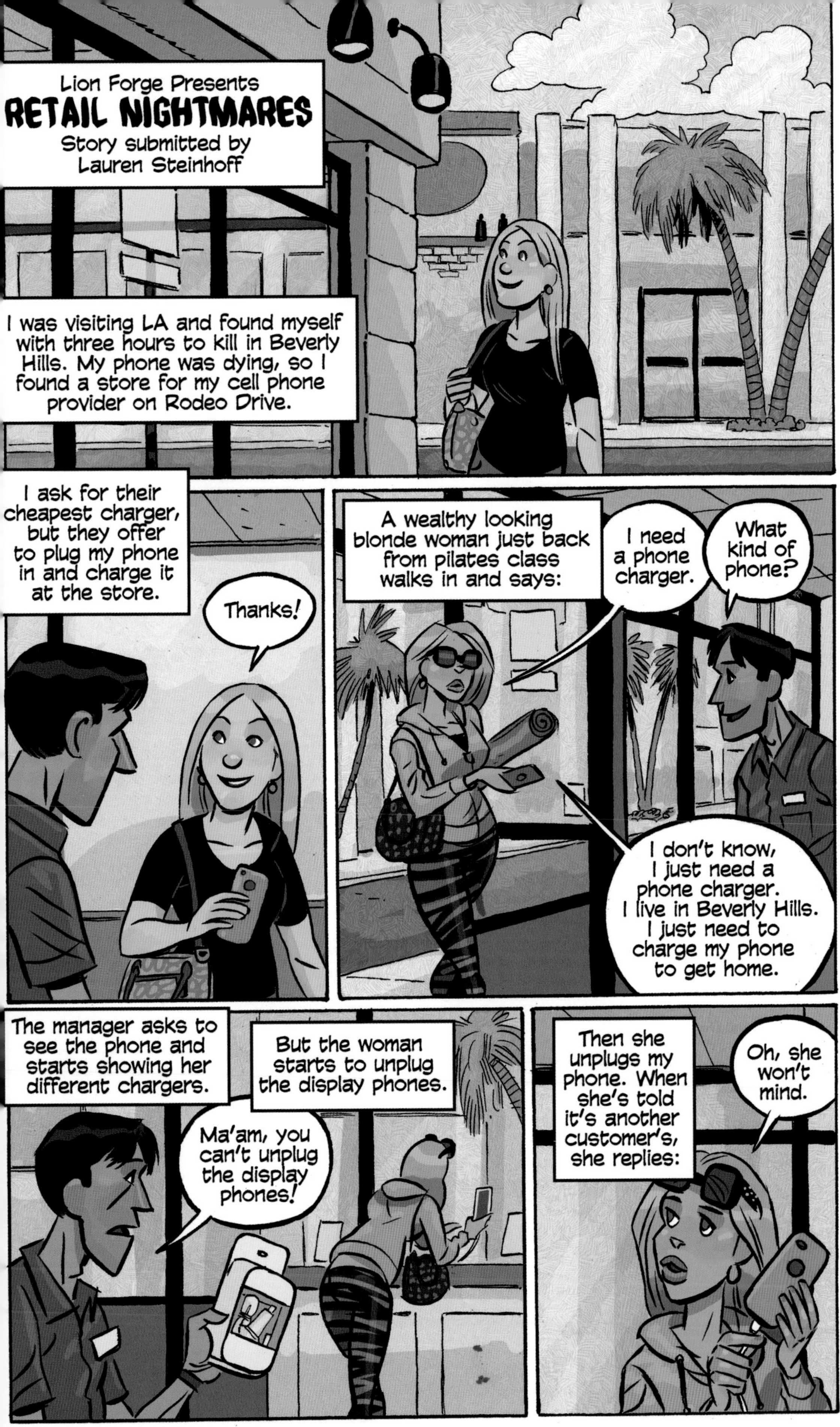

Lion Forge Presents
RETAIL NIGHTMARES
Story submitted by Lauren Steinhoff
I was visiting LA and found myself with three hours to kill in Beverly Hills. My phone was dying, so I found a store for my cell phone provider on Rodeo Drive.
I ask for their cheapest charger, but they offer to plug my phone in and charge it at the store.
Thanks!
A wealthy looking blonde woman just back from pilates class walks in and says:
I need a phone charger.
What kind of phone?
I don't know, I just need a phone charger. I live in Beverly Hills. I just need to charge my phone to get home.
The manager asks to see the phone and starts showing her different chargers.
But the woman starts to unplug the display phones.
Ma'am, you can't unplug the display phones!
Then she unplugs my phone. When she's told it's another customer's, she replies:
Oh, she won't mind.

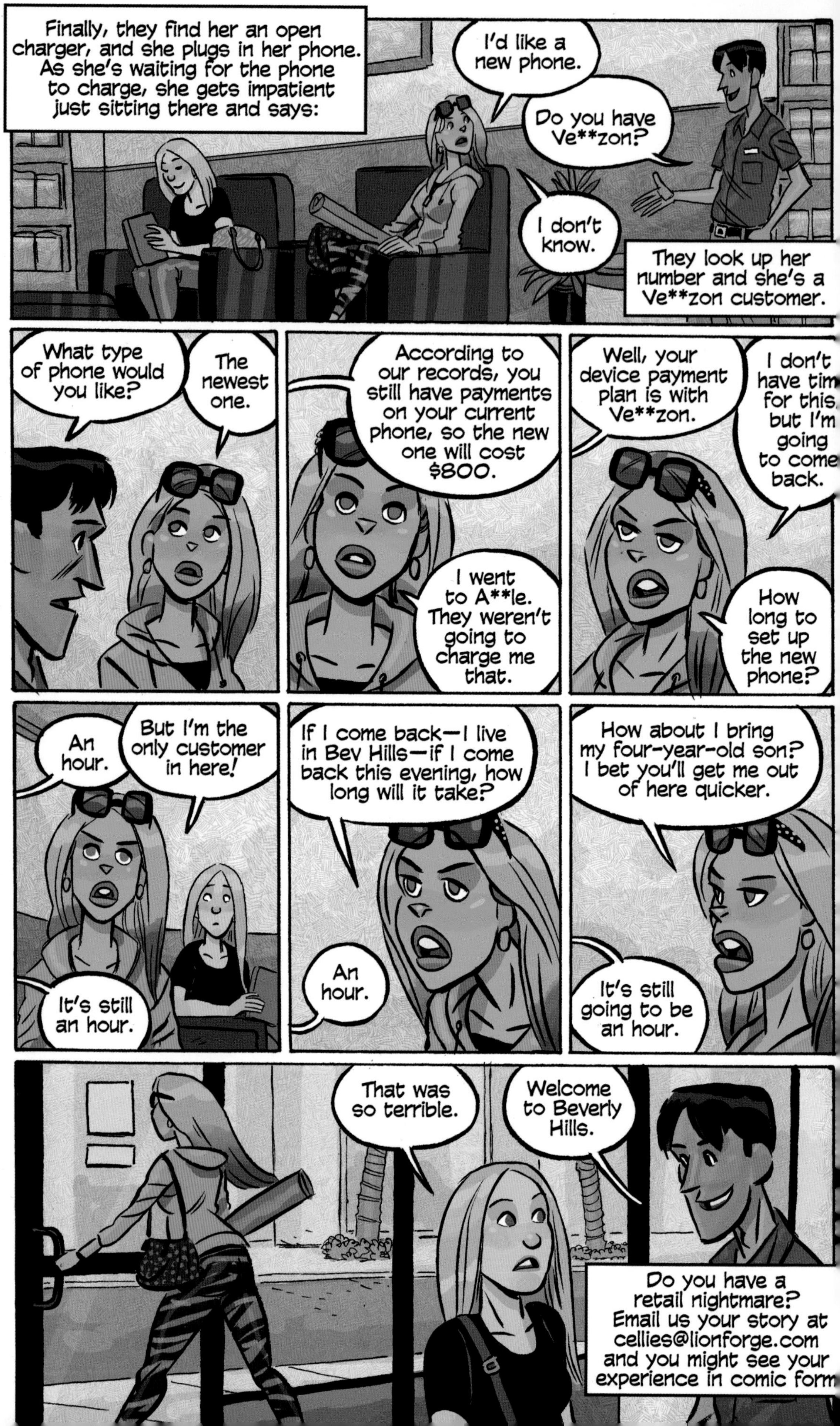
Finally, they find her an open charger, and she plugs in her phone. As she's waiting for the phone to charge, she gets impatient just sitting there and says:
I'd like a new phone.
Do you have Ve**zon?
I don't know.
They look up her number and she's a Ve**zon customer.
What type of phone would you like?
The newest one.
According to our records, you still have payments on your current phone, so the new one will cost $800.
I went to A**le. They weren't going to charge me that.
Well, your device payment plan is with Ve**zon.
I don't have tim for this but I'm going to come back.
How long to set up the new phone?
An hour.
But I'm the only customer in here!
It's still an hour.
If I come back—I live in Bev Hills—if I come back this evening, how long will it take?
An hour.
How about I bring my four-year-old son? I bet you'll get me out of here quicker.
It's still going to be an hour.
That was so terrible.
Welcome to Beverly Hills.
Do you have a retail nightmare? Email us your story at cellies@lionforge.com and you might see your experience in comic form

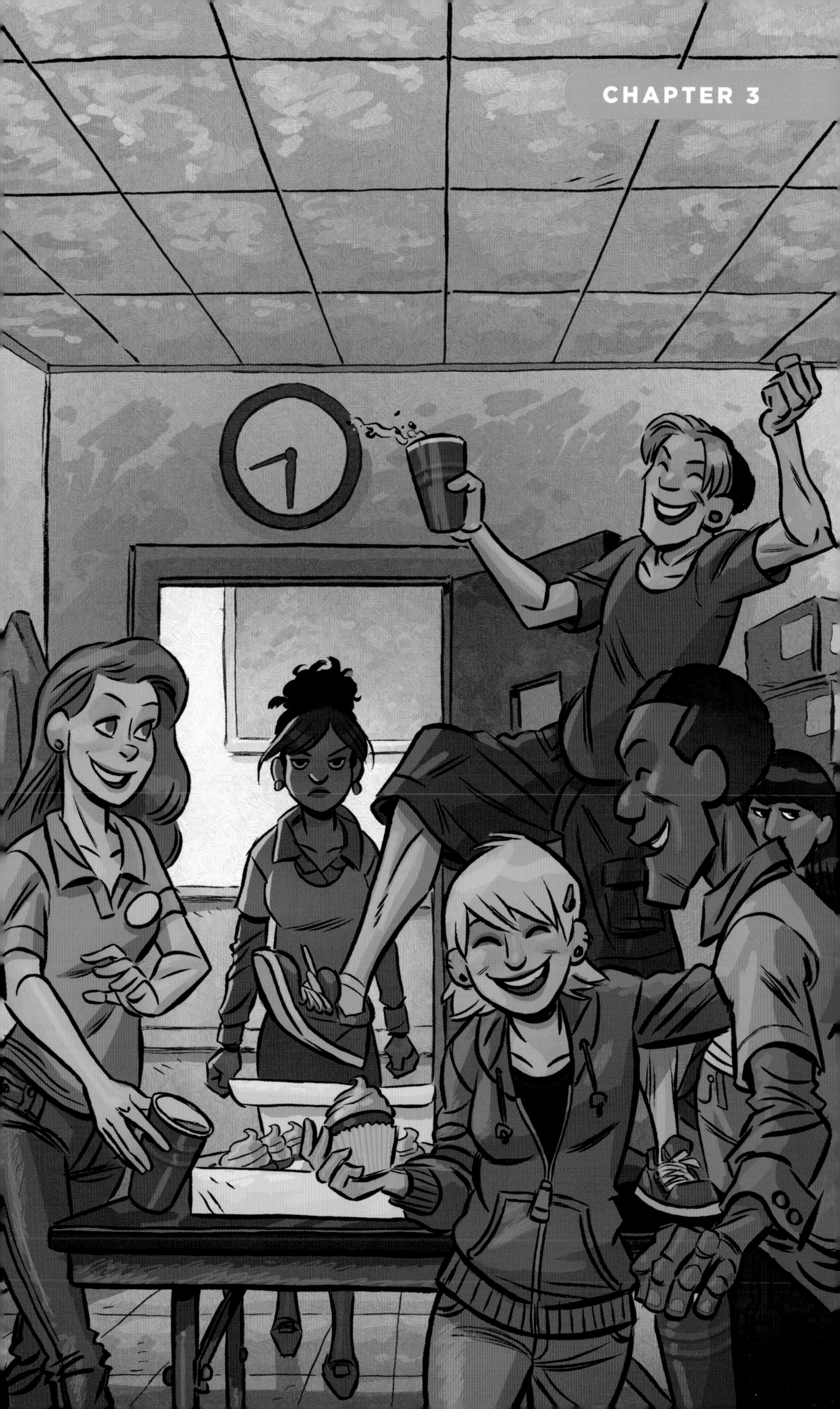
CHAPTER 3

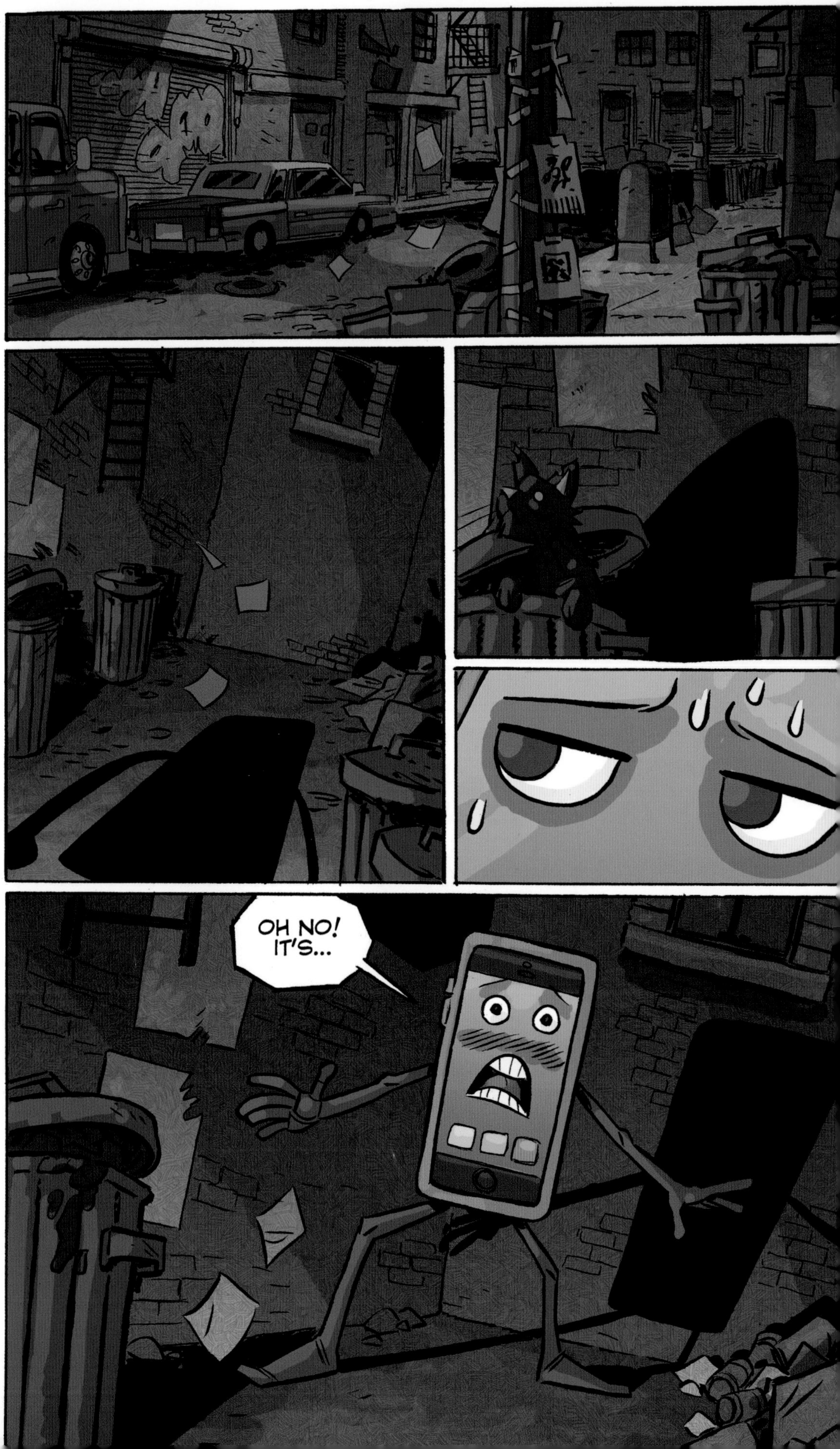
OH NO! IT'S...

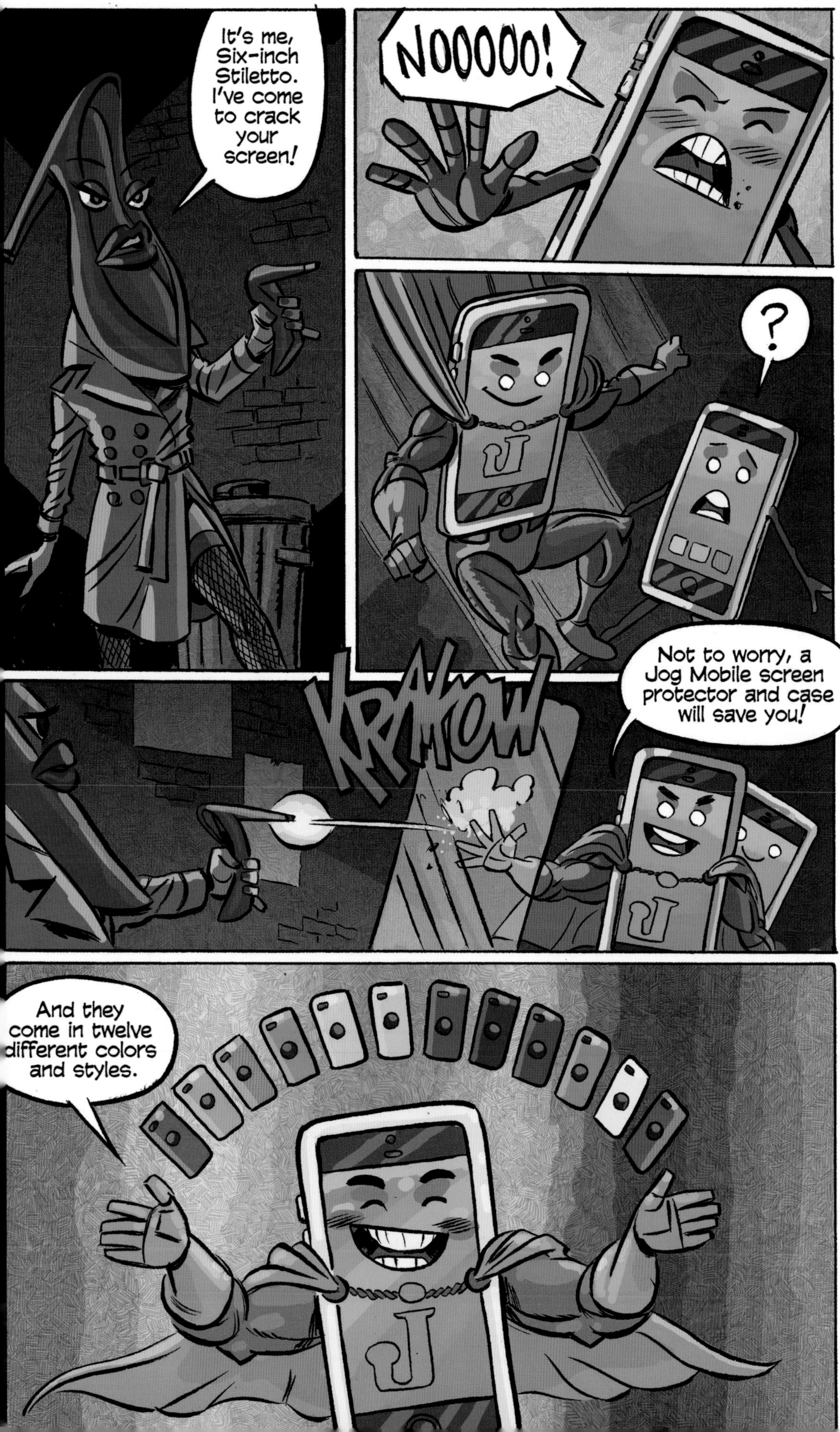

It's me, Six-inch Stiletto. I've come to crack your screen!
NOOOOO!
?
KRAKOW
Not to worry, a Jog Mobile screen protector and case will save you!
And they come in twelve different colors and styles.

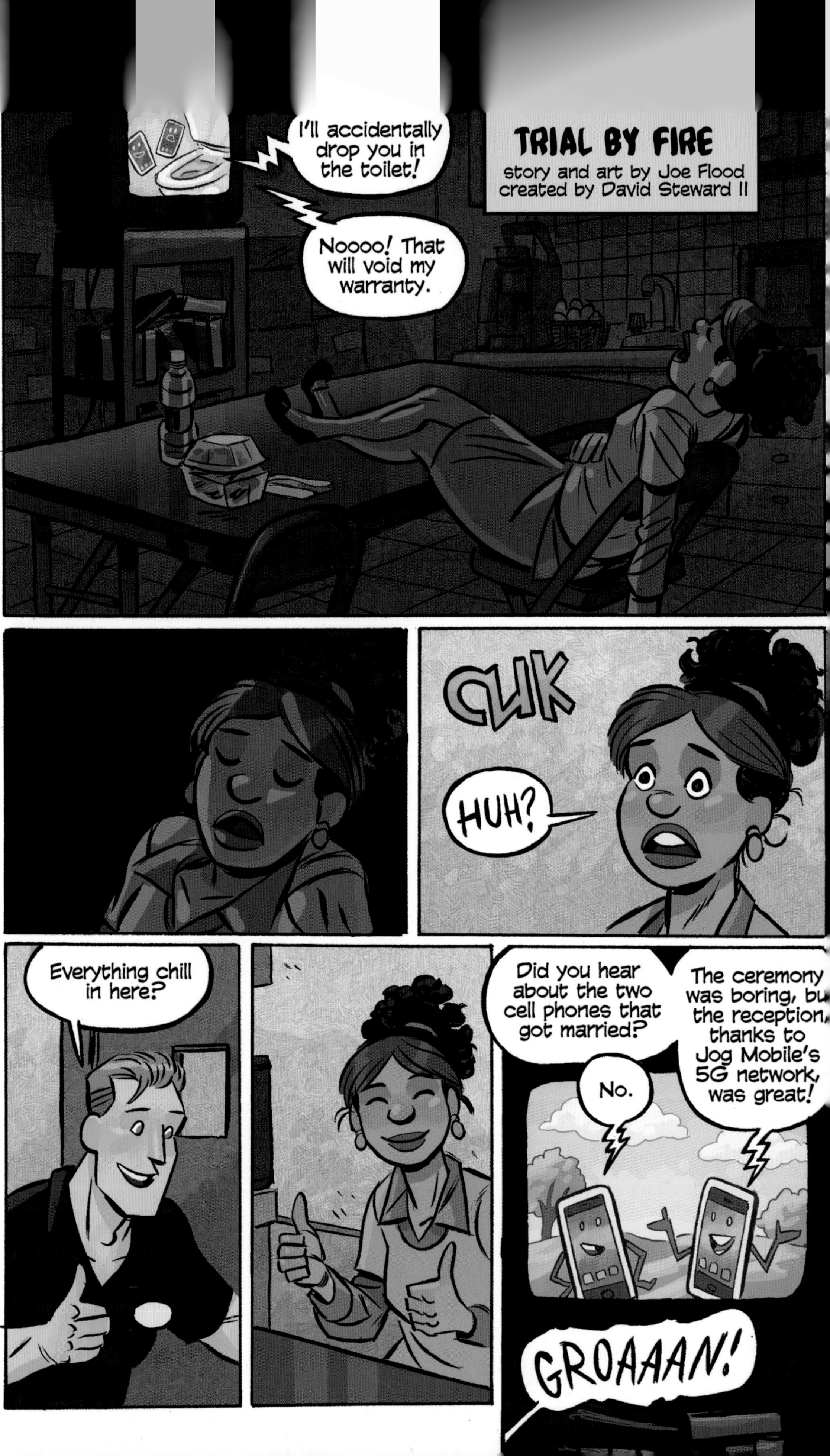

TRIAL BY FIRE
story and art by Joe Flood
created by David Steward II
I'll accidentally drop you in the toilet!
Noooo! That will void my warranty.
CLUK
HUH?
Everything chill in here?
Did you hear about the two cell phones that got married?
No.
The ceremony was boring, bu the reception, thanks to Jog Mobile's 5G network, was great!
GROAAAN!

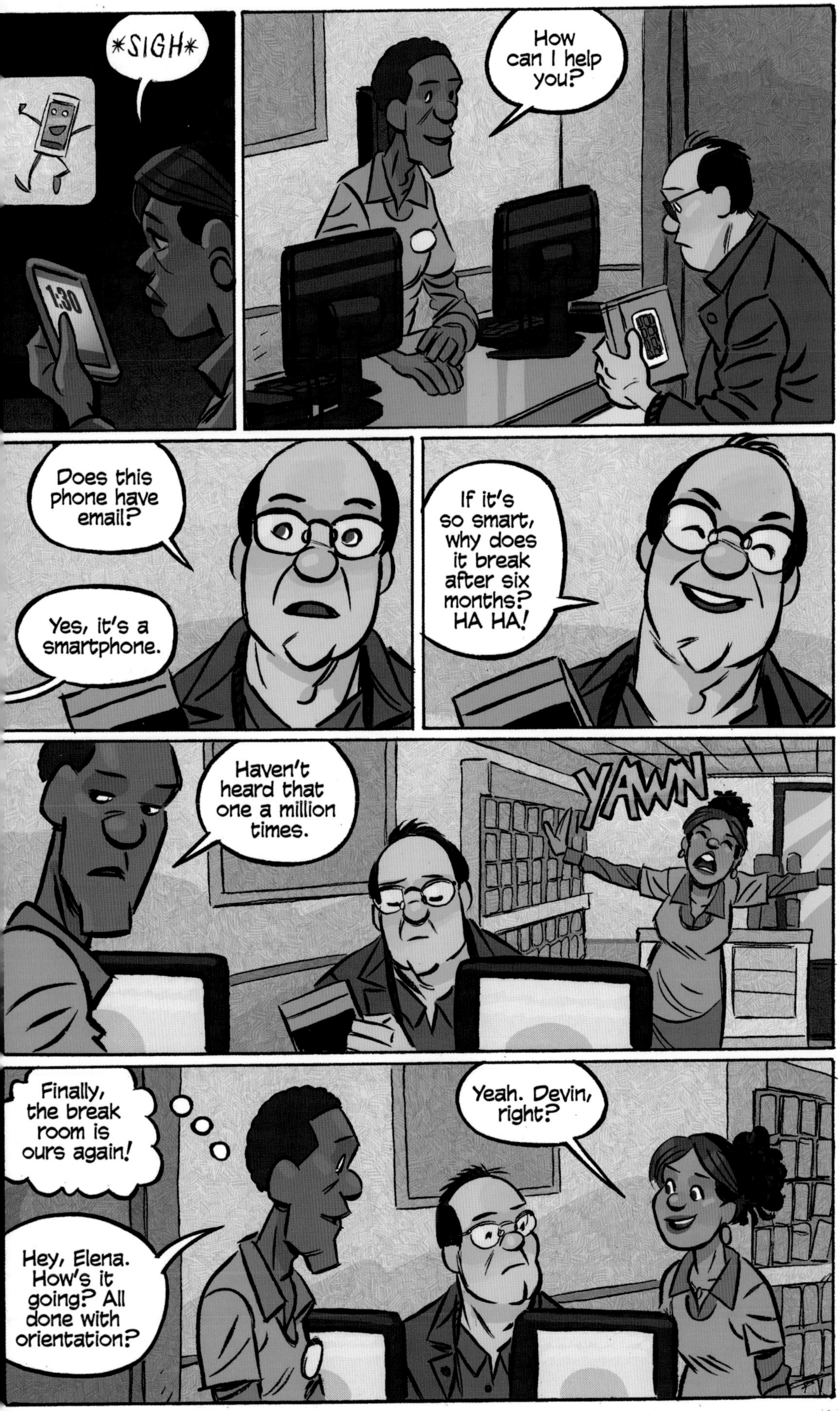

*SIGH*
1:30
How can I help you?
Does this phone have email?
Yes, it's a smartphone.
If it's so smart, why does it break after six months? HA HA!
Haven't heard that one a million times.
YAWN
Finally, the break room is ours again!
Hey, Elena. How's it going? All done with orientation?
Yeah. Devin, right?

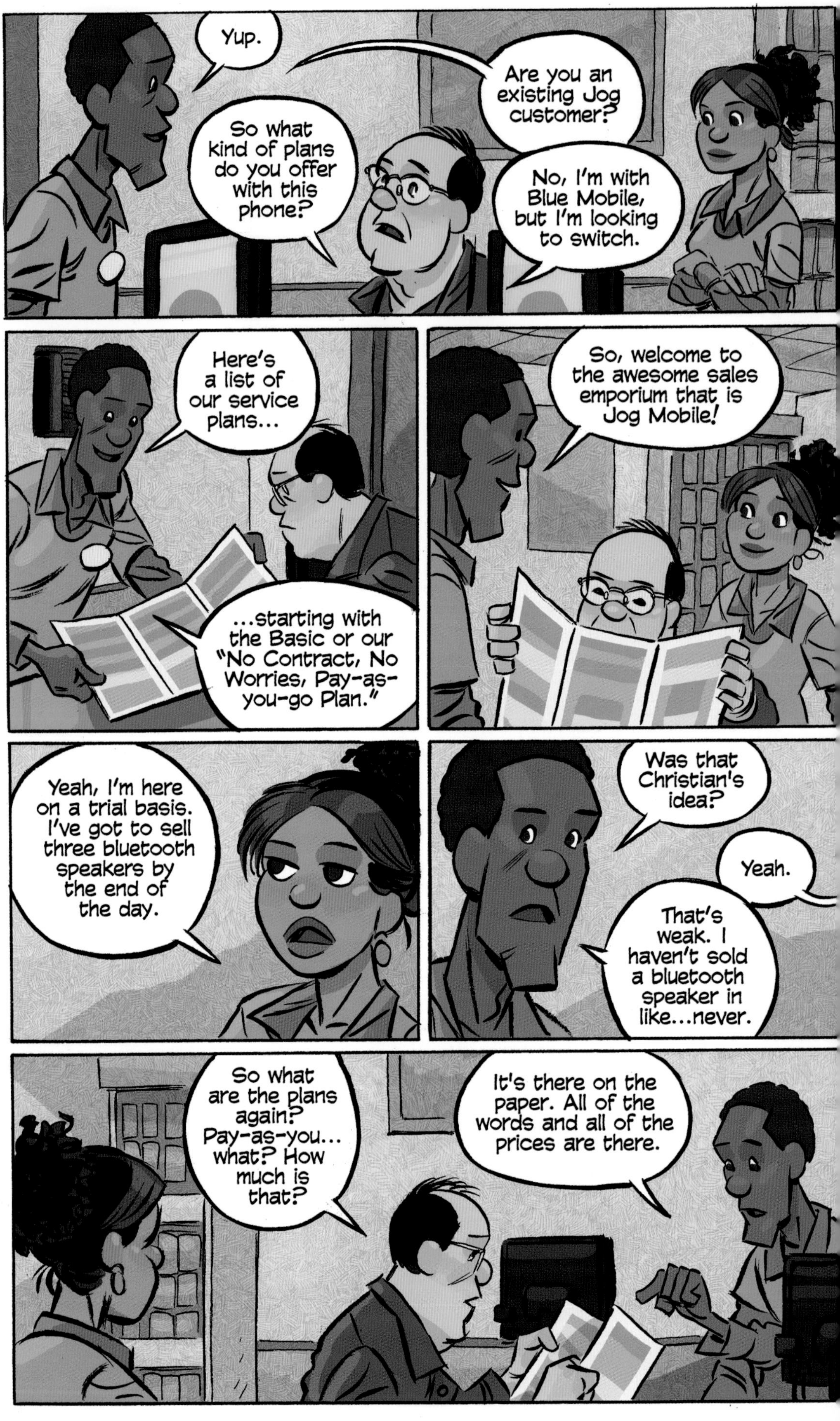
Yup.
Are you an existing Jog customer?
So what kind of plans do you offer with this phone?
No, I'm with Blue Mobile, but I'm looking to switch.
Here's a list of our service plans...
...starting with the Basic or our "No Contract, No Worries, Pay-as-you-go Plan."
So, welcome to the awesome sales emporium that is Jog Mobile!
Yeah, I'm here on a trial basis. I've got to sell three bluetooth speakers by the end of the day.
Was that Christian's idea?
Yeah.
That's weak. I haven't sold a bluetooth speaker in like...never.
So what are the plans again? Pay-as-you... what? How much is that?
It's there on the paper. All of the words and all of the prices are there.

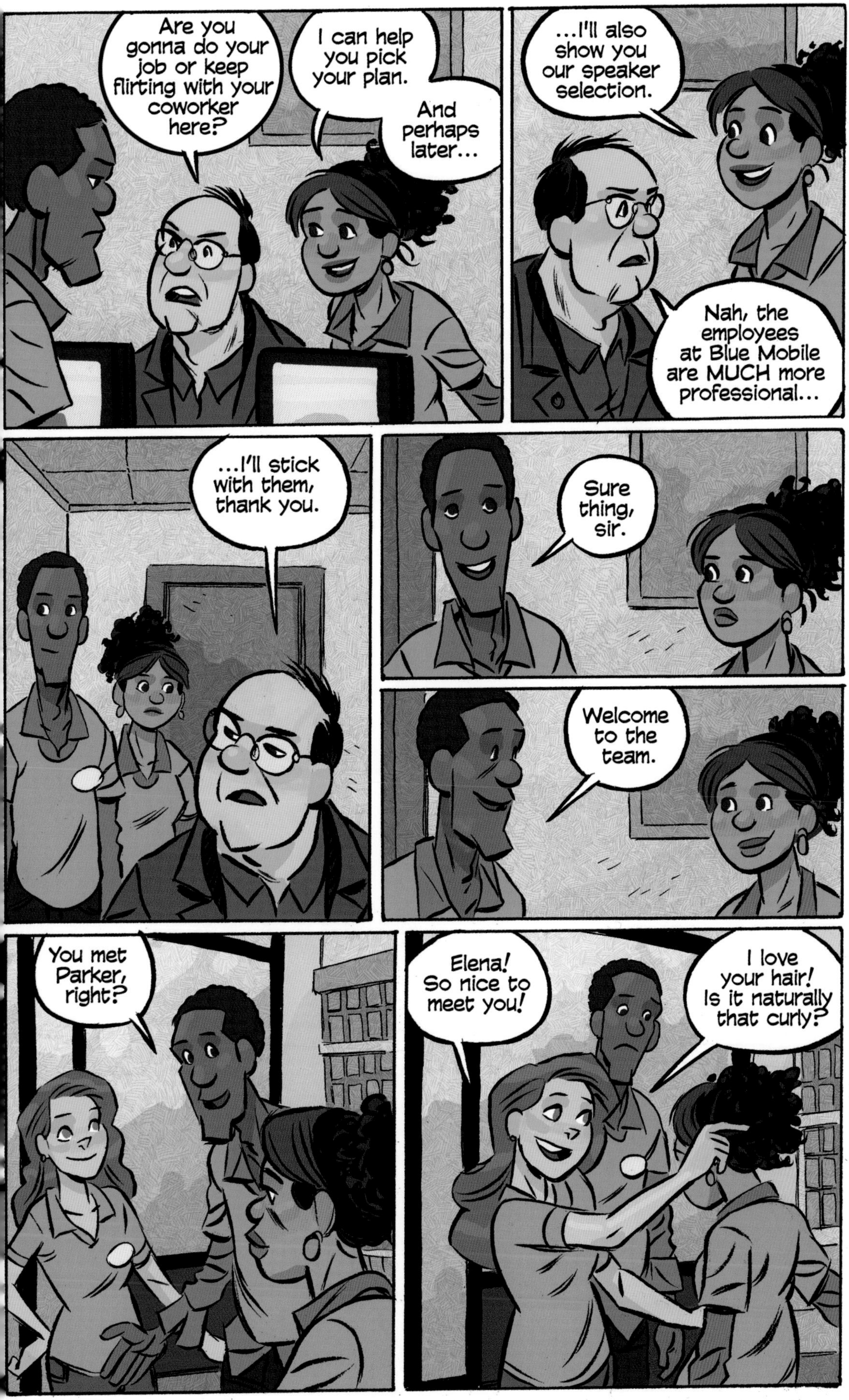
Are you gonna do your job or keep flirting with your coworker here?
I can help you pick your plan.
And perhaps later...
...I'll also show you our speaker selection.
Nah, the employees at Blue Mobile are MUCH more professional...
...I'll stick with them, thank you.
Sure thing, sir.
Welcome to the team.
You met Parker, right?
Elena! So nice to meet you!
I love your hair! Is it naturally that curly?

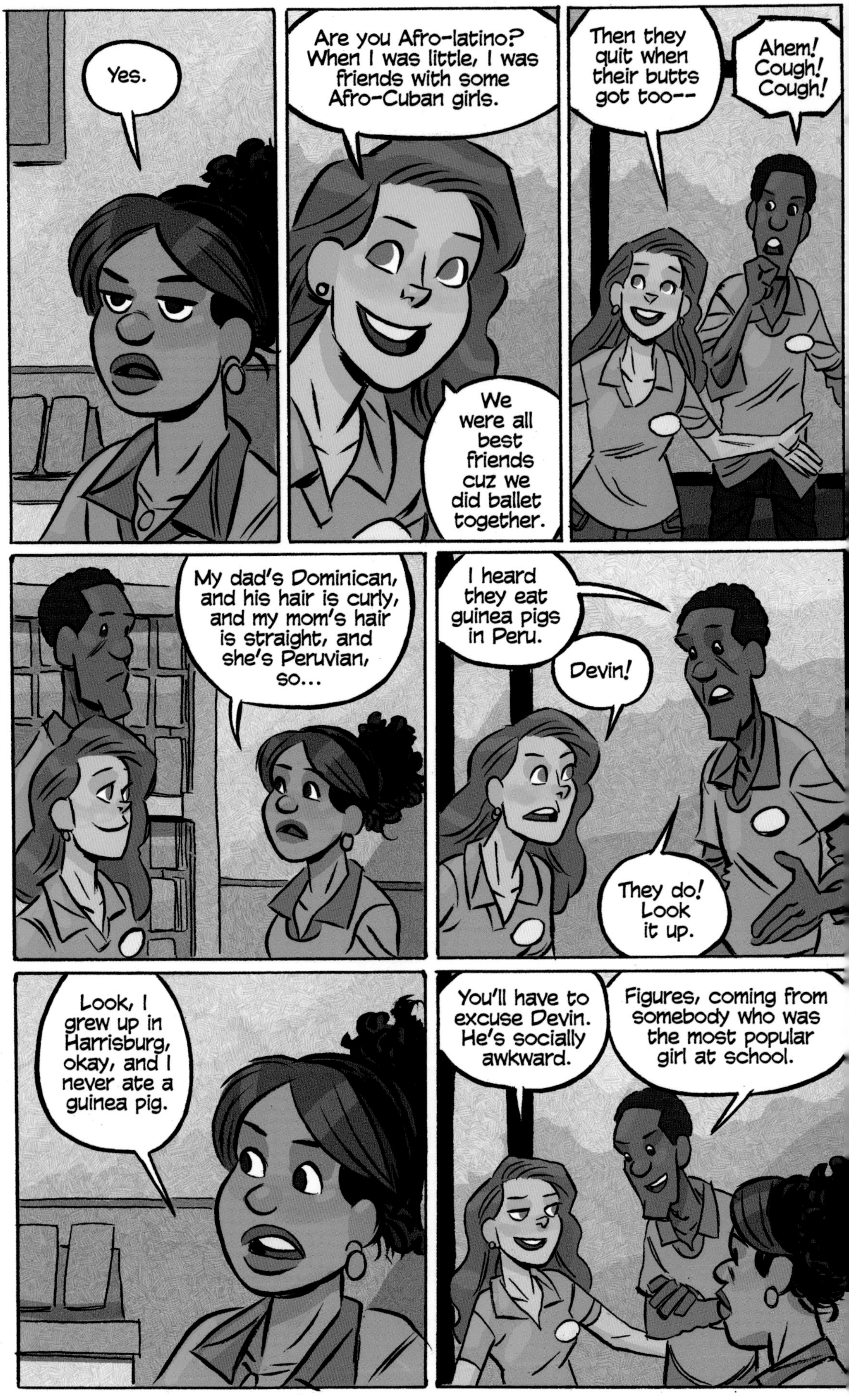
Yes.
Are you Afro-latino? When I was little, I was friends with some Afro-Cuban girls.
We were all best friends cuz we did ballet together.
Then they quit when their butts got too--
Ahem! Cough! Cough!
My dad's Dominican, and his hair is curly, and my mom's hair is straight, and she's Peruvian, so...
I heard they eat guinea pigs in Peru.
Devin!
They do! Look it up.
Look, I grew up in Harrisburg, okay, and I never ate a guinea pig.
You'll have to excuse Devin. He's socially awkward.
Figures, coming from somebody who was the most popular girl at school.

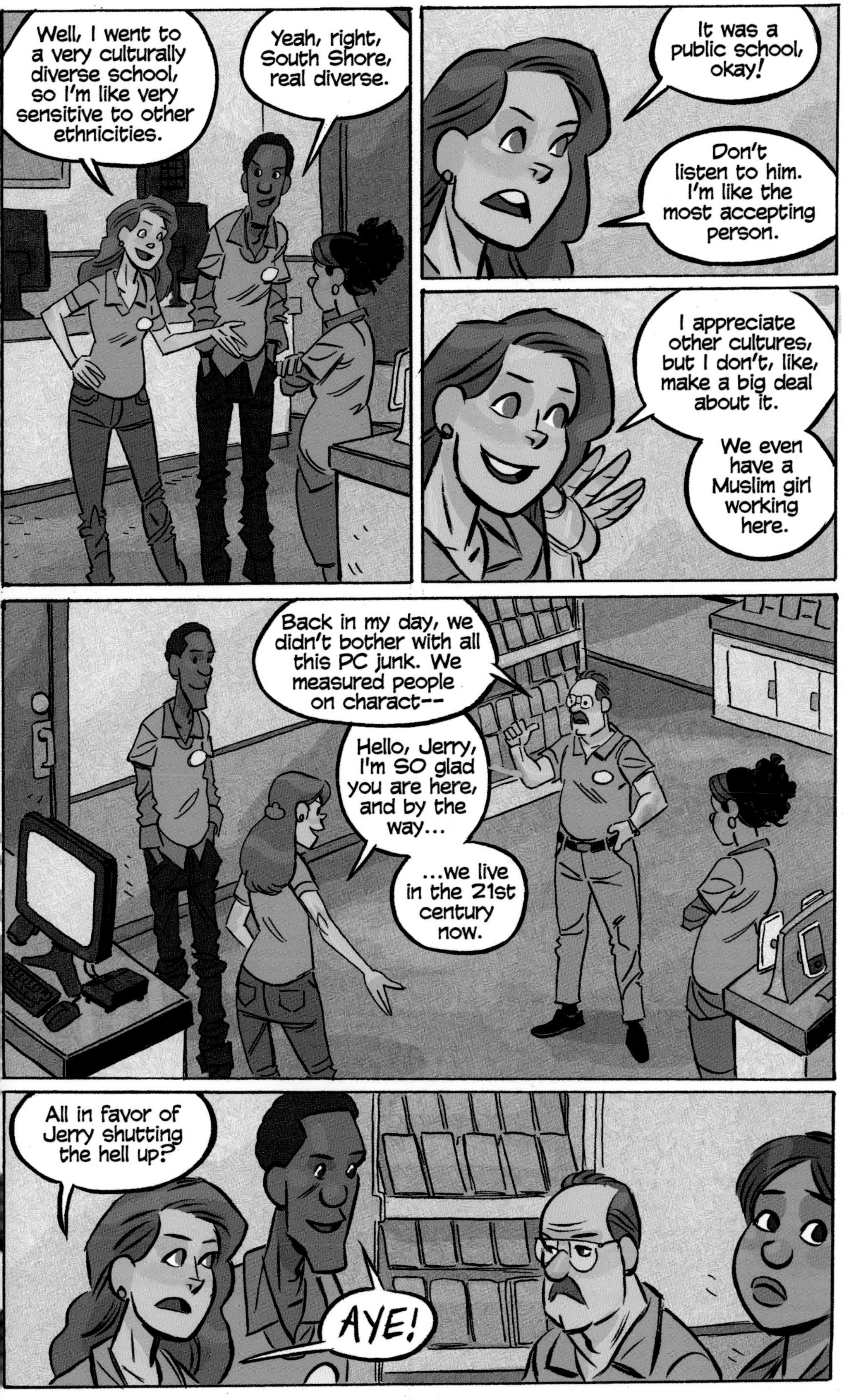
Well, I went to a very culturally diverse school, so I'm like very sensitive to other ethnicities.
Yeah, right, South Shore, real diverse.
It was a public school, okay!
Don't listen to him. I'm like the most accepting person.
I appreciate other cultures, but I don't, like, make a big deal about it.
We even have a Muslim girl working here.
Back in my day, we didn't bother with all this PC junk. We measured people on charact--
Hello, Jerry, I'm SO glad you are here, and by the way...
...we live in the 21st century now.
All in favor of Jerry shutting the hell up?
AYE!

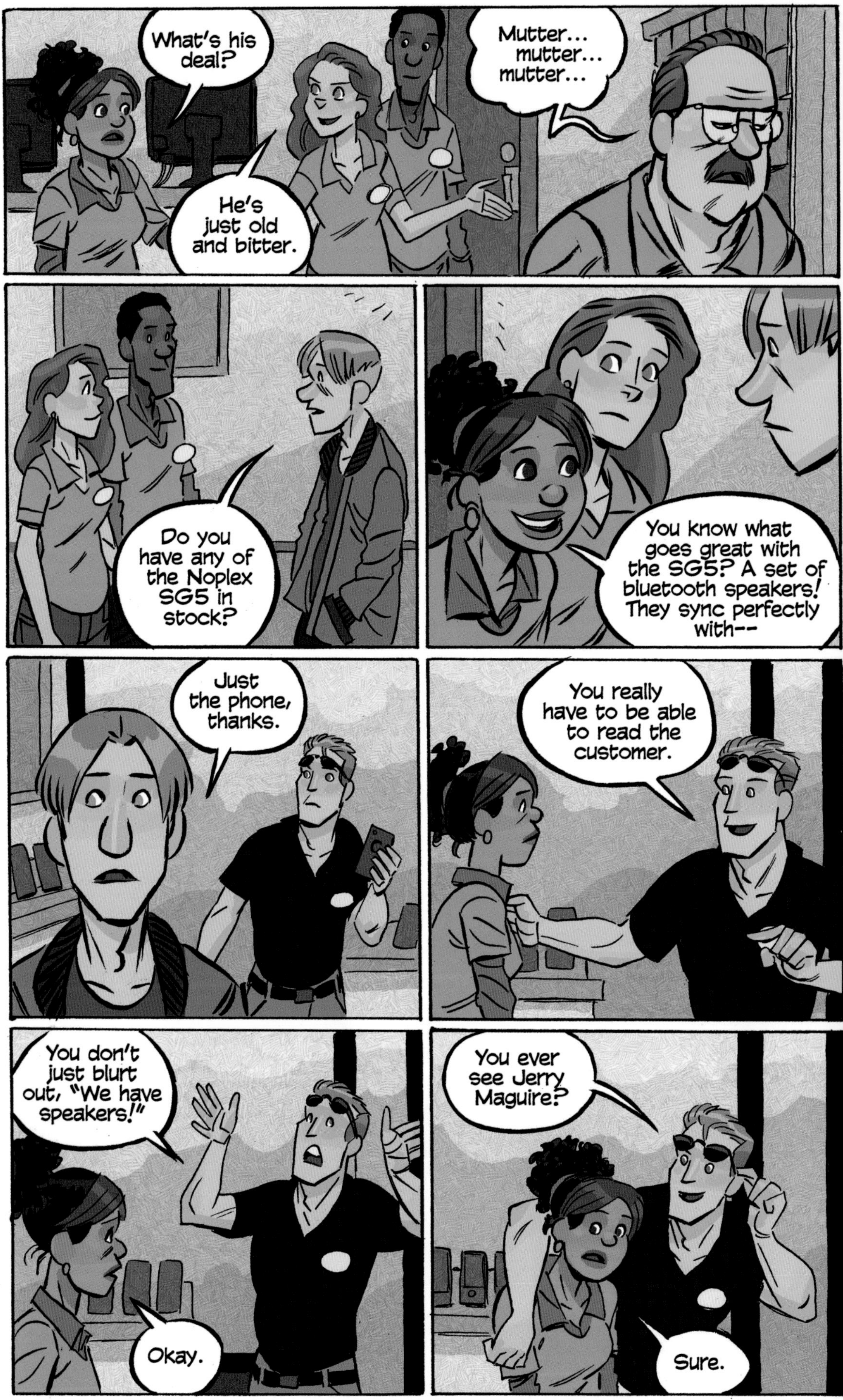
What's his deal?
He's just old and bitter.
Mutter... mutter... mutter...
Do you have any of the Noplex SG5 in stock?
You know what goes great with the SG5? A set of bluetooth speakers! They sync perfectly with--
Just the phone, thanks.
You really have to be able to read the customer.
You don't just blurt out, "We have speakers!"
Okay.
You ever see Jerry Maguire?
Sure.

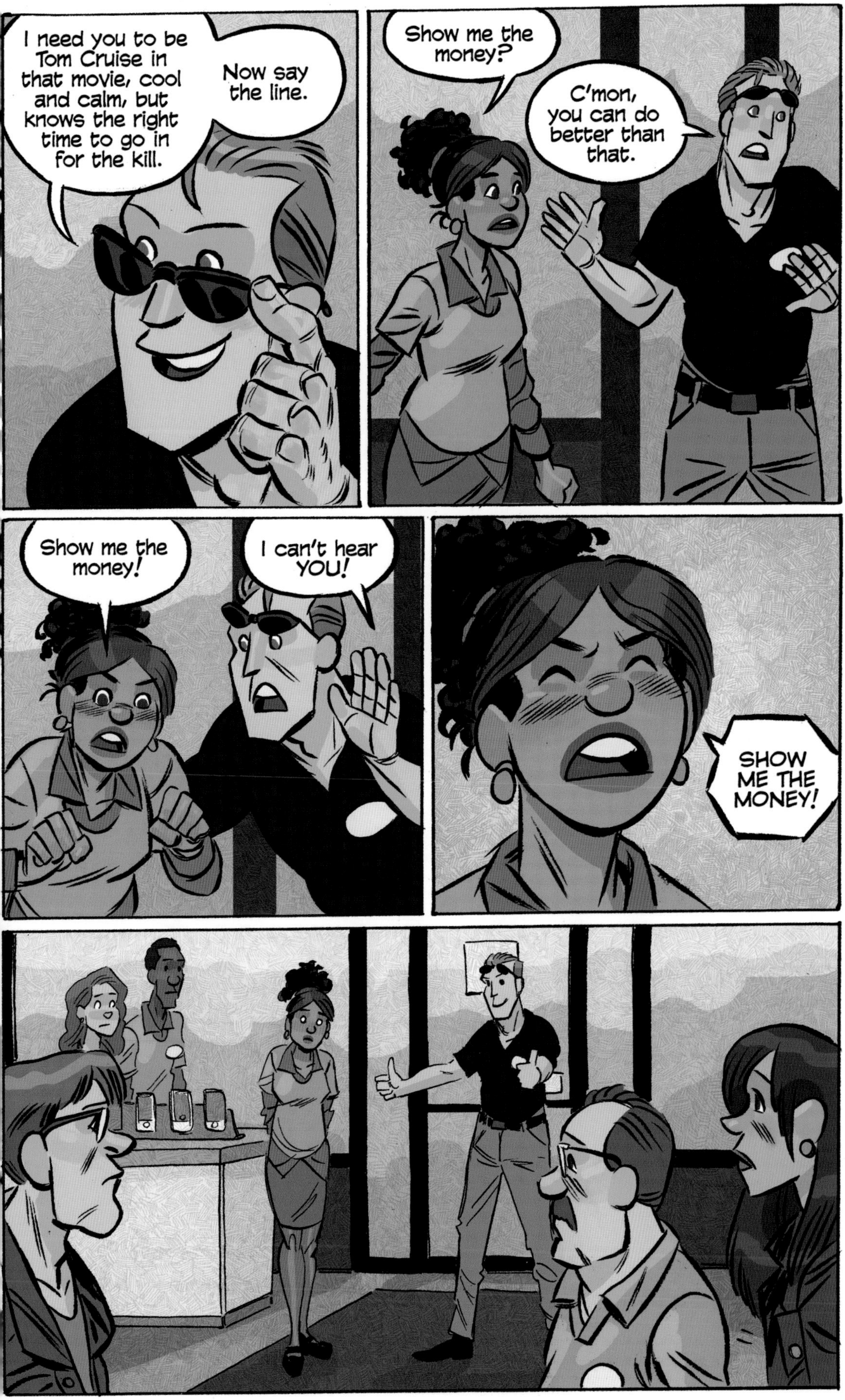
I need you to be Tom Cruise in that movie, cool and calm, but knows the right time to go in for the kill.
Now say the line.
Show me the money?
C'mon, you can do better than that.
Show me the money!
I can't hear YOU!
SHOW ME THE MONEY!

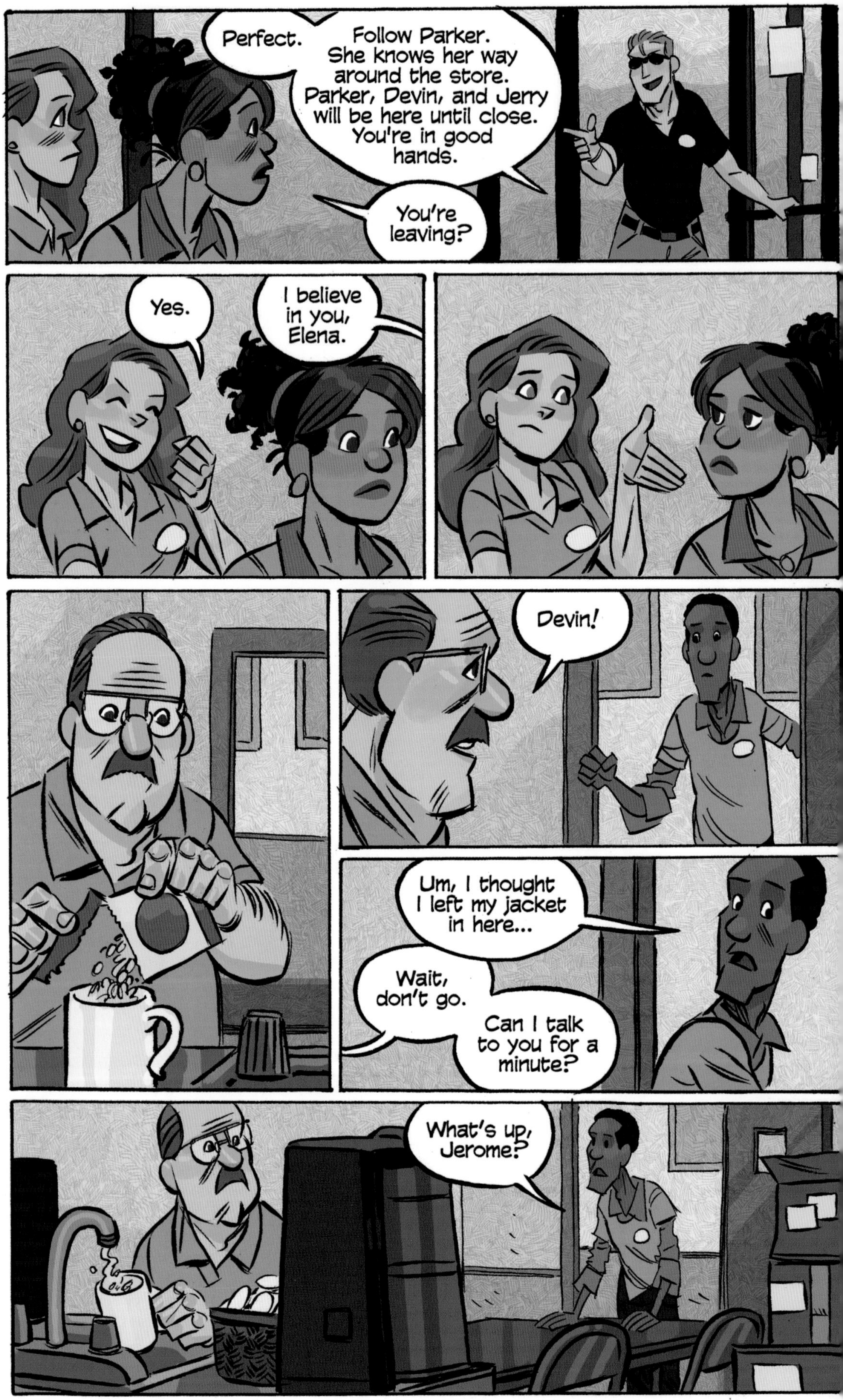
Perfect.
Follow Parker. She knows her way around the store. Parker, Devin, and Jerry will be here until close. You're in good hands.
You're leaving?
Yes.
I believe in you, Elena.
Devin!
Um, I thought I left my jacket in here...
Wait, don't go.
Can I talk to you for a minute?
What's up, Jerome?

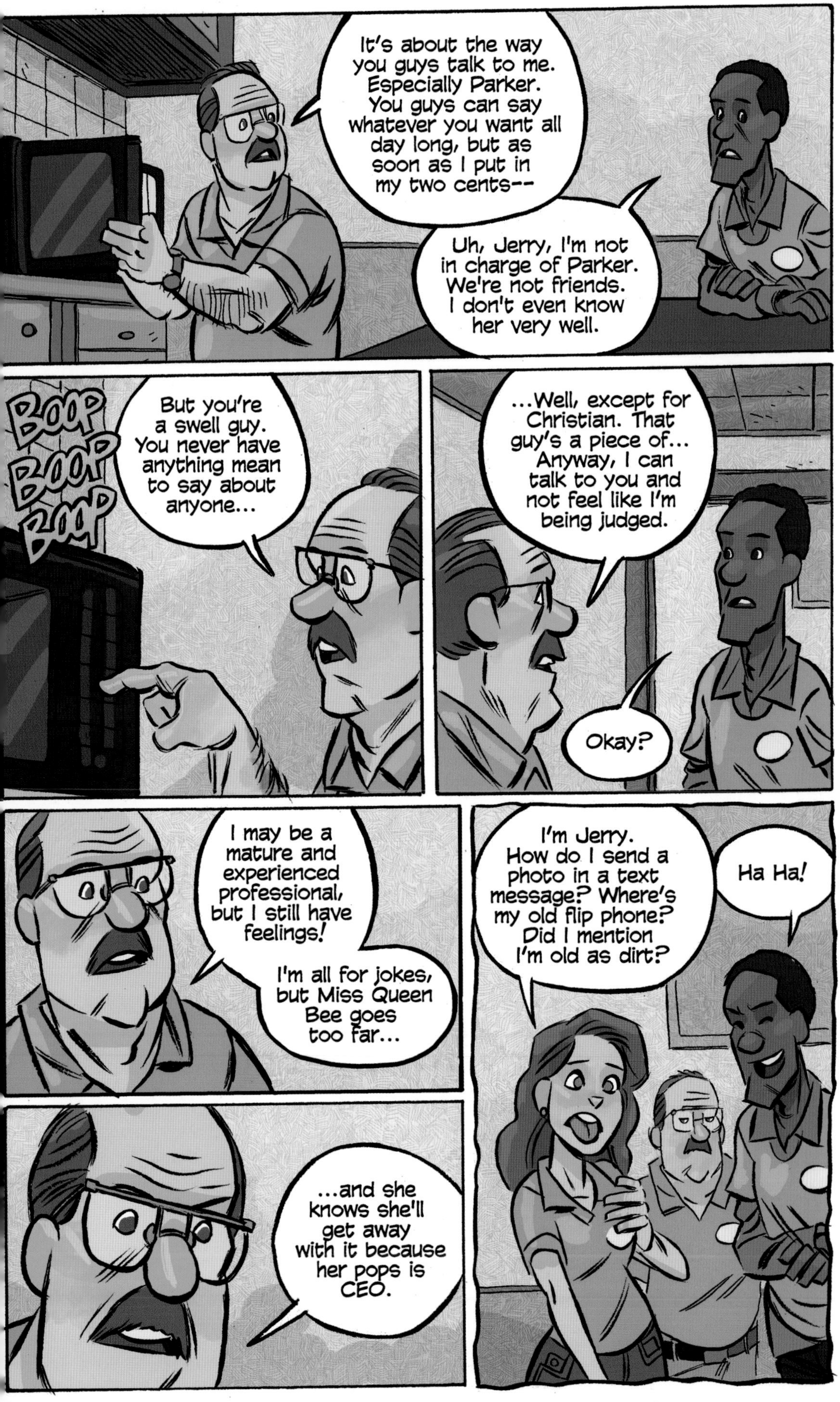
It's about the way you guys talk to me. Especially Parker. You guys can say whatever you want all day long, but as soon as I put in my two cents--
Uh, Jerry, I'm not in charge of Parker. We're not friends. I don't even know her very well.
BOOP BOOP BOOP
But you're a swell guy. You never have anything mean to say about anyone...
...Well, except for Christian. That guy's a piece of... Anyway, I can talk to you and not feel like I'm being judged.
Okay?
I may be a mature and experienced professional, but I still have feelings!
I'm all for jokes, but Miss Queen Bee goes too far...
...and she knows she'll get away with it because her pops is CEO.
I'm Jerry. How do I send a photo in a text message? Where's my old flip phone? Did I mention I'm old as dirt?
Ha Ha!

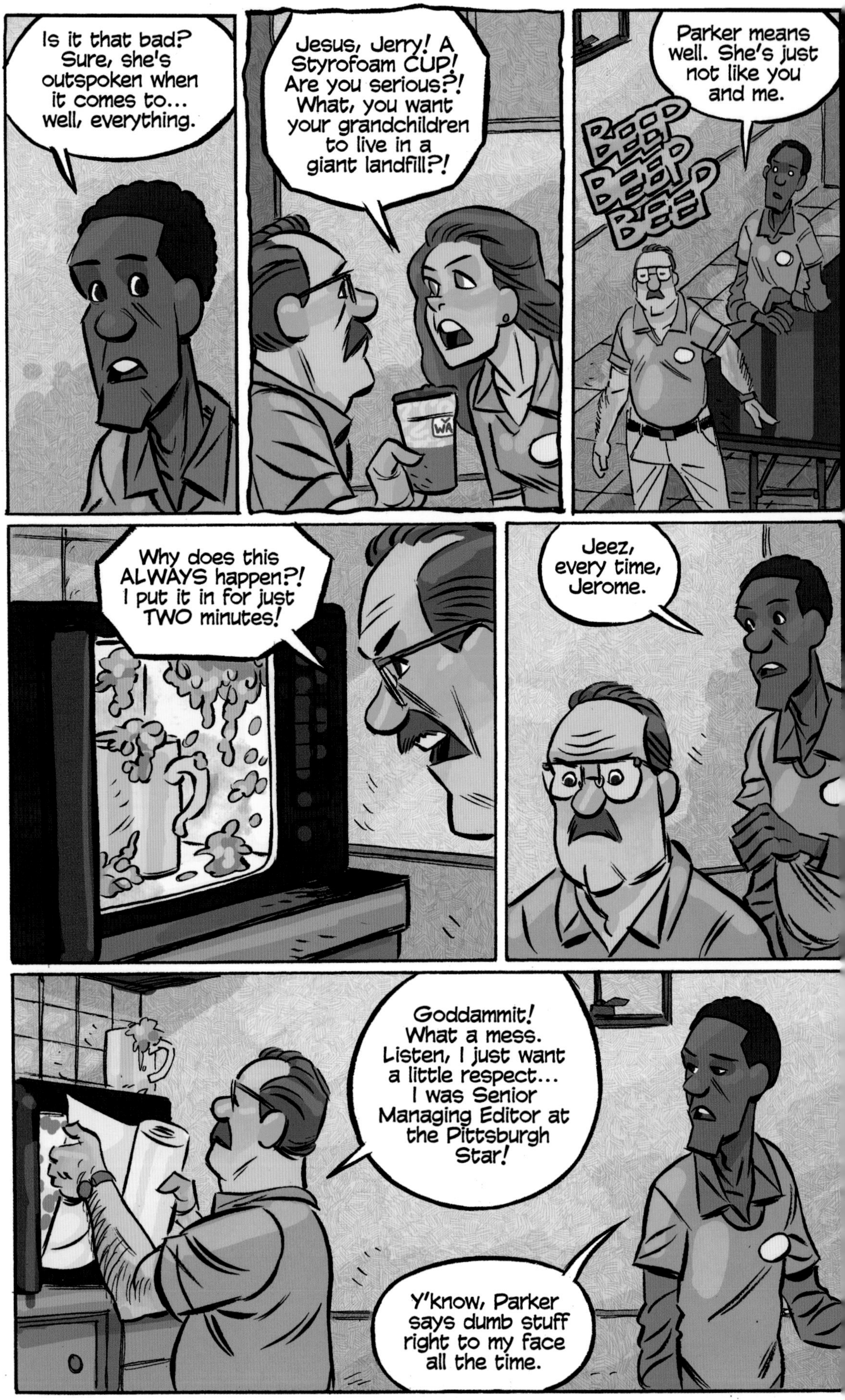
Is it that bad? Sure, she's outspoken when it comes to... well, everything.
Jesus, Jerry! A Styrofoam CUP! Are you serious?! What, you want your grandchildren to live in a giant landfill?!
Parker means well. She's just not like you and me.
BEEP BEEP BEEP
Why does this ALWAYS happen?! I put it in for just TWO minutes!
Jeez, every time, Jerome.
Goddammit! What a mess. Listen, I just want a little respect... I was Senior Managing Editor at the Pittsburgh Star!
Y'know, Parker says dumb stuff right to my face all the time.

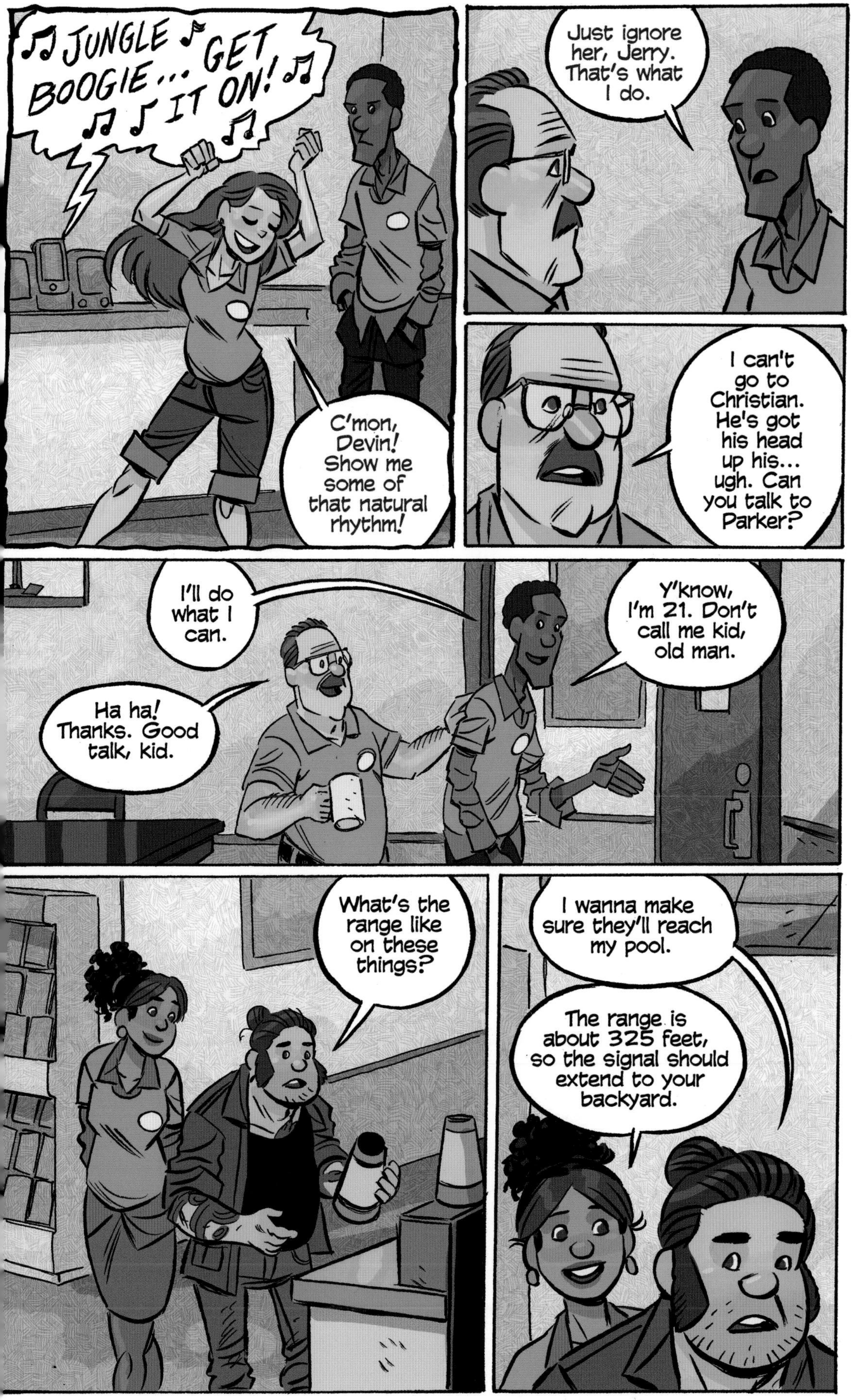
JUNGLE BOOGIE... GET IT ON!
C'mon, Devin! Show me some of that natural rhythm!
Just ignore her, Jerry. That's what I do.
I can't go to Christian. He's got his head up his... ugh. Can you talk to Parker?
I'll do what I can.
Ha ha! Thanks. Good talk, kid.
Y'know, I'm 21. Don't call me kid, old man.
What's the range like on these things?
I wanna make sure they'll reach my pool.
The range is about 325 feet, so the signal should extend to your backyard.

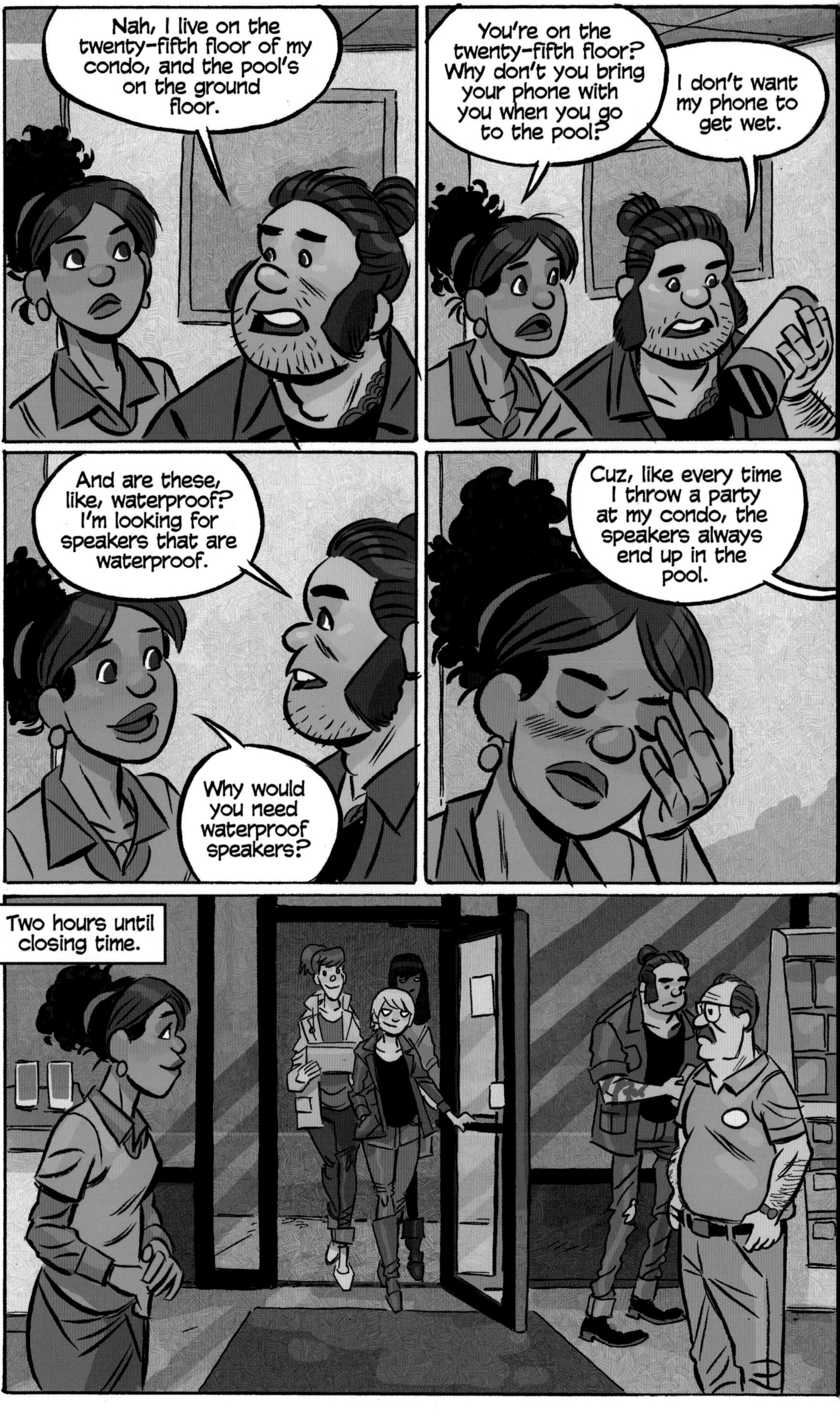
Nah, I live on the twenty-fifth floor of my condo, and the pool's on the ground floor.
You're on the twenty-fifth floor? Why don't you bring your phone with you when you go to the pool?
I don't want my phone to get wet.
And are these, like, waterproof? I'm looking for speakers that are waterproof.
Why would you need waterproof speakers?
Cuz, like every time I throw a party at my condo, the speakers always end up in the pool.
Two hours until closing time.

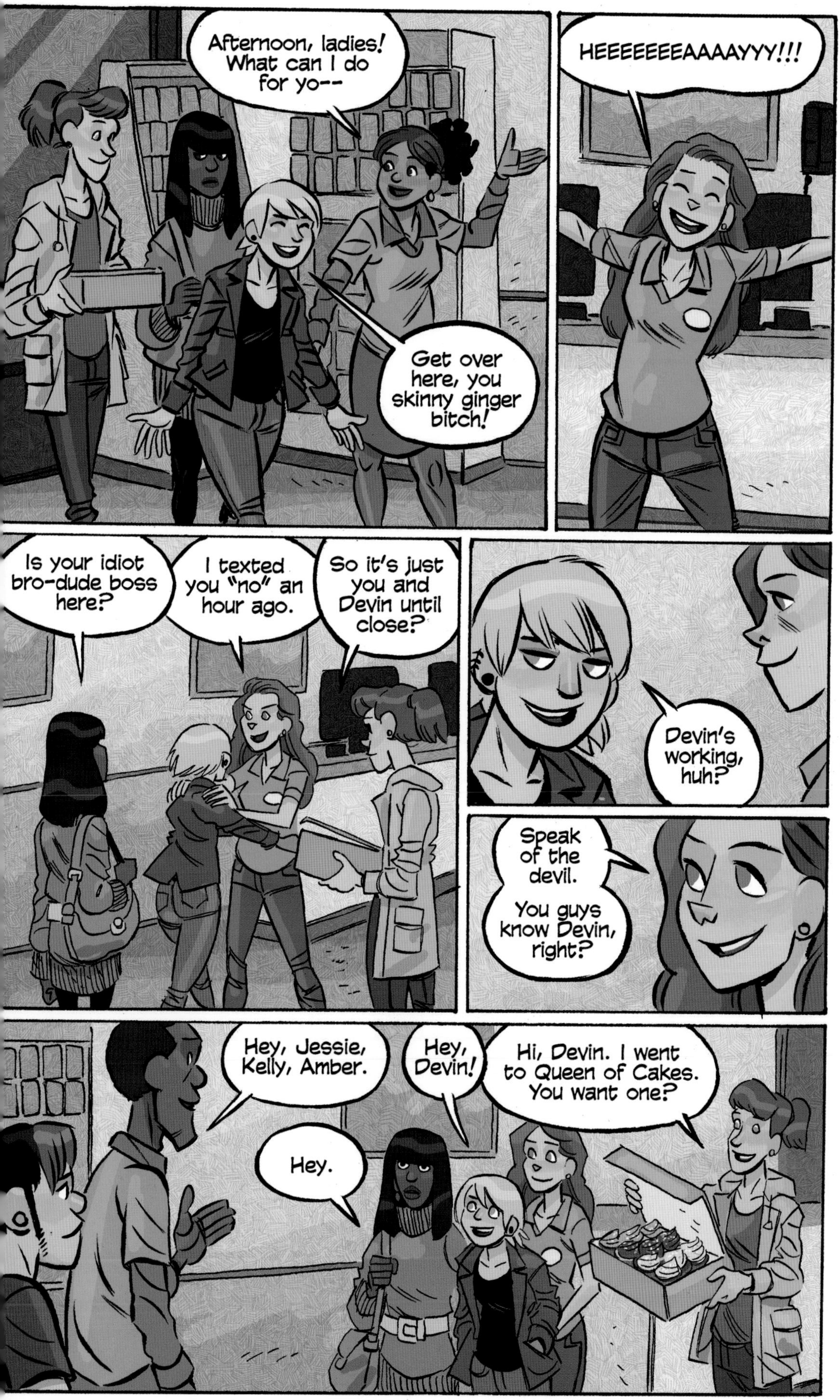

Afternoon, ladies! What can I do for yo--
Get over here, you skinny ginger bitch!
HEEEEEEEAAAAYYY!!!
Is your idiot bro-dude boss here?
I texted you "no" an hour ago.
So it's just you and Devin until close?
Devin's working, huh?
Speak of the devil.
You guys know Devin, right?
Hey, Jessie, Kelly, Amber.
Hey, Devin!
Hey.
Hi, Devin. I went to Queen of Cakes. You want one?

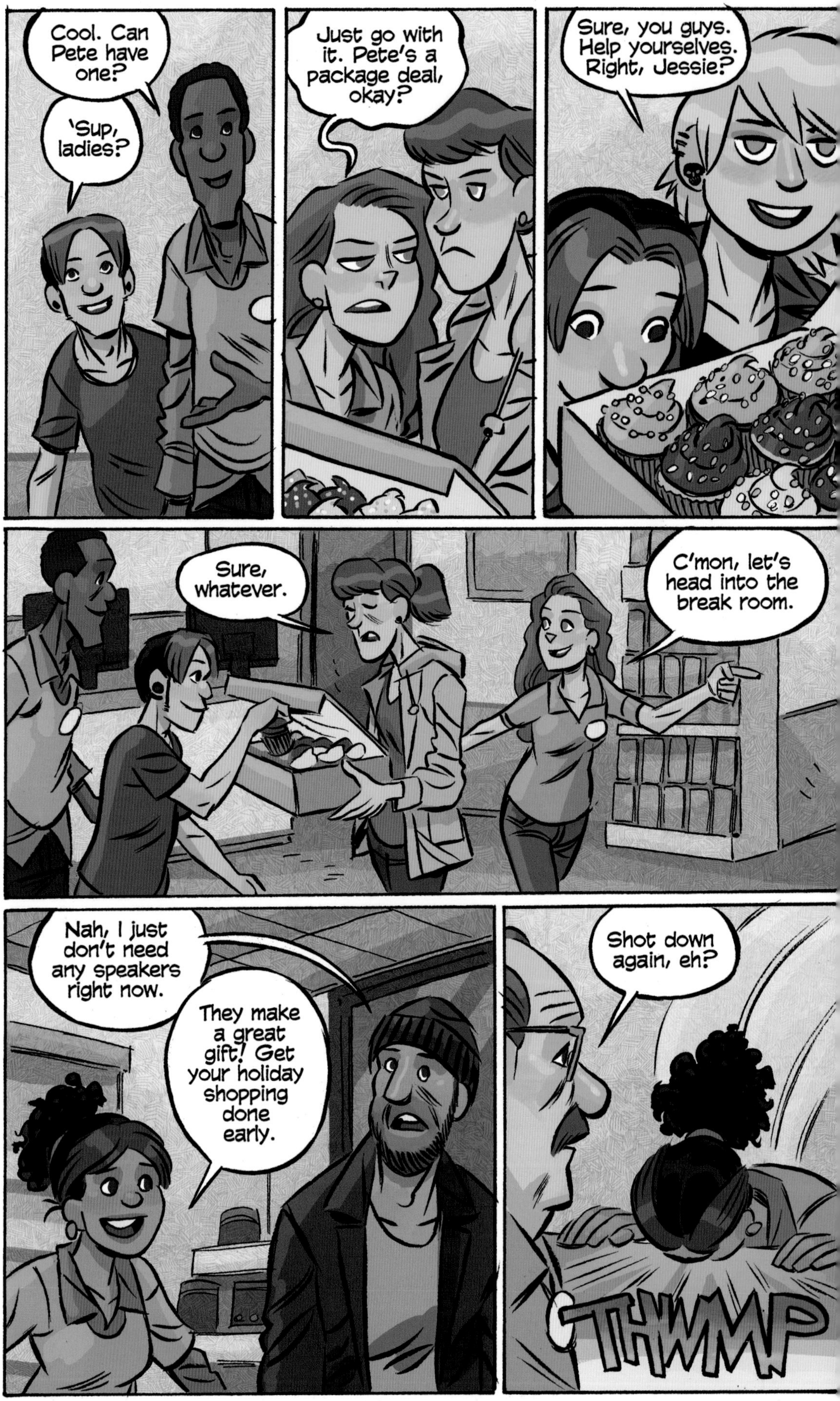
Cool. Can Pete have one?
'Sup, ladies?
Just go with it. Pete's a package deal, okay?
Sure, you guys. Help yourselves. Right, Jessie?
Sure, whatever.
C'mon, let's head into the break room.
Nah, I just don't need any speakers right now.
They make a great gift! Get your holiday shopping done early.
Shot down again, eh?
THWMP

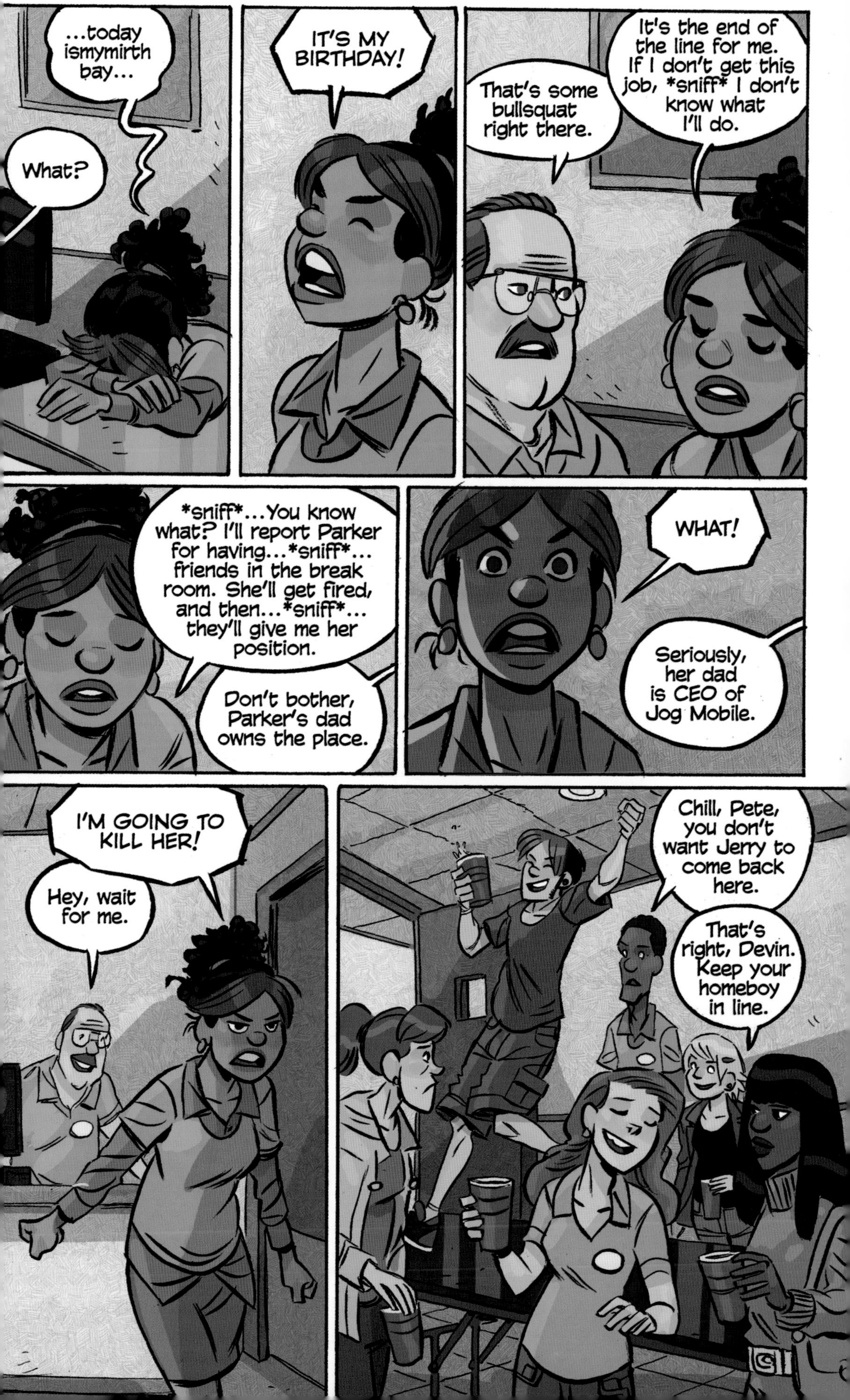
...today ismymirth bay...
What?
IT'S MY BIRTHDAY!
That's some bullsquat right there.
It's the end of the line for me. If I don't get this job, *sniff* I don't know what I'll do.
*sniff*...You know what? I'll report Parker for having...*sniff*... friends in the break room. She'll get fired, and then...*sniff*... they'll give me her position.
Don't bother, Parker's dad owns the place.
WHAT!
Seriously, her dad is CEO of Jog Mobile.
I'M GOING TO KILL HER!
Hey, wait for me.
Chill, Pete, you don't want Jerry to come back here.
That's right, Devin. Keep your homeboy in line.

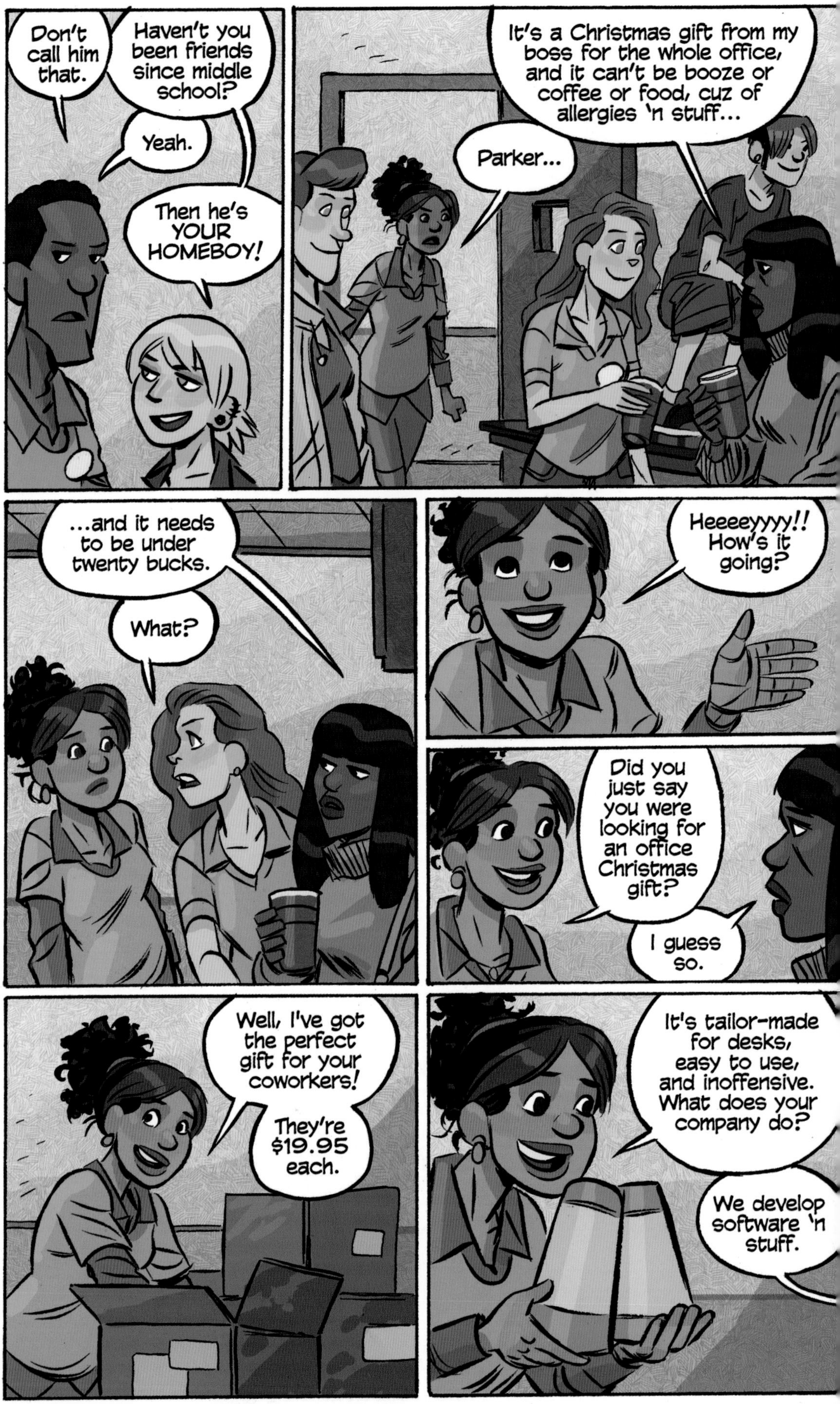
Don't call him that.
Haven't you been friends since middle school?
Yeah.
Then he's YOUR HOMEBOY!
It's a Christmas gift from my boss for the whole office, and it can't be booze or coffee or food, cuz of allergies 'n stuff...
Parker...
...and it needs to be under twenty bucks.
What?
Heeeeyyyy!! How's it going?
Did you just say you were looking for an office Christmas gift?
I guess so.
Well, I've got the perfect gift for your coworkers!
They're $19.95 each.
It's tailor-made for desks, easy to use, and inoffensive. What does your company do?
We develop software 'n stuff.

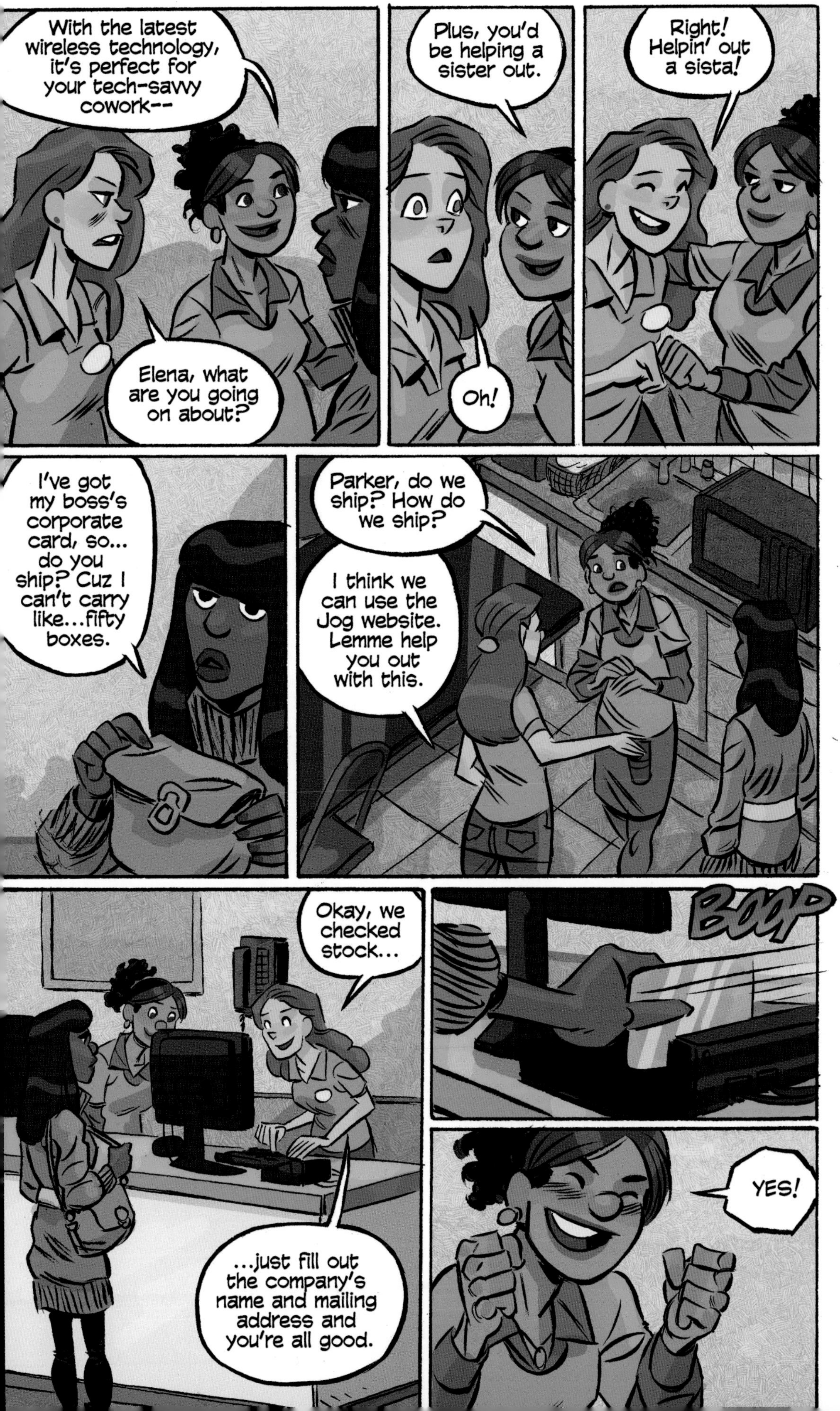
With the latest wireless technology, it's perfect for your tech-savvy cowork--
Elena, what are you going on about?
Plus, you'd be helping a sister out.
Oh!
Right! Helpin' out a sista!
I've got my boss's corporate card, so... do you ship? Cuz I can't carry like...fifty boxes.
Parker, do we ship? How do we ship?
I think we can use the Jog website. Lemme help you out with this.
Okay, we checked stock...
...just fill out the company's name and mailing address and you're all good.
BOOP
YES!

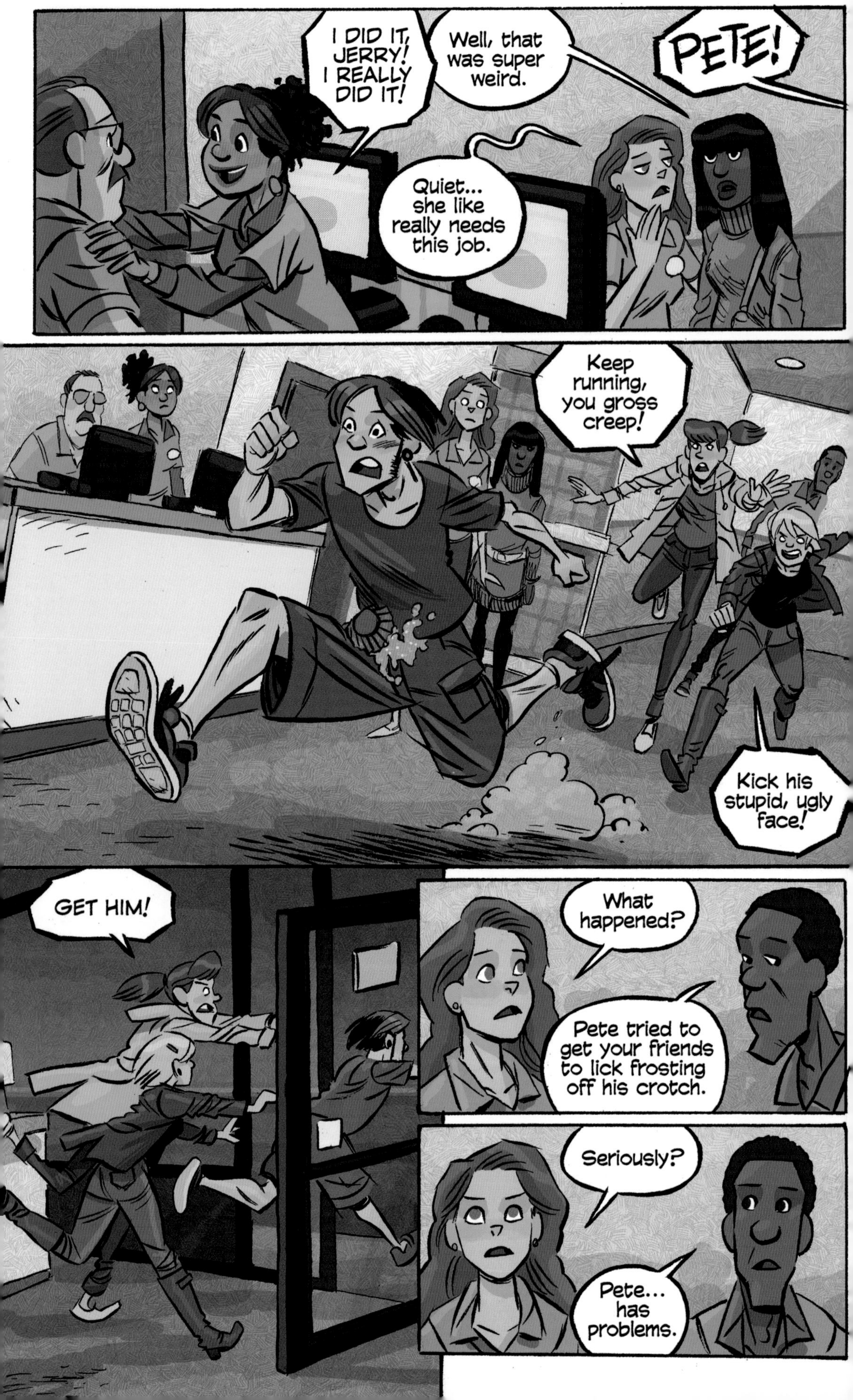

I DID IT, JERRY! I REALLY DID IT!
Well, that was super weird.
PETE!
Quiet... she like really needs this job.
Keep running, you gross creep!
Kick his stupid, ugly face!
GET HIM!
What happened?
Pete tried to get your friends to lick frosting off his crotch.
Seriously?
Pete... has problems.

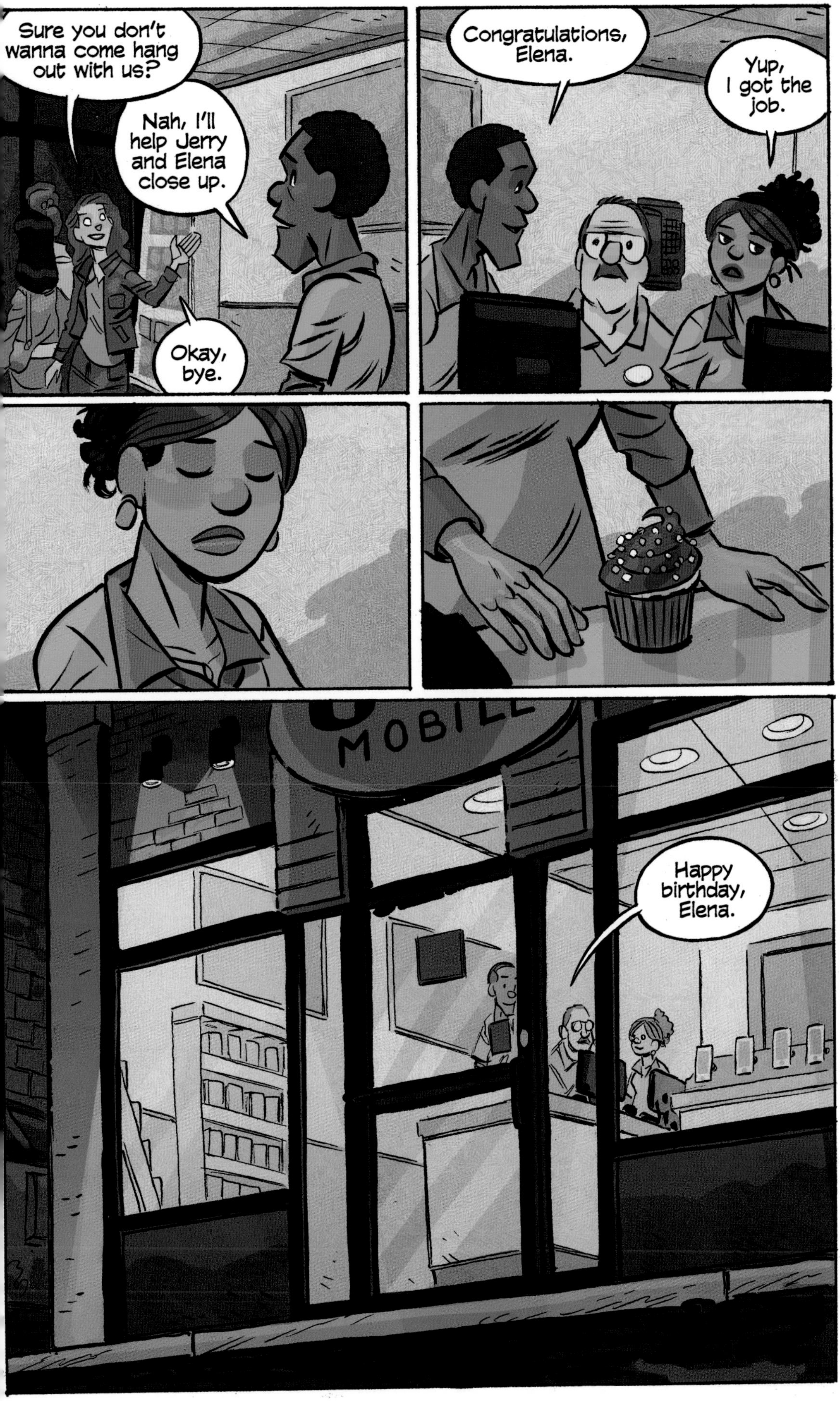
Sure you don't wanna come hang out with us?
Nah, I'll help Jerry and Elena close up.
Okay, bye.
Congratulations, Elena.
Yup, I got the job.
MOBIL
Happy birthday, Elena.

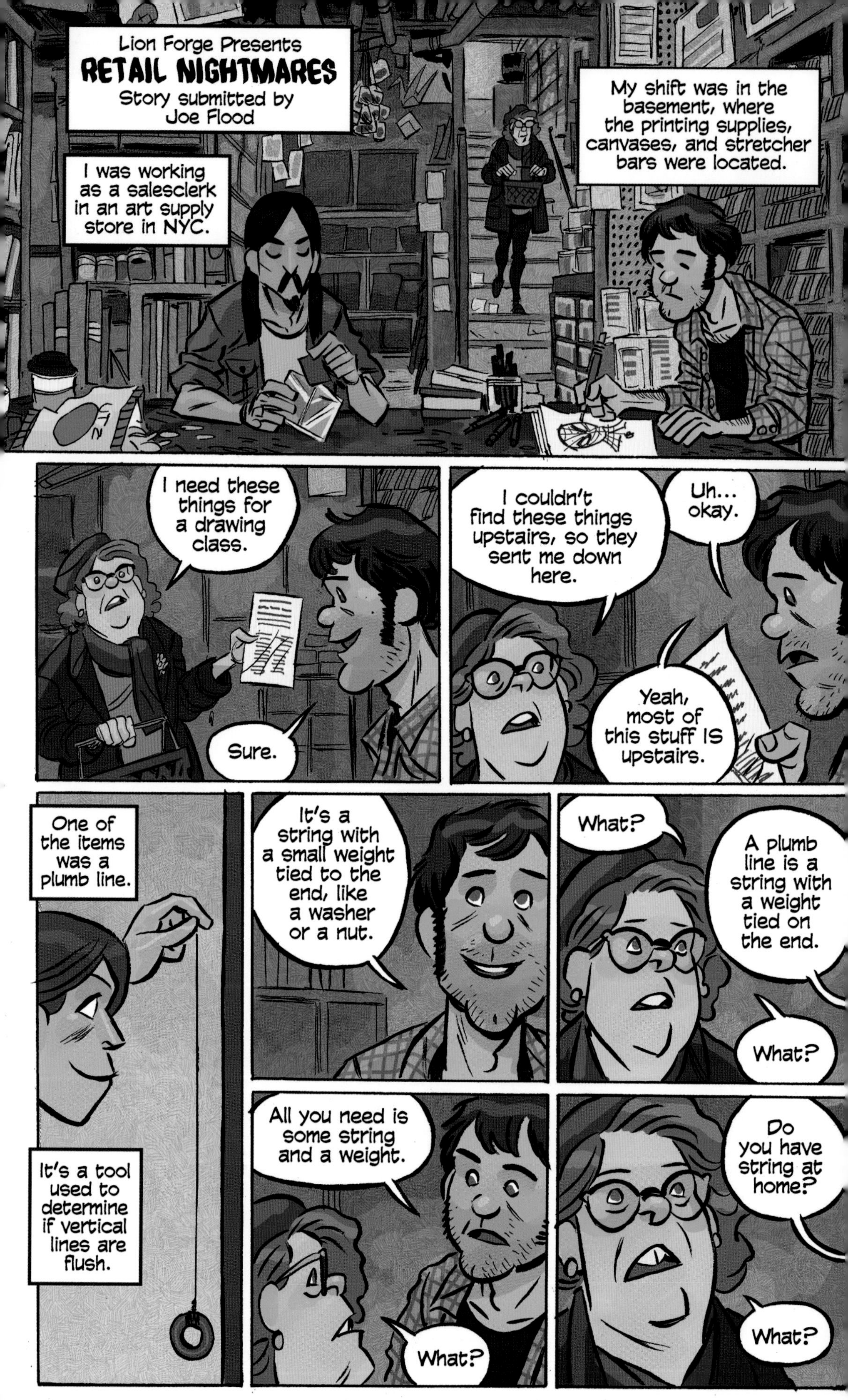
Lion Forge Presents
RETAIL NIGHTMARES
Story submitted by
Joe Flood
I was working as a salesclerk in an art supply store in NYC.
My shift was in the basement, where the printing supplies, canvases, and stretcher bars were located.
I need these things for a drawing class.
Sure.
I couldn't find these things upstairs, so they sent me down here.
Uh... okay.
Yeah, most of this stuff IS upstairs.
One of the items was a plumb line.
It's a tool used to determine if vertical lines are flush.
It's a string with a small weight tied to the end, like a washer or a nut.
What?
A plumb line is a string with a weight tied on the end.
What?
All you need is some string and a weight.
What?
Do you have string at home?
What?

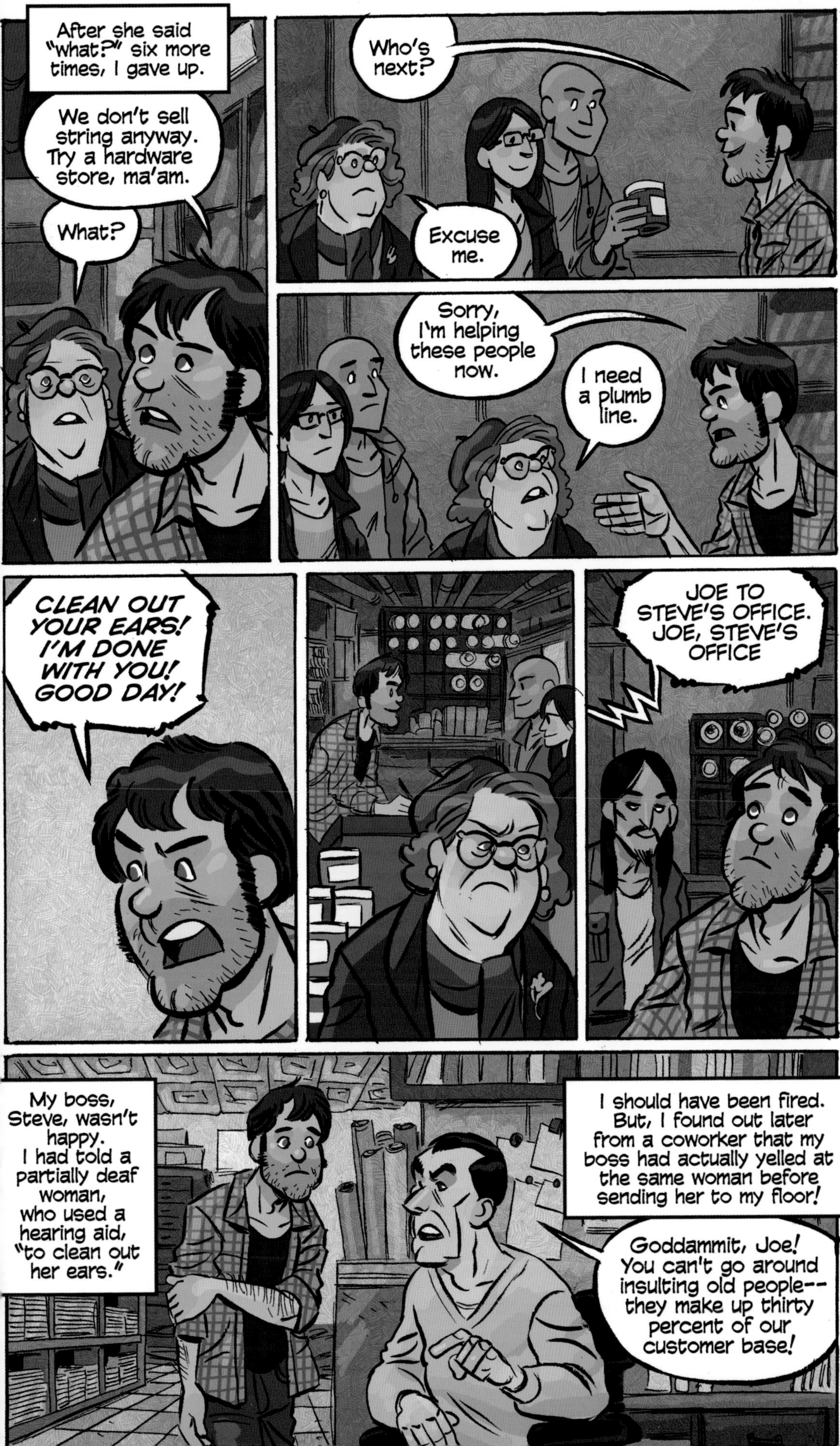
After she said "what?" six more times, I gave up.
We don't sell string anyway. Try a hardware store, ma'am.
What?
Who's next?
Excuse me.
Sorry, I'm helping these people now.
I need a plumb line.
CLEAN OUT YOUR EARS! I'M DONE WITH YOU! GOOD DAY!
JOE TO STEVE'S OFFICE. JOE, STEVE'S OFFICE
My boss, Steve, wasn't happy. I had told a partially deaf woman, who used a hearing aid, "to clean out her ears."
I should have been fired. But, I found out later from a coworker that my boss had actually yelled at the same woman before sending her to my floor!
Goddammit, Joe! You can't go around insulting old people-- they make up thirty percent of our customer base!

# CHAPTER 4

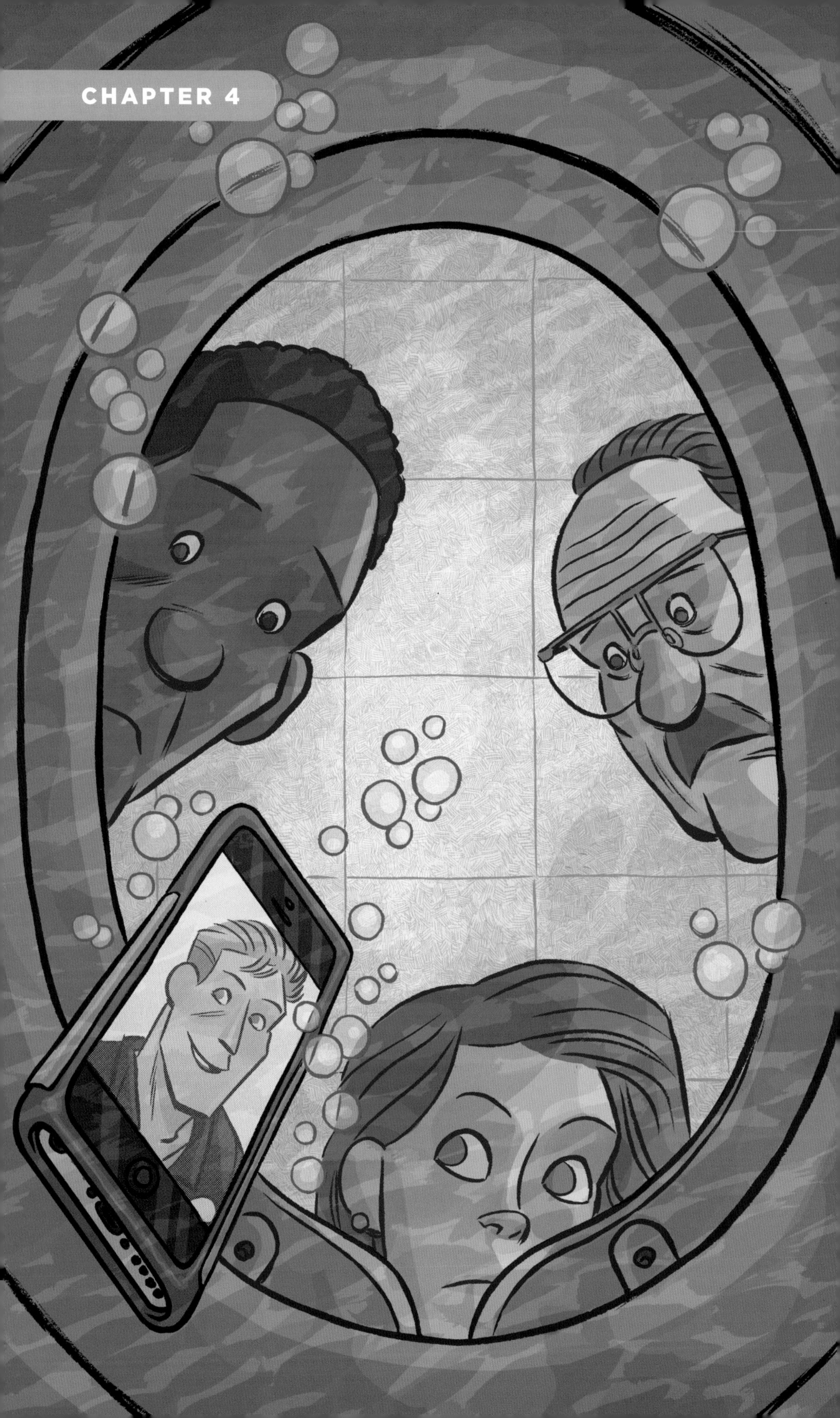

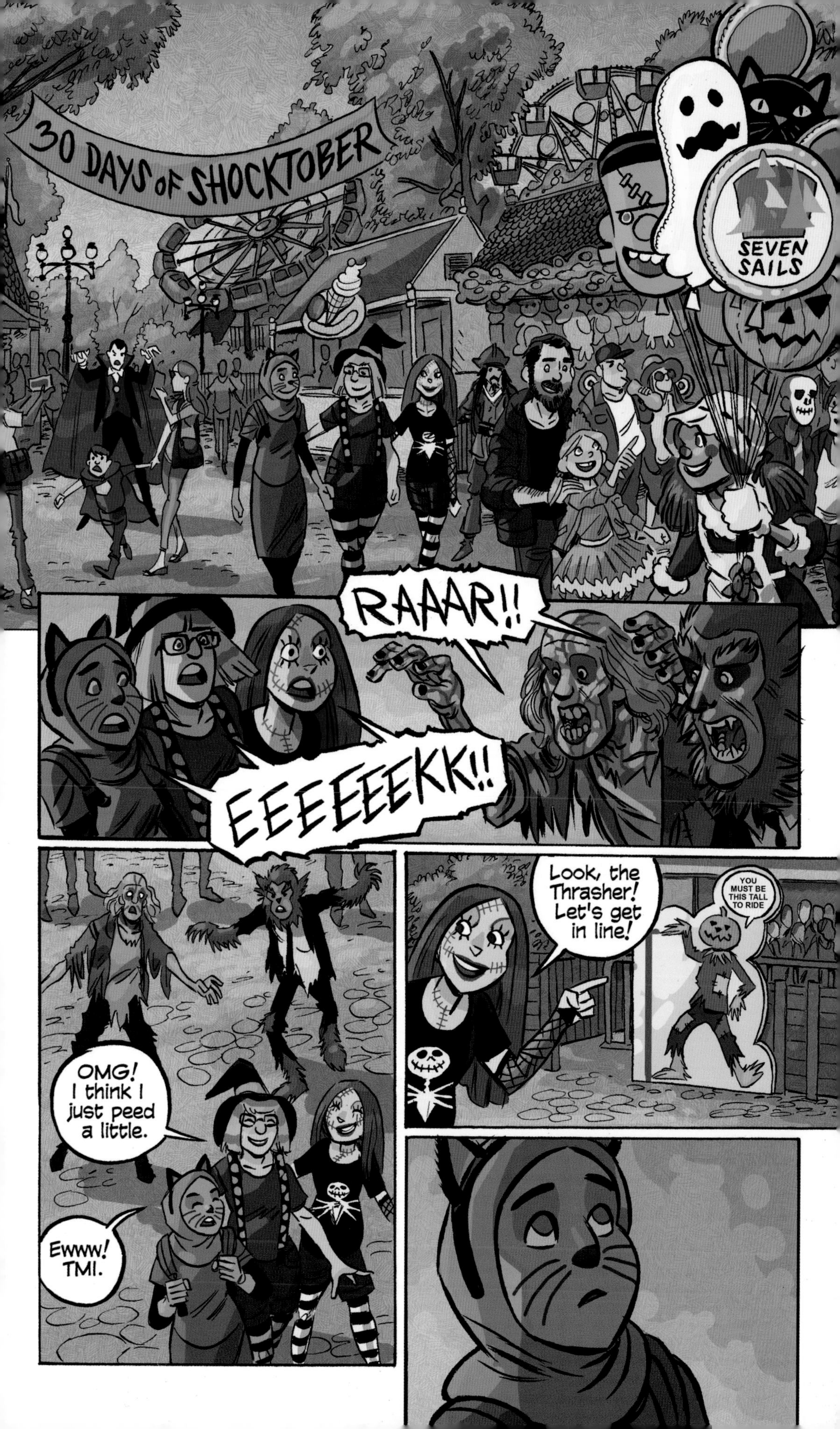
30 DAYS OF SHOCKTOBER
SEVEN SAILS
RAAAR!!
EEEEEEEKK!!
OMG! I think I just peed a little.
Ewww! TMI.
Look, the Thrasher! Let's get in line!
YOU MUST BE THIS TALL TO RIDE

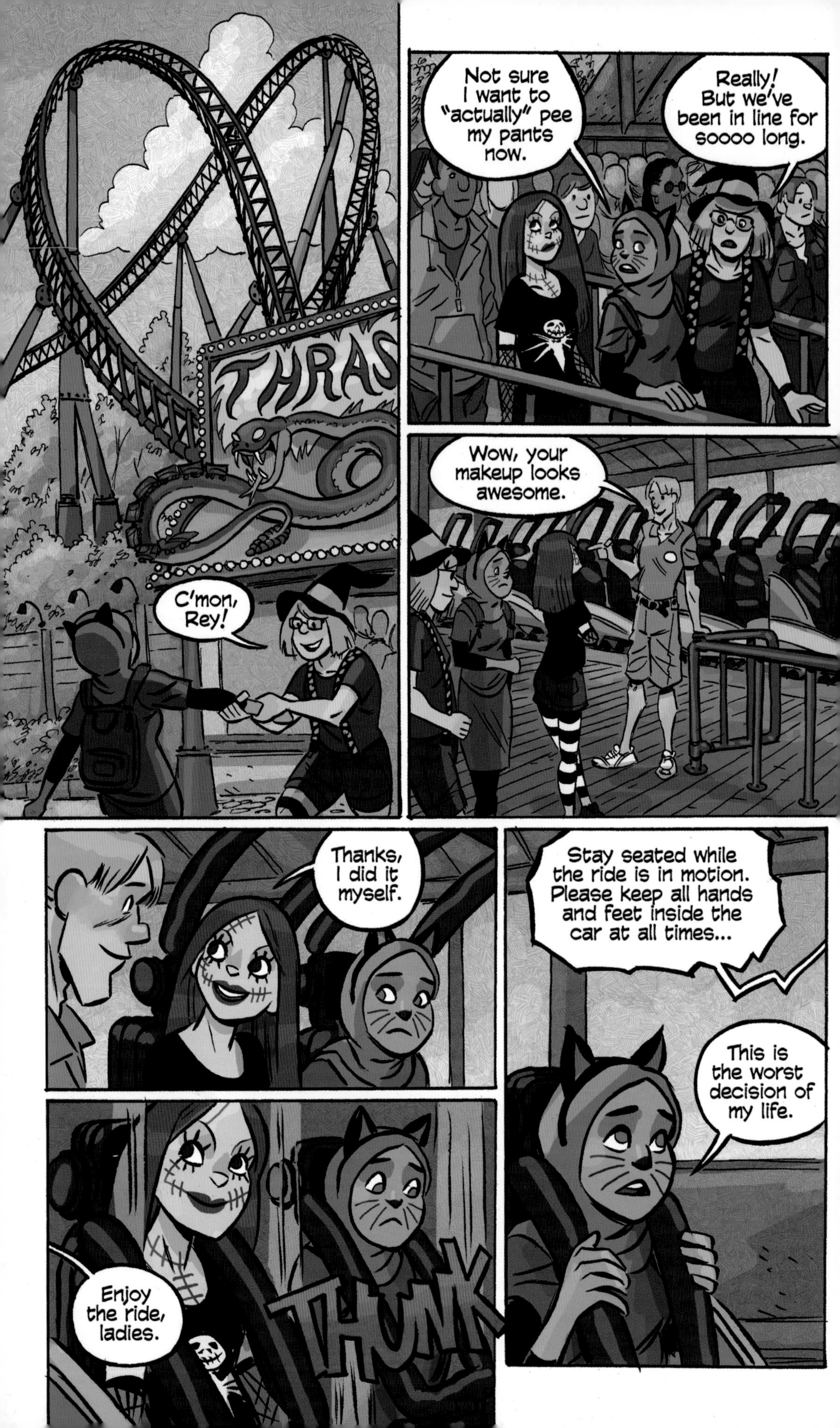
THRAS
C'mon, Rey!
Not sure I want to "actually" pee my pants now.
Really! But we've been in line for soooo long.
Wow, your makeup looks awesome.
Thanks, I did it myself.
Enjoy the ride, ladies.
THUNK
Stay seated while the ride is in motion. Please keep all hands and feet inside the car at all times...
This is the worst decision of my life.

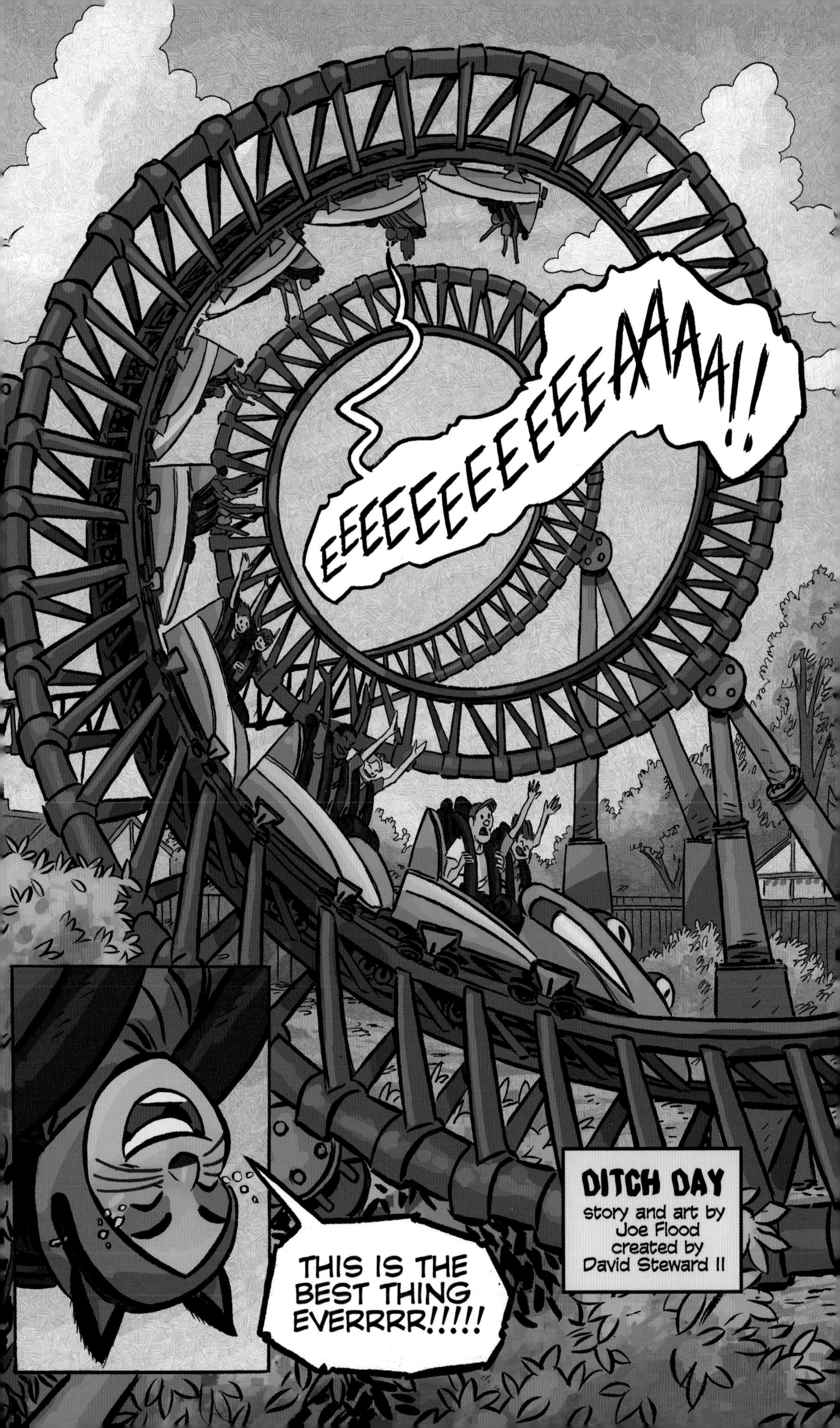
EEEEEEEEEEEEEAAAAA!!
THIS IS THE BEST THING EVERRRR!!!!!
DITCH DAY
story and art by Joe Flood
created by David Steward II

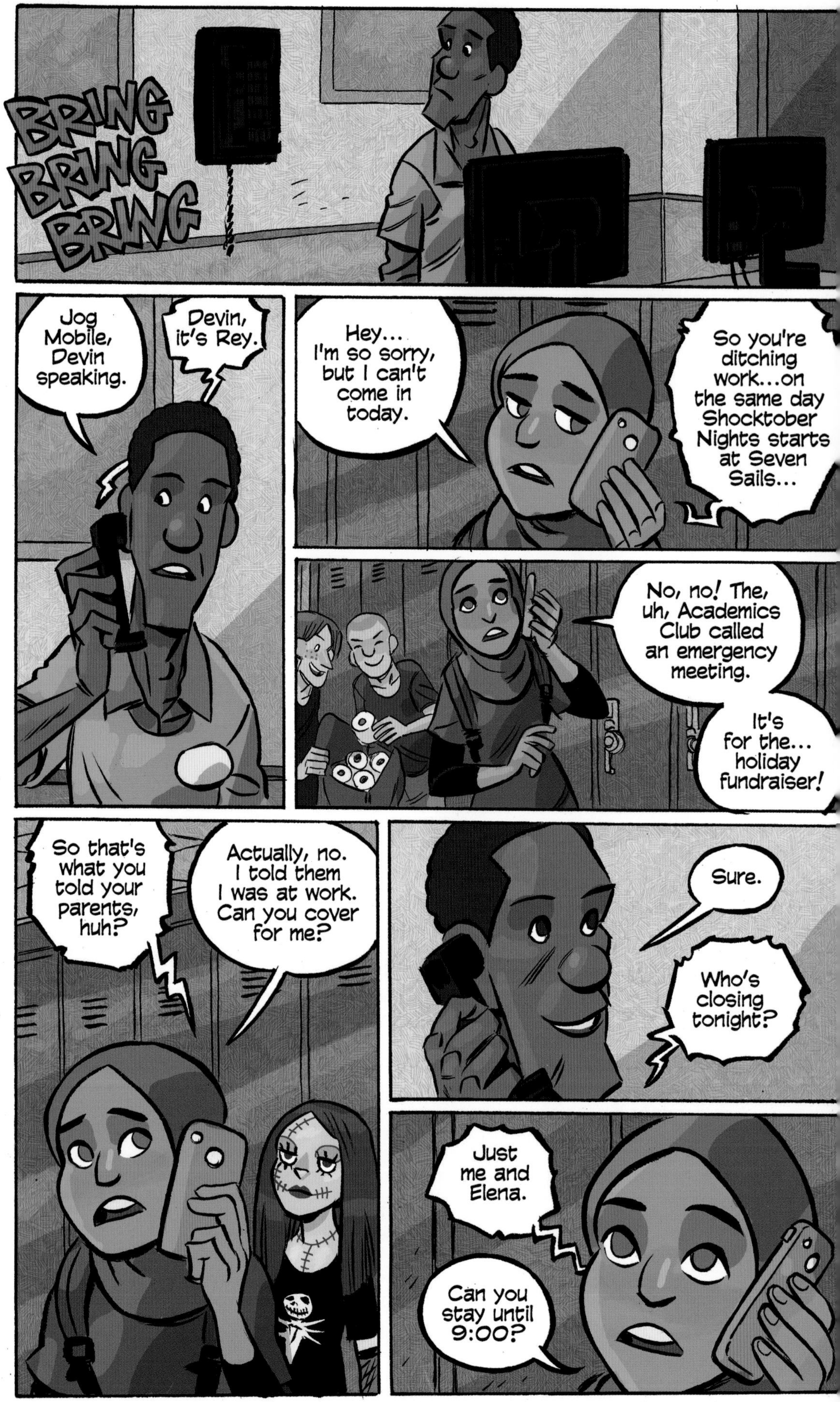
BRING
BRING
BRING
Jog Mobile, Devin speaking.
Devin, it's Rey.
Hey... I'm so sorry, but I can't come in today.
So you're ditching work...on the same day Shocktober Nights starts at Seven Sails...
No, no! The, uh, Academics Club called an emergency meeting.
It's for the... holiday fundraiser!
So that's what you told your parents, huh?
Actually, no. I told them I was at work. Can you cover for me?
Sure.
Who's closing tonight?
Just me and Elena.
Can you stay until 9:00?

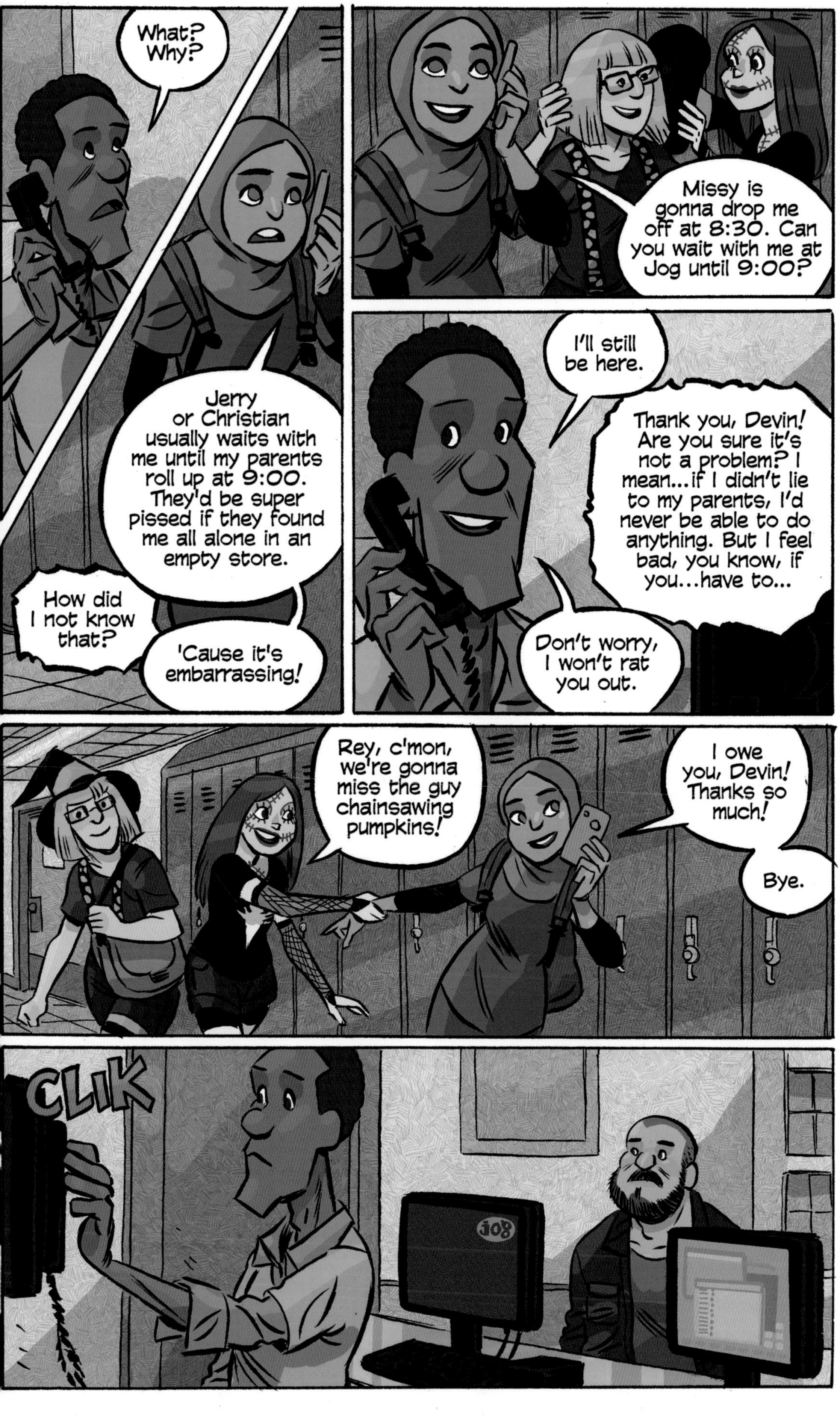
What? Why?
Jerry or Christian usually waits with me until my parents roll up at 9:00. They'd be super pissed if they found me all alone in an empty store.
How did I not know that?
'Cause it's embarrassing!
Missy is gonna drop me off at 8:30. Can you wait with me at Jog until 9:00?
I'll still be here.
Thank you, Devin! Are you sure it's not a problem? I mean...if I didn't lie to my parents, I'd never be able to do anything. But I feel bad, you know, if you...have to...
Don't worry, I won't rat you out.
Rey, c'mon, we're gonna miss the guy chainsawing pumpkins!
I owe you, Devin! Thanks so much!
Bye.
CLIK

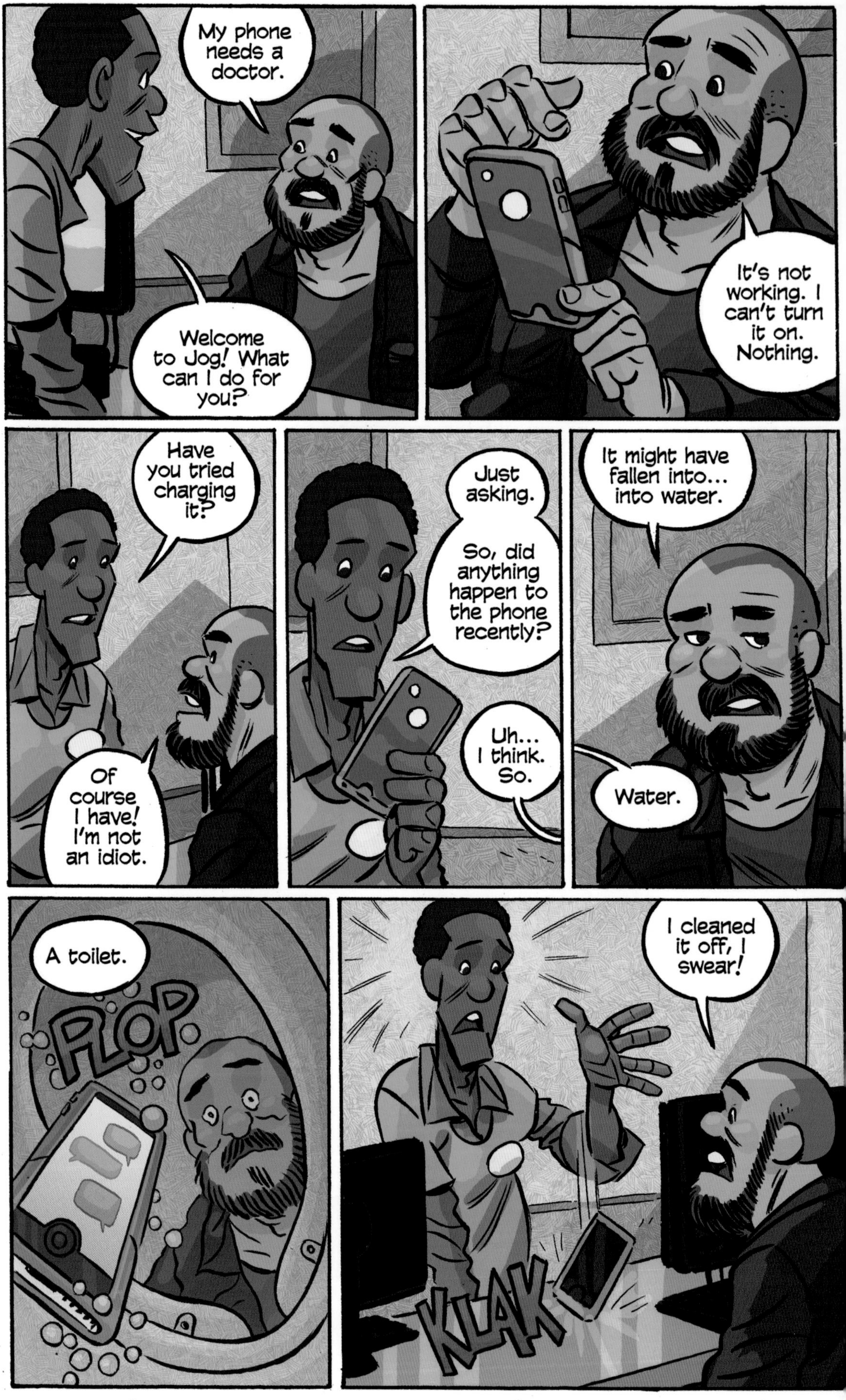
My phone needs a doctor.
Welcome to Jog! What can I do for you?
It's not working. I can't turn it on. Nothing.
Have you tried charging it?
Of course I have! I'm not an idiot.
Just asking.
So, did anything happen to the phone recently?
Uh... I think. So.
It might have fallen into... into water.
Water.
A toilet.
PLOP
I cleaned it off, I swear!
KLAK

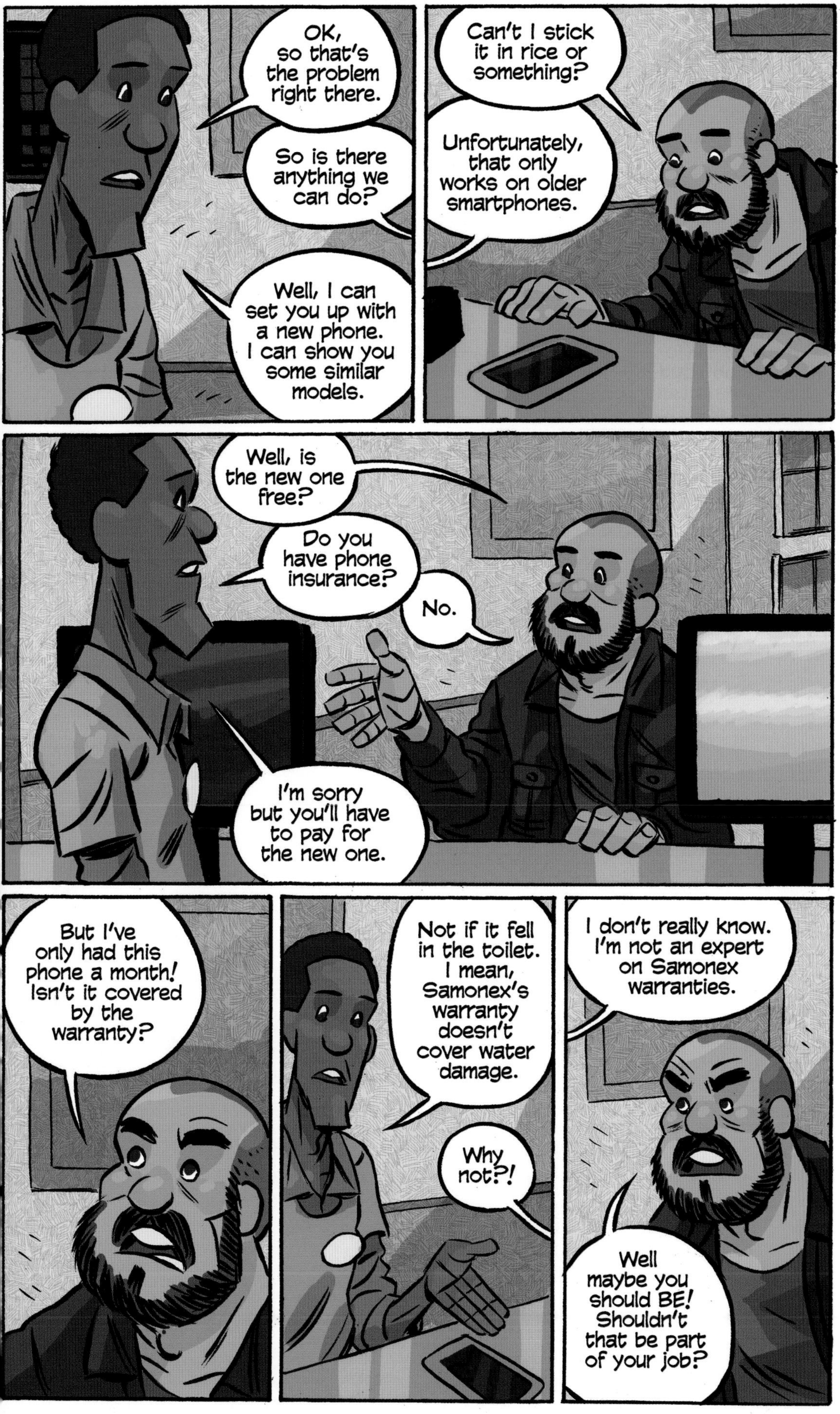
OK, so that's the problem right there.
So is there anything we can do?
Well, I can set you up with a new phone. I can show you some similar models.
Can't I stick it in rice or something?
Unfortunately, that only works on older smartphones.
Well, is the new one free?
Do you have phone insurance?
No.
I'm sorry but you'll have to pay for the new one.
But I've only had this phone a month! Isn't it covered by the warranty?
Not if it fell in the toilet. I mean, Samonex's warranty doesn't cover water damage.
Why not?!
I don't really know. I'm not an expert on Samonex warranties.
Well maybe you should BE! Shouldn't that be part of your job?

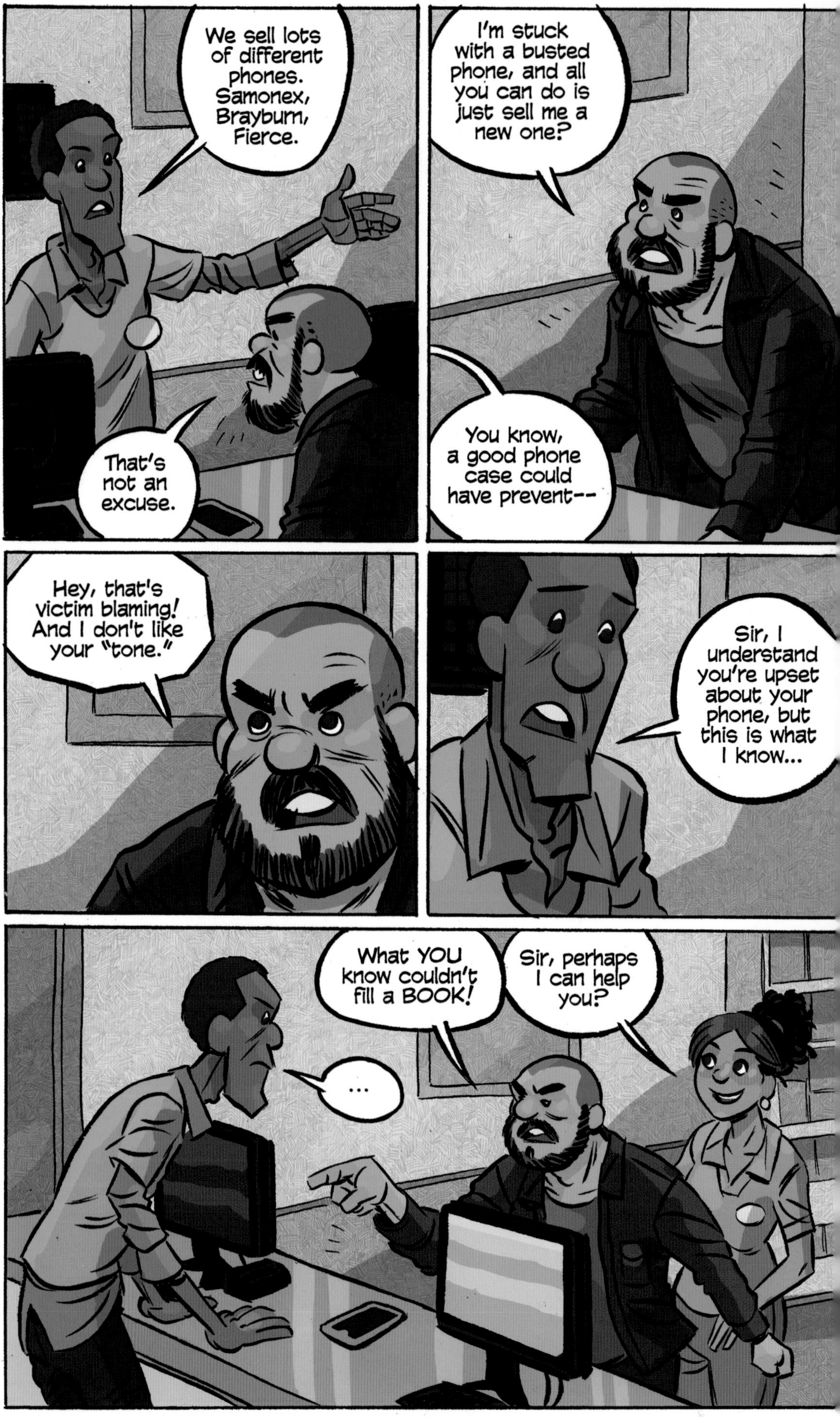
We sell lots of different phones. Samonex, Brayburn, Fierce.
That's not an excuse.
I'm stuck with a busted phone, and all you can do is just sell me a new one?
You know, a good phone case could have prevent--
Hey, that's victim blaming! And I don't like your "tone."
Sir, I understand you're upset about your phone, but this is what I know...
What YOU know couldn't fill a BOOK!
Sir, perhaps I can help you?
...

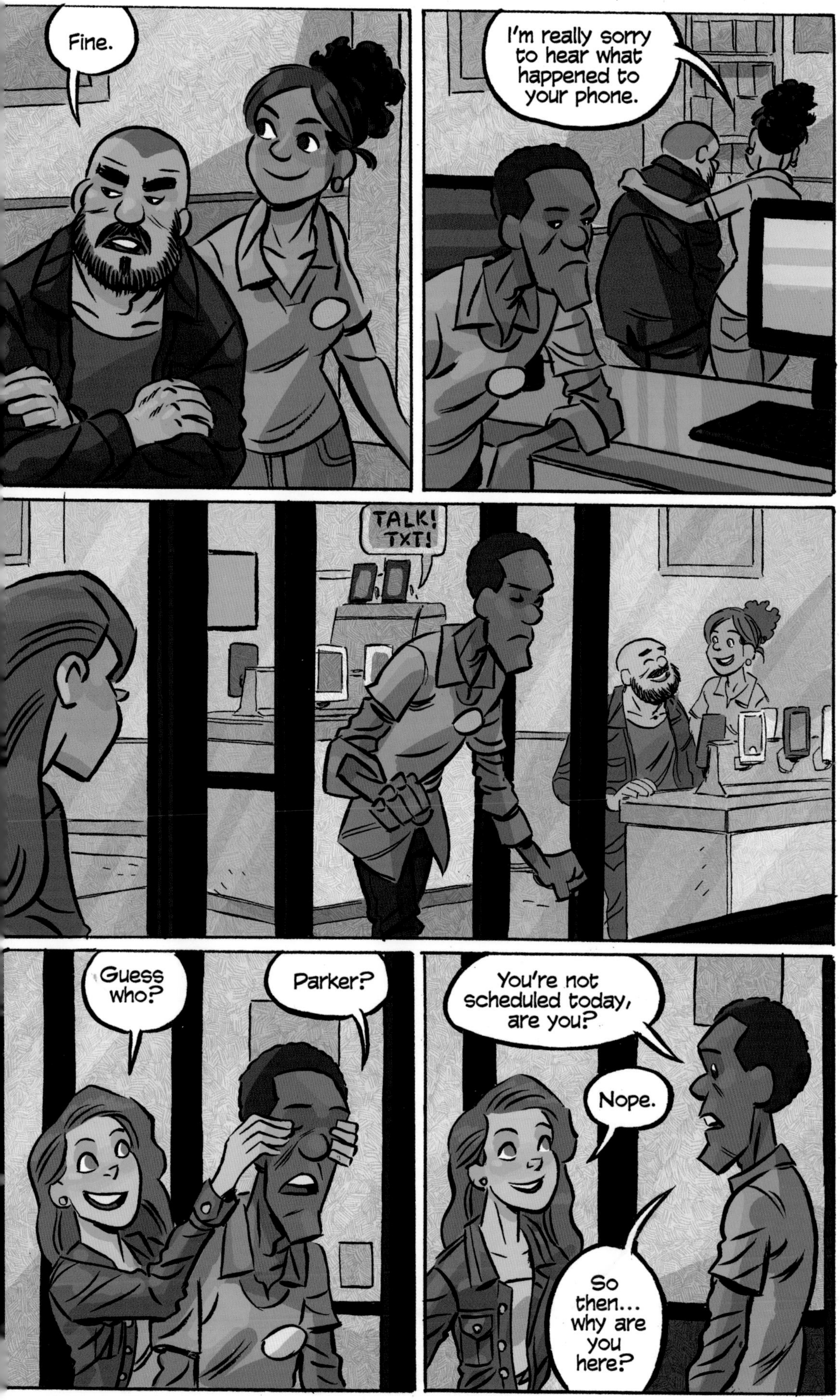
Fine.
I'm really sorry to hear what happened to your phone.
TALK! TXT!
Guess who?
Parker?
You're not scheduled today, are you?
Nope.
So then... why are you here?

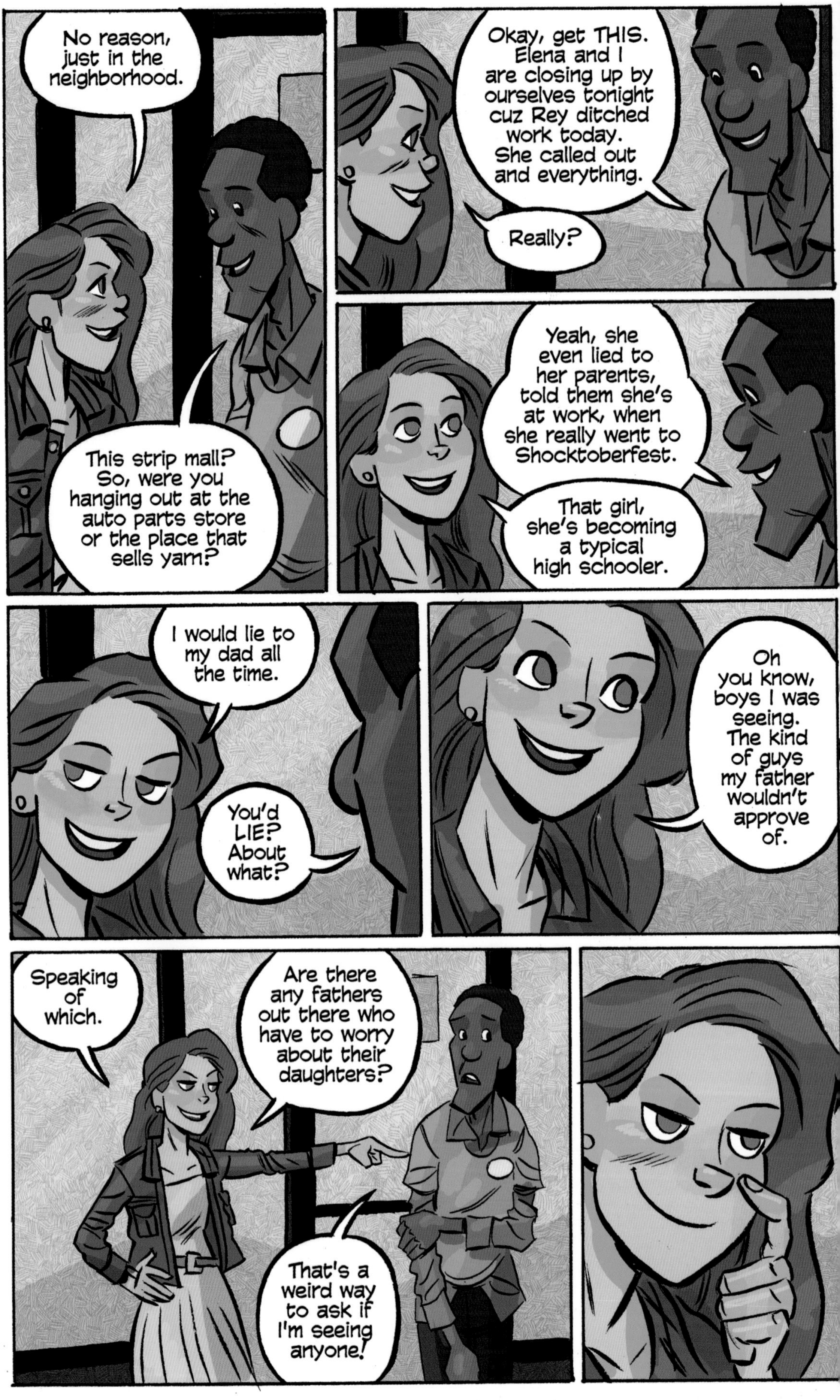
No reason, just in the neighborhood.
This strip mall? So, were you hanging out at the auto parts store or the place that sells yarn?
Okay, get THIS. Elena and I are closing up by ourselves tonight cuz Rey ditched work today. She called out and everything.
Really?
Yeah, she even lied to her parents, told them she's at work, when she really went to Shocktoberfest.
That girl, she's becoming a typical high schooler.
I would lie to my dad all the time.
You'd LIE? About what?
Oh you know, boys I was seeing. The kind of guys my father wouldn't approve of.
Speaking of which.
Are there any fathers out there who have to worry about their daughters?
That's a weird way to ask if I'm seeing anyone!

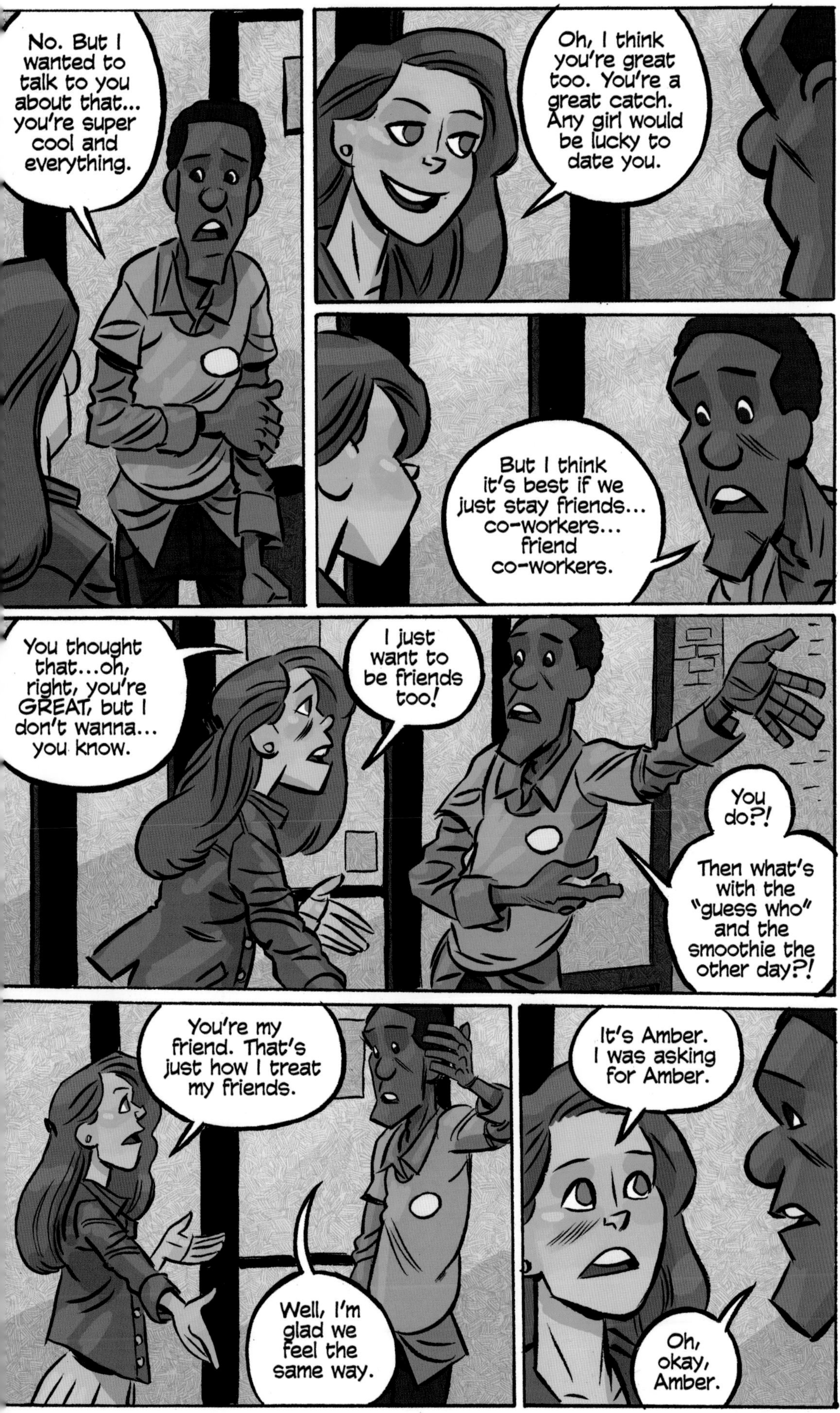
No. But I wanted to talk to you about that... you're super cool and everything.
Oh, I think you're great too. You're a great catch. Any girl would be lucky to date you.
But I think it's best if we just stay friends... co-workers... friend co-workers.
You thought that...oh, right, you're GREAT, but I don't wanna... you know.
I just want to be friends too!
You do?!
Then what's with the "guess who" and the smoothie the other day?!
You're my friend. That's just how I treat my friends.
Well, I'm glad we feel the same way.
It's Amber. I was asking for Amber.
Oh, okay, Amber.

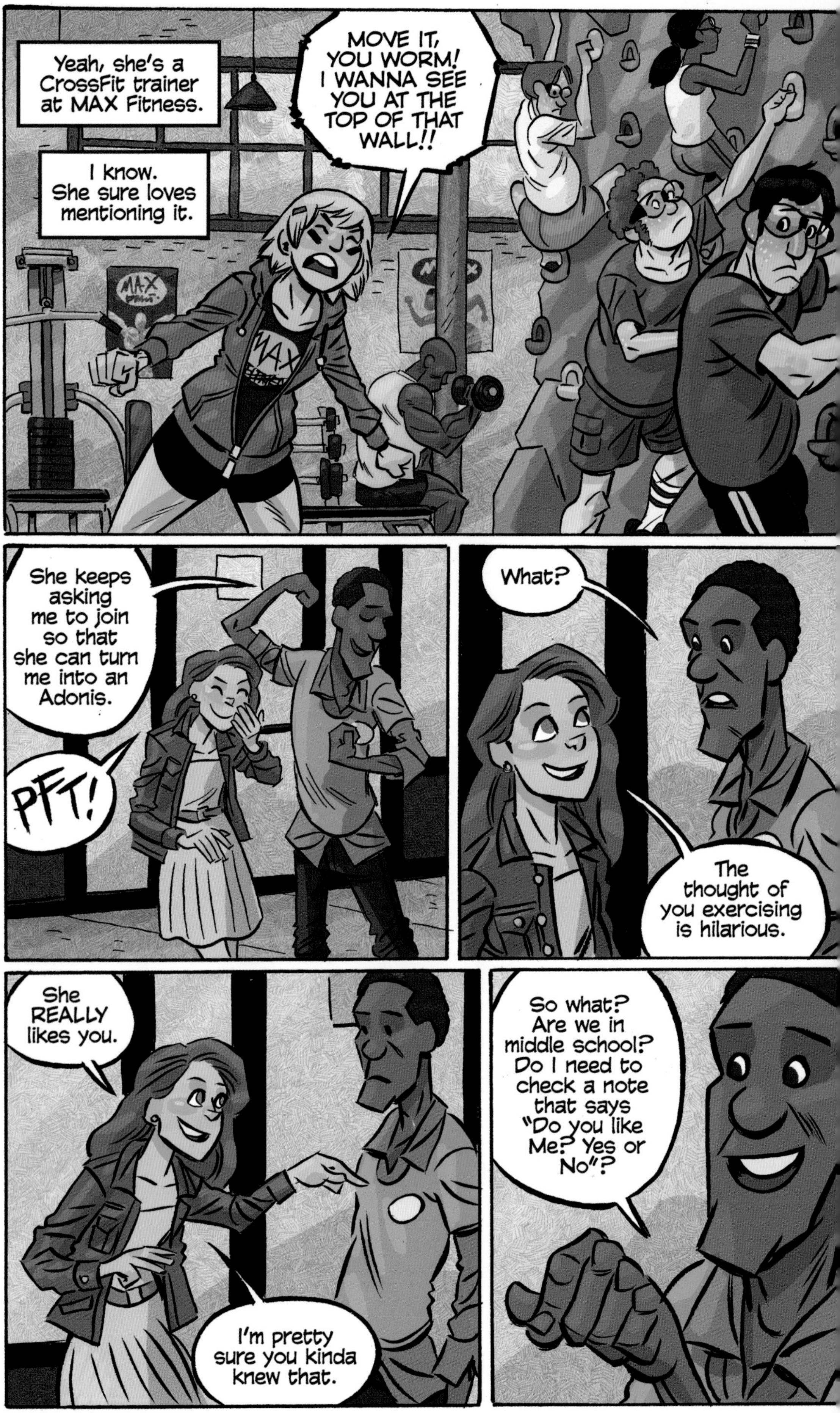

Yeah, she's a CrossFit trainer at MAX Fitness.
I know. She sure loves mentioning it.
MOVE IT, YOU WORM! I WANNA SEE YOU AT THE TOP OF THAT WALL!!
MAX
She keeps asking me to join so that she can turn me into an Adonis.
PFT!
What?
The thought of you exercising is hilarious.
She REALLY likes you.
I'm pretty sure you kinda knew that.
So what? Are we in middle school? Do I need to check a note that says "Do you like Me? Yes or No"?

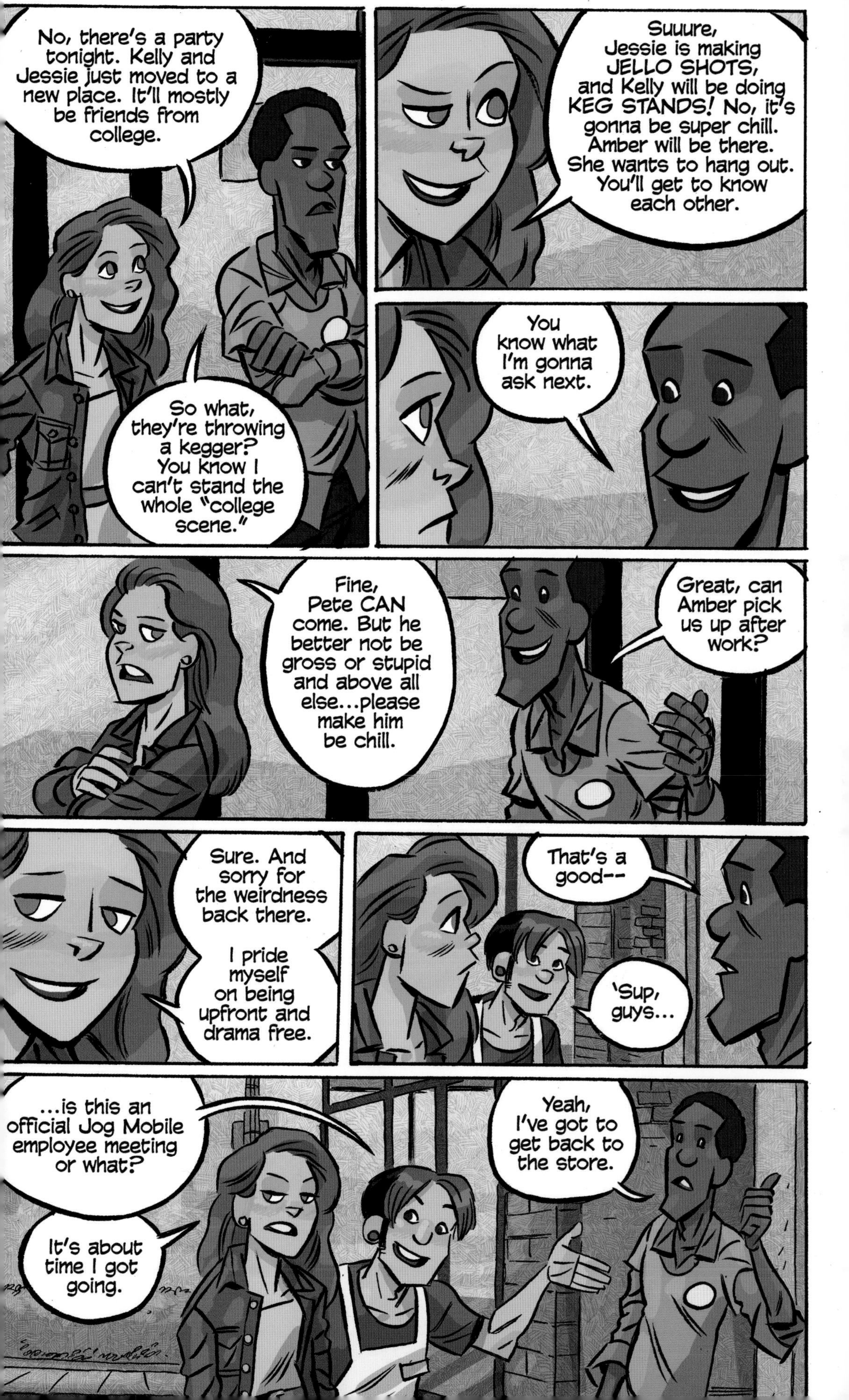
No, there's a party tonight. Kelly and Jessie just moved to a new place. It'll mostly be friends from college.
So what, they're throwing a kegger? You know I can't stand the whole "college scene."
Suuure, Jessie is making JELLO SHOTS, and Kelly will be doing KEG STANDS! No, it's gonna be super chill. Amber will be there. She wants to hang out. You'll get to know each other.
You know what I'm gonna ask next.
Fine, Pete CAN come. But he better not be gross or stupid and above all else...please make him be chill.
Great, can Amber pick us up after work?
Sure. And sorry for the weirdness back there.
I pride myself on being upfront and drama free.
That's a good--
'Sup, guys...
...is this an official Jog Mobile employee meeting or what?
It's about time I got going.
Yeah, I've got to get back to the store.

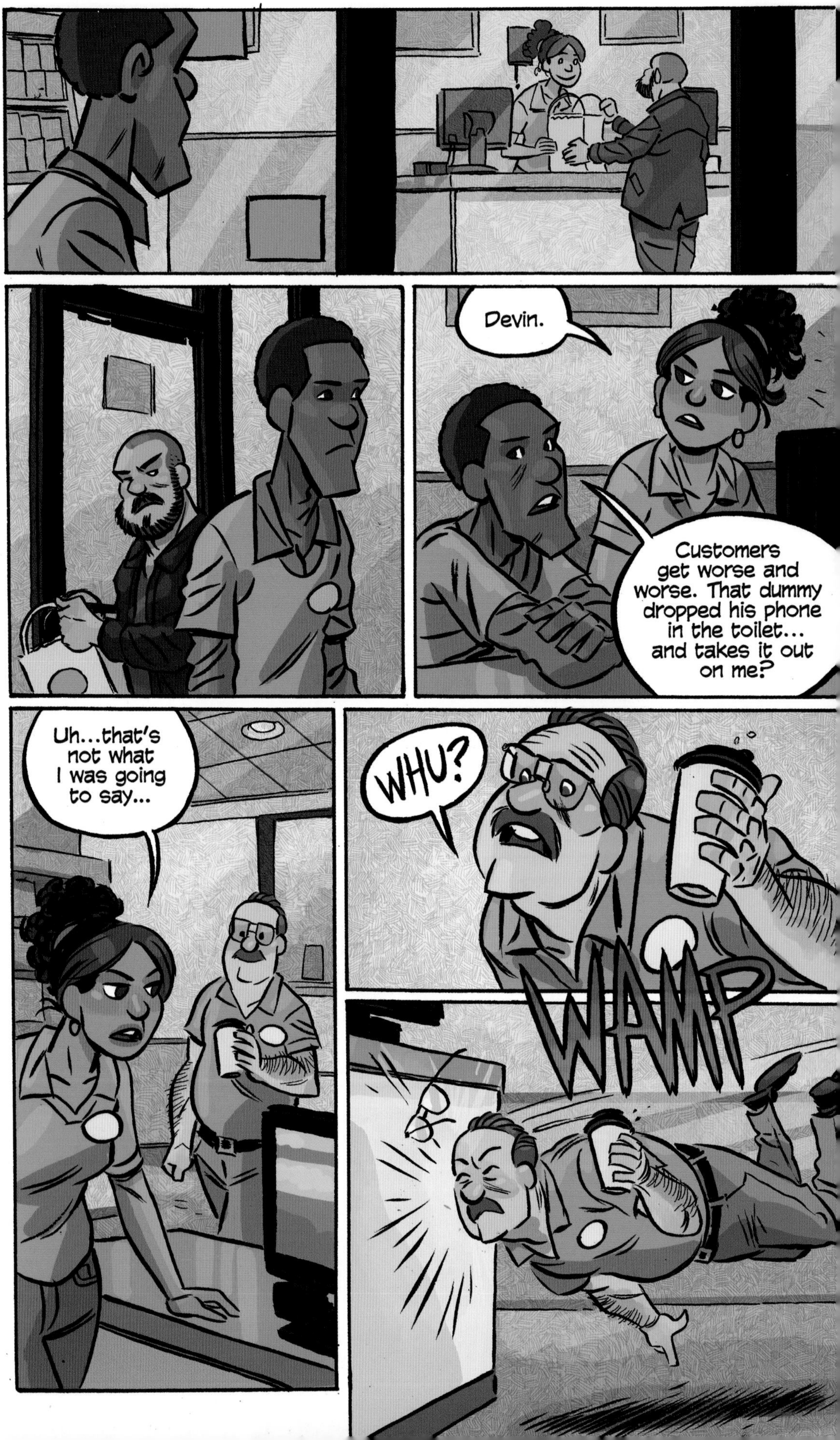
Devin.
Customers get worse and worse. That dummy dropped his phone in the toilet... and takes it out on me?
Uh...that's not what I was going to say...
WHU?
WAMP

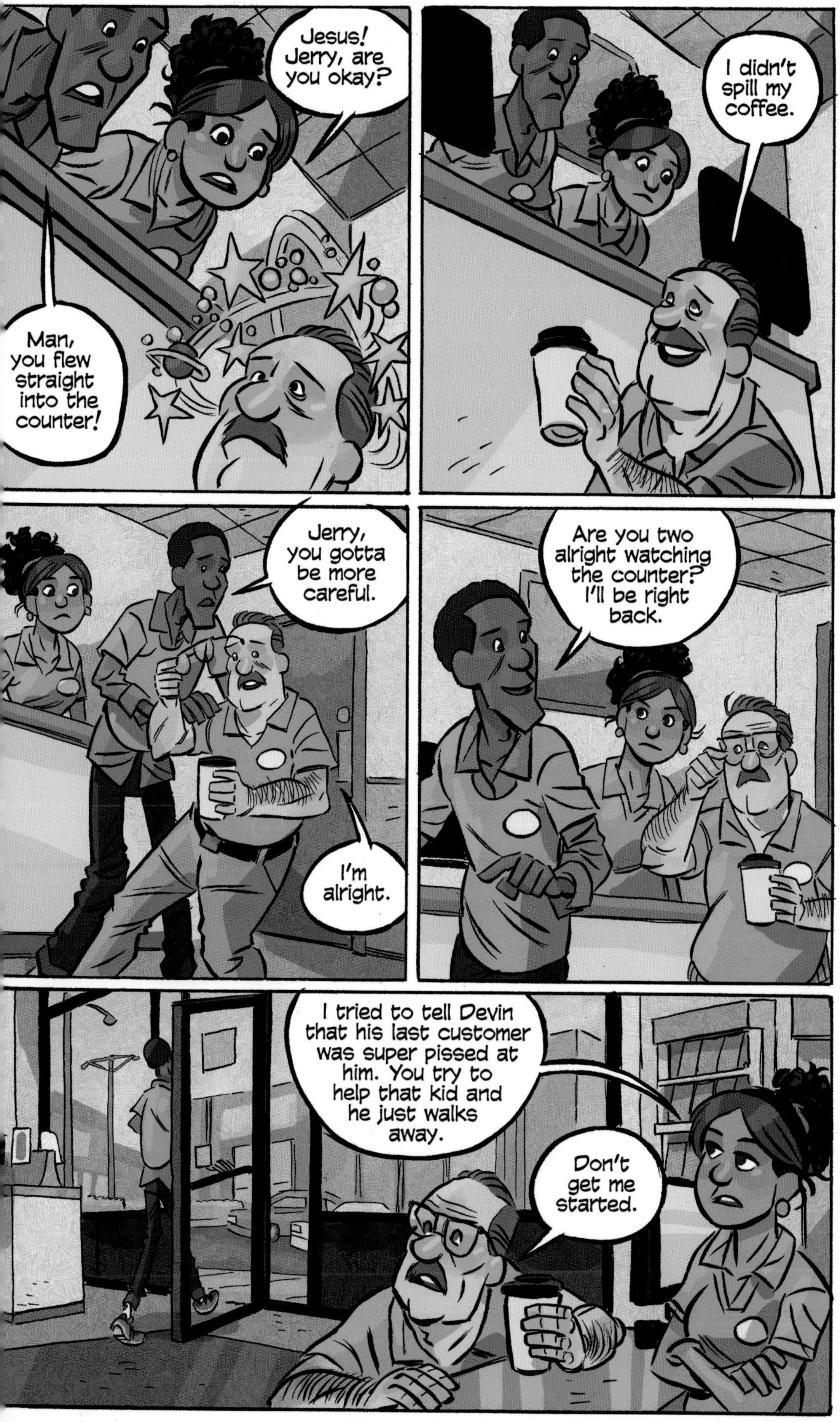
Jesus! Jerry, are you okay?
Man, you flew straight into the counter!
I didn't spill my coffee.
Jerry, you gotta be more careful.
I'm alright.
Are you two alright watching the counter? I'll be right back.
I tried to tell Devin that his last customer was super pissed at him. You try to help that kid and he just walks away.
Don't get me started.

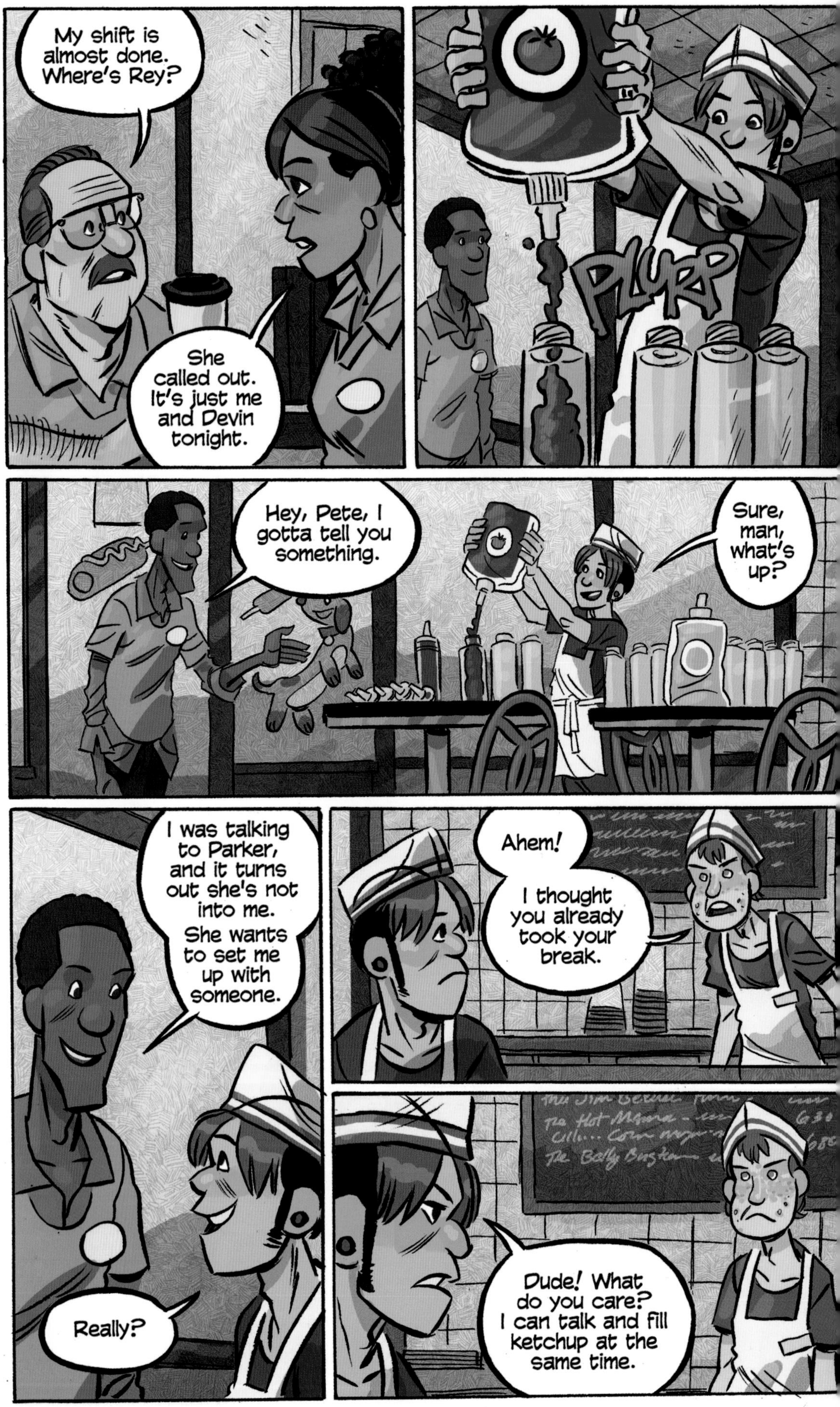
My shift is almost done. Where's Rey?
She called out. It's just me and Devin tonight.
PLURP
Hey, Pete, I gotta tell you something.
Sure, man, what's up?
I was talking to Parker, and it turns out she's not into me.
She wants to set me up with someone.
Really?
Ahem!
I thought you already took your break.
Dude! What do you care? I can talk and fill ketchup at the same time.

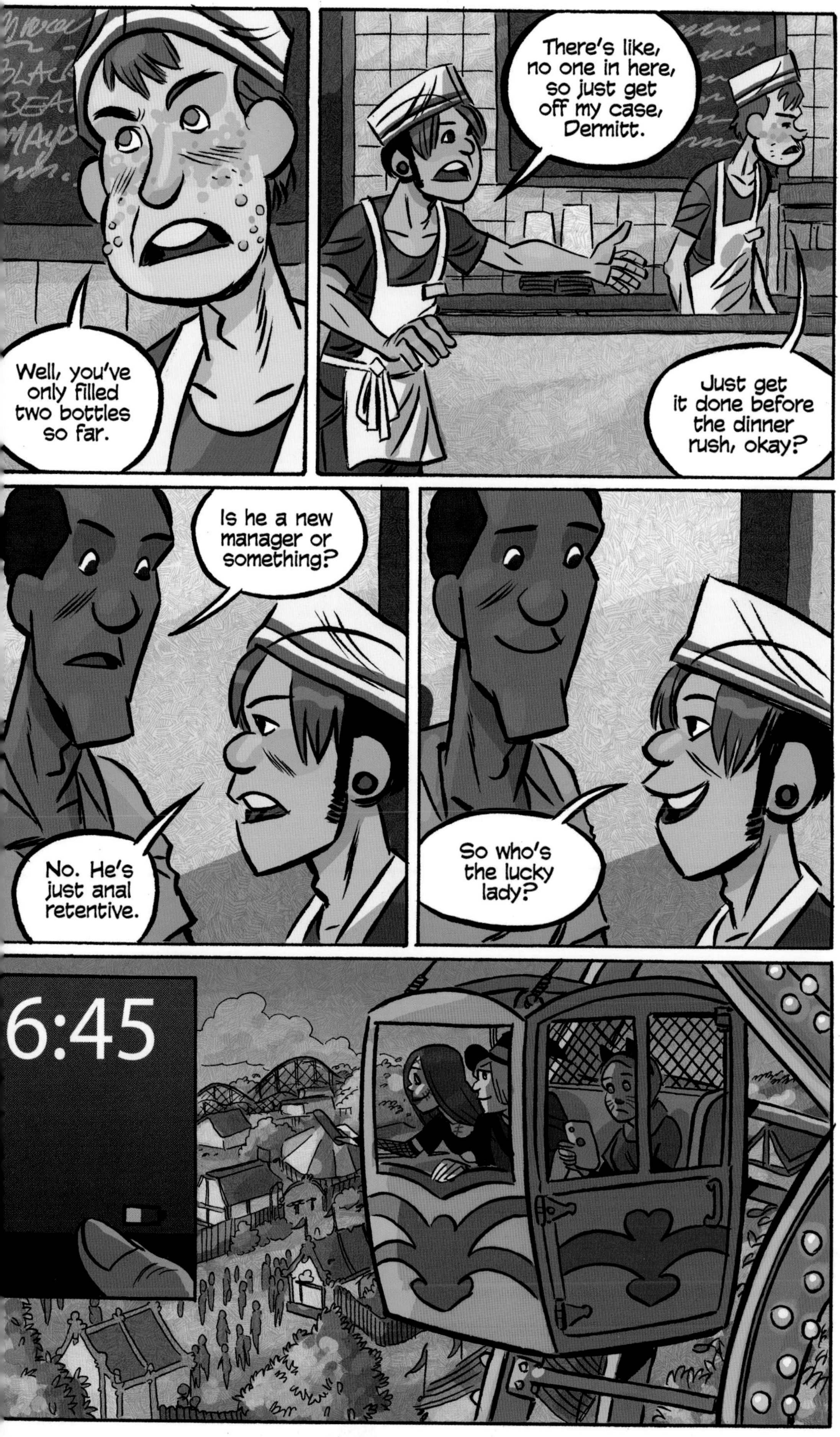
Well, you've only filled two bottles so far.
There's like, no one in here, so just get off my case, Dermitt.
Just get it done before the dinner rush, okay?
Is he a new manager or something?
No. He's just anal retentive.
So who's the lucky lady?
6:45

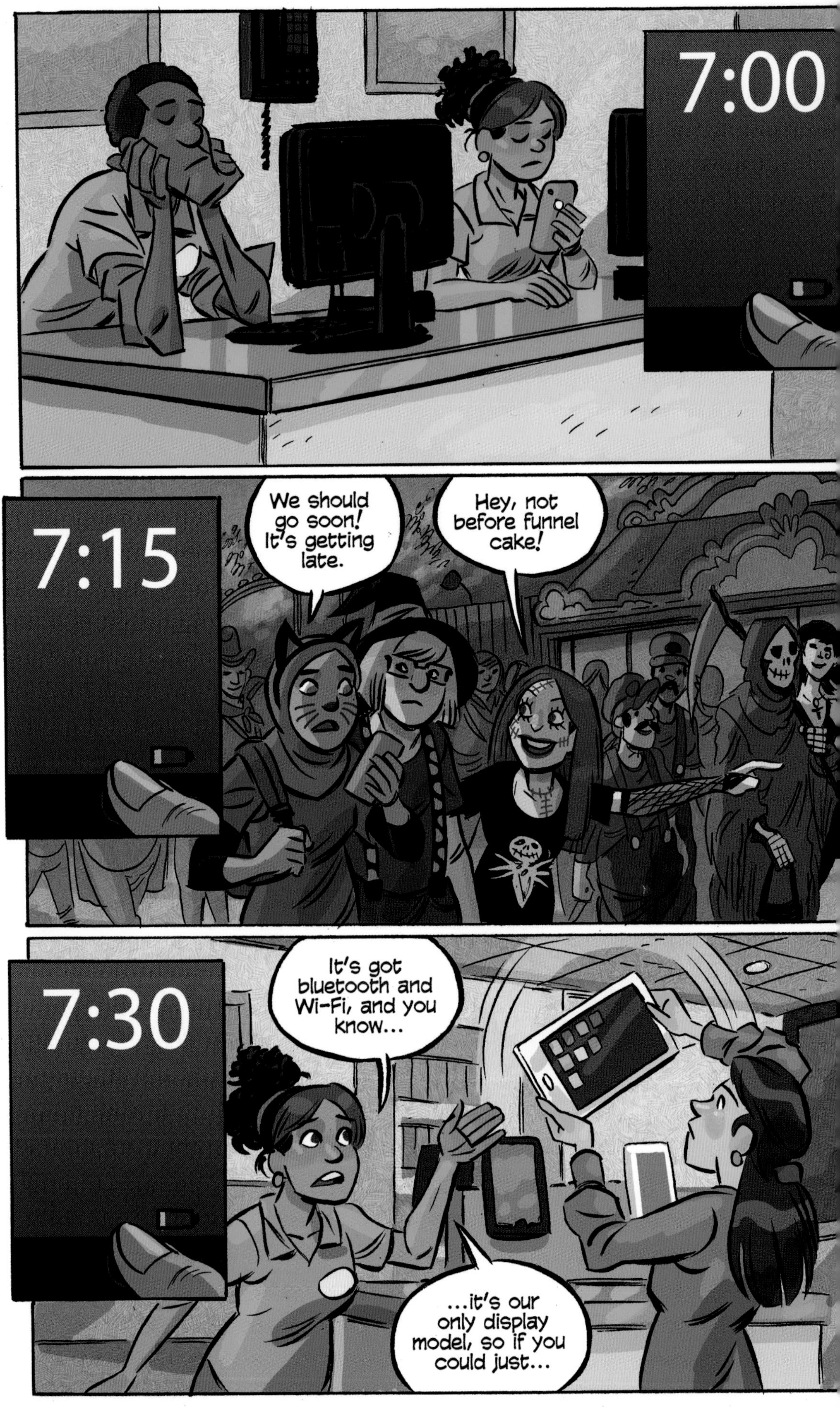
7:00
7:15
We should go soon! It's getting late.
Hey, not before funnel cake!
7:30
It's got bluetooth and Wi-Fi, and you know...
...it's our only display model, so if you could just...

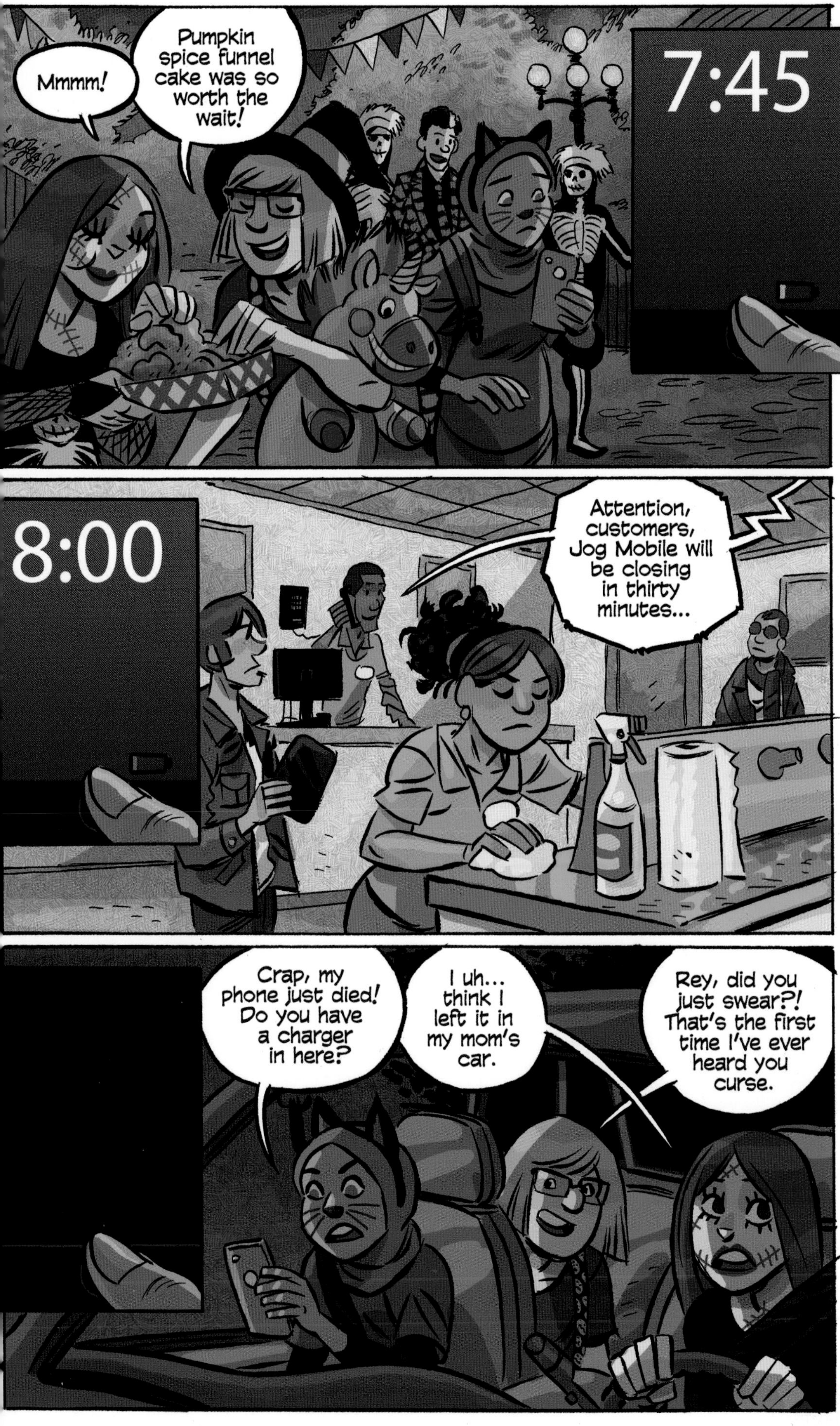
7:45
Mmmm!
Pumpkin spice funnel cake was so worth the wait!
8:00
Attention, customers, Jog Mobile will be closing in thirty minutes...
Crap, my phone just died! Do you have a charger in here?
I uh... think I left it in my mom's car.
Rey, did you just swear?! That's the first time I've ever heard you curse.

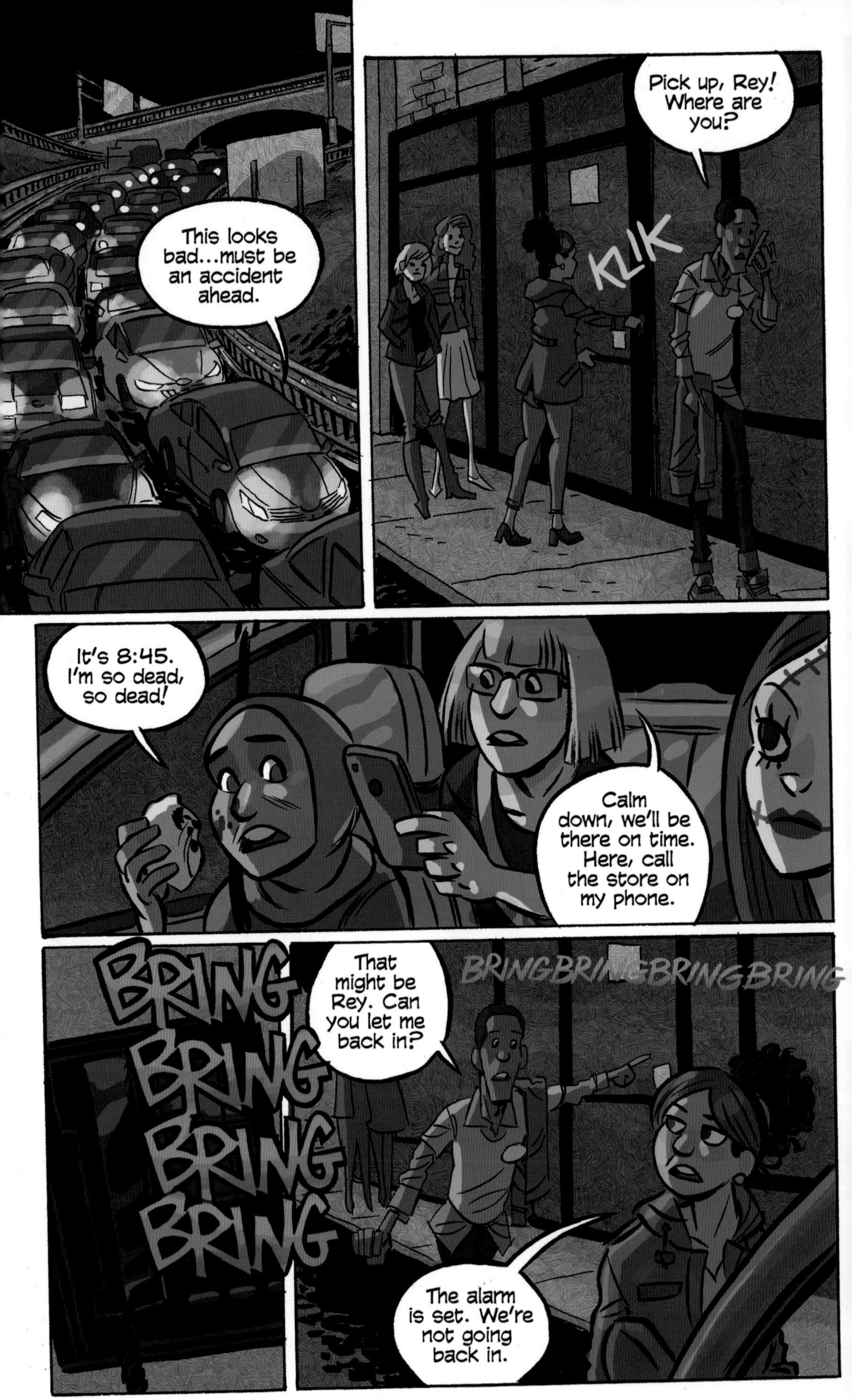
This looks bad...must be an accident ahead.
Pick up, Rey! Where are you?
KLIK
It's 8:45. I'm so dead, so dead!
Calm down, we'll be there on time. Here, call the store on my phone.
BRING BRING BRING BRING
BRINGBRINGBRINGBRING
That might be Rey. Can you let me back in?
The alarm is set. We're not going back in.

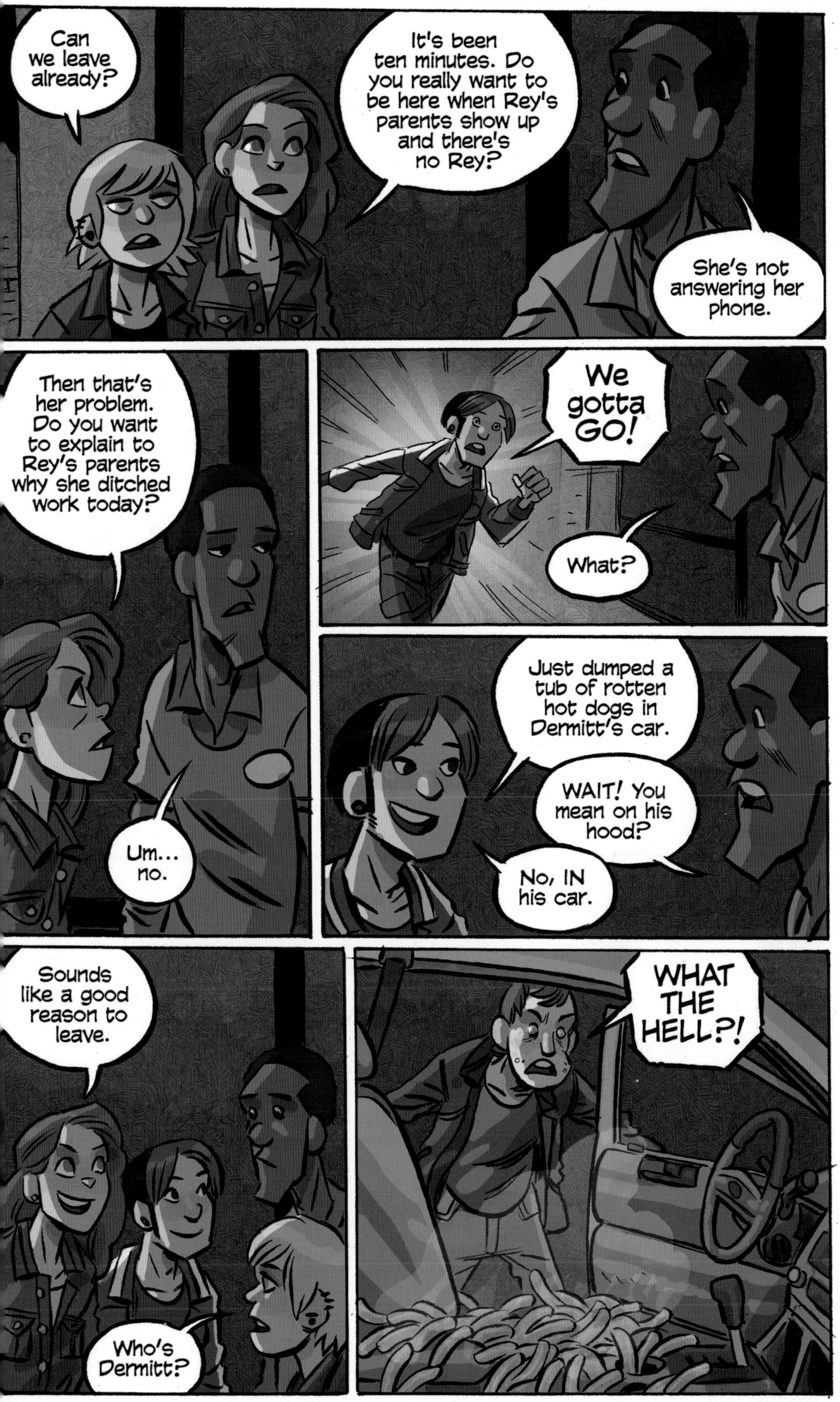

Can we leave already?
It's been ten minutes. Do you really want to be here when Rey's parents show up and there's no Rey?
She's not answering her phone.
Then that's her problem. Do you want to explain to Rey's parents why she ditched work today?
Um... no.
We gotta GO!
What?
Just dumped a tub of rotten hot dogs in Dermitt's car.
WAIT! You mean on his hood?
No, IN his car.
Sounds like a good reason to leave.
Who's Dermitt?
WHAT THE HELL?!

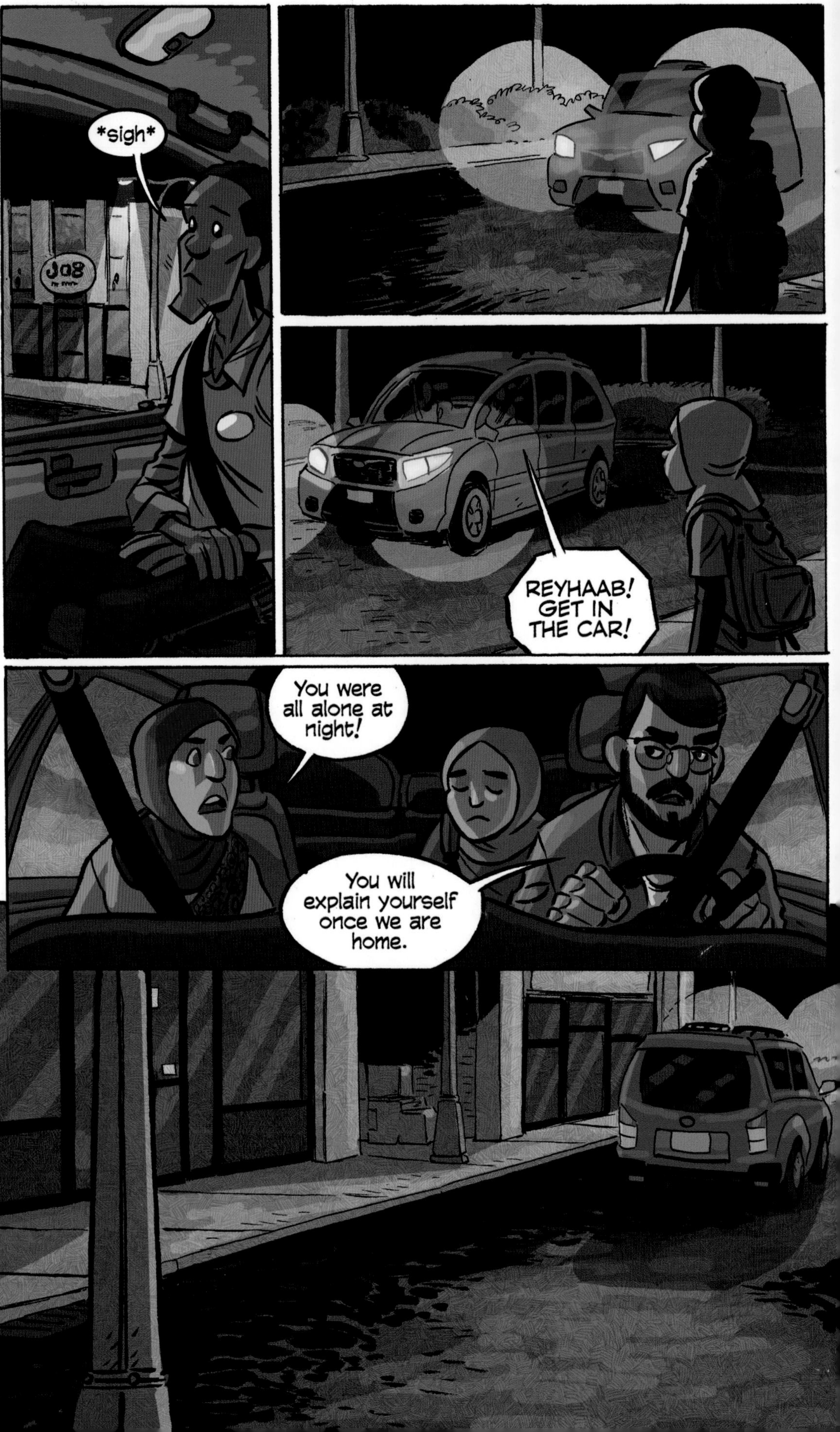
*sigh*
REYHAAB! GET IN THE CAR!
You were all alone at night!
You will explain yourself once we are home.

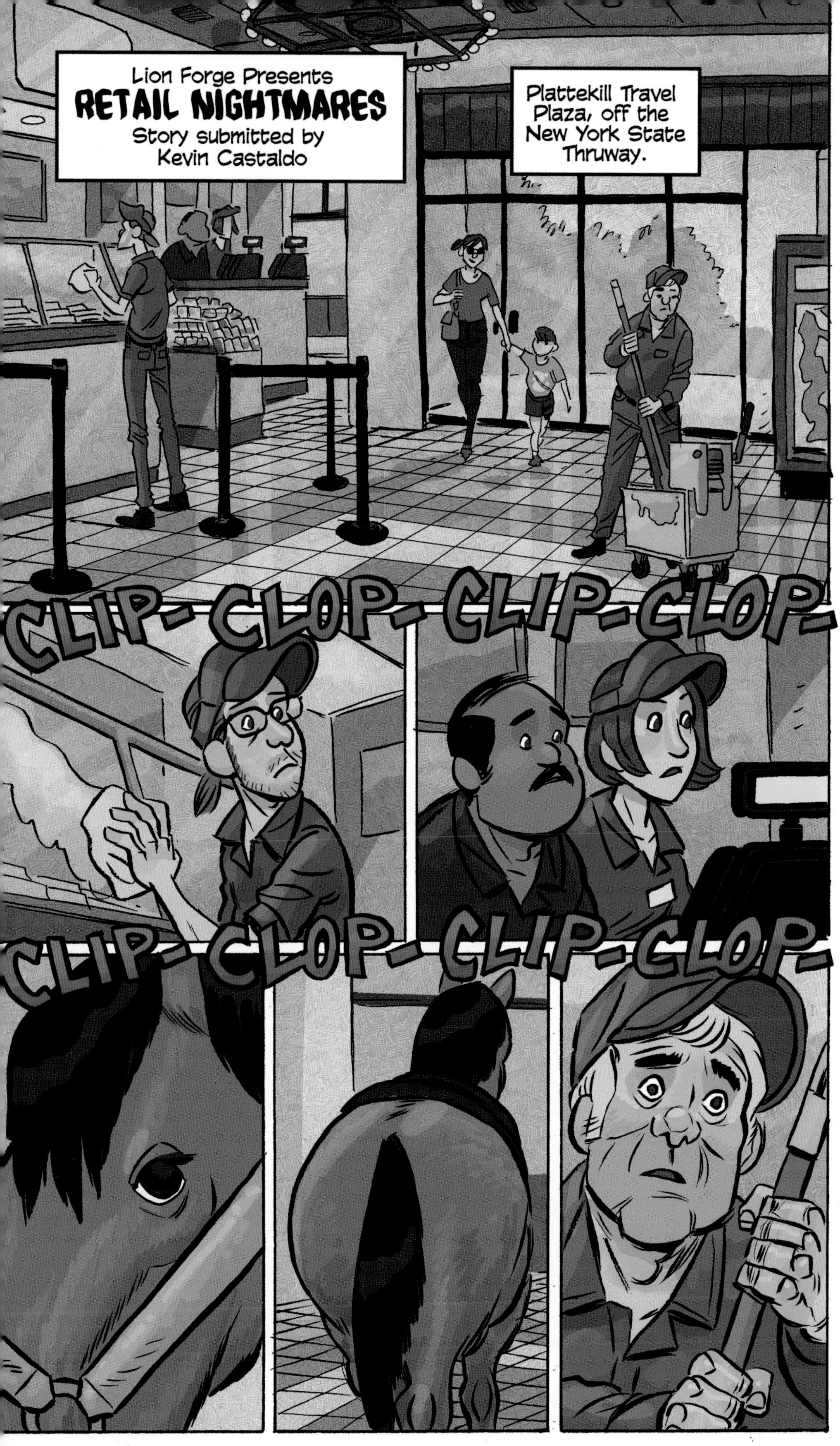
Lion Forge Presents
RETAIL NIGHTMARES
Story submitted by
Kevin Castaldo
Plattekill Travel Plaza, off the New York State Thruway.
CLIP-CLOP-CLIP-CLOP-
CLIP-CLOP-CLIP-CLOP-

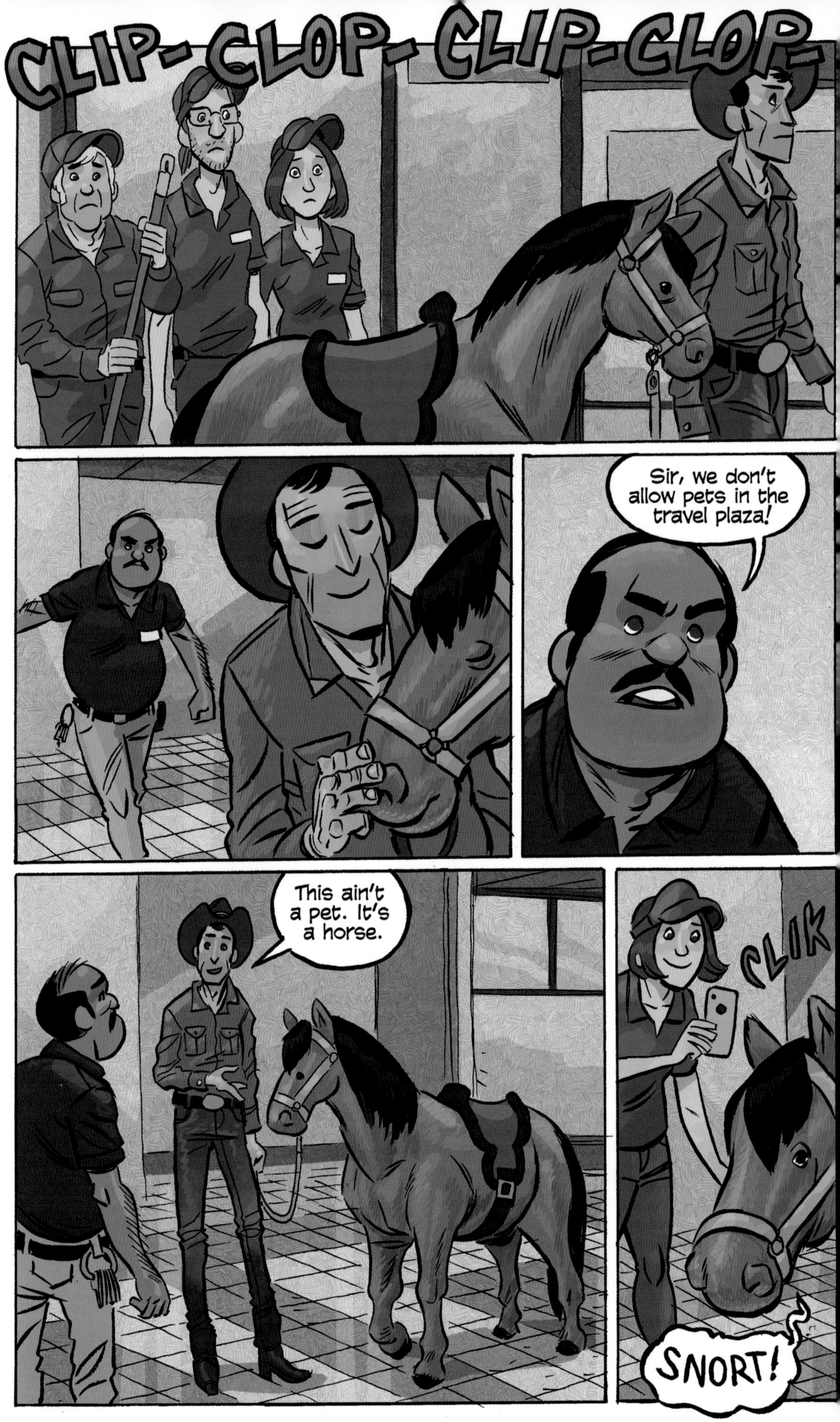
CLIP-CLOP-CLIP-CLOP-
Sir, we don't allow pets in the travel plaza!
This ain't a pet. It's a horse.
CLIK
SNORT!

# CHAPTER 5

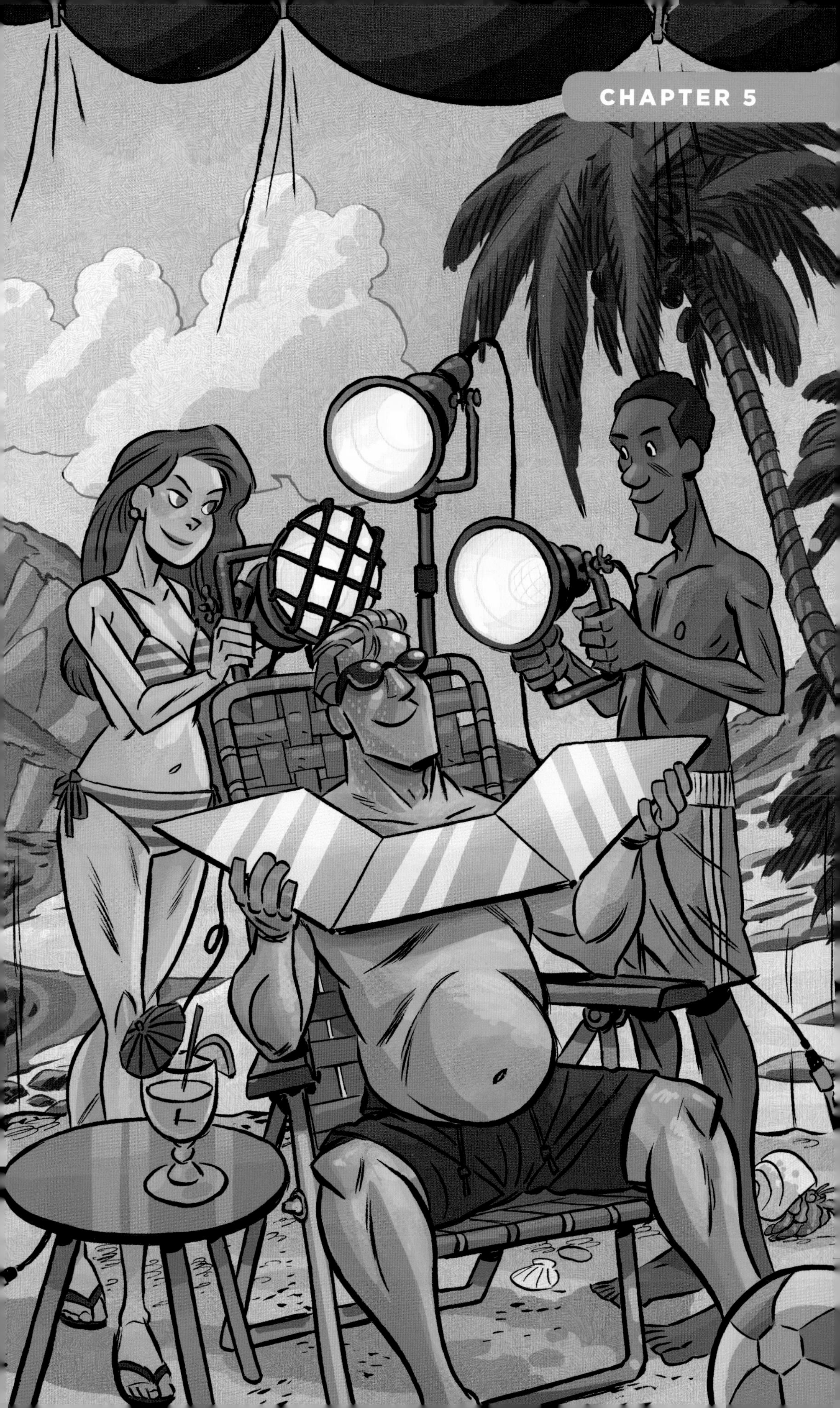

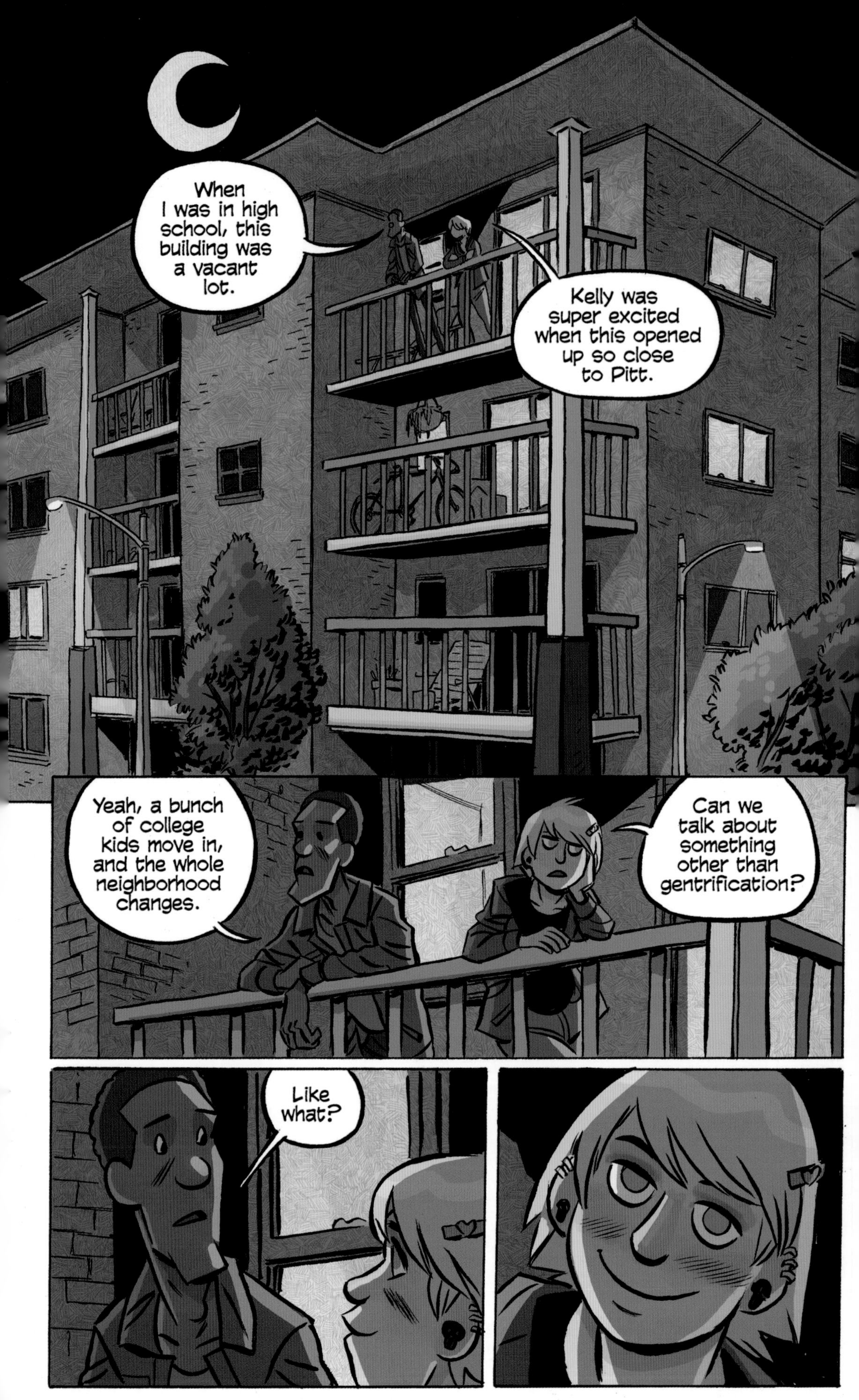
When I was in high school, this building was a vacant lot.
Kelly was super excited when this opened up so close to Pitt.
Yeah, a bunch of college kids move in, and the whole neighborhood changes.
Can we talk about something other than gentrification?
Like what?

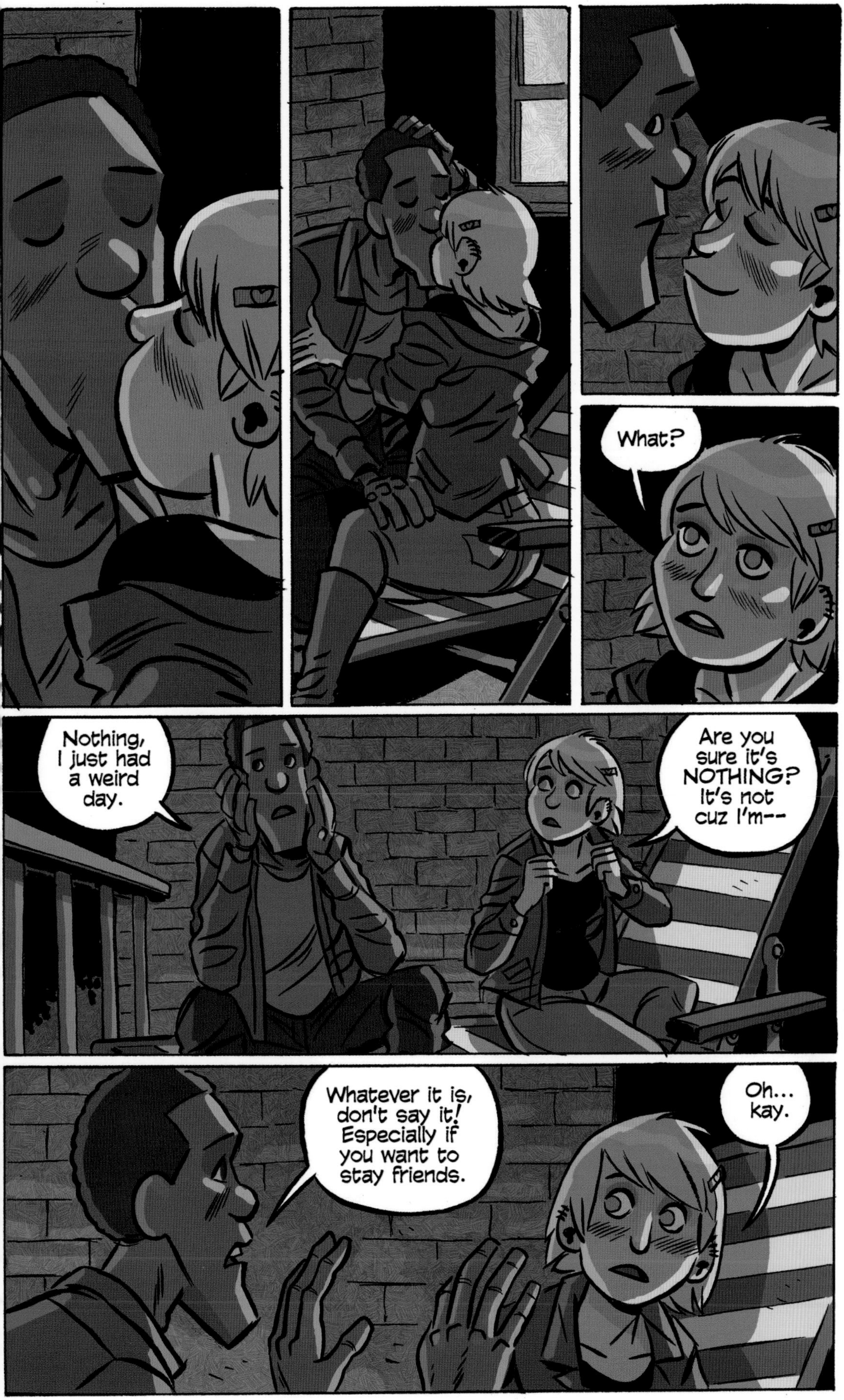
What?
Nothing, I just had a weird day.
Are you sure it's NOTHING? It's not cuz I'm--
Whatever it is, don't say it! Especially if you want to stay friends.
Oh... kay.

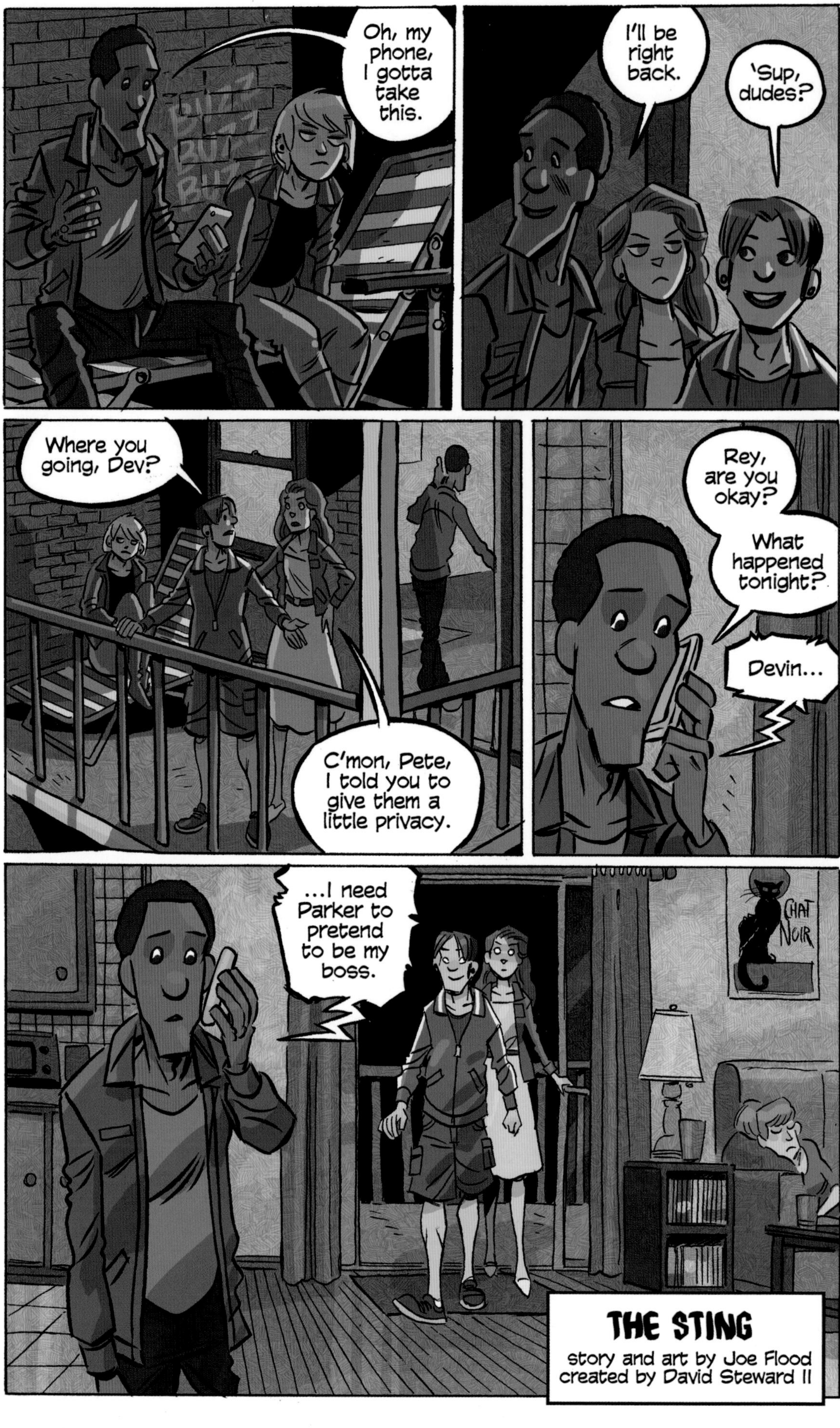
Oh, my phone, I gotta take this.
I'll be right back.
'Sup, dudes?
Where you going, Dev?
C'mon, Pete, I told you to give them a little privacy.
Rey, are you okay?
What happened tonight?
Devin...
...I need Parker to pretend to be my boss.
CHAT NOIR
THE STING
story and art by Joe Flood
created by David Steward II

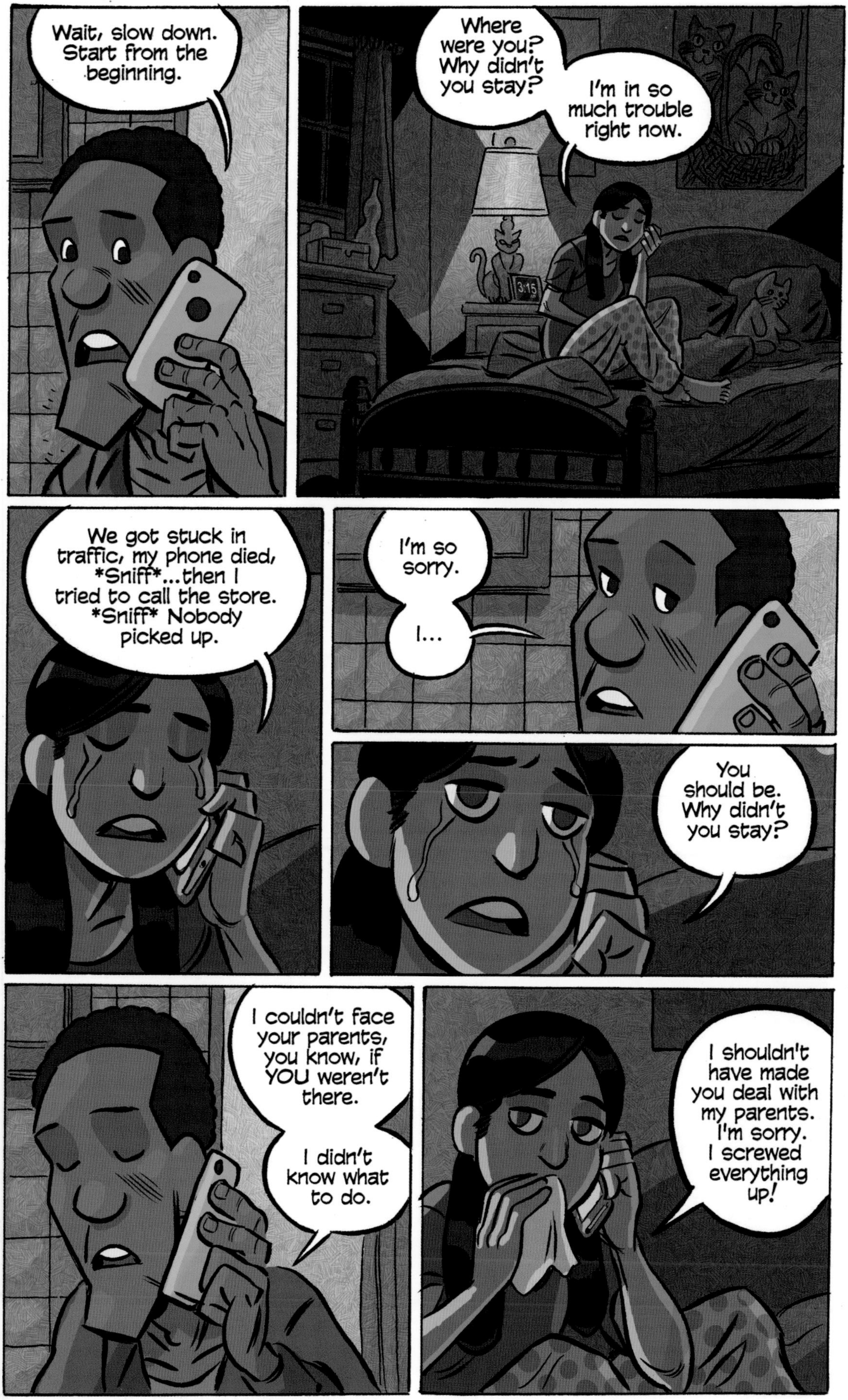

Wait, slow down. Start from the beginning.
Where were you? Why didn't you stay?
I'm in so much trouble right now.
3:15
We got stuck in traffic, my phone died, *Sniff*...then I tried to call the store. *Sniff* Nobody picked up.
I'm so sorry.
I...
You should be. Why didn't you stay?
I couldn't face your parents, you know, if YOU weren't there.
I didn't know what to do.
I shouldn't have made you deal with my parents. I'm sorry. I screwed everything up!

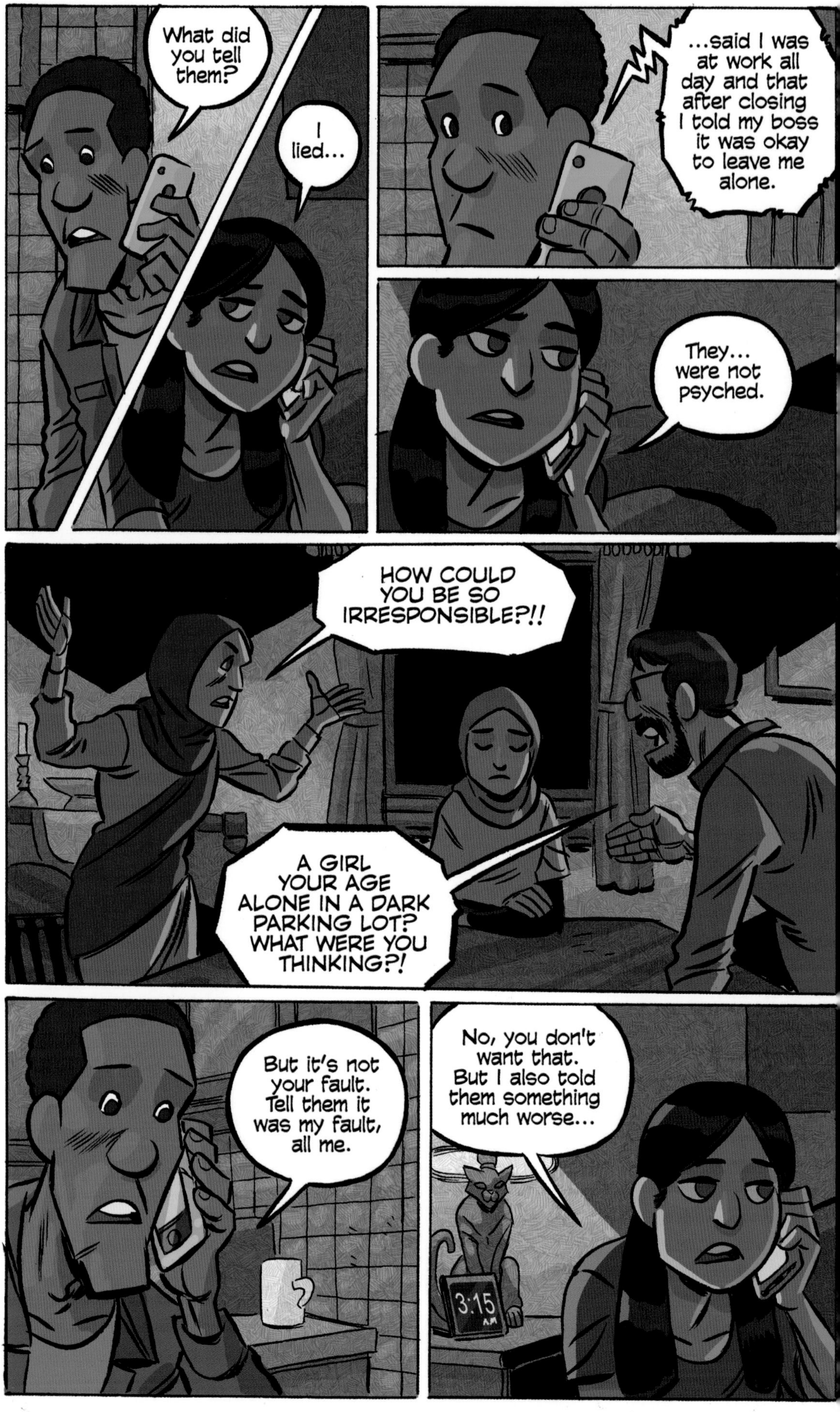
What did you tell them?
I lied...
...said I was at work all day and that after closing I told my boss it was okay to leave me alone.
They... were not psyched.
HOW COULD YOU BE SO IRRESPONSIBLE?!!
A GIRL YOUR AGE ALONE IN A DARK PARKING LOT? WHAT WERE YOU THINKING?!
But it's not your fault. Tell them it was my fault, all me.
No, you don't want that. But I also told them something much worse...
3:15 AM

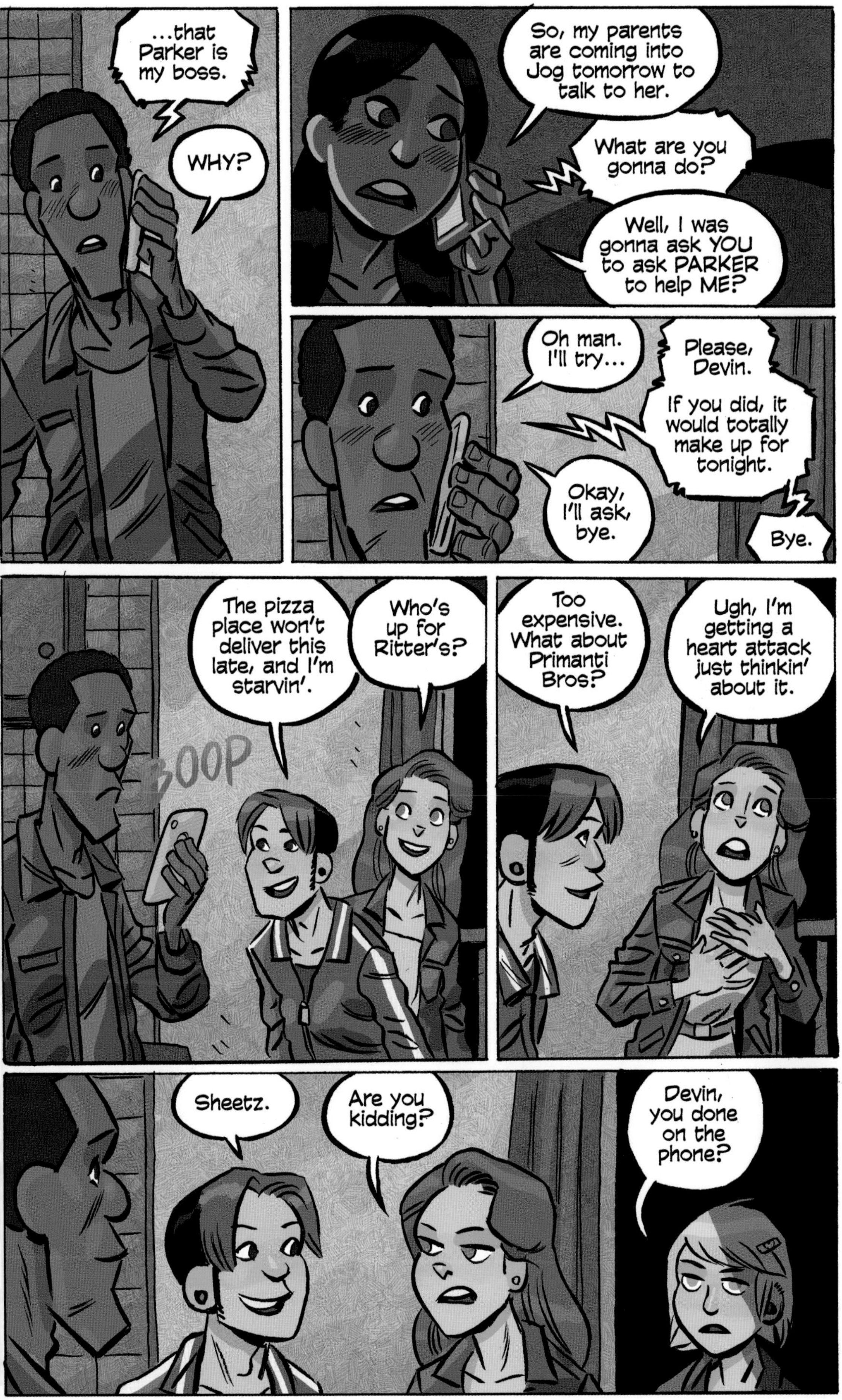

...that Parker is my boss.
WHY?
So, my parents are coming into Jog tomorrow to talk to her.
What are you gonna do?
Well, I was gonna ask YOU to ask PARKER to help ME?
Oh man. I'll try...
Please, Devin.
If you did, it would totally make up for tonight.
Okay, I'll ask, bye.
Bye.
BOOP
The pizza place won't deliver this late, and I'm starvin'.
Who's up for Ritter's?
Too expensive. What about Primanti Bros?
Ugh, I'm getting a heart attack just thinkin' about it.
Sheetz.
Are you kidding?
Devin, you done on the phone?

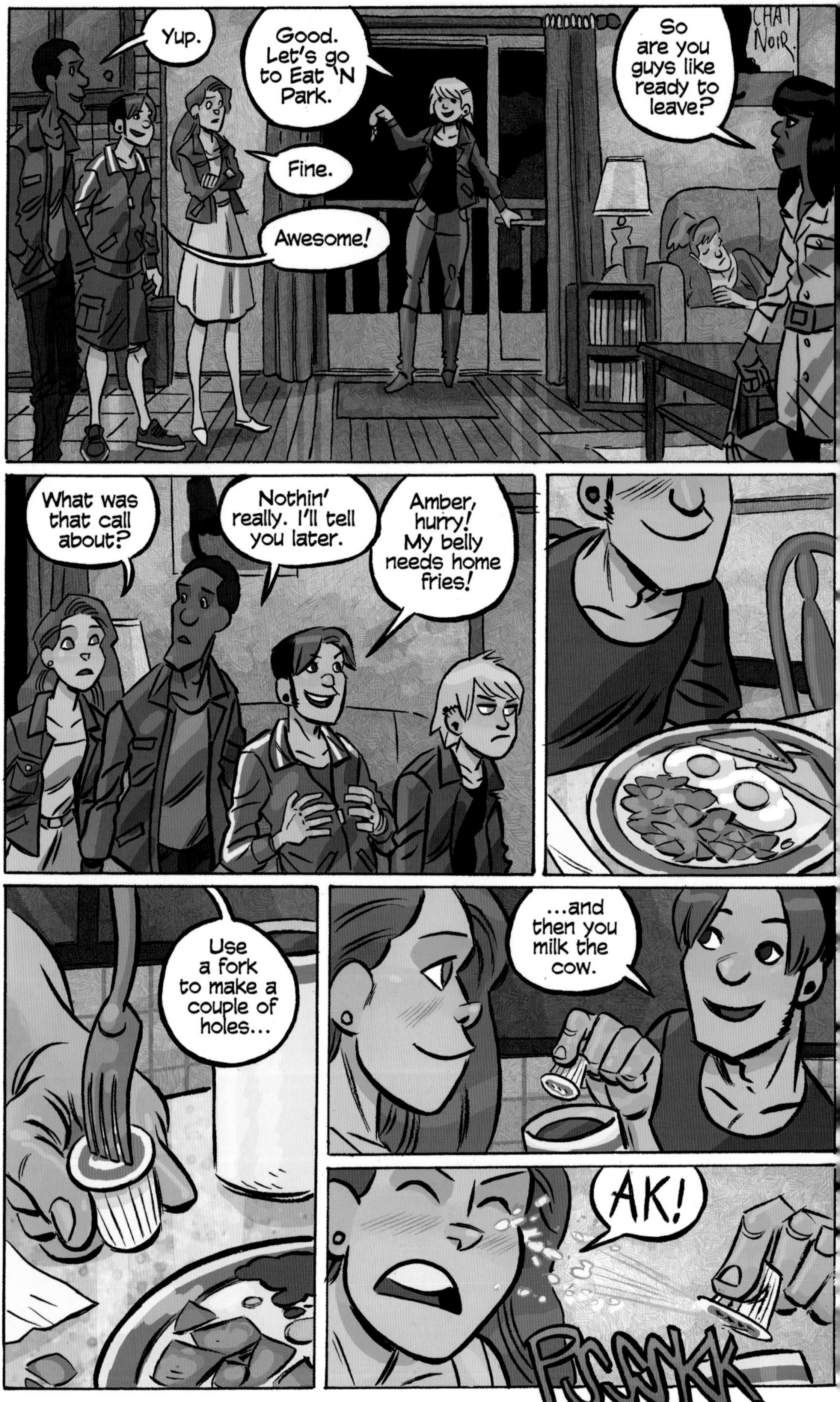
Yup.
Good. Let's go to Eat 'N Park.
Fine.
Awesome!
So are you guys like ready to leave?
CHAT NOIR
What was that call about?
Nothin' really. I'll tell you later.
Amber, hurry! My belly needs home fries!
Use a fork to make a couple of holes...
...and then you milk the cow.
AK!
PSSSHKK

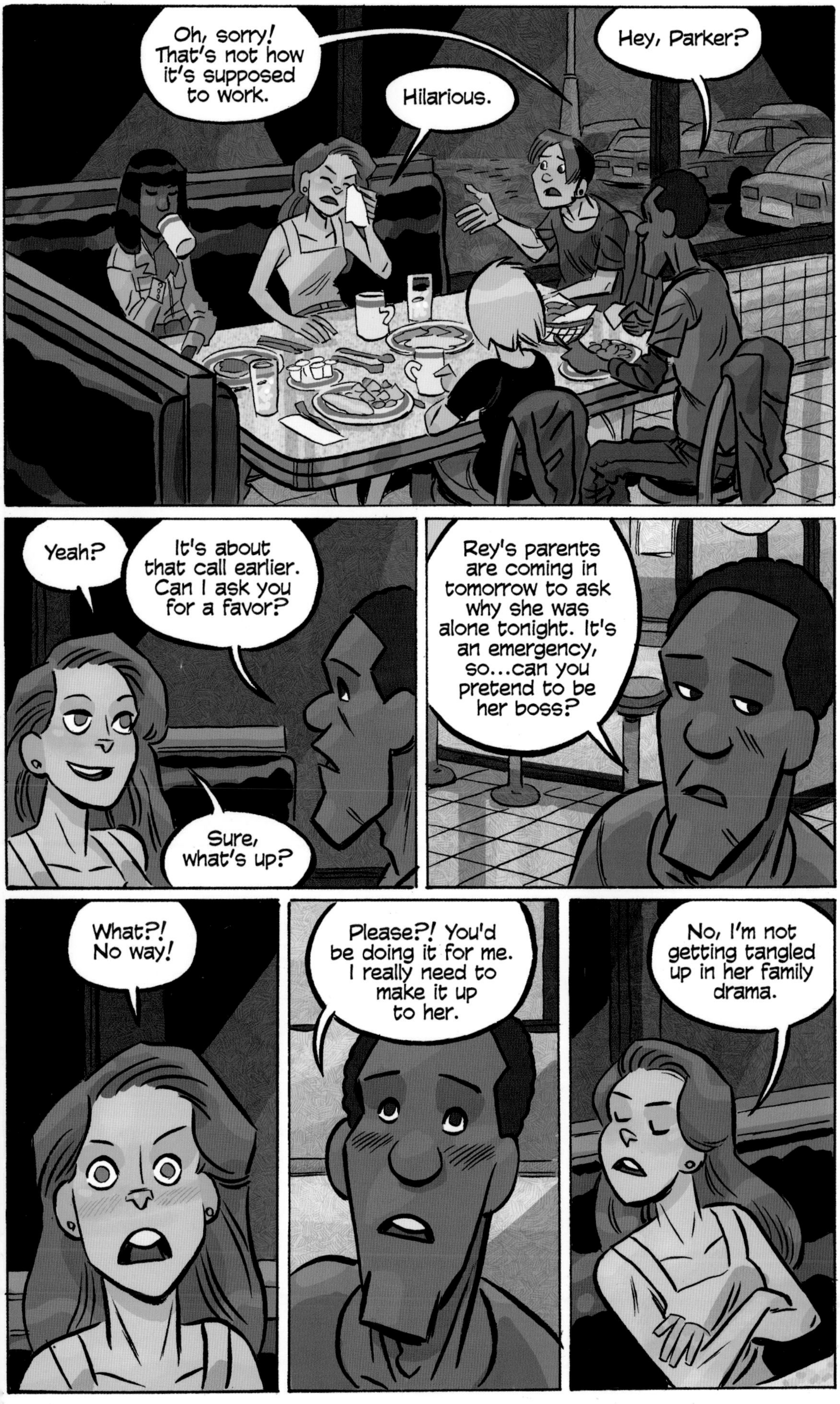
Oh, sorry! That's not how it's supposed to work.
Hilarious.
Hey, Parker?
Yeah?
It's about that call earlier. Can I ask you for a favor?
Sure, what's up?
Rey's parents are coming in tomorrow to ask why she was alone tonight. It's an emergency, so...can you pretend to be her boss?
What?! No way!
Please?! You'd be doing it for me. I really need to make it up to her.
No, I'm not getting tangled up in her family drama.

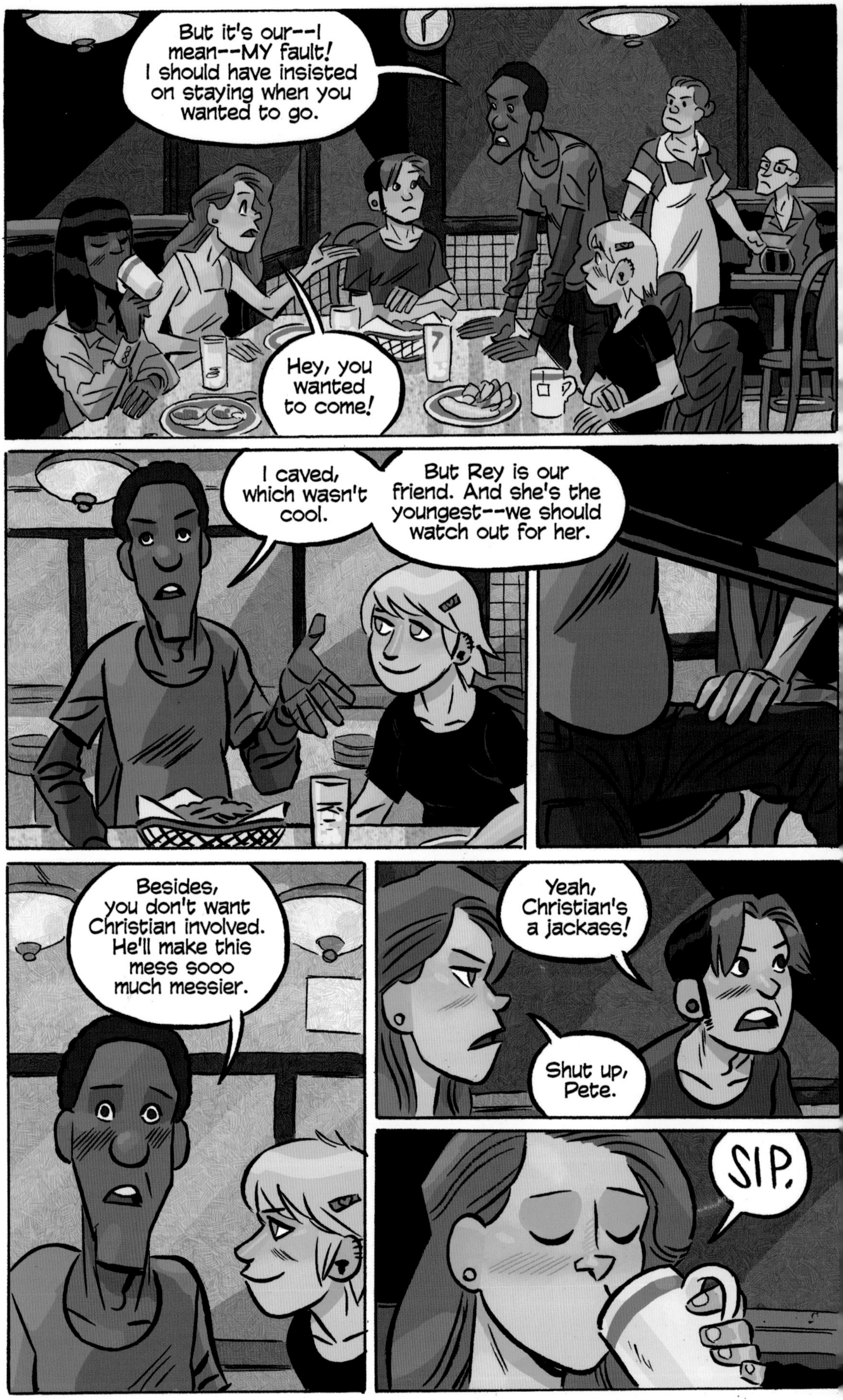
But it's our--I mean--MY fault! I should have insisted on staying when you wanted to go.
Hey, you wanted to come!
I caved, which wasn't cool.
But Rey is our friend. And she's the youngest--we should watch out for her.
Besides, you don't want Christian involved. He'll make this mess sooo much messier.
Yeah, Christian's a jackass!
Shut up, Pete.
SIP.

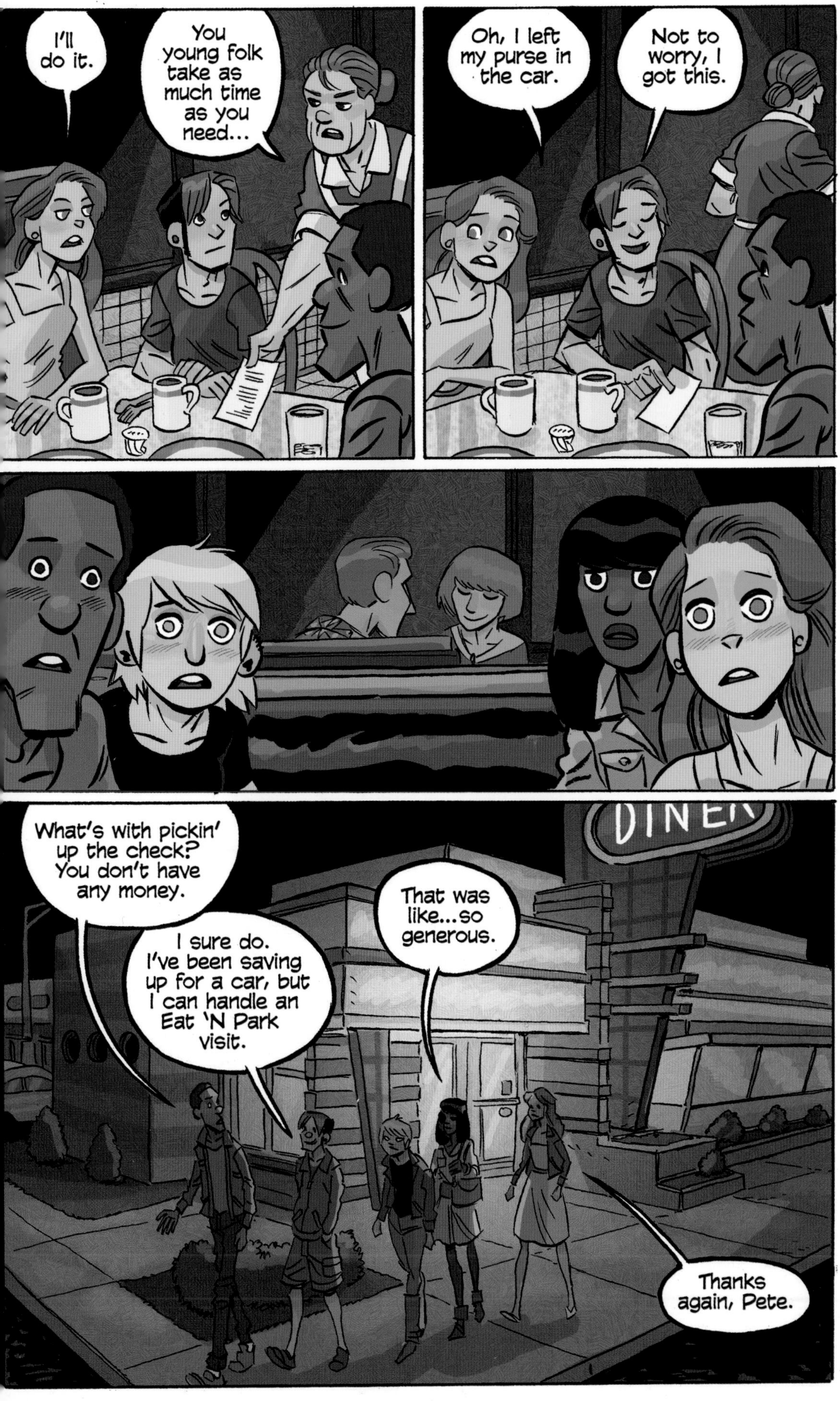

I'll do it.
You young folk take as much time as you need...
Oh, I left my purse in the car.
Not to worry, I got this.
DINER
What's with pickin' up the check? You don't have any money.
I sure do. I've been saving up for a car, but I can handle an Eat 'N Park visit.
That was like...so generous.
Thanks again, Pete.

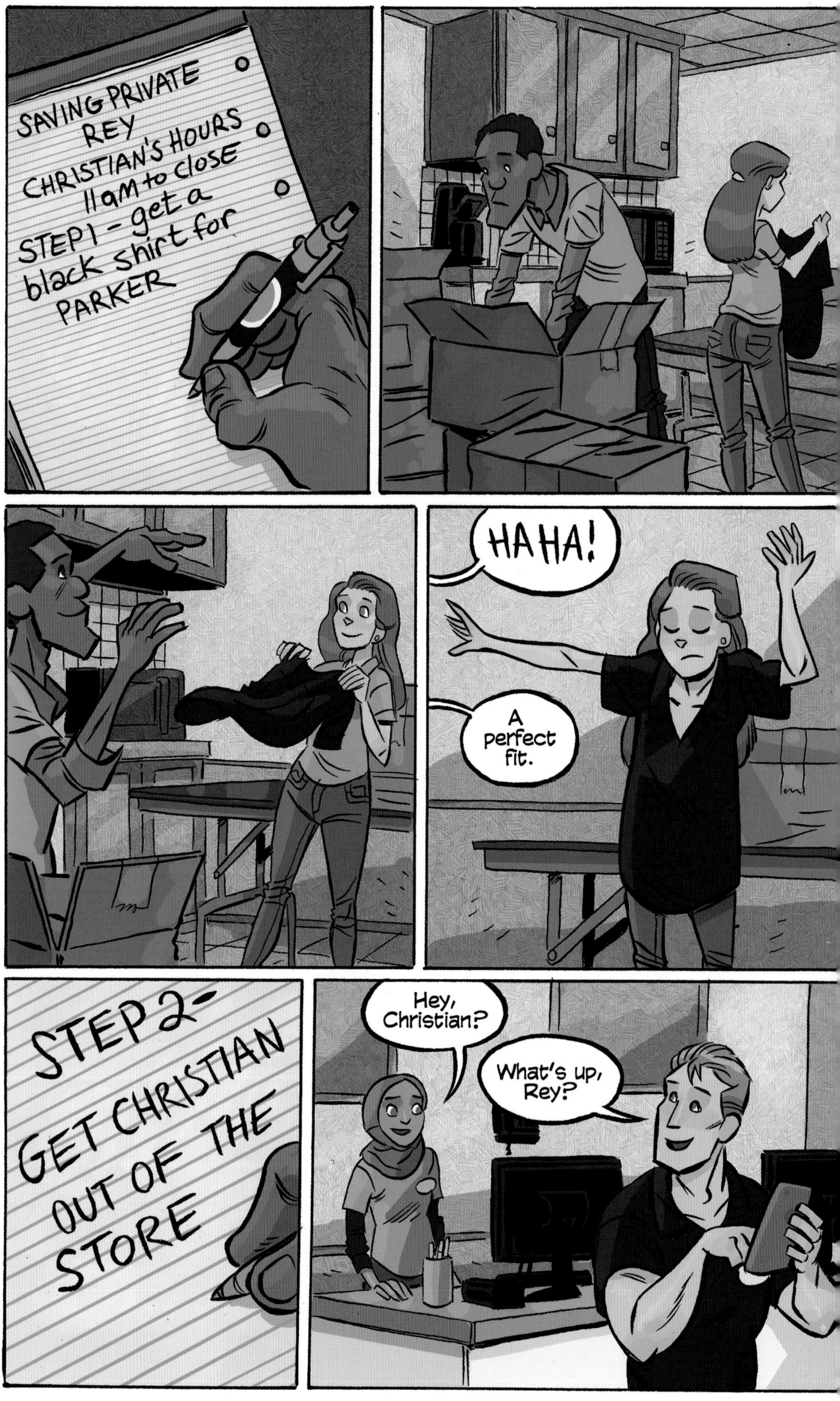
SAVING PRIVATE REY
CHRISTIAN'S HOURS
11am to close
STEP1 - get a black shirt for PARKER
HAHA!
A perfect fit.
STEP 2-
GET CHRISTIAN OUT OF THE STORE
Hey, Christian?
What's up, Rey?

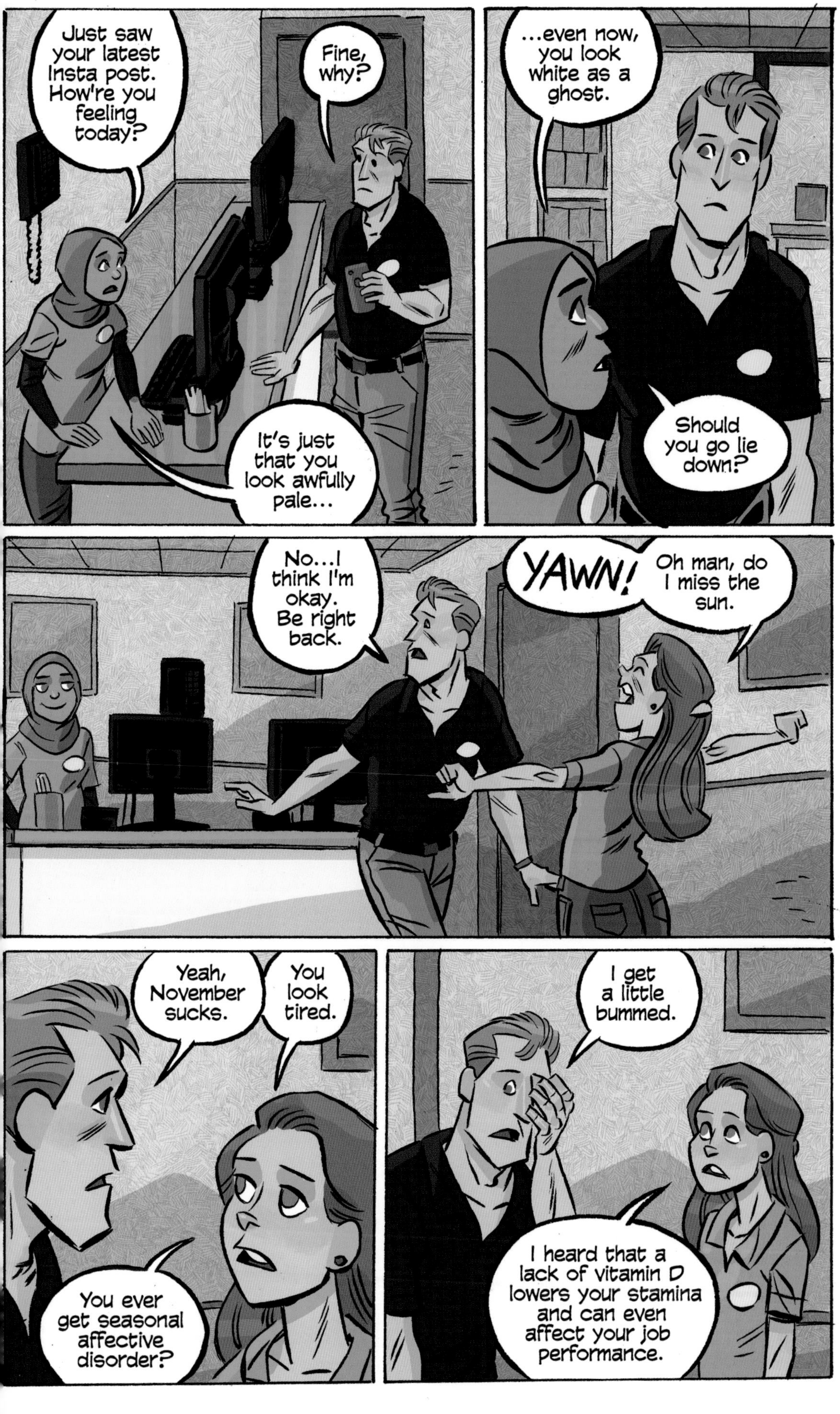

Just saw your latest Insta post. How're you feeling today?
Fine, why?
It's just that you look awfully pale...
...even now, you look white as a ghost.
Should you go lie down?
No...I think I'm okay. Be right back.
YAWN!
Oh man, do I miss the sun.
Yeah, November sucks.
You look tired.
You ever get seasonal affective disorder?
I get a little bummed.
I heard that a lack of vitamin D lowers your stamina and can even affect your job performance.

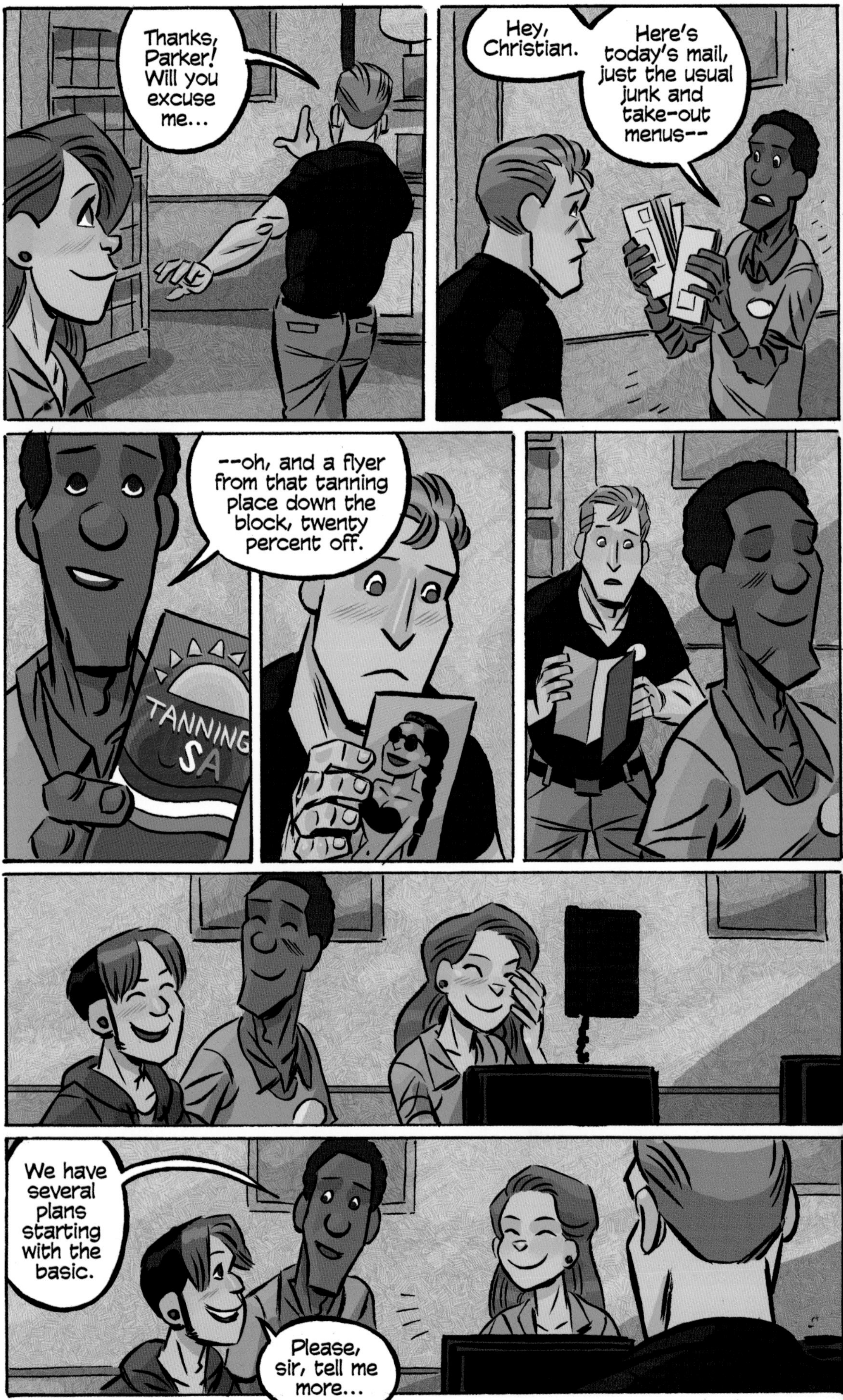
Thanks, Parker! Will you excuse me...
Hey, Christian.
Here's today's mail, just the usual junk and take-out menus--
--oh, and a flyer from that tanning place down the block, twenty percent off.
TANNING USA
We have several plans starting with the basic.
Please, sir, tell me more...

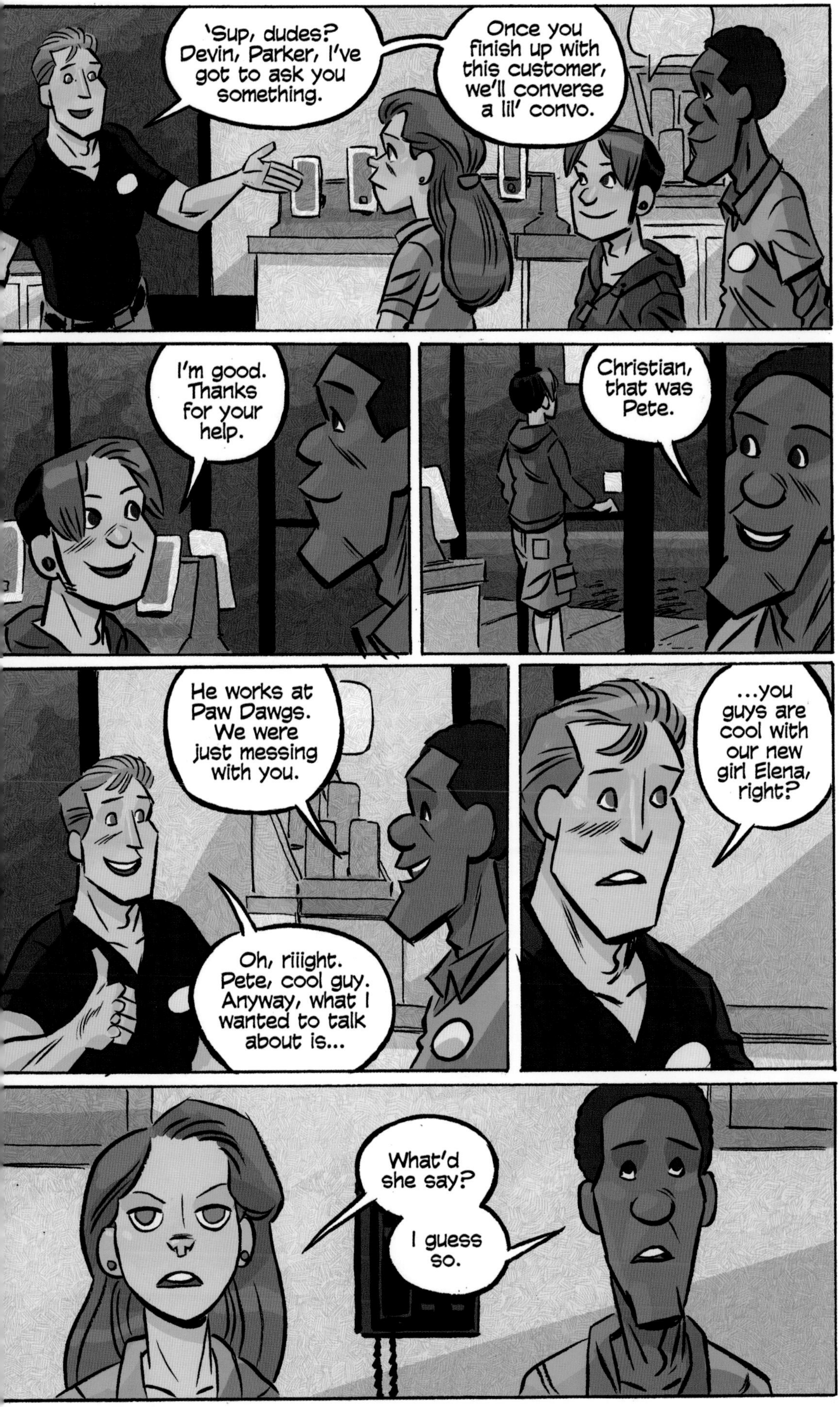
'Sup, dudes? Devin, Parker, I've got to ask you something.
Once you finish up with this customer, we'll converse a lil' convo.
I'm good. Thanks for your help.
Christian, that was Pete.
He works at Paw Dawgs. We were just messing with you.
Oh, riiight. Pete, cool guy. Anyway, what I wanted to talk about is...
...you guys are cool with our new girl Elena, right?
What'd she say?
I guess so.

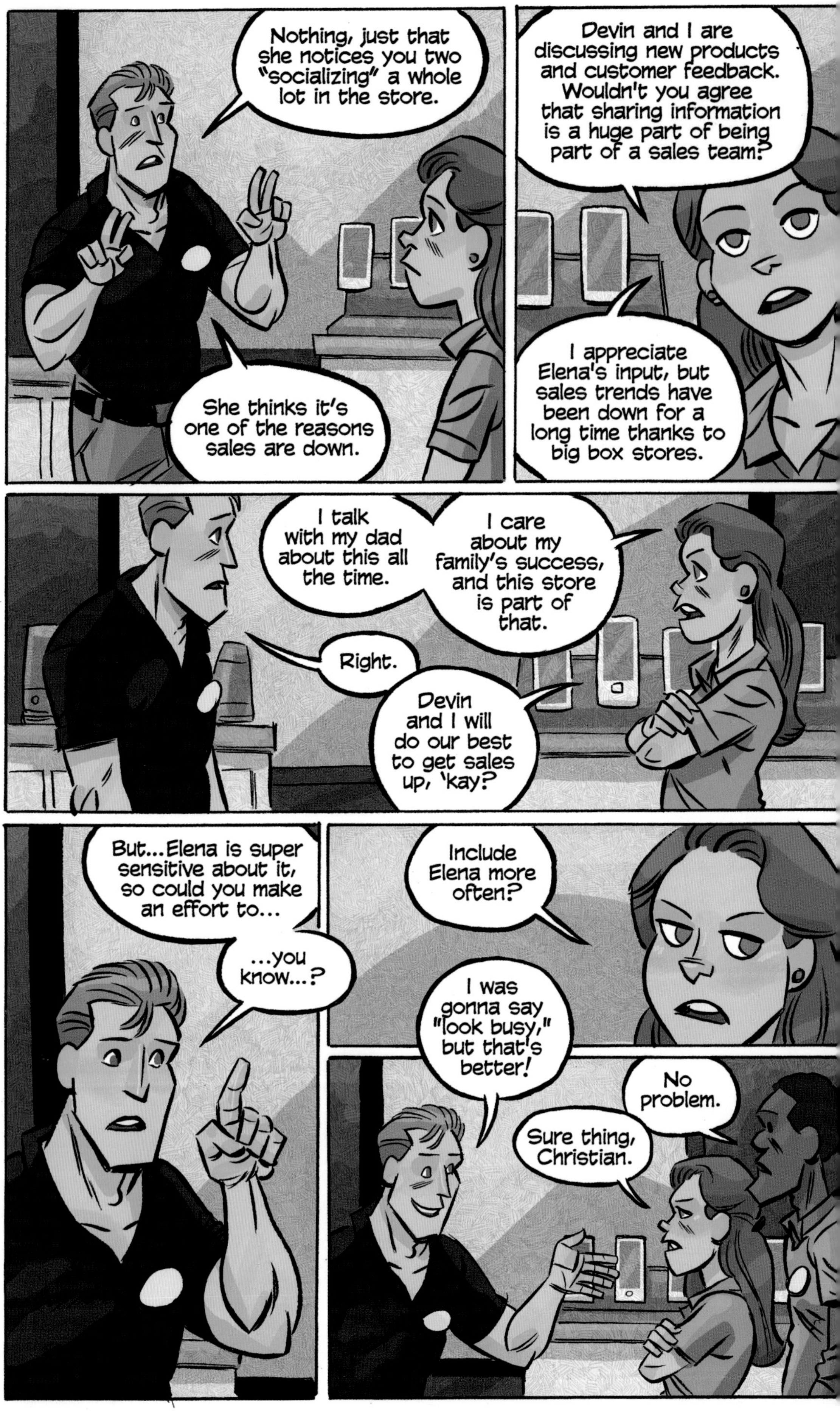
Nothing, just that she notices you two "socializing" a whole lot in the store.
She thinks it's one of the reasons sales are down.
Devin and I are discussing new products and customer feedback. Wouldn't you agree that sharing information is a huge part of being part of a sales team?
I appreciate Elena's input, but sales trends have been down for a long time thanks to big box stores.
I talk with my dad about this all the time.
I care about my family's success, and this store is part of that.
Right.
Devin and I will do our best to get sales up, 'kay?
But...Elena is super sensitive about it, so could you make an effort to...
...you know...?
Include Elena more often?
I was gonna say "look busy," but that's better!
No problem.
Sure thing, Christian.

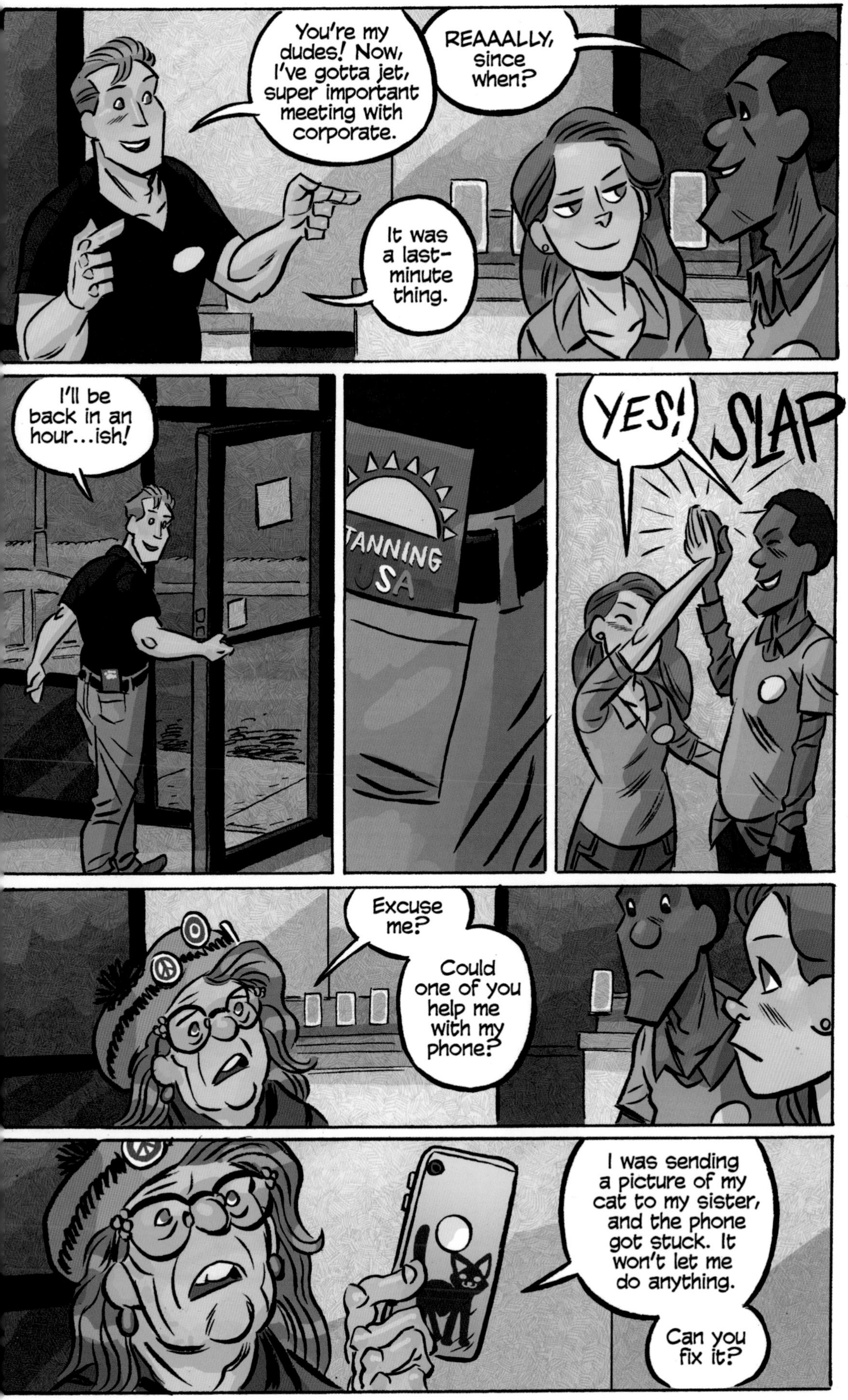
You're my dudes! Now, I've gotta jet, super important meeting with corporate.
REAAALLY, since when?
It was a last-minute thing.
I'll be back in an hour...ish!
TANNING USA
YES!
SLAP
Excuse me?
Could one of you help me with my phone?
I was sending a picture of my cat to my sister, and the phone got stuck. It won't let me do anything.
Can you fix it?

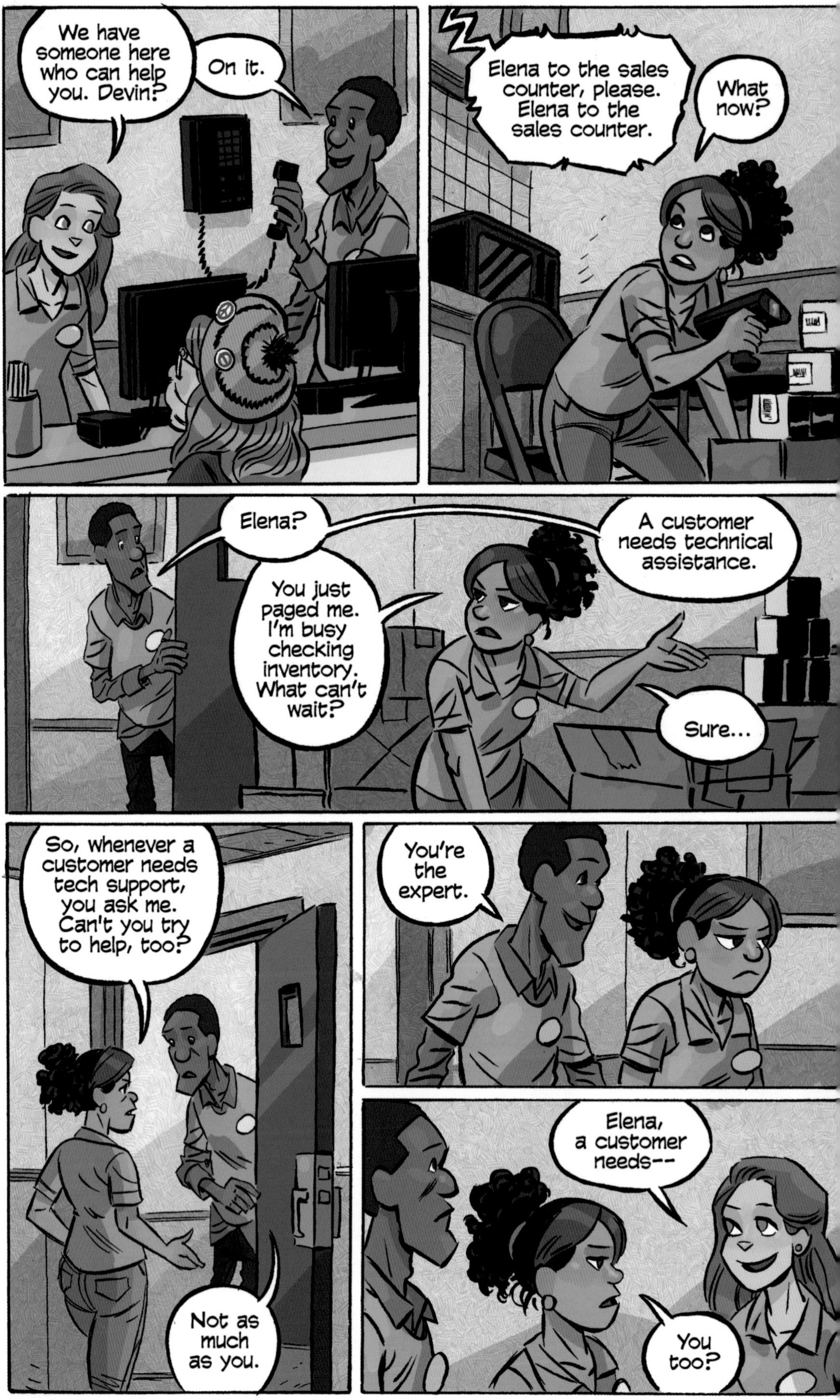
We have someone here who can help you. Devin?
On it.
Elena to the sales counter, please. Elena to the sales counter.
What now?
Elena?
A customer needs technical assistance.
You just paged me. I'm busy checking inventory. What can't wait?
Sure...
So, whenever a customer needs tech support, you ask me. Can't you try to help, too?
Not as much as you.
You're the expert.
Elena, a customer needs--
You too?

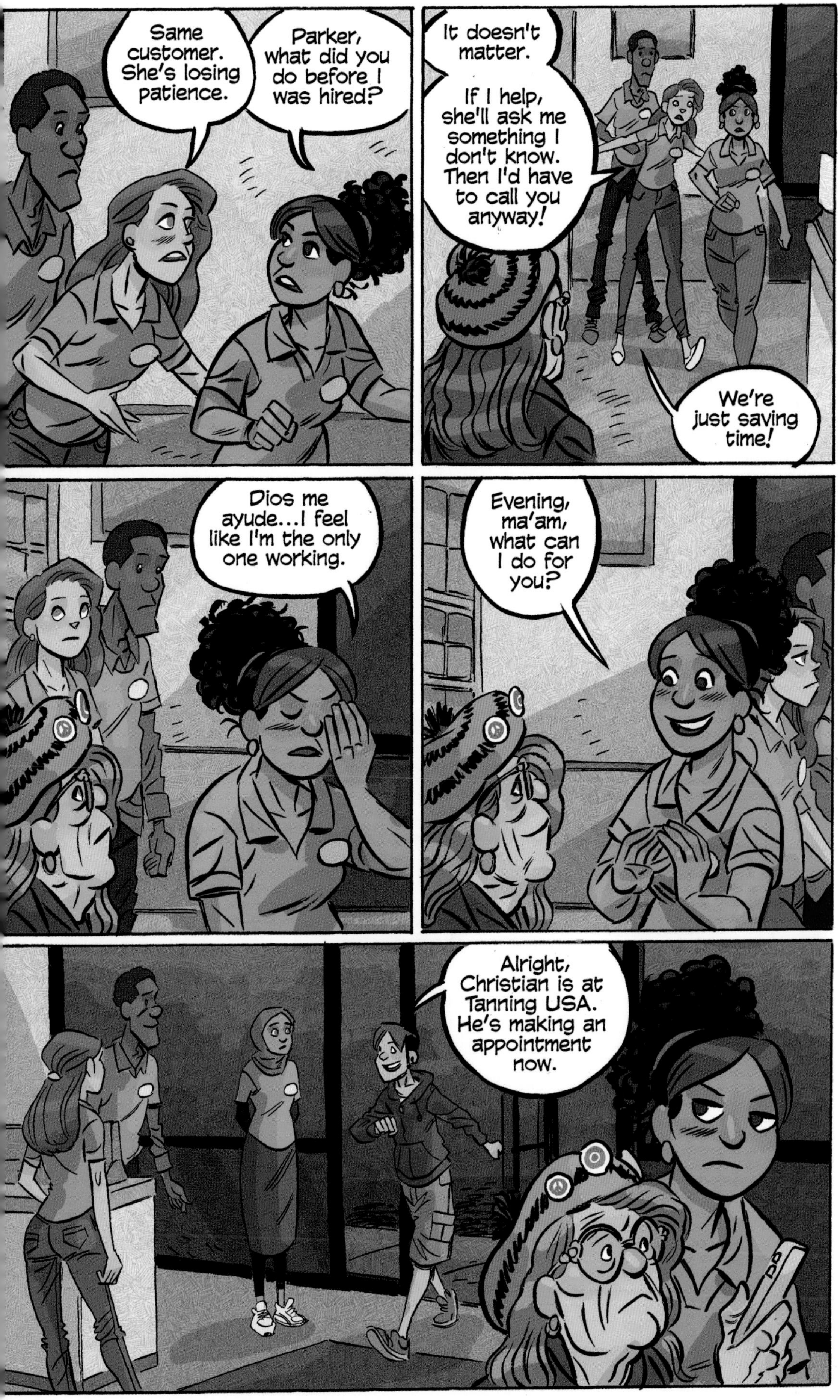
Same customer. She's losing patience.
Parker, what did you do before I was hired?
It doesn't matter.
If I help, she'll ask me something I don't know. Then I'd have to call you anyway!
We're just saving time!
Dios me ayude...I feel like I'm the only one working.
Evening, ma'am, what can I do for you?
Alright, Christian is at Tanning USA. He's making an appointment now.

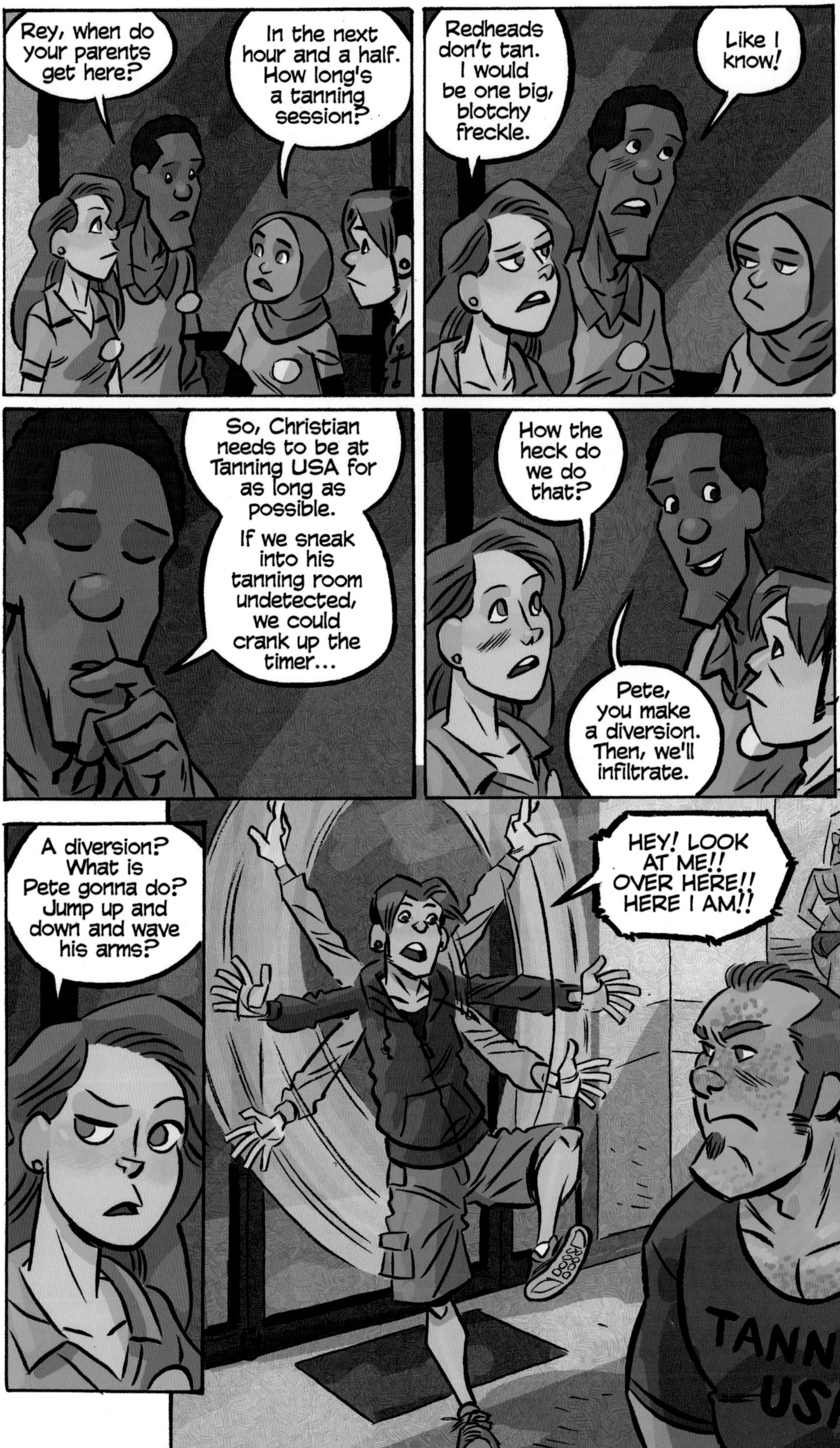
Rey, when do your parents get here?
In the next hour and a half. How long's a tanning session?
Redheads don't tan. I would be one big, blotchy freckle.
Like I know!
So, Christian needs to be at Tanning USA for as long as possible.
If we sneak into his tanning room undetected, we could crank up the timer...
How the heck do we do that?
Pete, you make a diversion. Then, we'll infiltrate.
A diversion? What is Pete gonna do? Jump up and down and wave his arms?
HEY! LOOK AT ME!! OVER HERE!! HERE I AM!!
TANN USA

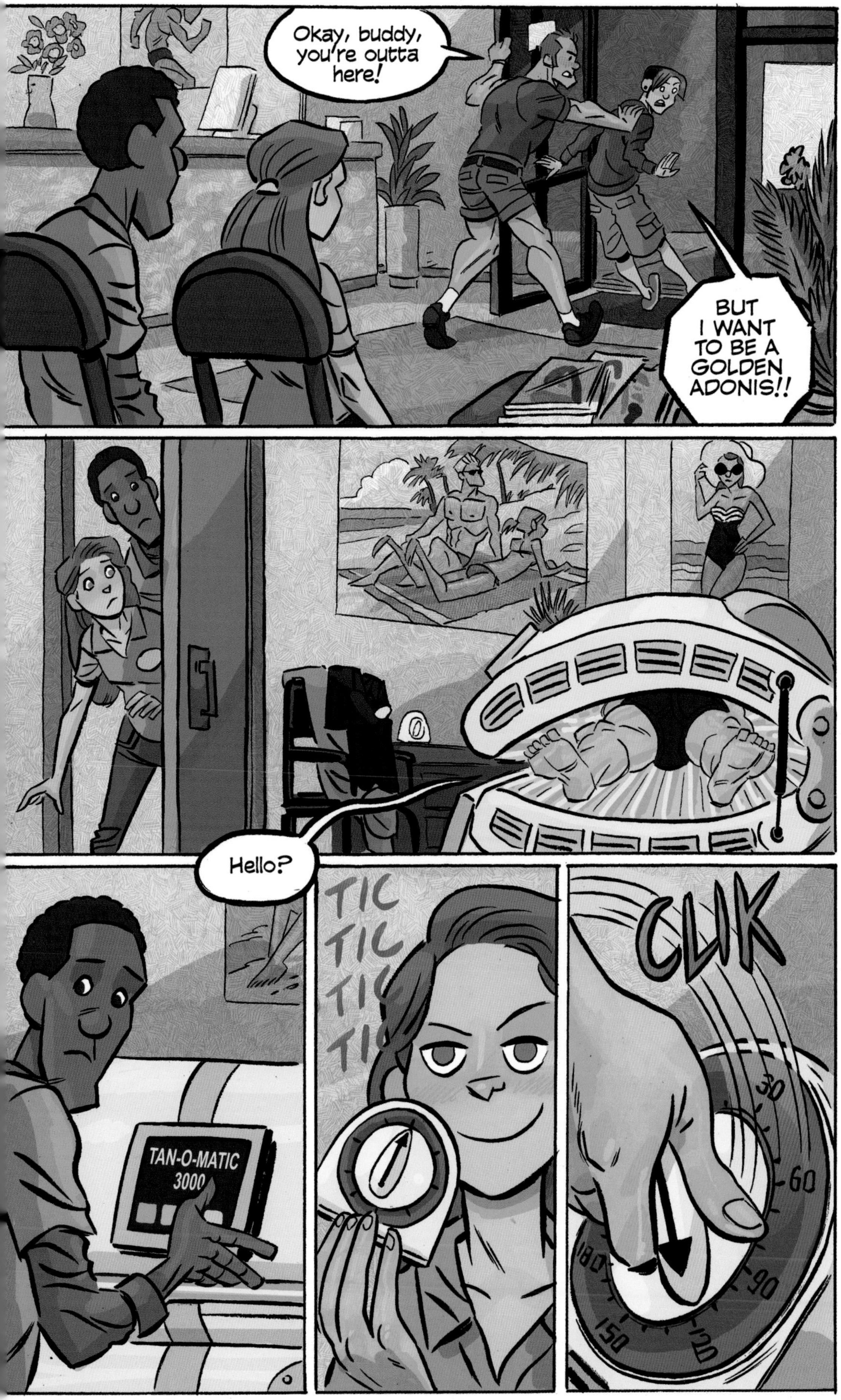
Okay, buddy, you're outta here!
BUT I WANT TO BE A GOLDEN ADONIS!!
Hello?
TAN-O-MATIC 3000
TIC
TIC
TIC
TIC
CLIK
30
60
90
120
150
180

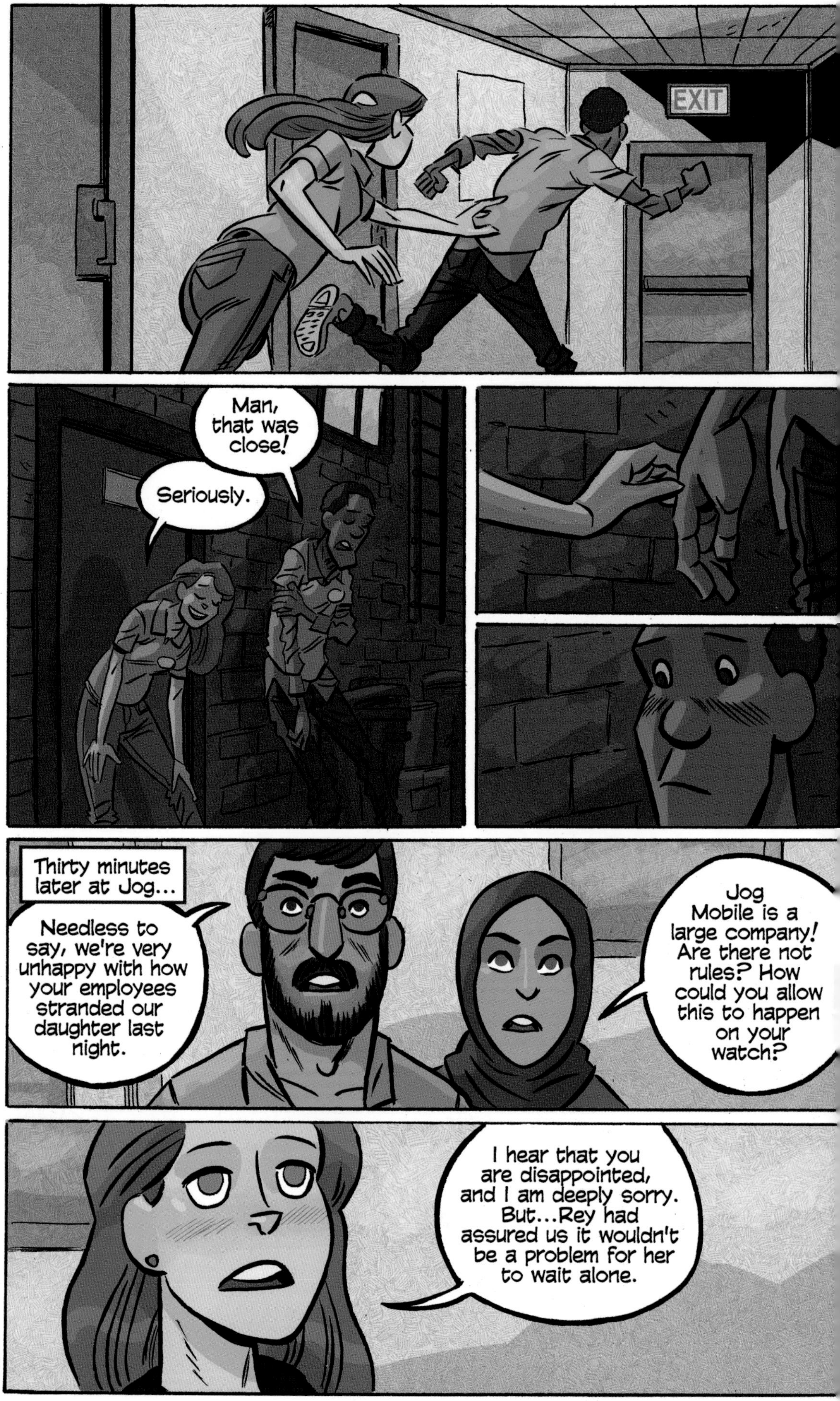
EXIT
Man, that was close!
Seriously.
Thirty minutes later at Jog...
Needless to say, we're very unhappy with how your employees stranded our daughter last night.
Jog Mobile is a large company! Are there not rules? How could you allow this to happen on your watch?
I hear that you are disappointed, and I am deeply sorry. But...Rey had assured us it wouldn't be a problem for her to wait alone.

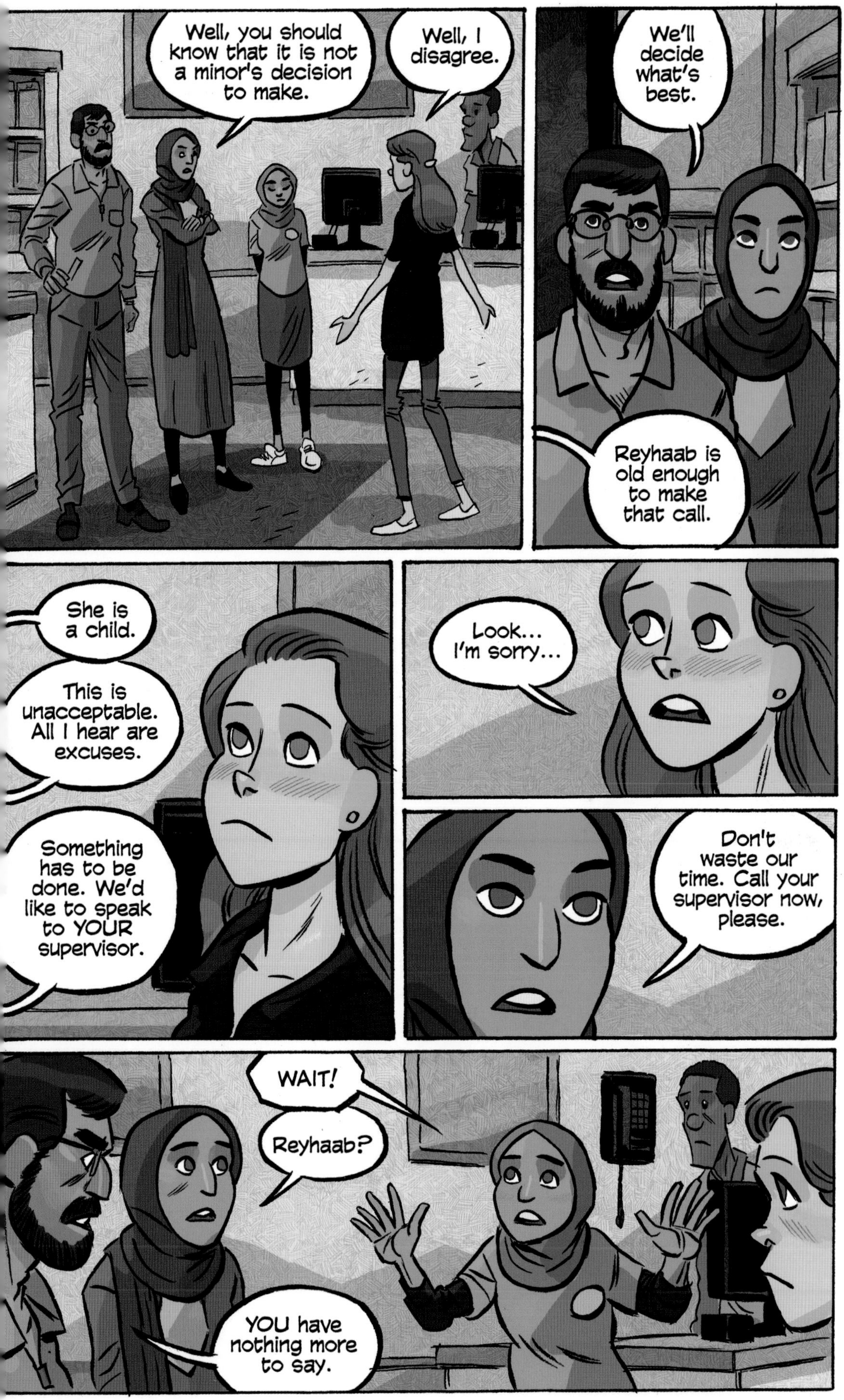

Well, you should know that it is not a minor's decision to make.
Well, I disagree.
We'll decide what's best.
Reyhaab is old enough to make that call.
She is a child.
This is unacceptable. All I hear are excuses.
Something has to be done. We'd like to speak to YOUR supervisor.
Look... I'm sorry...
Don't waste our time. Call your supervisor now, please.
WAIT!
Reyhaab?
YOU have nothing more to say.

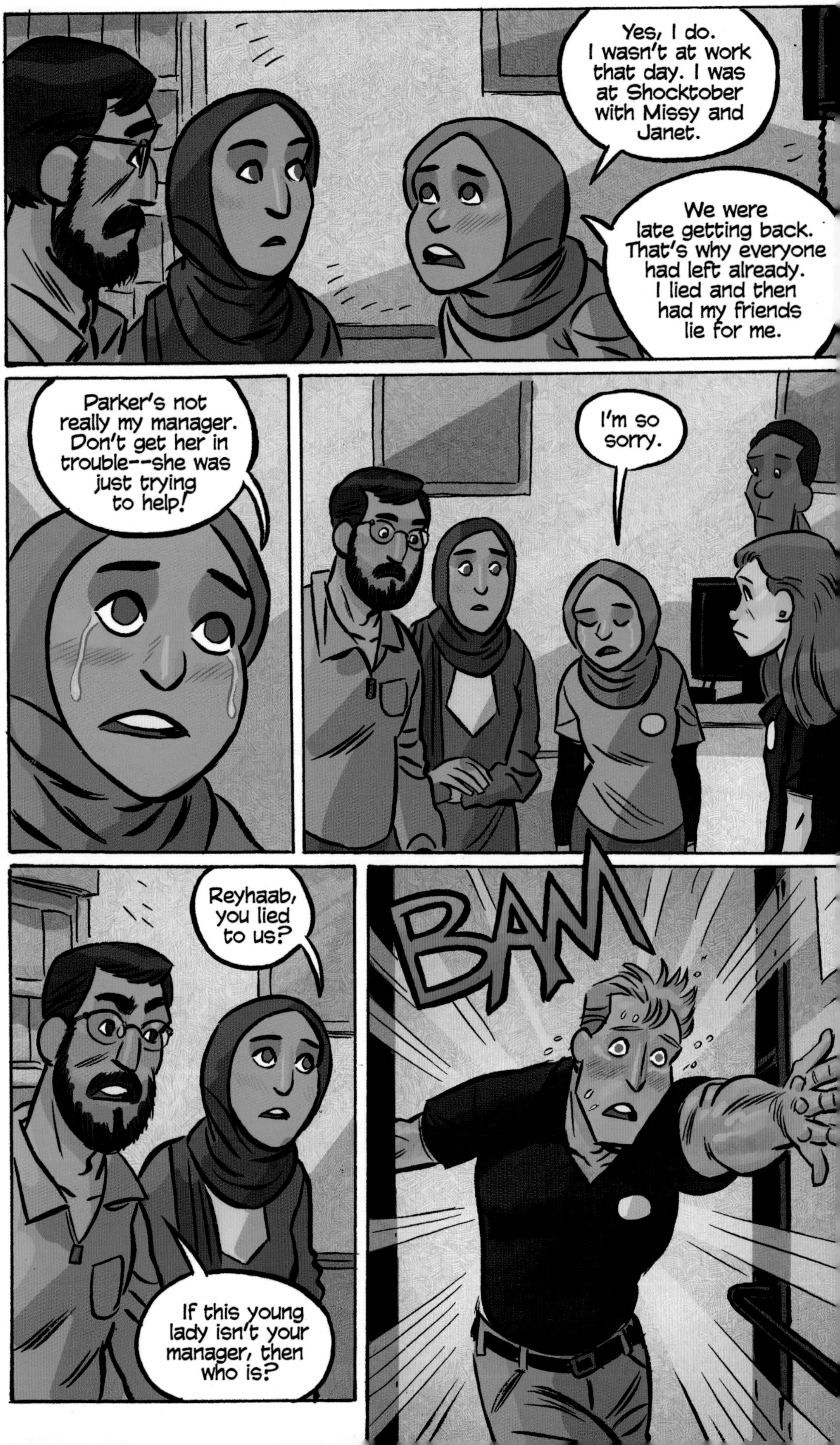
Yes, I do. I wasn't at work that day. I was at Shocktober with Missy and Janet.
We were late getting back. That's why everyone had left already. I lied and then had my friends lie for me.
Parker's not really my manager. Don't get her in trouble--she was just trying to help!
I'm so sorry.
Reyhaab, you lied to us?
If this young lady isn't your manager, then who is?
BAM

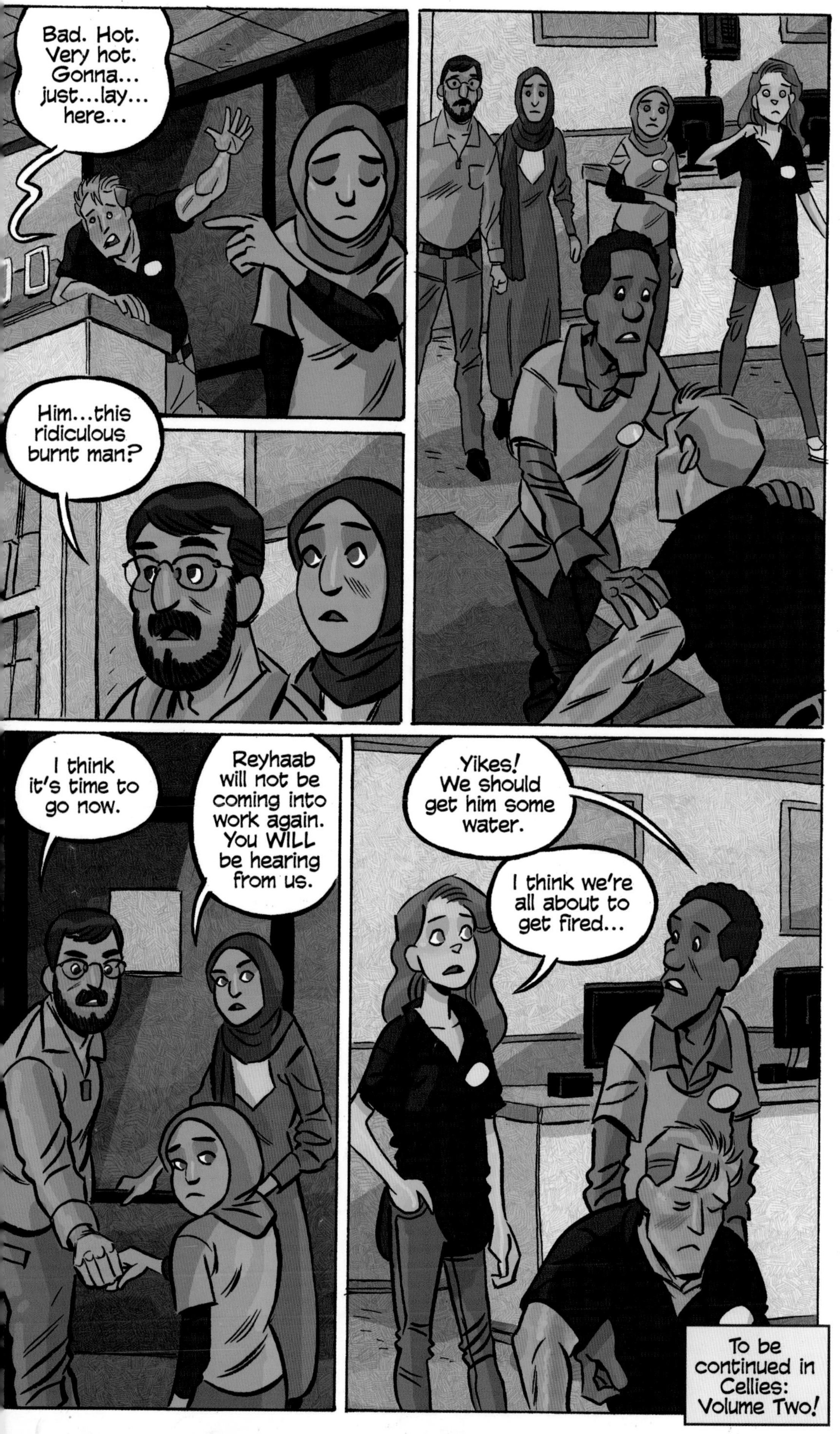
Bad. Hot. Very hot. Gonna... just...lay... here...
Him...this ridiculous burnt man?
I think it's time to go now.
Reyhaab will not be coming into work again. You WILL be hearing from us.
Yikes! We should get him some water.
I think we're all about to get fired...
To be continued in Cellies: Volume Two!

**JOE FLOOD** is a comic book writer and artist whose work includes the graphic novels *Orcs: Forged for War, The Cute Girl Network, Dinosaurs: Of Fossils and Feathers,* and *Sharks: Nature's Perfect Hunter.* His other work includes Disney's *Pirates of the Caribbean.* Joe lives in New York's Hudson Valley with his wife and daughter.